Prologue

20 November, 1812

Elizabeth woke that morning to her sleeping sister Mary's elbow colliding with her face, and from there the day did not progress much better. Indeed, the three days since Elizabeth and Jane had returned from their stay at Netherfield Park had been abysmal, from the presence of their cousin Mr. Collins at Longbourn to the antics of their younger sisters, for the whole family had been confined indoors for the first two days by heavy rains. Today, at last, they had ventured out into the village for the monthly market day in Meryton, and again that evening for their Aunt Phillips' card party. Jane appeared recovered enough from the illness that had afflicted her at Netherfield, and so Elizabeth decided it was time to return to the room they shared. After all, they had much to discuss.

"I hope you are well enough that we might share," Elizabeth said as she slipped into their bedroom.

Jane was already in her dressing gown, sitting on the bed in a ponderous pose. "Of course, Lizzy. I have told you; I am perfectly well. It was just a trifling cold."

Elizabeth observed her sister with affectionate skepticism. Jane had not been herself since returning to Longbourn, Elizabeth was sure of it. Two days trapped indoors with the constant company of their obsequious cousin Collins, their officer-crazy sisters, and their matrimonially obsessed mother was enough to put anyone out of sorts, but Jane loved market day. So why did she seem so listless? "You are not ill anymore, perhaps, but lovesick?"

"Lizzy!" Jane blushed as she curled her knees up to her chest.

"You can tell me, Jane." Elizabeth met her sister's eye with a reassuring look before she began to dress for bed. "I have missed our nighttime conversations, you know."

As Elizabeth sat down at their dressing table, she glanced back at Jane in the mirror, and was relieved to see her sister soften. "Oh, Lizzy, so have I. It was kind of you to share with Mary, but perhaps I have been too much alone with my thoughts since we have been back at home."

Elizabeth turned and smiled at her sister. "Thoughts of Mr. Bingley?"

Jane flung a pillow, but the shy grin that crept across her face gave her away. "I do wish to speak of it, but if you mean to tease me, I shall remind you of Mr. Collins' attentions."

Elizabeth groaned and gave a dramatic roll of her eyes. "And I shall remind you that you were his first choice!"

"Well, I cannot say a great deal in favor of our cousin, but he is a man whose intentions are clear." Elizabeth let out a screech as she ran her brush through a tangled bit of hair, and Jane flew to her side at once. "Oh Lizzy, I am sorry. He *is* determined – but perhaps he will improve upon further acquaintance."

Elizabeth chortled. "Do you mean he will cease to rank us in order of attractiveness, and form some opinions that have not been provided by his noble patroness? Shall he improve in his *arranging little compliments that are always acceptable to the ladies*? I am sure our poor aunt must not have known his compliments this evening to be any such thing – I have never seen her so offended."

Madness in Meryton

Jayne Bamber

Madness in Meryton

Copyright 2020 by Jayne Bamber

Cover Art by Carl Herpfer and Amber Cheney

***

This book is a work of fiction. Any person or place appearing herein is fictitious or is used fictitiously.

All rights reserved, including the right to reproduce this book, or portions thereof, in any form. Please do not reproduce or transmit this book, in whole or in part, by any means without permission in writing from the author.

This book is licensed for your personal enjoyment only, and may not be re-sold or given away to other people. If you would like to share this book with another person, please purchase an additional copy for each person. If you're reading this book and did not purchase it, or it was not purchased for your use only, then please purchase your own copy.

Thank you for respecting the hard work of this author.

***

ISBN: 9798671438895

Acknowledgements

For Gertrude McGillicutty,
an indomitable force to be reckoned with.

Jayne Bamber

"It was not very well done," Jane admitted. "But his intentions were good."

"And what of his intentions in coming to Longbourn?"

Jane knit her brow, and began to brush Elizabeth's thick, tangly hair in silence for a moment. "I think *that* is kind of him, too. He had no obligation to pay us any such consideration, you know."

"If it was Lady Catherine de Bourgh's notion, I am sure he feels very obligated indeed to procure a Bennet bride for his patroness to assist in the same way she has *assisted* Mr. Collins."

"Let me finish, Lizzy – you are being unkind." Elizabeth flinched; she had hoped to speak more cheerfully with her sister after so strange a day. She nodded for Jane to continue.

"What I mean to say is that I feel sorry for being happy when I know that you are not. You spent several days in company with people you dislike, for my sake, when you nursed me at Netherfield. And now you must bear Mr. Collins' attentions because Mamma has clearly warned him away from me."

"Perhaps that is true, but it is not your fault that you fell ill at Netherfield, or that Mr. Bingley's sisters and friend are so disagreeable – at any rate, I would put up with much worse to see you looked after. And really, I think you may be right that Mamma has warned Mr. Collins away from you, but I am glad of it. Imagine poor Mr. Bingley trying to outwit a rival that has not any wits at all!"

"Lizzy!"

"Well, I do not blame you for Mr. Collins turning his eye to me. If he had any sense at all, he would see that we are ill-suited for one another – of course, if he had enough sense, we might not be so ill-suited. What a dreadful conundrum – but I am not unhappy." Elizabeth tried to laugh it off for Jane's sake, and fidgeted with the locket she had purchased at the market that morning.

"You had better hide that away somewhere," Jane chided her. "I saw Lydia eyeing it all day."

"Indeed, she has already asked to borrow it," Elizabeth agreed. She removed the locket, admiring the pretty rose and silver filigree on the heart-shaped pendant before she tucked it away under some stockings in her bureau. "She would have chosen it herself, she said, but she was too shocked by the lightning that struck the tree in the square."

"It was rather frightening," Jane observed. She smiled coyly at Elizabeth as the two sisters got into their bed. "What were you speaking of to Mr. Darcy? I saw you standing together just before the lightning struck and Sir William Lucas cried out."

She had almost enjoyed her brief conversation with Mr. Darcy that morning, for he had spoken of his sister, and even solicited Elizabeth's advice in purchasing some little trinket for Miss Darcy from the gypsy's cart. Elizabeth deflected her sister's question with a waggle of her eyebrows. "Poor Sir William – I am sure he jumped three feet into the air! However shall he recover his dignity? But at least it did not rain – I could not have borne another day of rain."

Jane agreed, and nudged Elizabeth. "Will you really refuse to admit you had a pleasant discussion with Mr. Darcy? I saw you smiling at him."

"Yes, I suppose he is to be congratulated for demonstrating the minimum requirements of civility. What a milestone for him."

"You surprise me, Lizzy. Mr. Bingley told me that Mr. Darcy said he enjoyed conversing with you at Netherfield."

"I am sure he thoroughly delighted in observing all my flaws and scorning me for taking pleasure in dancing!" Elizabeth let out a huff of indignation, but pressed on, for she had come to what she had really wished to tell her sister. "Jane, Mr. Wickham told me something this evening at our aunt's card party."

"About Mr. Darcy?"

"Yes." Elizabeth rolled over and drew closer to Jane as she began to recount Mr. Wickham's tale of woe; the poor man, despite his dashing looks and charming manners, had suffered a great deal at Mr. Darcy's hand. Mr. Darcy *had* been unusually civil that morning, but Elizabeth's initial dislike of him was more firmly fixed than ever.

After Elizabeth related what she had been told, Jane

appeared contemplative. "But how can this be possible? Oh Lizzy, I think there must be some mistake, some misunderstanding! Mr. Wickham certainly seems to be an amiable man, and I cannot imagine he would ever invent such a history – but I could no more believe that Mr. Darcy would go against his father's wishes, ignore his duty, and really ruin the life of another man! And surely Mr. Bingley would not be friends with such a man, if Mr. Darcy *had* done such a thing."

Elizabeth laughed and shook her head. "Of course you wish to frame them both as good, but I cannot see how it is to be done. I could more easily see Mr. Bingley's being imposed upon, but Mr. Darcy's villainy is not so unfathomable. As to Mr. Wickham, I cannot question the veracity of his information, for there was truth in all his looks."

Jane was quiet for a moment. "Poor Mr. Bingley. If the story were to be made public, imagine his distress!"

"I suppose you are quite perfect for one another," Elizabeth teased her. "You are both too inclined to think well of others."

Another pretty blush spread across Jane's face. "I do not know if we are perfect for one another, but I like him, Lizzy."

"And he is half in love with you already."

Jane sighed. "I wish he had been invited to our aunt's card party. I am sure she was on the point of inviting him when they went away."

"Yes, and you have Mr. Darcy to thank for that," Elizabeth huffed. "I think you are right. Aunt Phillips had just invited the officers, and it did seem she meant to speak to Mr. Bingley, until Mr. Darcy dragged him off."

"I am sure he did not do it on purpose," Jane said with a frown. "He must have thought the lightning meant rain would follow."

"No indeed, Jane. Mr. Darcy saw Mr. Wickham, and he could not face the man he had wronged, and so he ran away like a coward. Besides, if he sensed the invitation was coming, he would have no wish to allow his friend to accept it. He thinks himself far too superior for such company, and with the way our mother and sisters were behaving – and our dreadful cousin – I can hardly blame him."

"Surely not, Lizzy. What could it matter to Mr. Darcy, if he did think so meanly of us? Mr. Bingley might have attended the party without him."

"Then how can you explain Mr. Darcy's hasty departure? There is no excuse that could acquit him of rudeness and lack of feeling."

"I hardly know," Jane muttered. She rolled over and snuffed out the candle beside their bed. "I only wonder at why Mr. Bingley followed him."

1

Elizabeth woke the next morning to her sister Mary's elbow colliding with her face. She yelped in surprise, and then sat up with no little alarm, staring down at her sleeping sister. She had gone to sleep in her own bed, the one she had always shared with Jane – but here she was. Elizabeth had heard of sleepwalking, but she had never experienced it. And yet, yesterday had been so very strange a day, she could hardly dismiss the notion that it had ended on an even stranger note.

Mary was still sleeping soundly; Elizabeth crept back to her own room and, careful of waking Jane, she dressed for a morning walk. It had not rained the day before, and she hoped it would not be too muddy for a trek to Oakham Mount before breakfast. She peered out the curtains only to find that the ground still appeared very damp – it must have rained at some point in the night.

She had not meant to groan so loudly at the notion of being confined to the house again, and Elizabeth was sorry indeed when Jane began to stir. "Lizzy, is that you?" Jane stretched and sat up with a wide, lazy smile.

"Sorry, Jane. I meant to be quieter."

"No matter; I ought to get up and start getting ready. Mamma will be wanting us in fine looks today."

Elizabeth snorted with laughter. "When does she not?"

Jane made the same face she always did when she had not the heart to contradict an ungenerous truth, her eyes shifting sideward as she pasted a smile on her face. "I happen to agree – today at least."

Elizabeth smiled knowingly – Jane must be hoping to see Mr. Bingley again. Mr. Darcy had whisked him away so quickly yesterday at the market, and Mr. Bingley *had* said he had intended to call at Longbourn. Elizabeth only hoped that Mr. Bingley would come alone, that he might remain as long as he wished this time.

Jane got out of bed and began dressing, and as Elizabeth went about her toilette, another idea occurred to her. "Jane, what if we assist Mary in her preparations this morning? Perhaps we might convince her to try a new hair style or borrow a dress from one of us."

"Why, Lizzy?" Jane's eyes lit with sudden comprehension before Elizabeth could answer. "Oh! Has it anything to do with Mr. Collins?"

"Yes, exactly. I thought about what you said last night, and the remarks our cousin made at breakfast yesterday – perhaps if Mary put herself forward more...."

Jane furrowed her brow. "I agree with you about Mary, but what remarks? What did Mr. Collins say about Mary – and what did I say to you last night about it? I do not recall discussing it with you."

Elizabeth felt an unaccountable sense of unease for the second time that morning. "Yesterday at breakfast Mr. Collins essentially rated us all in order of appearance – but I am sure you heard him, for you looked just as uncomfortable as I felt. And last night, you said that Mamma has likely warned Mr. Collins away from you on account of Mr. Bingley, and you were sorry if I was unhappy about being our cousin's next choice."

Jane's reaction was terribly bizarre – for though she

disclaimed any recollection of either conversation, it was clear that she had certainly thought of such things.

"Jane, are you well?"

"I am perfectly well, Lizzy. Really – you may resume sleeping in our bed tonight, I am entirely recovered from my trifling cold."

"No, I meant...." Elizabeth stopped herself. Jane had no recollection of their conversation last night, and Elizabeth herself had woken in Mary's bed. Had she dreamt up their bedtime chat? "Perhaps *I* am not quite well."

Jane had just put on the same sprigged muslin day dress she had worn the day before, and she crossed the room to place a hand on Elizabeth's forehead. "You are not feverish. That is a relief."

"Yes, I suppose so," Elizabeth muttered, still feeling entirely bewildered. Jane had moved on to admiring herself in the mirror, and though she looked very well indeed, Elizabeth blurted out, "You mean to wear that again? Would you not prefer Mr. Bingley to see you in something else?"

"Oh!" Jane looked stricken. Why she would think to wear the same dress two days in a row was beyond Elizabeth, but she could see she had offended Jane.

"I only meant that with all the mud, the dress might be ruined if you go outdoors." Elizabeth hesitated, suddenly wondering why Jane's dress was not soiled from their excursion to Meryton the day before.

"You are right," Jane admitted. "And of course I shall be going outside, silly."

Elizabeth smirked to herself – with Mr. Collins present, an escape to the garden with Mr. Bingley would be a welcome respite for Jane, if their family remained as determined to expose themselves as they had been the day before. And after what Jane had said last night, Elizabeth was determined to ensure her sister would get some time with Mr. Bingley.

And yet... *had* Jane really said any such thing? Elizabeth might have dreamt it up, which would explain why Jane had spoken so candidly of her feelings for Mr. Bingley, but Elizabeth was sure of what Jane must be feeling.

Jane was changing gowns, and she snapped Elizabeth out of her reverie when she asked for some assistance in dressing. "Could you do the back, Lizzy? Good Heavens, what is the matter?"

Elizabeth fastened the buttons idly, and then leaned in and rested her chin on Jane's shoulder. "I know I must be acting so oddly – I had the strangest dream last night."

"Oh?" Jane leaned her head against Elizabeth's. "I think it has upset you."

"A little. I suppose I am only adjusting my sensibilities – it felt so real, but it did not really happen. It is a queer feeling, but I suppose I need not be so alarmed." Elizabeth had no wish to feel so disconcerted, but she ran her fingers along the spotless hem of the sprigged muslin her sister had worn to the village yesterday, and her confusion persisted.

"You are frightening me, Lizzy," Jane sighed. "Here, sit down, and I will arrange your hair. Tell me what you dreamed of, perhaps it will make you feel better."

As Elizabeth sat down and considered where to begin, she laughed to think of her own foolishness. "I dreamt of speaking with you before bed. Perhaps I have only been missing our nightly conversations."

Jane began brushing out Elizabeth's hair and pinning it up. "What did we speak of in your dream?"

"Everything that happened over the course of the day." She let out a heavy sigh, and Jane motioned for Elizabeth to continue. "We spoke of the market, our aunt's card party, and of Mr. Bingley and Mr. Collins – and what Mr. Darcy has done to poor Mr. Wickham."

"Well, after the last two days at home, I can well imagine you would dream of market day and the card party. I have been looking forward to it, too."

"Looking forward to it?" Had the whole day been a dream? Elizabeth flinched, and Jane put her hand atop Elizabeth's head to gently still her.

"Of course. I hope I might encounter Mr. Bingley at the market – I was thinking perhaps our aunt would invite him to attend the party tonight."

Her hair was finished, though simply arranged; Elizabeth turned around to face her sister. "That is exactly what you said in my dream."

"Did I?" Jane's voice was calm, but her countenance betrayed the same mounting anxiety that Elizabeth felt.

"Yes. You said that you were sure our aunt was on the point of inviting him when he suddenly went away."

"He suddenly went away?" Jane let out a little, panicked groan.

"Only because Mr. Darcy led him off – no doubt because he could not face Mr. Wickham."

"And who is Mr. Wickham, Lizzy?"

Elizabeth shook her head as if to dislodge the confusion in her mind. It had all been so real – never had she experienced such a vivid dream, with every detail so clear the next day. She let out a nervous laugh. "I suppose I *would* invent a handsome officer to flirt with me and share my grievances against Mr. Darcy. My mind must have conjured him up for its own amusement."

Jane offered her a weak smile. "I hope you feel better now, Lizzy. It was all just a dream, but now we shall enjoy all the reality of a lovely and full day."

Elizabeth rallied her spirits enough to smile back at her sister. "Of course. It was just a dream. Well, shall I do your hair?"

"No, I think I will ask Hill. I liked your notion of helping Mary try something new. I suppose you must have dreamt of Mr. Collins saying something about Mary's looks, but there is merit in the idea. I think she is the most suited to him out of all of us."

"I will go to her at once," Elizabeth said. She left the room just as Hill was coming to do Jane's hair.

As Elizabeth passed by Lydia and Kitty's room, she heard the same sounds of squabbling that the sisters had made in her elaborate dream, but this was not an unusual occurrence. On an impulse, she slipped into the room, where her sisters were arguing over a bonnet. They took little notice of her, and with a sly grin Elizabeth helped herself to a pink floral dress and pink ribbon that were heaped on a chair nearby. She slipped out unnoticed and went to knock at Mary's door.

***

Half an hour later, Elizabeth and Mary joined the rest of their family for breakfast. Mary had been coaxed into wearing a far more feminine dress than was her usual custom, and Elizabeth was prodigiously proud of the flattering hairstyle she had cajoled Mary into allowing. The effect struck everyone at once, to varying effect.

"Well now! How well you look, Mary," Mrs. Bennet cried. "I knew you could not be so immune to all the officers in our midst! Come here, my dear girl!"

At this, Mr. Bennet looked up at Mary, and then gave Elizabeth a wink and a smirk, and Jane mirrored the same approval. Mr. Collins had also looked up and taken notice, though he was not so surprised as to preclude him from eating his kippers. Lydia and Kitty were the loudest, of course.

"Mary," Lydia cried. "That is my pink ribbon!"

"And my dress," Kitty whined.

Lydia nudged Kitty with her shoulder. "Hang your dress, Kitty! You can only wear one at a time, anyhow!"

"Well, it is the same with ribbons," Kitty protested.

"Indeed it is not! I can wear as many ribbons as I like. Anyhow, ribbons are smaller and more easily lost – and I do not trust Mary with mine! But it does not signify – I am sure the officers will still like me better!"

"And me," Kitty agreed.

"Hush, girls! There are plenty of officers to go around, and we shall get new ribbons at the market, I am sure," Mrs. Bennet scolded them.

"Your mother is right to chastise you, dear cousins," Mr. Collins said loftily. "My noble patroness, Lady Catherine de Bourgh, would never tolerate such behavior at a family meal. Though you are comely girls, you must learn some of your older sisters' modesty and propriety. And really, I cannot think why you would wish to put yourself forward for the officers. They have little prospects, compared to *some*, you know."

Elizabeth coughed to cover her laughter, for she was astonished to actually agree with her inane cousin for once.

Here her agreement came to an end, however, for Mr. Collins was not yet done. "You eldest sister's superior graces may be beyond imitation, but dear Cousin Elizabeth is one to be admired, to be sure, for she combines beauty and charm with modest sense and decorum, as befitting a woman with little fortune to recommend her. You would do well, my young cousins, to look to Cousin Elizabeth as your guide before you speak so boldly. Cousin Mary is quite right to look to her in matters of appearance – and see what very proper improvements *she* has made."

Mr. Bennet looked up from his newspaper to roll his eyes at Mr. Collins' speech. "Yes, well done, Lizzy. Well done, Mary."

"*Well done Mary?* She has spent the last two days sermonizing at us all, and now she steals my ribbon," Lydia persisted.

The argument resumed, with Kitty and Lydia carrying on about fripperies and officers, and Mary and Mr. Collins talking over one another about morality and propriety, while Mrs. Bennet scolded them all and Mr. Bennet resumed reading the paper.

Jane leaned in and whispered to Elizabeth. "I think your dream must be a prophecy, Lizzy. You said that Mr. Collins ranked us all by our appearance, and so he has done. It is uncanny."

"I cannot think how he can say such things, and then speak of decorum," Elizabeth whispered back as the rest of their family squabbled. "But I daresay it is not *so* uncanny that I would have dreamed of such a similar scene unfolding. I suppose I have taken the measure of all our family well enough, especially after two days of being confined indoors with them. We have heard of little else than officers, fripperies, and Lady Catherine – I cannot even escape it in my sleep!"

***

An hour later saw the Bennet ladies, accompanied by Mr. Collins, arriving in Meryton for the delights of the monthly market day. Just as in her dream, Mr. Collins had spent the walk into the village attempting to recommend himself to her, but this time Elizabeth had a little more success in drawing his attention to Mary, who remained the only Bennet with any interest in what Mr. Collins had to say.

As they made their way through the crowded thoroughfare of the village, Elizabeth seized the opportunity to separate herself from Mr. Collins; she latched onto Jane's arm and led her sister in the direction she expected Mr. Bingley to approach from.

Jane smiled brightly at her sister. "Where shall we go first?"

"In my dream, I bought a pretty necklace from Baba Romilda, and that is where Mr. Bingley happened upon us." Elizabeth frowned, recollecting that she had actually dreamt of having a pleasant conversation with the odious Mr. Darcy.

Jane beamed at her. "Baba Romilda was in your dream? Oh, I do love it when she passes through the village – I hope she is really here!"

"Her cart was in front of Mr. Miller's shop – let us begin there." Elizabeth led the way, and though she was disappointed that there was no trace of the kindly old gypsy who frequently brought assorted wares from London and abroad, she was pleased enough when they did indeed encounter Mr. Bingley.

Mr. Darcy trailed behind him, looking more sour than he had even in her dream. Elizabeth muddled through the civilities, but avoided Mr. Darcy's eye, for though she had merely dreamt up Mr. Wickham's tale, she still had her own reasons for disliking the man. Fortunately, he was easy enough to ignore, with Mr. Bingley before them.

"Well, this is exciting," Mr. Bingley said affably. "I had no notion it was market day – Darcy and I were on our way to call at Longbourn to ask after your health, Miss Bennet, but we have stabled our horses to have a look around."

Elizabeth was disconcerted that Mr. Bingley should address them just as he had in her dream, but Mr. Darcy's scowl of disapproval provoked her to respond with even more affability than Jane, who was Mr. Bingley's principal object. "It is just what I expected you to say, sir. You have settled in so agreeably to country life since coming to Netherfield."

"I hope I have," Mr. Bingley replied. "Indeed, I mean to distinguish myself as really part of the neighborhood by giving a ball very soon – now that you are so beautifully recovered, Miss Bennet, I am sure you must name the day."

"That is very kind of you, sir," Jane said with a blush, and for a moment she and Mr. Bingley simply stared at one another, smiling.

Elizabeth was resolved to help her sister on. It would likely vex Mr. Darcy, and that pleased her almost as much as doing Jane a good turn. "We must repay you with an invitation of our own, Mr. Bingley. Our aunt – I believe you have met Mrs. Phillips – is giving a card party tonight. I am sure we should all be delighted if you would attend."

"Oh, yes," Jane agreed, looking nervously at Mr. Darcy. "You are all very welcome."

"That sounds splendid, does it not, Darcy?" Mr. Bingley clapped his friend on the back. "But I daresay the invitation must come from your aunt – I believe I see her just over there, speaking with your mother."

Mr. Darcy looked far less pleased than his friend, and Elizabeth quickly understood why. She heard her mother's voice and her cousin's as well, and glanced over her shoulder to see them approaching. Lydia had latched onto Mrs. Forster and her husband the colonel, and was laughing boisterously with them as they trailed behind Mrs. Bennet and Mr. Collins.

It was near enough what had transpired in her dream that Elizabeth began to feel anxious indeed, for all her family seemed on the verge of exposing themselves, and she had no wish to see it. She knew Mr. Bingley was too amiable to think ill of her family, least of all when he was so preoccupied with Jane, but Elizabeth wished to spare herself the mortification of Mr. Collins introducing himself and her sisters fawning over the officers; she unwittingly began inching away, and looking around for some escape.

Mr. Darcy caught her eye, his expression stern, and

Elizabeth realized that she had no wish for him to witness her family's behavior, either. Surely it would only make him dissuade his friend from attending the card party. She forced a smile at him, reminding herself that though he was unpleasant, he was at least not as villainous as she had dreamt.

"Forgive me, Jane, Mr. Bingley – after two days cooped up at home, I am longing to look around – I still mean to see if Baba Romilda is about. Do excuse me." She cast a hesitant glance back at Mr. Darcy, and for Jane's sake she swallowed her loathing and asked him, "I wonder if you might wish to accompany me, sir? Perhaps a closer look at Meryton might improve your opinion of the place."

Mr. Darcy looked shocked, perhaps even affronted, but he nodded and offered her his arm. "I would by no means suspend any pleasure of yours, Miss Elizabeth."

Mr. Wickham's ill-use was just a dream, she reminded herself, schooling the disgust from her face as she accepted Mr. Darcy's arm. Much as it annoyed her, it was rather helpful to hold his elbow, as the thoroughfare was still very muddy from the recent rain. He led her away from the rest of her family, and after Elizabeth overcame her surprise that her ruse had worked, she was left wondering what to say to Mr. Darcy.

After a moment of uncomfortable silence, Elizabeth began to grow embarrassed – how odd it must have seemed, not only to Mr. Darcy but to all her companions, when she had singled him out and asked him to escort her! She certainly had no wish for him to presume she had any particular desire for his company, not after his slight to her at the assembly, and all of their arguments at Netherfield. Alas, the man looked miserable, and though this was not a reaction she wished her company to arouse, it was just what he deserved.

At length Mr. Darcy overcame his ill-humored silence and said, "I believe you meant to seek out a particular vendor, Miss Elizabeth."

"Oh, yes. Baba Romilda – she is an old friend."

Mr. Darcy gave her a querulous look. "Baba Romilda?"

"She is Romany," Elizabeth explained. "She travels a great deal, but she passes through the village sometimes to see her niece, and occasionally on market day she is out with her cart selling all sorts of trinkets and curio from parts unknown."

"Sounds fascinating." Darcy's look was inscrutable; Elizabeth was not sure whether he was mocking her. Strangely, in her dream he had been surprisingly friendly to her old friend, and Baba Romilda had been so well pleased with him as to give Elizabeth a suggestive waggle of her eyebrows behind Mr. Darcy's back.

Elizabeth was curious to compare what might transpire, with what had happened in her dream; there had been such uncanny similarities already, but unfortunately she could not see Baba Romilda anywhere. What did catch her eye was Sir William Lucas, who was seated on a bench near the large oak tree at the center of the village square. She halted in her steps, staring at the tree as she was struck with the vivid recollection of it being struck by lightning in her dream. "So strange," she muttered.

"Pardon? I did not hear you, Miss Elizabeth," Mr. Darcy said.

"Oh – I only meant...." Elizabeth chewed her lip for a moment. She could hardly say something as odd as that she had already experienced nearly this very situation in a dream. "I saw Sir William, and wondered if Charlotte was about," Elizabeth covered. "But perhaps she has already found my sisters."

They lapsed into silence again, and then Mr. Darcy said, "I am glad to see your sister appears recovered since her stay at Netherfield."

"Thank you, she is much better now." Elizabeth continued looking about for Baba Romilda, who was nowhere to be found. She knew she ought to be relieved, for if the morning had continued to progress too much like her dream she might have really been alarmed, and yet she could not dispel some little disappointment. However, she was glad that she was not with her family, watching her sisters fawn over the officers while Mr. Collins fawned over *her* – even if it meant walking with Mr. Darcy.

"I hope your sister is well, too, sir."

"As well as can be expected," Mr. Darcy said, glancing over his shoulder at the old oak tree before they rounded the corner and continued past the market stalls. "That is, she is well, thank you."

"I understand she is fifteen? My sister Lydia's age."

Mr. Darcy gave her a strange look. "Yes."

Elizabeth instantly realized her mistake – he had said it in her dream, when they had been perusing Baba Romilda's wares. "Miss Bingley had much praise for her at Netherfield."

He smiled, and Elizabeth watched with disbelief as he actually smirked – and nearly laughed. "Yes, rather too much, I think."

"Oh!" Elizabeth had attributed many qualities to Mr. Darcy, but never humor; she knew not what to say.

"I do not mean to say that she is not worthy of praise," he added, glancing nervously at her. "Only that she is modest and does not enjoy such lavish compliments. It makes her quite shy."

"I see," Elizabeth replied, reminding herself to discount the description of Miss Darcy she had from the fictional Mr. Wickham in her dream. "I believe it is often the case that those worthiest of praise desire it the least," she added, thinking of her own sisters.

"Exactly," Mr. Darcy said, smiling again. "I can guess you would say the same of Miss Bennet."

"I would. Jane is the best person I know – I believe I could never run out of wonderful things to say about her, and yet I know she does not like it. She, too, is shy and modest, which of course only adds to her perfection."

"And it speaks well of you, Miss Elizabeth, that you are so devoted to her."

She blushed at his words, before asking herself if he would think it as much of a recommendation were she to sing the praises of any others in her family, for she knew he held them all in contempt. "Aha – and now you have verbally fenced me in, sir, for if I am to accept your compliment – the first, I believe, you have ever paid me – I must acknowledge your merit in expressing the same sentiments toward your own sister."

He laughed again. "I surrender, Miss Elizabeth. As I have not the same claim on your compliments as Miss Bennet, I thought to resort to trickery. It was very wrong of me." His look was far from repentant – there was something so warm in his expression, so vastly different from his usual solemnity, that Elizabeth had unconsciously drawn closer to him. But then his expression clouded. "But I am sure these were not the first kind words you have had from me."

Elizabeth arched an eyebrow at him. "I daresay it does not signify, for what does not please me might still amuse. I am *tolerable*, perhaps, but I do not expect this to tempt you into any manner of eloquence."

Mr. Darcy clearly understood the import of her words, even as Elizabeth wondered what had possessed her to say them. They had rounded another corner and were approaching the high street again, and though Mr. Darcy looked as though he might speak, Mr. Bingley broke off from his conversation with the other Bennets and several officers, to wave and approach Mr. Darcy.

Elizabeth was flustered with embarrassment and released her hold on Mr. Darcy's arm to go to Jane, who moved away from Mr. Bingley when she perceived Elizabeth's distress. All this had happened in an instant, and what followed was terribly awkward. Elizabeth was sorry indeed that she had so perversely spoiled what had briefly been a very amiable conversation with Mr. Darcy, and sorrier still that Jane and Mr. Bingley seemed to feel the tension.

"Well, Darcy," Mr. Bingley said, glancing nervously at Jane and Elizabeth before addressing his friend. "Any luck finding a gift for your sister? Did you see your old gypsy friend, Miss Elizabeth?"

"No," both Elizabeth and Darcy said in unison.

"Well, that is a shame," Mr. Bingley replied. "I would offer to help you both have a look around, but we really ought to get back to Netherfield, Darcy. We have an evening out to look forward to, thanks to Mrs. Phillips."

Elizabeth roused herself from her sullen reverie to grin up at Jane, who looked very well pleased. Perhaps there was some silver lining to the offense Elizabeth had been unable to resist giving Mr. Darcy – now Mr. Bingley would come alone to the card party, and so much the better for Jane. For everyone, really!

"I am sure you have conveyed enough gratitude for the both of us," Mr. Darcy replied, and Mr. Bingley only laughed in agreement. "Like Miss Elizabeth, I am not especially fond of cards, but I shall look forward to attending. I might even hope there is some opportunity for dancing," Mr. Darcy said with a nod to Elizabeth. "I should find it refreshing."

Jane and Mr. Bingley were visibly surprised, but nobody more so than Elizabeth, who gaped up at the stoic and suddenly perplexing man. Again she knew not if he was mocking her, and she began to suspect he was not – he seemed to be in earnest, for he held her gaze with just the trace of a smile.

The moment was shattered by the sound of Lydia's laughter in the distance, and Elizabeth looked that way long enough to see her two younger sisters surrounded by officers. Mrs. Bennet caught Elizabeth's eye and waved her handkerchief in the air, shouting something inaudible. Mr. Darcy was looking that way, too, and his face set in a severe grimace before he turned and abruptly walked off.

Mr. Bingley laughed nervously. "I suppose that is my cue to bid you all farewell – until tonight, at least. Your mother must be wanting you. Give my thanks again to your aunt, Miss Bennet."

After Mr. Bingley hastened away, Jane linked her arm through Elizabeth's, slowly ambling toward the rest of their relations. "What was that about, Lizzy? I got the impression we had interrupted some manner of disagreement between you and Mr. Darcy."

"Disagreements between us are not especially scarce, though I had the strangest feeling he was very near apologizing, until Lydia provided such a timely reminder of why he might consider himself justified in thinking himself so very much above the rest of us."

Elizabeth instantly felt she ought not to have said such a thing, and it was clear Jane thought so. "Mr. Darcy seemed very gracious, Lizzy. But what was he about to apologize for?"

"I let him know I heard what he said at the assembly."

Jane gasped. "You did not!"

"I do not know what came over me. We had been conversing almost affably until then." Elizabeth could not bring herself to give voice to the fleeting suspicion that he had been flirting with her.

"Perhaps you might make amends at the card party tonight," Jane whispered as they rejoined their mother and sisters.

The evening's entertainment was being energetically discussed by Mrs. Phillips and the rest of the Bennet ladies, who were flanked by an increasing number of officers. One in particular caught Elizabeth's eye, for his was a familiar face. She felt her stomach sink, and saw Jane go white as a sheet, when Lydia introduced the newcomer as Mr. George Wickham.

***

Elizabeth had no chance to speak privately with her older sister that afternoon, though the many secret, significant looks exchanged between the sisters throughout the day indicated that Jane wished it. However, the afternoon continued much as Elizabeth had dreamt it, with her mother and sisters speaking of little else than the officers, and Mr. Collins seeking to recommend himself but achieving the opposite result.

It was only when they arrived at their Aunt Phillips' house that events began to transpire differently than how Elizabeth had dreamt, but by then it was already too late for Elizabeth's equanimity.

She did her best to stay close to Jane, hoping they might find some opportunity to sneak away and discuss the great shock of Elizabeth apparently dreaming a man into existence, but the presence of Mr. Bingley, which Elizabeth had orchestrated herself, made any confidence between the sisters impossible. Their amiable new neighbor approached them at once, and seemed determined to remain attached to Jane throughout the evening.

This ought to have been cause for both sisters to rejoice – certainly Jane was enjoying the company of such an attentive suitor, for she only ceased smiling to offer Elizabeth the occasional hesitant sideward glance.

Elizabeth did her best to push the dream from her mind and enjoy the evening, and she really did see how she *ought* to take pleasure in it. It was a fine thing that Mr. Bingley had been invited to the card party – and a finer thing, in Elizabeth's mind, that he had not brought his sisters. More likely, she knew, they had refused to come, but this was just as well, as they would have increased the enjoyment of the occasion for nobody.

Mrs. Phillips was in fine form, for she delighted in having company, and though she had been initially affronted by Mr. Collins' bumbling attempts to praise her home, she eagerly led him away to play whist, her look telling Elizabeth that the woman meant only to give her nieces some respite from their garrulous cousin.

On a whim, Elizabeth urged Mary to join them at cards. It had been easy enough to persuade Mary to exert the same effort for her evening toilette as she had done in the morning, and Elizabeth pressed her luck by extracting a promise that Mary would only play the instrument if no other ladies would oblige them. If she must exhibit, it would be a concerto she had practiced well – under no circumstances must she be pressed to indulge them with a tune they could dance to, for Mr. Darcy had threatened to dance with Elizabeth, and she could not countenance such a thing after the embarrassment she had caused herself that morning. Nor could she stomach the mortification she had felt in her dream, when her younger sisters had danced a reel with the officers, and with so much of the day unfolding so similarly, Elizabeth wished to avoid as much unpleasantness as she could.

To that end, she did her best to dodge Mr. Darcy, whose gaze followed her about the room. It was impossible not to notice and difficult to ignore; her only relief was that he did not seem inclined to converse with her.

Instead she moved about the room, ensuring Jane had ample time to speak with Mr. Bingley by intercepting any of their friends who approached to speak with them. For the first half hour of the party, Elizabeth remained thus occupied, and though it unnerved her that every conversation she had was nearly identical to her dream, she took comfort in the knowledge that the greatest difference between her dream and reality was that her family was not exposing themselves nearly as much as a result of her efforts.

Elizabeth had just deflected Colonel Forster and his young bride from interrupting Jane's tete-a-tete with Mr. Bingley, when Elizabeth's talent for distracting her companions began to wane. It was at this moment that Mr. Darcy seemed to tire of lurking about the perimeter of the room; he met her eye as he sought her out, and she did her best to ignore the man, and her thoughts of why he should do such a thing.

It was also at this moment that the lively game of whist came to an end, and the no longer distracted Mr. Collins also turned his attention back to Elizabeth. The two men crossed paths before they reached her, but Elizabeth was near enough to hear them speak; they had not been introduced at the market that morning, but Mr. Collins addressed Mr. Darcy nonetheless.

"Mr. Darcy," he said, bowing and simpering. "I have just made the most gratifying discovery – that you are indeed the nephew of my esteemed noble patroness, Lady Catherine de Bourgh. I have the honor of serving as her humble parson, for she has bestowed upon me the most valuable and estimable living of Hunsford. I can happily assure you that her Ladyship was in excellent health when I left the area three days ago."

Mr. Darcy regarded Mr. Collins with unrestrained wonder, offering a brief reply before shifting his gaze to Elizabeth. Mortified that he should look to her at such a moment, and that she had been found out observing them, Elizabeth quickly moved away, hiding her face as it turned pink. She looked around for Jane and Mr. Bingley, but it was too late. Mary had been entreated to open the pianoforte after her game of whist, and as a large group of officers had just arrived, Lydia and Kitty were loudly demanding music they could dance to.

It was all too much for Elizabeth. She rushed to Mary's side just as her sister had sat down on the piano stool. "Mary, you are not looking so lovely tonight for nothing," Elizabeth leaned in and whispered. "I am sure our cousin would dance, as he means to make amends for offending our aunt's hospitality when we arrived. Let me provide the music; you must have your share of the amusement."

Mary smiled gratefully, but hesitated after she relinquished her seat to Elizabeth. "Surely I cannot ask him to dance – and to put myself in his path so brazenly would go against what little praise he had for me this morning," she murmured.

"Do not vex yourself, Mary. It is only an informal gathering, and he *is* our relation. There is no impropriety in it – and I suspect he is rather floundering in his conversation with Mr. Darcy," Elizabeth said softly. "He may appreciate the rescue."

It was indeed a relief to see Mary detach their cousin from Mr. Darcy, who then turned to stare at Elizabeth again. He offered her the trace of a smile, and Elizabeth rolled her eyes as a smirk crept across her face. He may think she had done him some little favor, but it was all for her own dignity, which was rather short lived. Lydia and Kitty were still standing nearby, flirting with the officers, and Lydia resumed her clamoring for music.

"I do not care who plays, but you must play a jig," Lydia wailed, stamping her foot impatiently. "I wish to dance with Mr. Wickham – the poor man has not had a dance these three months at least!"

"So I have heard," Elizabeth muttered to herself, recollecting Lydia making the very same argument to Mary in her dream. Her fingers fumbled over the keys as she began to play; when she had finally composed herself enough to go on as if all were right and well, she made the mistake of looking up again.

Mr. Darcy was no longer staring at her, but at Mr. Wickham. *It must be true.* Elizabeth could not account for how, but if she had dreamed up the very image of the man dancing now with Lydia, the man who inspired such ominous looks from Mr. Darcy, then surely what he had told her in the dream must also be real. Either that, or she was, quite possibly, simply running mad.

Now Mr. Darcy crossed the room and began to speak with Mr. Bingley, actually interrupting his friend's dance with Jane. Odious man! Their exchange was a brief one before Mr. Darcy stalked away with a scowl – he began to look in Elizabeth's direction, but she quickly looked down at the instrument, for she could not bear to meet his eye. The next time she looked up, he was nowhere to be seen.

After she had indulged her companions with a second performance, she was content to relinquish the instrument to Mary; Elizabeth was far less embarrassed now that Mr. Darcy was gone, and exhausted from caring so much about her family exposing their want of propriety in his presence. A man who put others so constantly on edge ought not to go out into society – he did not appear to take pleasure in it at all, and certainly nobody desired his company!

Still angry with Mr. Darcy, she was eager to speak with Mr. Wickham, both to compare her dream with the man himself, and because he was really quite handsome. Lydia had moved on to flirting with Captain Denny, and Elizabeth stepped away from the instrument, positioning herself in the very same nook where she had spoken with Mr. Wickham in her dream. It did not take much to summon him – she met his gaze and offered a genuine smile at the sight of his interest in her.

With a grin, Mr. Wickham broke away from his fellow officers at once and made a very gallant approach. "Miss Elizabeth," he said, taking her hand in his as he bowed. "At last we speak. I ought to commend your performance – and thank you for playing for us, but I am sorry we have not danced."

"There is no need to apologize – I had not planned on dancing tonight, but I am content enough now – now that some others have departed."

Elizabeth was baiting him, but she could not help it. She was anxious to discover whether he really had any history with Mr. Darcy, but she thought she had brought it up naturally enough.

Mr. Wickham took a seat beside her. "You did seem distressed, before. Forgive me – I should never say such a thing to a beautiful woman, but I had a particular reason for noticing. I, too, was uncomfortable in Mr. Darcy's presence."

"I daresay we all were, with the exception of poor Mr. Bingley."

Mr. Wickham laughed. "Poor he is not, I am sure – else he

would be no friend of Mr. Darcy's. But I am surprised to hear you say such a thing – it is not often the case that I find others who share my opinion, when generally Mr. Darcy's status and fortune are enough to blind others to his defects."

What followed was just what Elizabeth suspected, a nearby verbatim recitation of what she had dreamt. Mr. Wickham revealed his connection with the Darcy family, Mr. Darcy's refusal to honor his father's wishes, and Wickham's struggle after being denied the living of Kympton. It was just as disturbing to hear of even for a second time – perhaps *because* she had heard it all before, but this time it was real. It was undeniably true, and Elizabeth's outrage all the greater when she considered that her dreaming of such a conversation before it occurred must certainly lend the encounter some great import and significance. But what could it all mean?

Elizabeth was no nearer an answer when she laid down beside Jane in bed that night, discussing the day's events. She was relieved, of course, that the day was nearly over, for the resemblance to her dream had made it impossible to take any real enjoyment in anything. The only exception was Jane's satisfaction in spending the evening with Mr. Bingley, which entirely made up for the rest in Elizabeth's estimation. Jane was tired from dancing and they did not speak long, but Elizabeth drew just enough comfort from her sister's happiness and her own vindication of despising Mr. Darcy, that she fell asleep quickly, looking forward to waking to some return to normalcy.

2

To Elizabeth's dismay, she awoke once again to Mary's elbow landing on her face. She did not cry out this time, but laid motionless on her back beside Mary, drawing the covers around her as if to dispel the trepidation she felt. As her sister continued to toss and turn, Elizabeth kept still and silent, fighting the urge to scream.

She gave in to the silent panic that gripped her until Mary had fallen back into a restful sleep, and then Elizabeth slowly eased her way out of bed, the cold floor on her bare feet even more startling than Mary's elbow. *I am not crazy*, she told herself. *I went to sleep in my own room last night, and woke up with Mary. Again.*

Elizabeth tiptoed over to the window and drew back the curtains just enough to peek through. Yesterday had been market day, and it had not rained – but the ground was soggy. Again. She let the curtain slip through her fingers and raised both hands to her head, which had begun to throb. *What is going on?*

Some part of her wanted to crawl back into bed – her own bed – but she could not let the matter rest. She slipped out of Mary's room, and back into her own. Jane was still sleeping, though Elizabeth recalled how easily her elder sister had woken the day before. She sat down at the dressing table and picked up her brush; she held it for a moment, torn between the opposing desires of wanting to postpone confirming her fears, and simply getting it over with. She let the hairbrush clatter to the floor and busied herself with retrieving it as Jane roused and sat up with a sleepy smile.

"Lizzy, is that you?" Jane stretched her arms above her head and yawned.

"Sorry to wake you," Elizabeth said as she brushed her hair out.

"No matter; I ought to get up and start getting ready. Mamma will be wanting us in fine looks today."

Elizabeth closed her eyes and sighed. "Yes. Market day."

Jane was holding her sprigged muslin dress up against herself in front of the mirror, but she turned and looked over her shoulder at Elizabeth. "I expected more enthusiasm from you, Lizzy. You love market day."

"I used to," Elizabeth sighed. "It rained in the night; you ought to wear something else, you will soil that."

Jane frowned down at her dress and set it aside. "I suppose you are right."

"The dark blue one, perhaps? It looked lovely on you yesterday, and Mr. Bingley seemed to like you well enough in it."

Jane screwed up her face. "Lizzy, whatever are you talking about?"

"We had the same conversation yesterday," Elizabeth replied, too weary to conceal what troubled her. "You want to look nice for Mr. Bingley. You are hoping our aunt will invite him to her party this evening. And you feel guilty because you like him and he likes you, which has made you exempt from Mamma's machinations regarding Mr. Collins. You believe Mary is the best suited for him out of all of us, and you would think it a wonderful idea if I assisted Mary in her toilette this morning. Am I wrong?"

Jane stared at Elizabeth, her eyes wide as she sank down onto the bed, her posture deflated. "I must be very transparent," she said softly.

"No, Jane." Elizabeth felt awful for upsetting her sister, and went to sit beside her. "Listen to me, Jane. I told you we have already had this conversation – you do not remember it, and I suppose I did not expect you to, but it is true."

"Lizzy, what are you talking about?"

"I do not know exactly – that is, I cannot explain what is happening to me. Yesterday morning I awoke believing it to be Thursday, with vivid memories of market day being the day before. I spoke with you yesterday, and you said it was market day. I thought I had dreamt everything up – but then the day passed in so similar a fashion to what I thought had been a dream.... and now it is happening again. For me, this is the third consecutive day I have woken up on the twentieth of November."

Jane knit her brows in concern and shifted uncomfortably. "I... I do not think you are teasing me...."

"I am not."

"I see." Jane raised her hand to Elizabeth's forehead, checking for fever.

"You did that yesterday, too," Elizabeth said with a bitter laugh.

Jane pulled her hand away. "Oh."

"I do not know what to do, Jane. I cannot explain what is happening – it cannot be a dream, surely."

"I cannot say. Perhaps you have dreamed of having a dream – oh dear, that is complicated."

"But you believe me?" Elizabeth clutched her sister's hand. It felt vitally important that Jane believed her.

"I wish to. You would not lie or invent such a trick. But there must be some explanation."

"Like what?"

Jane crossed her legs and leaned her shoulder against Elizabeth. "I do not know, Lizzy. I am trying to understand. You say you have experienced market day twice already – did anything of import occur?"

Elizabeth shrugged. "There were many similarities between the two versions of the day, but differences as well."

"Start with what was the same. That seems more significant, somehow."

"Mr. Collins made several ill-judged comments at breakfast about us and our sisters. Then we walked to the village, and Mr. Collins paid me more attention than I would have liked. We saw Mr. Bingley and Mr. Darcy at the market. Our sisters behaved as one might expect around all the officers, and our aunt invited them to her card party. I had a surprisingly civil conversation with Mr. Darcy, but then he abruptly left, and Mr. Bingley went with him. We met a Mr. Wickham, who has come to enlist in the militia, and he attended our aunt's party. Mr. Collins compared our aunt's home to Rosings, but in such a way as to accidentally give offense. Lydia and Kitty were boisterous in demanding music they could dance to. It all sounds rather urbane – exactly the sort of things anybody might guess – but there was one event of particular significance, I suppose."

Jane was listening in eager attention. "What is that?"

"Mr. Wickham told me that Mr. Darcy's father was his godfather, and desired him to join the church, but Mr. Darcy cheated him out of his inheritance."

Jane gasped. "Impossible!"

"I knew you would say so. We have had this conversation already, as well. You will say that there must be some mistake, that Mr. Darcy could not have ruined another man's life, and that Mr. Bingley could not be so deceived in his friend."

Jane nodded. "Yes – that is... I do think that. But could there not have been some misunderstanding? I know Mr. Darcy has offended you, and you have every right to resent him for it, but to go against his father's wishes and destroy a man's future is so extreme! And poor Mr. Bingley, if it is true! What a scandal, what mortification for him if his friend's history were made public!"

Elizabeth laughed ruefully. "Yes, I know."

"This is... shocking, Lizzy. I am overwhelmed – I am speechless."

Elizabeth pressed Jane's hand in hers. "I am sorry for burdening you – if you are feeling half the panic I have felt since yesterday, I can well understand your dismay. I hope you do not resent me for confiding in you."

"Resent you? Never, Lizzy!" Jane leaned in to embrace her. "I only wish I could help! But what is to be done? What *should* be done?"

"Nothing, I hope," Elizabeth replied with a shrug. "I only want it to be over. I want the day to pass quickly, and to wake up tomorrow in this bed, and hear that it is Thursday. And then we shall never speak of this again."

"I suppose that is all you can do," Jane agreed. "But if there is anything I can do for you today, you have only to ask, Lizzy."

"Oh, Jane." Elizabeth snuggled up to her sister. "It is enough that you believe me, for if you did not, I could not have believed it all myself."

***

Elizabeth and Jane had tarried too long in dressing themselves to be of any assistance to Mary before they went down for breakfast. Their family conversed much as they had done on the previous versions of that morning, and Jane sat at Elizabeth's side with an air of protective curiosity.

Breakfast at Longbourn was often chaotic, and some degree of silliness was not unusual, but the conversation this morning was exactly what Elizabeth had described to Jane. Mr. Collins began to compare the five sisters to one another in both appearance and comportment, and then compare them all to Lady Catherine de Bourgh's singular ideal of womanhood.

Elizabeth heard Jane draw in a sharp breath, and felt somewhat vindicated. Jane believed her, and though Elizabeth was no closer to figuring out what was happening to her or why, it was enough, for now, to have an ally.

When the Bennet ladies walked to Meryton after their repast, Jane remained close to Elizabeth, but Mr. Collins was determined to do the same. Elizabeth was eager to confide further in her sister and make sense of the strange repetition she was experiencing, and she could not put the matter from her mind sufficiently to listen to her cousin's inanities.

Desperate to put him off, Elizabeth adopted her younger sisters' method for repulsing their cousin: open disdain. It only took a few rolls of her eyes and snorts of derision, peppered with outlandish exaggeration about her interest in the officers, to convince him she was not up to Lady Catherine de Bourgh's standards. Elizabeth could see that Jane did not approve of her stratagem, but she was only a little repentant.

"I know, it was very wrong of me," Elizabeth admitted to her sister after Mr. Collins had abandoned his efforts. "But I have had to put up with him for many days longer than the rest of my family."

Jane offered her a look of dubious commiseration. "Well, Mary seems to appreciate his company more," she observed.

"Poor Mary," Elizabeth laughed.

"And poor Lizzy, too," Jane said. She gave Elizabeth's hand a gentle squeeze, and then her expression took an almost mischievous turn. "So, does your sudden interest in the officers have aught to do with this Mr. Wickham who has come to enlist?"

Elizabeth swatted playfully at her sister. "He is handsome, if that is what you really wish to know, but I have many reasons to think well of him. Aside from his affability and his charm and ease in conversation, I believe he is a man of great feeling, who has suffered immensely – and his pain is of Mr. Darcy's infliction."

"And what exactly does he claim occurred?"

"Claim! Oh Jane, there can be no doubting it," Elizabeth whispered, her ire rising at the thought of it. She glanced around to ensure that nobody else could hear before relating the story to Jane in full.

"The curious thing," Elizabeth continued once she had given Jane every particular, "is that his story was identical on both occasions. This, too, must lend him some credulity. If he was lying, surely there must have been some difference from one day to the next. And Mr. Darcy has boasted to me himself of his own pride – no, it *must* be true."

Jane, of course, made all the same protestations as she had done the day before, and the day before that – and Elizabeth said so. "Oh dear," Jane sighed. "Shall you know what I am about to say all day?"

"I suppose it depends. If it is a conversation we have had before, then I suppose I will. For instance, when Mr. Bingley sees us at the market, he will say that he was on his way to Longbourn to ask after your health."

Jane blushed. "That is very kind of him."

"Yes, that is just what you tell him," Elizabeth laughed, and put an arm around her sister's shoulders. "I am not laughing at you, I promise. Only at the peculiar situation I am in."

"Oh, Lizzy." Jane gave her a reassuring smile. "What do you mean to do?"

Elizabeth thought for a moment, screwed up her face, and shrugged. "I have not decided. I suppose if I am to repeat the day, I must make it an improvement of the previous versions I have experienced, and if I can avoid those that vex me the most, I shall be satisfied."

Jane made a droll face. "Mr. Collins and Mr. Darcy?"

"Precisely."

"I see," Jane said with a wry smile. "How convenient that you have adopted such a ruse – your *feigned* interest in the officers."

"It was very clever of me, to be sure," Elizabeth replied with equal mirth. "And I mean to make the most of it." They had nearly reached the village now, and ahead of them Lydia and Kitty quickened their pace. "You will encounter Mr. Bingley coming from the direction of the stables at the inn. I have no wish to quarrel with Mr. Darcy again, but if you lead them the other way, I will make sure our aunt seeks them out to invite them to the card party this evening."

"And am I to meet your Mr. Wickham?"

Elizabeth grinned, feeling flustered at the thought of his charming gaze. "He is not *my* Mr. Wickham – but I am sure you shall. Knowing Lydia, it will be impossible to keep him all to myself."

At that, Elizabeth ran ahead to catch up with her two

youngest sisters. They were already speculating on where to look for their favorites amongst the militia, Captain Carter and the charming Mr. Denny.

"I hope you do not mean to spoil our fun, Lizzy," Lydia pouted.

"No indeed! I only want my share in it," Elizabeth replied with a roguish waggle of her eyebrows. After all, if there was any chance of Lydia not remembering this tomorrow, Elizabeth might as well enjoy herself.

Kitty eyed Elizabeth with some suspicion. "You are not going to scold us or make a fuss about manners?"

Lydia laughed this off. "As if she could! La! I am hardly worried about *that* – I only hope you do not mean to steal their attention all for yourself."

Elizabeth laughed. "I would not dare! Indeed, I have no designs at all upon Carter or Denny. But perhaps I might meet a new officer...."

They had rounded a corner and the opposite side of the square from where Elizabeth had walked the day before – in the distance she could see Mr. Bingley hastening to greet Jane. A group of officers approached from further down the street, and Lydia let out a squeal of excitement. "Oh! Here they come!"

Elizabeth laid a hand on Lydia's arm. "There is no need to run, Lydia. *They* must come to *us*."

Though Lydia grimaced, Kitty laughed. "Oh, yes! They must come to us!"

A slow smile spread across Lydia's face, and she nodded knowingly at Elizabeth. "Yes, I shall conceal *my* interest to increase theirs – what a fine joke!" She straightened her posture, her chest and shoulders rising, poised to meet them and determined to be everybody's favorite. Elizabeth gave a little shake of her head at Lydia's determination, and looked for Mr. Wickham amongst the approaching officers.

He must have sensed her looking, for he turned and met her eye, and his look of surprise was quickly replaced with a confident smile that bespoke of her interest being returned.

Of course, Lydia made the greatest fuss over him when they all met and began to converse. She batted her eyelashes, clung to his arm, and giggled a vast deal, and though it annoyed Elizabeth, she was sure she only resented Lydia's behavior out of a sense of decorum.

Before long the sisters were joined by their mother and Mrs. Phillips, and it was not long before an invitation to the card party was issued. Amidst the great excitement that followed, Mr. Wickham broke away from his companions to approach Elizabeth. She had hinted to her aunt that the party at Netherfield must be invited, and with her duty to Jane now dispensed with, Elizabeth beheld Mr. Wickham with a determination to please and be pleased.

They had exchanged several glances of mutual appreciation when Lydia and Denny had dominated the conversation, and it had been clear that he wished to speak to her. Elizabeth was obliged to school her countenance and recollect that for him this was their first meeting.

"It is a relief to be so well received," he said with an easy gait as he stepped closer. "I was not sure what to expect of the locals."

"Meryton is always kind to newcomers," Elizabeth replied. "Whether they are as kind in return...." she cast a glance across the square at Mr. Darcy, who was standing at some remove from Jane and Mr. Bingley, scowling in their direction.

Mr. Wickham followed her gaze and betrayed a look of discomfort. "I hope the warm welcome continues," he said as he recovered himself. "I am in want of society, and it appears Meryton to be just the place for it. Your aunt is exceedingly kind."

"She is a dear woman," Elizabeth agreed. "Her card parties are always enjoyable – I hope you mean to attend."

"I shall look forward to it. Tell me, is there likely to be dancing? I should be all eager anticipation if there is any chance of dancing a reel."

"I can say with absolute certainty that there will be dancing," Elizabeth said with private amusement.

"Absolute certainty? Well, I am sure you have not the proxy to answer on anybody's behalf but your own, therefore I must hope this means that you will be the first to stand up with me, if there is dancing."

"*When* there is dancing," Elizabeth said, her face coloring.

Mr. Wickham held her eye for a moment, smiling down at her the way Mr. Bingley often did to Jane, and Elizabeth was blissfully flustered by his obvious attraction to her. However, the moment was spoiled when Mr. Wickham looked away – at Mr. Darcy.

Elizabeth was startled by the odious man's approach. He had not sought Mr. Wickham out in the previous iterations of the day, and she could not account for why he would do so now, but it was clear that poor Mr. Wickham had no wish to meet with him, and neither did she.

"I feel a sudden chill," Elizabeth observed. "I ought to keep walking – have you had much of a look about the market?"

"No, not at all, but I should like to." He cast one final glance at Mr. Darcy before offering Elizabeth his arm, and she happily accepted – despite the look of unrestrained envy Lydia shot her. She allowed Mr. Wickham to lead her up the high street, feeling very well satisfied with how the day was unfolding.

***

Elizabeth's good cheer remained undiminished as she and her sisters arrived at her Aunt Phillips' house that evening. Jane's faith in Lizzy had been cemented upon her meeting with Mr. Wickham that morning, and the look Jane gave her when both sisters heard Mr. Collins bumbling through a shabbily rehearsed compliment to their aunt reaffirmed it.

Strange as it all was, Elizabeth was far less distressed about it all than she had been that morning. The card party, she was sure, must hold some key to the mystery; Jane had wished Mr. Bingley to attend, and Elizabeth was sure Mr. Wickham's confidence in her bore some little significance.

She considered her earlier conversation with Jane, wherein she had resolved to evoke some manner of improvement upon the previous versions of the day. Though her younger sisters may require some interference later in the evening, Elizabeth considered that she had done well enough in orchestrating the day to greater satisfaction on this occasion. She had thoroughly repulsed her cousin, avoided Mr. Darcy at the market, and received such charming encouragement from Mr. Wickham. Perhaps all would be put right.

Mr. Bingley arrived shortly after the Bennets, and though he was accompanied by Mr. Darcy and Miss Bingley, Jane appeared not to mind at all. Elizabeth paid them all exactly the degree of civility she felt them due – she was affable as ever to Mr. Bingley, and spoke only the barest of greetings to his sister and friend.

Mr. Wickham and the officers arrived soon after, and though Elizabeth was gratified at Mr. Wickham searching her out in the crowd from afar, Lydia quickly thwarted Elizabeth by latching onto Mr. Wickham almost immediately. She called for Mary to play a jig, and Elizabeth chastised herself for forgetting to ensure that this particular moment was handled with more delicacy.

She had some consolation in perceiving that though Lydia was to claim the first dance with Mr. Wickham, he had eyes only for Elizabeth as he moved to the center of the room to join the set that was forming. This pleasure was fleeting, however, for as Elizabeth moved about the room, sipping a glass of wine, she unexpectedly encountered Mr. Darcy in her path. "Oh!" She stopped just sort of colliding with him.

Mr. Darcy collected himself, his cool reserve only momentarily disrupted. "I beg your pardon."

"No indeed," she said, taking a step backward. She had been very close to him, and he was so very tall – it was rather disconcerting. "I had not realized Miss Bingley had released you from her clutches." She let out a little gasp as soon as the words were spoken, and raised her hand to her mouth before anything worse could come out.

Mr. Darcy appeared indignant, or so she thought, until he laughed softly. "Yes, it is the first thing to surprise me all day."

Elizabeth was taken aback by his unforeseen humor, and then again at the recollection of her two pleasant conversations with him on the previous market days. She recovered herself, and her eyes flicked to Mr. Wickham – surely *that* must have surprised him as well, for Mr. Darcy had been glaring at the poor man since the moment the officers arrived.

She recollected all his offenses against Mr. Wickham, though she had yet to hear the recitation of them yet tonight – and Elizabeth began to hasten away.

"Miss Elizabeth," Mr. Darcy said as she began to move away.

"Sir?"

"I find I am unable to resist the temptation of dancing," he said, making an awkward gesture to those of their party who were reeling merrily together. "Would it be tolerable to you to stand up with me?"

Elizabeth felt a surge of panic at his phrasing, and was searching her mind for the right way to refuse him – as disdainfully as possible – when she saw her cousin approaching them. She could not determine which possibility was worse, standing up with Mr. Darcy, or witnessing another recurrence of Mr. Collins adding fuel to the flame of Mr. Darcy's derision. In the end, she gave a silent nod and accepted Mr. Darcy's hand as they joined the dance.

The surprise of the rest of the party when they entered the set was evident, and it occurred to Elizabeth that to some it must seem as though Mr. Darcy had paid her a great compliment, but she rather felt it a punishment, for he was silent and stoic as ever, and stared ineffably at Mr. Wickham as they began the movements of the dance.

She mused for a moment on whether her dislike of him ought to be expressed by refusing conversation, or by initiating it, and at length she settled on the latter. "You are much to be admired," she began innocuously. "To be going out in such confined and unvarying society must take tremendous forbearance – but at least your friend is happy." She made a subtle gesture toward Mr. Bingley, who stood at some remove with Jane; the two were completely engrossed in one another.

Mr. Darcy looked down at her with consternation. "There are few who would say that such an evening as this is any comparison to the social occasions of London, and though this is a fact, it does not follow that it must be an unpleasant thing."

The dance obliged them to turn, and they both clapped along with their companions, but Elizabeth felt none of the same joyful energy that she usually experienced when dancing. Mr. Darcy was gazing intently at her, and beyond them Mr. Wickham was looking on in some dismay.

Poor man! How it must pain him to see her standing up with his nemesis! She hoped it would not sway his opinion of her, for she would have rather danced with Mr. Wickham, had not Lydia been moved into competing for his attentions.

"And did you find our market to be pleasant this morning?"

Mr. Darcy's face took on a very strange expression, and after a pause he replied, "It was just what I expected it might be, I suppose; I daresay I did not find it as pleasant as some."

Elizabeth glared at him before the dance obliged her to turn again. "Perhaps you have some particular reason for thinking so – and more the pity. For my family, it is always a cheerful occasion – and an opportunity to make new acquaintance."

Mr. Darcy frowned, his color rising. "Mr. Wickham is blessed with such happy manners as may ensure his *making* friends – whether he may be equally capable of *retaining* them is less certain." He cast a glance over at the gentleman in question, his jaw clenched.

"He has been so unlucky as to lose your friendship," Elizabeth spat, "and in a manner he is likely to suffer from all his life."

His eyebrows knit together as he sneered down at her, and he was on the verge of making some reply when Mrs. Phillips passed that way, and called out to Elizabeth.

"What superior dancing, Mr. Darcy," said she, actually interrupting their steps to converse with them. "We were all so very shocked when you did not dance at the assembly, but I daresay it is only natural that Meryton must be growing on you. I am sure we shall hope to see such merriment often repeated, particularly when a *certain event* takes place!" Here she motioned you Jane and Mr. Bingley. "But I shall not detain you any longer," Mrs. Phillips laughed. "I see my niece's bright eyes upbraiding me!"

Mr. Darcy appeared not to hear this last part, for when his attention had been called to Jane and Bingley, he had begun to stare in their direction with evident disapproval. He went through the steps by rote, and it was a very long minute indeed before he seemed to recollect Elizabeth. "My apologies – I have grown distracted since your aunt spoke with us."

"It is of little matter," Elizabeth said coolly. "I am sure she could not have interrupted any two people with less to say to one another."

Mr. Darcy seemed chastened by her speech, and Elizabeth smiled. She caught a glimpse of Mr. Wickham further down the set, and he seemed to perceive that she was even more miserable dancing with Mr. Darcy than he was with Lydia. He made a droll face at her, and smirked.

Mr. Darcy had not perceived this silent exchange, but he may have guessed who had caught her eye. He made another attempt to converse. "What think you of books?"

Elizabeth began to suspect he only wished to engage her to vex his rival, and she refused to cooperate. Keeping her expression grim, that he might not claim any triumph in pleasing her, she replied, "I am sure we never read the same, or not with the same feelings."

"I am sorry you think so; but if that is the case, there can at least be no want of discourse between us. We may compare our different opinions."

Elizabeth peered over at Mr. Wickham again, eager for this dance to end, that she might stand up with an infinitely preferable partner. Looking back at Mr. Darcy, she arched an eyebrow. "Of which we have an inexhaustible supply, I am sure. But I can hardly speak of books while dancing at a party – my head is sure to be somewhere else."

"The *present* always occupies you in such scenes, does it?"

"Yes, always," she said without much thought. She missed a step, then, reminded of her unusual dilemma. "Especially just now."

Now Mr. Darcy missed a step, and as he corrected his movements, he looked at her with some discomposure. "There we must agree – I hope you are not too terribly shocked."

"It is *you* that has claimed to be nearly past surprise," Elizabeth reminded him.

"Trust me, Elizabeth, if you but knew...." Mr. Darcy had not the opportunity to finish his sentence, for Elizabeth reacted at once to his use of her Christian name. Without even attempting to make it appear an accident, she trod on Mr. Darcy's foot very hard, and muttered a paltry apology before moving away.

She fled across the room, seating herself on the same sofa where she had previously conversed with Mr. Wickham. As she had hoped, he sought her out when the dance ended a couple minutes later. "I hope you do not fault me for not honoring our promised dance – it seems we were both rather prevailed upon."

Elizabeth smiled up at Mr. Wickham and motioned for him to sit with her. "I am relieved that you understand me, sir – Heaven forbid anybody get the impression I enjoyed my last partner!"

His face lit with delight as Mr. Wickham took a seat at Elizabeth's side. "You are a remarkable discovery, Miss Elizabeth. I fear there are too many women who would consider a dance with Mr. Darcy in a much different light, no matter how disagreeable he is."

Across the room, Mr. Darcy was speaking with Miss Bingley; the two were staring at Mr. Bingley, no doubt conspiring to draw him away from Jane. Elizabeth moved a little closer to Mr. Wickham, hoping Mr. Darcy might see the growing esteem she felt for her present companion; she listened with alacrity and empathy as he told her of his history with Mr. Darcy, and though she had heard it all before, she was still moved to feel a great surge of compassion for the handsome gentleman who had singled her out.

The Netherfield party had departed by the time Mr. Wickham had finished his tale, which still had not varied, and though Elizabeth wished Mr. Darcy still present, if only to see him instantly and publicly disgraced, she was content to enjoy Mr. Wickham's company. For his part, he appeared perfectly at ease with her, and his open approbation was bestowed as they moved on to other subjects, chatting happily and flirting just enough, until the evening came to its inevitable conclusion.

Elizabeth had a great deal to think on when she returned home and dressed for bed with Jane, who naturally had much to say for herself, and more to ask of her sister. They talked together later than they had in previous days, and though neither could sway the other's opinion on the dispute between Mr. Darcy and Mr. Wickham, they remained in complete and harmonious agreement on the matter of Mr. Bingley's perfection.

***

Elizabeth was far less surprised the fourth time she awoke to Mary's elbow connecting with her face. She was disheartened, but bitterly dispassionate. Where yesterday she had hoped to find some meaning in what was happening to her, today she wanted only to put an end to the maddening repetition that plagued her.

The day proceeded just as it had before, beginning with Elizabeth quickly telling Jane what she must, in order to convince her sister of the strange redundancy she was experiencing. Breakfast, too, was just what she knew to expect; she made no endeavor to change the course of conversation, and so it proceeded in so identical a fashion as the day before as to make Elizabeth feel utterly hopeless.

Only when they arrived at the market did Elizabeth discern any difference, and it was not, strictly speaking, an improvement in any way; Mr. Bingley met them, but it was his sister who had accompanied him – Mr. Darcy had remained at Netherfield.

As she had done before, Elizabeth took measures to ensure Mr. Bingley was invited to the card party, and she did her best to be agreeable when they were introduced to Mr. Wickham, but she found the whole endeavor rendered exhausting in its pointlessness.

She walked on her own and soon encountered Charlotte Lucas – it was a pleasant change, and a greater relief than she might have guessed.

"Lizzy," Charlotte greeted her.

"Charlotte!" Elizabeth eagerly embraced her friend. "How do you do? It feels like an age since I have seen you!"

Charlotte attached herself to Elizabeth with all the ease and affection of a long-standing friend, and the two began ambling down the high street arm in arm. "I hear you were at Netherfield for several days – but you must tell me all about it, for we are very dull at Lucas Lodge. How did Jane and Mr. Bingley get on? And how did Mr. Darcy behave?"

"Much the same," Elizabeth said, her grin fading as the weight of her words struck her. She longed to confide in Charlotte, wondering what her pragmatic friend might make of it all. "Indeed, the last few days have all been so much the same, it is as if I am living the same day over and over again."

Accustomed to all of Elizabeth's odd humors and sardonic japes, Charlotte grinned and shook her head. "You shall not convince me, dear Lizzy, that there has not been *some* excitement."

"I have no intention of making any such claim," Elizabeth laughed. "Quite the reverse."

Charlotte squeezed Elizabeth's arm. "Tell me."

Before Elizabeth could do so, several of the officers broke away from her sisters, across the village square, and began to walk in that direction. Mr. Wickham was amongst them; he held Elizabeth's gaze as he came toward her, and as he was passing her, he smiled broadly and gave her a nod of acknowledgement. She returned his obvious admiration with a bright smile of her own.

"Why Lizzy, you sly thing!" Charlotte giggled merrily. "Who – and what – was that?"

"That was Mr. Wickham – I met him this morning. He has come to Meryton to join the regiment."

"I should like to see him in a red coat," Charlotte said appreciatively. "I suppose this must be a popular opinion in the village this morning."

Elizabeth chortled at her friend's cheek. "If my younger sisters are to be trusted...."

"Your sisters?"

"Do not look at me like that, Charlotte!"

"Shall I look at you like this?" Charlotte began to mimic the flirtatious gaze of Mr. Wickham, and Elizabeth could not stop herself from laughing. "Another admirer – well done, Lizzy!"

"Another?" Elizabeth had been watching Mr. Wickham make a circuit about the open square, and nearly tripped as she wracked her brain to understand – Charlotte could not know about Mr. Collins yet, surely.

"Really, Lizzy, you must know I mean Mr. Darcy."

Elizabeth snorted and scoffed in one odd sound. "No indeed!"

"He is not so bold as your handsome officer, but I have often observed Mr. Darcy staring at you a great deal, and he speaks to you more than any other local lady."

"Only to declare me less than tolerable, and to accuse me of willfully misunderstanding everybody," Elizabeth replied, rolling her eyes.

"Did he say that to you?"

"Yes, at Netherfield. We did little but quarrel while I was there. Vexing man!"

Charlotte smiled, almost smug now. "Ah, but perhaps he is right, Lizzy. You misunderstand me, and perhaps you even misunderstand Mr. Darcy – he must have meant to hint that you have misjudged him."

Elizabeth laughed ruefully. "A prettier explanation, perhaps, than his evident desire to insult me."

"Laugh as much as you choose," Charlotte teased. "You shall not laugh me out of my opinion. Oh! Look, there is Mr. Darcy now – and what do you know? He is looking this way."

Elizabeth peered out across the square, and just beyond the ancient oak at the center of it, she discerned Mr. Darcy in the distance. He was indeed staring at her, but looked away as he perceived her returning his gaze. "I know it is abominably rude to stare at people in such a way," Elizabeth quipped. "I wonder what he is about, leering at people like that! Mr. Bingley told us Mr. Darcy had stayed at Netherfield – would that he had, odious man!"

Charlotte only shook her head in amusement at Elizabeth's

indignation, and the two went on their way. They had meandered toward where the rest of the Bennet and Lucas ladies were clustered; Mrs. Bennet called out to them, waving her handkerchief in the air. Elizabeth was weary indeed of the sight before her: her younger sisters flirting, laughing and shrieking wildly for all the village to see, her cousin Collins eyeing her with disjointed pomposity, and her mother testing the limits of Mr. Bingley's interest in Jane.

Unable to resist, Elizabeth glanced back over her shoulder to see if Mr. Darcy had taken in the mortifying tableau, but instead she glimpsed him across the square, speaking – arguing, to be exact – with Mr. Wickham. Filled with a sense of unease, Elizabeth laid her hand atop Charlotte's. "I hope you will come to the card party tonight. There are some particulars I must acquaint you with."

"How very wicked of you," Charlotte whispered as they approached their mothers. "I can hardly press you about your secrecy now, and must spend many hours in private conjecture." She twisted her lips into a smirk, before schooling her countenance into perfect innocence.

"Take care that you arrive early, then," was all Elizabeth could say in return.

***

Elizabeth received an unexpected scolding from her mother for inviting the Lucases to Mrs. Phillips' party. "Well, what a fine thing for your sisters!" Mrs. Bennet's voice was heavy with sarcasm. "What a *relief* your sisters will have two more young ladies in the party, else they might have suffered the *misfortune* of having the officers all to themselves!"

This in no way diminished Elizabeth's pleasure in seeing her friend Charlotte at the party on this version of the evening. She arrived just after Elizabeth and her sisters; the two friends sought one another out directly. Elizabeth led Charlotte to a quiet part of the room, away from the rowdy game of whist. "I have so much to acquaint you with," she whispered to Charlotte.

"You must do so before either of your beaux arrive," Charlotte chided her softly.

"No," Elizabeth said with an eyebrow arched as she sat down on the sofa beside her friend. "What I must do is wait just a moment."

Charlotte knit her brow with skeptical humor in her eyes. "Why must we wait?"

Elizabeth scanned the room; it was a familiar scene by now. Only a few of the officers had arrived yet, and they were all clustered around Kitty and Lydia, who played whist with Mrs. Phillips and Mr. Collins. Mary was finishing up her first piece of the evening at the pianoforte, and seeming somewhat to transition to the second.

"In a moment, my aunt will chastise Mr. Collins for playing the wrong suit, and Lydia will crow very loudly over his error," Elizabeth whispered. "He will apologize with greater verbosity than strictly necessary, and then Lydia will play her trump card, and lean very far over as she does it – affording the officers standing by Kitty a view of her décolletage. Mary will perceive this from the instrument and scowl before she begins a new song. She will sing poorly, I am afraid, and then Lydia will be the one to wince. A moment after that, Colonel Forster will arrive, and his wife will be wearing a very over-trimmed green dress and a feather in her hair. My uncle will greet them very eagerly, but Mrs. Forster will pay him little mind and make straight for Lydia."

"Have you grown clairvoyant, Lizzy?"

Elizabeth made no reply, and when she heard her aunt begin to fuss at Mr. Collins, Elizabeth gestured for Charlotte to watch – the scene unfolded just as she had described.

"Well," Charlotte breathed, her eyes wide as she looked over at Elizabeth. "Apparently you have. Pray, did Miss Bingley instruct you in the dark arts while you were staying at Netherfield?"

"I am not clairvoyant, I do not think," Elizabeth said, wondering how to proceed.

"But you knew what would happen. How is this possible?"

"If I tell you, you must promise to believe me. Jane believed me, for I have done some little foretelling this morning at Longbourn." Elizabeth glanced over at Jane, who was speaking with Mary and Maria Lucas in the corner. She wished to wave her sister over, but she knew that Mr. Bingley would soon arrive, and she had no wish to prevent him from attaching himself to Jane at once.

"I do promise." Charlotte leaned forward impatiently.

"Very well. I have been repeating the same day over again, Charlotte. Every day I wake up, and it is the twentieth of November all over again. Nobody but myself seems much aware of it."

"Repeating the same day?"

"That is how I knew what would occur just now – it is the fourth time I have seen it."

"And everything is the same, from one day to the next?"

"Generally, yes. Everyone will say and do just what they did the day before, unless I cause any alteration myself. We always walk to the market, we meet with Mr. Bingley and Mr. Wickham, my sisters flirt with the officers, Mr. Collins vexes me greatly. And here at the card party, there has been some variance, but usually it is of my own making."

Charlotte nodded and fell silent, her eyes darting about as she considered it all. "You say it is *usually* of your own making when events transpire differently from one day to the next – have there been any occasions where something is different, that is unconnected with you?"

Elizabeth was struck by the insight of her friend's question, and gave the matter some thought. "Well, on the first occasion, lightning struck the tree in the village square, but it has not happened since."

"That is ominous."

"I suppose it is. Let me think. Caroline Bingley came to the market this morning, that was new. And she was at the card party last night. The day before that it was only Mr. Darcy and Mr. Bingley, and the day before that nobody from Netherfield was invited."

Charlotte tapped her chin. "I am sure we might puzzle it all out."

They were quiet for a moment, and Elizabeth looked around the room. By now Mr. Bingley ought to have arrived, and it occurred to her that one thing she could not predict was who else might arrive with him.

With a rueful shake of her head, Charlotte observed, "I can hardly believe I am seriously entertaining such a notion. Lizzy, if this is a jest, please tell me at once."

"I assure you, it is not. I wish it were; I would happily confess. No, Charlotte, I am experiencing the twentieth of November for the fourth consecutive day – either that or I am gone mad."

"I cannot think you mad, Lizzy." Charlotte sighed. "Well, we must work it out. I cannot help but only that there must be some connection with Netherfield, if you have seen them appear in such varied groupings. And then there was something.... this morning, when we observed Mr. Darcy staring at you, you said that Mr. Bingley believed him to be at Netherfield. Has anything like that occurred before?"

"No. The last three days, they have come to the village together."

"Has Mr. Bingley seemed any different from one day to the next?"

"No, he always greets us just the same. Here at the party he does vary, but it is because something else has caused the conversation to go a different way – a long term effect of my own varied actions."

"Hmm. I still think there must be a Netherfield connection. And the lightning – that must be significant."

Elizabeth considered. Miss Bingley's behavior had altered independently of anything Elizabeth could have caused – perhaps the woman *was* practicing dark arts. It seemed no less likely than any other explanation, and yet just as preposterous as the situation itself.

"I have been wondering if Mr. Wickham has aught to do with it – if there is some significance to my meeting him."

Charlotte gave her a knowing look. "You *like* him."

"It is more than that," Elizabeth insisted. "Every evening, we have the most remarkable conversation." She related Mr.

Wickham's story in full, as Charlotte listened attentively.

"He tells you this every evening?"

"Yes – you cannot doubt it, surely!"

"I can understand why *you* do not," Charlotte replied. "A handsome young man who shares your favorite complaint – happy thought indeed!"

"What motive could he have for inventing such a history?"

"What motive could he have for speaking so candidly to a perfect stranger?" Charlotte gave Elizabeth a stern look. "If he has only just met you this morning, why should he reveal such private information? And with Mr. Darcy actually present!"

"On the first occasion, Mr. Darcy was not present. And then, the other times, Mr. Darcy had gone away before Mr. Wickham spoke."

"You only lend strength to my argument," Charlotte persisted. "He says these things when Mr. Darcy is not present to defend himself. I wonder, Lizzy, if you have given Mr. Wickham any hints of your dislike for Mr. Darcy before hearing this tale of woe?"

"Well...." Elizabeth hesitated, and let out a heavy sigh. "Oh dear," she muttered.

It was just as Elizabeth realized she might have given too much credit to Mr. Wickham's assertions, that the man himself entered the room. He smiled in her direction before following his fellow officers to greet his hostess. Lydia made her way to them at once and began demanding Mary play music fit for dancing. Elizabeth looked around in some panic. "Mr. Bingley ought to be here by now," she murmured. "He has always arrived before Mr. Wickham."

"That confirms it, then," Charlotte said. "There must be some element beyond your control, to account for any difference that is not your own doing."

Elizabeth nodded in pensive agreement, still considering her sudden misgivings about Mr. Wickham. "He will speak to me after his dance with Lydia, I believe. I shall attempt an experiment – I shall say something favorable about Mr. Darcy, and study how that affects what he chooses to confide."

Charlotte smiled. "And I shall be eavesdropping nearby, for

I cannot miss such a historic first."

***

Jane and Elizabeth left the card party in low spirits. Jane was merely disappointed that Mr. Bingley had not attended, and though Elizabeth shared her sister's feelings, she had a great deal besides that to discourage her.

Charlotte had been right about Mr. Wickham; he was easily repulsed when Elizabeth had betrayed every impulse and made a few favorable mentions of Mr. Darcy. To her immense chagrin, she called him handsome, amiable, and intelligent – and though she had fleetingly witnessed such qualities in the man during their acquaintance, given voice to such thoughts had left a sour taste in her mouth.

Just as Charlotte had predicted, Mr. Wickham did not confide his history to her that night, for she had not shown herself to be predisposed to believe him. It was some consolation to Elizabeth that Charlotte had taken no satisfaction in being right; she had only observed that if Mr. Darcy was really such a villain, Mr. Wickham ought to have made some effort to warn her. This was, somehow, much worse.

Elizabeth's head whirled with confusion as she settled into bed with Jane, trying to make sense of it all. Confiding in Charlotte had been a relief, at first, but her wise friend had given her so much to think upon that she could not bear it.

Jane was just as sullen, and after a companionable but heavy silence, Jane leaned her head against Elizabeth's shoulder. "Well, Sister, I hardly know what to think. Why would Mr. Bingley give his word this morning, and then not attend the party?"

"I cannot say. I did not speak with him this morning, as I had done on previous occasions."

"Perhaps that is why," Jane sighed. "Oh – I am sorry. I did not mean to blame you."

Elizabeth wrapped one arm around her sister. "I know, Jane. But perhaps you are right. Perhaps I must be directly involved, as I was before. I let my desire to speak with Mr. Wickham get the better of me."

"You did not speak much to him this evening."

"No. I tried something new, to see what difference it would make. I cannot like the outcome."

"Oh, Lizzy. I am sorry." Jane gave Elizabeth's hand a gentle squeeze. "Have you changed your opinion of him?"

"I do not know – perhaps. I must think on it. That, and... something Charlotte said."

"I saw you speaking together for quite some time. Did you tell her what you told me this morning?"

"I did. She thought it odd that Mr. Wickham would share his history with me; she did not believe it as implicitly as I did, and I suppose her skepticism has worn off on me."

"I did not believe it either."

Elizabeth regarded her sister with shame. "I ought to have trusted your instincts. Charlotte framed it in a way... well, anyhow, she cast the first shadow of doubt, and Mr. Wickham himself did the rest."

"I see," Jane said slowly. "What a pity. You seemed so optimistic this morning that you could improve upon the days' events."

"I should be satisfied if I woke up and it was all just a dream," Elizabeth said. "At any rate, I have little hope of waking to find it is the twenty-first of November." At that, she leaned over and blew out the candle on her nightstand. "I think I must sleep now, Jane. Better to put an end to the day and take my chances for the morning."

3

Elizabeth had not expected to wake beside Jane, and she did not. She laid next to Mary, silently agonizing over her inescapable plight. Yesterday had been the worst iteration of market day yet, from her disillusionment with Mr. Wickham to Mr. Bingley's absence from the card party, and all that Charlotte had led Elizabeth to consider.

It took her some time to muster the will to get out of bed. She had been optimistic at times yesterday, but it required all her energy to rouse the same sentiments again. She knew not what else she could do about her predicament, beyond trying to make the most of the day but it troubled her to know that the occupants of Netherfield Park may yet present complications.

Mary began to stir and sat up beside Elizabeth. "Good morning, Lizzy," she said with a yawn.

Elizabeth groaned. She closed her eyes, and gave herself exactly one minute to loathe everything, before she sat up at Mary's side, determined to get on. "I hope it shall be," she said. "What if I dress in here with you today?"

***

Elizabeth worked her magic on Mary once again, and made some suggestions for how her younger sister might converse with Mr. Collins. Mary accepted it all with speculative calm, though she, too, seemed to fall short of real optimism. "I will try, to please you, Lizzy," she said, trying out a few different smiles in the mirror before her face resumed its usual setting.

"Do not attempt it if it will not please *you*," Elizabeth urged. "I mean to make the most of the day, Mary, and I long for you to do the same. The rains have ceased, the market is sure to be exciting, I suppose – and Lydia and Kitty will have others to annoy besides ourselves."

Mary laughed without any trace of the guilt Jane might have felt, and Elizabeth appreciated Mary's complicity. "I hope Lydia will not be angry that I am wearing one of her gowns."

"I am sure she will fuss about it," Elizabeth said. "But Mamma will placate her, for she has the prospect of meeting with the officers, and is confident in her belief that she is the best of all of us, though I am sure our cousin thinks otherwise." Elizabeth hesitated, briefly considering taking Mary into her confidence, but at the last moment she decided against it. She wished to make a sort of study of her sister on this day, without Mary being aware of it.

Instead Elizabeth rolled her eyes at her own impertinence and gave Mary a reassuring pat on the shoulders. "You look lovely, so it will be worth a little bit of nonsense."

Mary took in her reflection. "I feel different – very conscious of myself. Do you think... do you think Mr. Collins will like it all?"

"Depend upon it, sister, and remember what I have told you. And consider, this evening, that if you relinquish the pianoforte to another performer, you might have some opportunity to dance yourself."

"I think he likes you better," Mary said flatly.

"That will not be the case for much longer, mark my words," Elizabeth said firmly. "I am convinced I am the last woman in the world who could make him happy – and I mean to make him see it."

Mary raised her eyebrows in surprise, but Elizabeth said no more; they were very near being late for breakfast, and she did not wish to chance a delay in their departure, lest it interrupt the events of the marketplace.

***

Elizabeth managed to catch Jane on the stairs, and she drew her sister aside, knowing she must speak before their repast. She quickly relayed much of what she had said to convince Jane of her plight on the previous days, and though she was more succinct and abbreviated, she succeeded in her purpose. Jane watched her closely throughout breakfast, giving herself away by subtle measures every time something Elizabeth had spoken of came to pass.

When Mrs. Bennet began to direct her daughters to the village, Mary was happily positioned to address Mr. Collins, and after a moment he offered her his arm. Elizabeth was gratified, for clearly Mary was pleased with herself.

With Jane at her side, Elizabeth watched Mary with their cousin; Lydia and Kitty were still walking too near for Elizabeth to speak freely yet, though she was sure Jane was wishing it. To Elizabeth's chagrin, Mr. Collins chanced to look around, and met her eye with a repellant smile. He was just conceited enough to presume she was looking on with envy, Elizabeth was sure of it – and the dreadful toad actually left Mary directly to walk alongside Elizabeth.

"My dear cousin," he said with a strange flourish. "What wonders you have worked on Miss Mary. I understand you have styled your own hair more simply today, that you might devote your time to your sister's aid. And yet your natural allurements shine as bright as ever! Commendable indeed! I am sure I have heard Lady Catherine extol on the virtues of simplicity, of simple, natural elegance in a young lady – when nature has been generous, no artifice be necessary – yes, that is it. Indeed."

Elizabeth was too astonished to reply, but Mr. Collins was

not daunted by her silence. He began to congratulate himself on the compliment he had just arranged for her, and repeated several very pretty comments he had made for the benefit of Lady Catherine and her daughter....

At length Jane cleared her throat, for Elizabeth had briefly ceased to attend what was passing at all. Jane looked anxious; Elizabeth suspected her sister wished some opportunity to discuss what Elizabeth had so hastily revealed before breakfast. For a few minutes more, the two sisters attempted to deflect Mr. Collins and repulse him with their lack of interest, but to no avail.

Finally, it occurred to Elizabeth that she cared so little for what Mr. Collins thought that perhaps honesty might truly be the best way to put paid to his interest in her. She gave Jane's hand a squeeze and met her eye with a significant look before addressing her cousin. "Cousin Collins, I can go no longer without confiding in you," Elizabeth said, slipping her arm through his.

Mr. Collins' eyes lit with pompous gratification, and his chin raised several inches. "Cousin Elizabeth, ought we not speak privately?" He flicked his gaze to Jane with a smarmy smile.

Elizabeth held fast to her sister with her free hand. "No indeed – Jane knows all the particulars of what I wish to confide, and I have always relied upon her wisdom. But you, as a man of God, may have some particular insight to help me with my problem."

Mr. Collins began to nod, and then stopped abruptly. "Your problem?"

"Yes. If the right honorable Lady Catherine de Bourgh has entrusted you with such distinction, surely you are capable enough to advise me in a matter of tremendous existential import." It was all Elizabeth could do to keep her voice quite serious.

"I see. I had thought – but perhaps it would not be delicate to say – there is still time yet for us to discuss...." Mr. Collins blushed as he trailed off, and he attempted to affect a mien of intelligent concern. "Perhaps you had better clarify what you mean, dear Cousin."

Elizabeth glanced back at Jane, who was watching with no little astonishment. "It would not be so awful if he simply decides I am mad," Elizabeth whispered to her sister. Jane knit her brow in distress, but finally nodded her agreement.

"Very circumspect of you," Elizabeth said to Mr. Collins. "I shall explain my situation to you in full, and then I quite long to hear your opinion."

Mr. Collins gave an exaggerated nod of his head and motioned for her to proceed.

"I am reliving the same day again that I have already experienced four times before," Elizabeth said. She detailed her plight in the same abbreviated fashion as she had done for Jane, but offered her cousin all the salient points, as she understood them.

Elizabeth did not expect him to believe her, though she would have welcomed his assistance and insight if he *had*, but she was at least willing to bear his disgust if he did not. She watched Mr. Collins' reaction carefully as she spoke, and in the end she was not disappointed.

His expression became amused, shocked, confused, and finally he settled upon indignation. "Cousin Elizabeth, if this is your notion of a joke, I think it a very odd one. That you would attempt a jest at my expense, as so near a relation, shows a want of respect I find quite alarming. As a clergyman, what you have described is grotesque and irreligious – I should not have even listened to such blasphemy."

Jane let out a small gasp, but Elizabeth only laughed. *At least he will leave me be, that I might make sense of it without his constant prattling on.*

"Furthermore," he continued, "I must own that I am obliged to reevaluate my interest – that is, I am sure you have noticed the marked attentions I have paid you since my arrival, but as you are either insolent in the extreme, or perhaps even mad – either of which, I am sure you must know, would hardly earn you the approval of my noble patroness – I must, with gracious apologies, withdraw any such intentions toward you. I am sorry if it shall cause you any dismay, but after what your own behavior has been, I trust this may yet yield some contrition, once you have had time to reflect on how your own intransigence has rendered you so beyond my notice. Take heart, Cousin Elizabeth, for your situation is such that another opportunity may never come your way."

Mr. Collins gave a hasty, grimacing bow before he moved away from them to walk the rest of the way with Mary. Elizabeth burst out laughing and turned to Jane, who was wide-eyed and pale.

"Forgive me, Lizzy, if I cannot laugh about it," Jane said, wringing her hands. "It was such a shock to hear, and I do believe you – if we do indeed encounter a Mr. Wickham in the village, I may faint dead away. But I worry at your telling our cousin about it. When *he* sees you proved right, I fear he might do something unpleasant."

"It was a rash decision, but really, Jane, I should rather be an object of derision to him, than a prospective bride – and I should rather face his contempt than the prospect of repeating this day again."

Jane tipped her head thoughtfully. "Do you expect that you will?"

"Expecting otherwise has begun to feel like too much to hope for."

"Then what will you do?"

"I keep coming back to the idea that I have to improve upon the previous occurrences of the day – that I must strive to make this the best version. I have attempted it before and failed miserably, but perhaps I might apply myself a little more today."

"The best version of the day," Jane mused. "How so?"

"Well, I have assisted Mary – she actually wishes for our cousin's attentions, and she is very welcome to them! And of course, I must ensure that Mr. Bingley is invited to the card party, because you wish it. I have not yet decided what to make of Mr. Wickham, though I am not so favorably disposed as I once was."

"Oh? I had understood that the day is always the same – how can you have changed your opinion of him?"

Elizabeth hesitated. She had not revealed Mr. Wickham's sad history when she had told Jane of him before, and she had no wish to speak of it now. Her mind was too unsettled on the matter, and she rather feared Jane might sway her.

"It is difficult to explain," Elizabeth said lamely. "I suppose I have begun to question everything – I still cannot account for why this is happening, or how I am to escape the endless repetition."

Jane gave a slow, pensive nod. "It is quite a wild tale – if I heard such a thing from anyone else but you, I am sure I could not believe it. But you must be right, about making some improvement upon the day. Certainly there can never be any ill in doing one's best."

Full of sudden mischief, Elizabeth grinned wickedly at her sister. "I am off to a poor beginning, with Mr. Collins suspecting me of blasphemy!"

Jane's mouth hung agape; a moment later she broke into laughter. "I am sorry, Lizzy – it is too ridiculous!"

Elizabeth joined her sister in laughing at the absurdity of it all. "Yes," she agreed. "That is just why I had hoped it would appeal to our cousin's sensibilities."

It felt good to make light of her strange dilemma with Jane, and Elizabeth was in good cheer as they arrived at the village market. Mr. Collins kept a distance from Elizabeth – indeed, he would not so much as look at her – and better still, Mr. Bingley appeared, and on this occasion he was alone.

"I had meant to call upon you at Longbourn, to ask after your health, Miss Bennet," Mr. Bingley said.

Jane's eyes darted over to Elizabeth, and she gave a slight nod in acknowledgement of what Elizabeth had told her Mr. Bingley would say.

He continued just the same. "I had no notion of it being market day, but I could not resist – I stabled my horse, that I might have a look around."

"I am much recovered, sir," Jane said with a blush.

"Splendid," Mr. Bingley cried. "I am so relieved. Perhaps you ought to walk with me – so I can see for myself that you are well – and I do wish to take it all in. I am sure you must know all the best vendors and stalls to visit." Jane, her cheeks very flushed now, was peering up at Mr. Bingley with a shy smile, and for a moment he only stared back at her with an endearingly stupid grin, before he recollected himself. "And Miss Elizabeth...."

She laughed and shook her head. "No indeed, you go along without me. I had meant to find my Aunt Phillips – she is to give a card party tonight, and I had intended to offer my assistance." She gave Jane a knowing look before bobbing in a curtsey and moving away.

Elizabeth was as good as her word, but Mrs. Phillips cried off any such assistance when Elizabeth approached her across the square. "Pah, Lizzy! Everything has been seen to, and it is not to be so grand an affair! But I would not have you wearing yourself out, you know." She leaned in confidentially. "Your mother would be very cross with me if you appeared tired in front of all the officers, or if you had rushed in dressing yourself. You must enjoy yourself, my dear. There is nothing so fetching, I am sure, as a pretty lady at leisure. Ah, I see how you blush – I wonder if any of the officers have caught your eye?"

"No indeed," Elizabeth cried, for her thoughts had taken a much different turn. She had begun to reassess her preference for Mr. Wickham, and the sight before her – her youngest sisters flirting brazenly with a cluster of officers – now gave Elizabeth some discomfort.

Besides this, Elizabeth was very pleased with this iteration of their market excursion. Jane and Mr. Bingley were walking happily together down the high street, and Mr. Collins had redirected his attention to Mary. Denny and Mr. Wickham had just joined her younger sisters and, in the spirit of making what improvements she could, Elizabeth made her way to their side.

"I hope your colonel will give a ball," Lydia was saying as Elizabeth approached. She hung on Mr. Wickham's arm, her chest thrust forward; far from singling Elizabeth out as he had done before, Mr. Wickham looked perfectly content, so much so that it unsettled Elizabeth.

"I do long for a ball," Lydia continued, gazing up at Mr. Wickham with an evident desire to be admired.

With tremendous willpower, Elizabeth managed not to roll her eyes – she had heard Lydia make the same statement to Mrs. Forster four evenings in a row. Instead she attempted the same tactic that had worked the day before with her youngest sister. "You have hardly been deprived, Lydia. I am sure you danced every dance at the assembly last month, and never wanted for partners before the militia came to Hertfordshire."

She hesitated as the officers looked over at her, realizing that she had painted Lydia in a rather bad light; Elizabeth, struggling to make her point, grasped at some means of expressing what she wished. "That is, I am sure we are happy the officers are amongst us, of course, but we have not been so dull before. As a gentleman's daughters we are not so starved for society and amusement." Elizabeth let out a sigh of impatience with herself. *Oh dear, this is not going as I meant it.*

It was clear from the expressions of her sisters and the officers that Elizabeth had not inspired Lydia to restrain herself and play hard to get, she had only presented herself as very priggish. After Lydia had recovered from her astonishment, she laughed and snorted. "La! Lizzy, you sound as snobbish and rude as snooty Mr. Darcy!"

This was enough to make Elizabeth curl her lips in disdain, and she nearly missed the sparkle of recognition in Mr. Wickham's eye before he looked down at Lydia. "I suppose your sister is right. I understand you have just gained some very grand new neighbors – we are but lowly soldiers, and it is true, you know, that we ought to be more desirous of company such as yours, than the reverse."

Lydia knit her brow for a moment, before she understood how Mr. Wickham had turned the tables on Elizabeth. "Oh, no! Poor Mr. Wickham, *I* do not think you are so lowly – and certainly *some* at Netherfield are not company I desire!"

Elizabeth groaned and moved away, for she could bear neither her own embarrassment nor her youngest sister. She hoped that she had done enough with her subtle maneuvering for Jane, and her much less subtle repulsion of Mr. Collins for Mary's sake – Lydia and Kitty might perhaps be subdued at the card party, once they had forgotten Elizabeth's first attempt.

***

This was not to be. Elizabeth had given some further counsel to Mary for sustaining Mr. Collins' interest throughout the evening, and smiling to herself as she returned to her room to begin dressing, when her mother sought her out. Mrs. Bennet's shrill voice accosted her as the two met in the hallway. "Well, Lizzy!"

"Yes, Mamma?"

"Oh, *yes Mamma* nothing," her mother cried, swatting at her. "And do not smirk at me! I know what mischief you have been up to today, and I will not tolerate it!"

"I beg your pardon?"

Mrs. Bennet put one hand on her hip and began scolding her daughter with the other. "You are always run away with your tongue, but I will not stand for such insolence as this! I have heard all about your rudeness to the officers, and I will not have it. And poor Mr. Collins, too! He had been very attentive to you, and might have continued on, if you were not determined to spoil your own good fortune! Telling him you can see the future or some such nonsense – what has come over you? I do not know, I am sure I do not, but you must be punished!"

Elizabeth could not help it – she laughed wildly. "Punished? I am being punished already, more than you could ever know." She turned to flee, but her mother pursued her.

"I am not finished, Lizzy! You are to be punished – you shall not be permitted to attend the party at your aunt's house tonight. You are to stay at home and think over what you have done. Mr. Collins was most shocked and distressed by what you said to him, and I cannot imagine what put such notions into your head! He begins to say you are mad, Lizzy – think of your reputation, and your poor sisters! Mr. Bingley will never propose to Jane if he thinks you are a lunatic who claims to see the future, and we shall all be listening to Mary sermonize about it forever! And the officers, you know, will want nothing to do with Lydia and Kitty if you are determined to vex and insult them!"

By now the rest of the family had begun to come out of their chambers to observe Mrs. Bennet's noisy hysterics. Even Mr. Collins had peeked out of the guest room, and as Mrs. Bennet paused to catch her breath, he seized the opportunity to speak. "Your mother is quite right to chastise you, Cousin Elizabeth." Mrs. Bennet puffed herself up and nodded with indignation, but Mr. Collins made a silencing gesture at her as he continued to lecture. "You do no credit to your family, and when Lady Catherine has heard of your impertinence and unchecked behavior, I am sure she will agree with me in casting judgement on all your family for allowing such behavior to fester, for it is clear to me that your temper must have always been thus."

"Now just a minute," Mrs. Bennet cried.

Her shriek was overcome by a great snarl from Elizabeth, whose frustration had finally boiled over. "Oh, for God's sake, I am sick of Lady Catherine," she shouted. "I am sick of all of you. Punish me if you like, I do not care." She stormed past Jane, who was quietly hanging back in the entrance to their bedroom and slammed the door.

***

After venting to her spleen to Jane for a few minutes, Elizabeth began to calm herself; by the time her sisters and cousin, accompanied this time by Mrs. Bennet, departed for the card party, Elizabeth was relatively tranquil again. She was no longer sorry to be left home, but almost serene about it.

After all, she might have already accomplished what she needed to, to have worked some sort of improvement on the day. Mary had made some little progress with Mr. Collins, Jane would have Mr. Bingley's company for the evening, and with any luck Mr. Darcy would not attend, just as he had not come to the market – her family would be safe from him, for the night. It was no great loss to Elizabeth that she would not have any opportunity to see Mr. Wickham, either. Even her mother's newfound awareness of the family's reputation must be a blessing, for though Mrs. Bennet's vexation with Elizabeth had been misplaced, if she applied the same attitude toward Lydia and Kitty's familiarity with the officers, it would be a very fine thing.

Jane's report of the evening, upon the family's return, seemed to indicate that all was well, and though Elizabeth was aware of Jane's tendency to see naught but good in the world, Elizabeth was determined to believe it.

"I can see that you are happy, Jane – but tell me, how did our sisters behave? Did Mary make an impression on Mr. Collins in my absence? Did Mamma's presence do anything to mitigate our younger sister's obsession with the officers?"

Jane laughed gently as she dressed for bed. "Dear Lizzy, I am relieved to see you serene – and so concerned for the rest of us. You were very cross at being excluded, before we all departed."

"Yes, but I am better now – optimistic even," Elizabeth replied.

"You mean, regarding your... problem?"

"Yes, exactly. That is why you must tell me how everybody behaved."

Jane came to sit beside Elizabeth on their bed. "I think you will be pleased, Lizzy. Mr. Bingley was very attentive to me, but then he is always so kind. Mary played only one song – the one you recommended to her, and I noticed our cousin listening very attentively to her. They even danced together, when Mary relinquished her seat at the pianoforte to Maria Lucas."

"The Lucases were there?"

"Oh, yes. Charlotte seemed rather glum – I suppose she was missing you. But she did just what I know you would have done – she spoke a great deal with Mr. Darcy and Miss Bingley, and I was incredibly grateful to her for it. Dear Mr. Bingley is so very amiable; I hope it was not terribly selfish of me to dominate his time as I did, but I could not help it!" Jane blushed and hid her face as she giggled. "Oh, and Mr. Darcy conveyed his wishes for your speedy recovery."

"My recovery?"

"Oh – well, Mamma was still very cross when we departed the house, but I convinced her not to speak of how she had disciplined you, for it would only remind our neighbors that you had behaved badly. I suggested she merely say that you are ill."

Elizabeth was gratified by this last part. "Well done, Jane. I will own I did let my temper get the better of me, but I am relieved indeed that half of Meryton is not aware of it."

Jane offered her sister an impish smile. "And will you not admit that it was very kind of Mr. Darcy to show such concern for your health?"

Elizabeth replied without a moment's consideration that she would do no such thing. "He is likely only concerned for himself. With you sick, and now me, he is likely afraid there is some outbreak in our remote country village – well, I hope it sends him packing for London at once, even if he was not really so cruel to Mr. Wickham!"

Jane knit her brows with confusion, and Elizabeth recollected herself; today she had given Jane a much briefer account of her dilemma, and had not gone into so much detail about Mr. Wickham. However, she had no wish to broach the subject now. There was still much she wished to know.

"And what of Kitty and Lydia? Were they noisy and flirtatious as ever?"

"No, I think they enjoyed themselves just enough; there was nothing terribly untoward about their behavior. I had expected Lydia to perhaps be a little more guarded around the officers, with Mamma present, and I think she was, really. She was friendly as ever, but she showed no great preference for anybody, except perhaps Mr. Wickham. They spoke a great deal, and I think she had finally met a man she likes well enough that she does not desire attention from any others. And Kitty, you know, is always quieter when she is separated from Lydia."

"Well," Elizabeth cried, surprised and relieved at her sister's account of the card party. "I feel no distress at all now about being made to stay home. I have attended the party four times already, and it has never gone as well as you describe it, Jane. I must be satisfied that all shall be well – that I shall wake up tomorrow and it will be Thursday, even if Mamma is still cross with me."

Jane smiled feebly, her eyes darting away – here was the face she always made when she had nothing appropriate to say, and chose instead to keep silent. It occurred to Elizabeth that perhaps Jane did not believe her as earnestly as she had the day before, and the day before that. This realization wounded Elizabeth, and yet she had not the will to convince Jane any further. It might soon all be over.

Though Elizabeth was determined to cling to this hope, her feelings were not to endure, for a tap on the door brought Lydia before them. She was dressed for bed but still appeared full of energy, and after closing the door she fairly jumped onto their bed, laughing as she disrupted Jane and Elizabeth.

"Well, Lizzy, I suppose you have had a very dull night compared to the rest of us, and I have had such great fun I can even pity you, for your rudeness to the officers made them like me better – *one* of them in particular, and you only told Mr. Collins what we have all been thinking since he arrived."

Lydia nudged her way between Jane and Elizabeth, that she might recline against their pillows. "I suppose I must thank you, Lizzy."

"Whatever for? Surely the officers would like you more than they ought to, even if I had been more civil – and I am not entirely convinced it is for the best."

Lydia laughed. "You must be wild with envy – and so you shall be after I tell you how Mr. Wickham confided in me, for he likes me above any other lady in the village! And Jane, I must tell you, too, for it concerns Mr. Bingley in an infamous way!"

"What?" Jane gasped. Elizabeth only groaned.

"Do not be like that, Lizzy. It is your own fault for acting like such a snob – but I suppose if you had not, Mr. Wickham would not have told me all about Mr. Darcy being a terrible villain and robbing him of his livelihood. He might have been a clergyman – and he is really handsome enough to make me rethink every ill thing I have said of their entire boring species – but now Mr. Wickham must go to war and be killed, and all because of wicked Mr. Darcy. You have got to warn Mr. Bingley, Jane, for I think Mr. Darcy may do something very dreadful to him, too."

What followed was Lydia's account of the same sad story Mr. Wickham had told Elizabeth, and Jane's reaction was just the same as ever. Elizabeth, however, felt completely nonplussed. Her first sentiment was envy, which quickly dissolved into disappointment, and no little chagrin. How special she had felt when *she* had been Mr. Wickham's confidante, how sure she was that it signified something of import. It seemed now to prove only that Charlotte was right, and Mr. Wickham merely wanted fertile ground to sow his seeds of malice.

Jane's attempt to reconcile the matter affected Lydia less than it had ever influenced Elizabeth; Lydia defended her new admirer staunchly, and applied to Elizabeth, whom she knew thought the worst of Mr. Darcy.

Elizabeth found herself in the unlikely position of defending the man she despised, if only to make her younger sister see sense. While Lydia took on the same stance that Elizabeth had lately taken, Elizabeth was obliged to argue as Charlotte had done.

"Lydia, you must not give credit to all Mr. Wickham's assertions. What sort of man shares such private information with a new acquaintance? Has it not occurred to you that he might have done so only because you spoke harshly of Mr. Darcy this morning, and Mr. Wickham sought to recommend himself to you by claiming to share your opinion?"

Lydia screwed up her face. "Good Heavens, Lizzy! You make him sound like Mary, prattling on about how wise Lady Catherine sounds, so that she might impress Mr. Collins, since she does not look well enough in *my* pink dress!"

Elizabeth let out a sigh of exasperation. "That is diff...." She stopped herself. Mary would never know, and Elizabeth knew she ought to seize her chance. "Yes," she said flatly. "Mr. Collins has not the wit to understand what is passing, but surely you know better."

Lydia appeared to consider this, and Elizabeth pressed on. "I know you are thinking what a pity it is that such a handsome man could be so duplicitous – and perhaps there is *some* truth in his tale, but I daresay he has not given you the full story, only the parts of it that present him in the best light. I was not wrong this morning, you know – we *are* a gentleman's daughters, and he a lowly soldier. Whether or not he was really so ill-used by Mr. Darcy, he could hardly support a wife on a soldier's pay, particularly not such a one as you, Lydia, dearest. Not with all the purchases you made at the market today! All his charm, and the sympathies he has aroused in you cannot change that, though he may wish you to forget the fact."

Lydia had appeared to be thinking quite seriously, but all she said was, "Oh!"

"And consider this," Jane added. "Why did Mr. Wickham remain at the same party as Mr. Darcy – why did he not confront him, or seek to warn any others besides you?"

Her face betrayed more concentration, and Elizabeth was torn between a hope that Lydia would see the error of her ways, and a sense of chagrin that Lydia could be convinced more easily than she herself had been.

In the end, however, Lydia seemed to tire of such weighty thoughts. "La! I only wished to tell you for a lark – I thought you would laugh, and not lecture me. Well, carry on as dull as you like, I am sure Kitty will hear me out." As Lydia fled the room, Elizabeth lost all hope of waking to up a bright and beautiful Thursday.

***

Mary's elbow still hurt, every time. Elizabeth sat up and rubbed at her face before hauling herself out of bed with resignation. She dressed quietly, not wishing to wake Jane, or even to confide in her. What was the point?

Breakfast was a monotonous exercise in forbearance, and the walk to Meryton a unique sort of agony – she had taken no measures to deter Mr. Collins' attention to her, beyond her inability to conceal the want of spirits she felt. This was evidently not enough to discourage him.

Elizabeth ignored him as much as she could, fantasizing about punching him right on the nose, or stamping his toes as she had done to Mr. Darcy. Mr. Wickham, too, bore some share of her private wrath, and Elizabeth scarcely trusted herself to encounter him in the village.

That he had told Lydia the same story he told Elizabeth, and that he had gone one night without speaking of it at all, did not expressly prove him false, but Elizabeth trusted Charlotte's instincts above her own after all that had occurred. To be sure, there was some riddle about Mr. Wickham she felt she must solve, but Elizabeth was in no humor for it today.

With such thoughts as these, Elizabeth was strangely amused to find that Mr. Darcy had again accompanied Mr. Bingley to the market. Elizabeth was reticent this morning, but the rest of her family was not, and Mr. Bingley was soon overcome by Mrs. Bennet's effusions, echoed by Kitty and Lydia, though they soon announced their intention to go off in search of the officers.

Mr. Collins finally left Elizabeth's side to put himself forward, and though his first greeting to Mr. Bingley and Mr. Darcy was courteous enough, he went on at some length, until it was surely impossible for either gentleman to consider him a sensible man.

"I understand Netherfield is much grander than Longbourn," he began, and then glanced back at the ladies, making a strange and servile gesture. "Of course, I have some reason to be partial to Longbourn, and my fondness for the place daily increases! But my own humble parsonage in Kent is so near the illustrious estate of Rosings Park, where I am a frequent guest – I have come to make a study of great houses, and happily enough as a clergyman I am quite comfortable in such settings, for it is my firm belief...."

Elizabeth could listen no further, though Mr. Bingley was too amiable to do otherwise. She noticed Mr. Darcy had betrayed no reaction to Mr. Collins' mention of Rosings, though she knew Lady Catherine to be Mr. Darcy's aunt. He likely had no wish to invite any further notice from the toady parson, and Elizabeth could hardly begrudge him such a sentiment – but she had not ruled out the possibility of mentioning the connection to Mr. Collins later, if it suited her purposes. Or if Mr. Darcy vexed her.

At present, she had borne quite enough mortification for one morning, and she wished to be away from her family. She remained resolved to do her best to help Jane along with Mr. Bingley – but how odd that today, in distracting Mr. Darcy, she was beginning to behave like him; she had grown silent and taciturn.

She said little at first as the two of them walked in the opposite direction of Jane and Mr. Bingley, and eventually Mr. Darcy broke the silence by asking after her health.

Elizabeth flinched, for it echoed what Jane had told her of Mr. Darcy's gracious inquiry the previous evening. *But that is quite impossible!* She assured him she was well, but she could hear the suspicion in her own voice, and looked away to hide what she knew must be a strange look upon her countenance.

"You nursed your elder sister so assiduously at Netherfield," he said after a minute of silence. "It would be a great pity if your kindness were repaid by catching cold yourself."

Of course, to Mr. Darcy, Jane's illness had only just happened. "I am quite hale, I assure you, sir." She glanced over at him again, feeling surprisingly at ease with Mr. Darcy, more so than she ever had before. It occurred to her that perhaps it was because she was so irascible herself this morning – what suitable companions they made at such a time!

She laughed to herself at a particularly impertinent notion, and though she was not inclined to share it, Mr. Darcy suddenly seemed unusually willing to converse with her. "May I ask what amuses you, Miss Bennet?"

"You may, perhaps, but it does not follow that I will answer you," she replied. She had not spoken in jest, but he seemed to believe she had, and he actually smiled down at her.

"I suppose I dare not hope I could have aroused such mirth. Only Miss Bingley laughs at my jokes before I have told them."

Elizabeth gaped up at Mr. Darcy before breaking into a wide smile. "Perhaps she is clairvoyant, sir – it would be a sort of accomplishment."

He laughed with her now, and Elizabeth felt her peevishness melting away. "What made me laugh before will do neither of us credit," she admitted. "Besides, your jape, which was an excellent one, has already disproven my theory."

He raised his eyebrows in a pose of exaggerated curiosity.

"My jest was tolerable, perhaps, but I am sorry I could not tempt you to be more candid with me, Miss Elizabeth. I am heartily sorry indeed." He met her eyes with something more than mirth, and Elizabeth quickly looked away. What was the world coming to when Mr. Darcy, of all people, was cheering her?

As if determined to sabotage any pleasant feelings toward him, Elizabeth finally decided to share her impudent musings. "I was amused before by my own petulance," she admitted. "It occurred to me that you often appear as surly as I felt this morning – I thought perhaps you, too, are plagued by relations who constantly disoblige you."

Mr. Darcy drew in a sharp breath and looked at her severely; she knew at once she had pressed him too far by insulting his family. She ought to apologize, but she supposed it would not matter tomorrow, for even if Thursday ever came, she would never have any great wish for Mr. Darcy's approbation.

The silence persisted a moment longer, and Elizabeth feared he might leave, and pull Mr. Bingley away from Jane. Finally, he gave a strange snort of laughter; she gasped up at him, almost wondering if she had imagined it.

"You are very near the truth," he said evenly. "More frequently than I can help it, I am caught by some distressing thought – I had not realized I was surly."

It seemed odd to Elizabeth that he took no offense on behalf of his family, only himself – but neither had she expected him to laugh about Miss Bingley. "Well, this morning is certainly full of surprises," she said.

"Ordinarily that should be a welcome relief," he said cryptically. "But what surprises *you*?"

He had wished her to be candid – well, she would oblige him. "You have made me laugh, you seemed before to be apologizing for what you said at the assembly, though I did not know you were aware I heard you – and now you take no offense at all when I imply your family drives you to distemper as mine does for me. I feared you might resent the comparison."

He laughed again; Elizabeth began to worry that perhaps she was truly growing a little madder with each repetition of this day. "It is not unjust, in fact. My cousin Richard is my dearest friend, but not always an ideal companion – we are very different. My aunt, Lady Catherine, can make me downright cantankerous – she has such an effect on nearly all her relations. I wonder if there is such a person in your family?"

Elizabeth was astonished by his candor, but past her own churlishness – she willingly offered him an encouraging smile. "How funny it is, that they have found one another."

"I suppose it was fate – they are well-suited, I think. Perhaps you would agree – another surprise." He arched an eyebrow at her in so similar a way as she had often done that Elizabeth instantly bubbled with laughter.

"My goodness, Mr. Darcy! We are of one mind – at last." She laughed a little more, and he looked very well pleased with himself.

"Stranger things have happened."

Elizabeth peered up at him. Strange things indeed. She briefly considered telling Mr. Darcy just how strange a thing had really occurred to her, several times now. Would he believe her, as Jane and Charlotte had? Or would he, like the man they had just mocked together, accuse her of blasphemy, and shun her completely? Well, there was only one way to find out.

"I have the uncanny feeling that today will be stranger still," she began, her lips twisting in a wry smile. "My aunt is to give a card party, where I can say with a certainty that...."

They were interrupted – Mrs. Bennet had come upon them, and was instantly fussing at Elizabeth. "There you are, Lizzy! Well! You must come at once and join your sisters. I am sure Mr. Darcy can have nothing to say to you," she said imperiously, "and you would get on much better with the officers."

Elizabeth peered across the square, and, as always, she saw her sisters on the other side, speaking with great animation to a cluster of soldiers. Mr. Wickham was already amongst them, clearly working his charms on Lydia. Mrs. Bennet fluttered her handkerchief in that direction, and he looked up as it caught his eye; noticing Elizabeth, he smiled and gave a nod of his head before turning back to his companions.

Mr. Darcy laid his hand atop Elizabeth's, for she was still holding his arm, and she longed to ask what truth there was in Mr. Wickham's tale.

"That is Mr. Wickham," Mrs. Bennet informed them. "He is just arrived – and what a charming young man! Oh – and there go the Lucases – your aunt has invited them to the card party – come along now, Lizzy."

She peered up at Mr. Darcy, and some perverse impulse led her to brush her hand subtly and deliberately against his before she drew it away. He had always looked upon Mr. Wickham with disdain, but this time Elizabeth wondered if there was more in it.

Now he looked back at her, again with some indiscernible feeling. "I shall bid you good day, then," he said softly.

Elizabeth began to follow her mother, but stopped after a couple of steps. She turned back to Mr. Darcy. "The card party – I hope I will see you there, sir. My Aunt Phillips would be delighted if you and Mr. Bingley would attend."

Mr. Darcy nodded, wearing the trace of a smile. "Thank you. Miss Bennet. I will mention it to Bingley – I foresee no objection on his part."

She watched him go, but her mother was ushering her forward. "Well, Lizzy, I suppose it was clever of you to think of Jane, just now! Very good of you!"

Elizabeth could barely look at her mother, after the quarrel they had had the day before – but her mother knew nothing of it today. "Thank you, Mamma," she muttered.

"And am I not to be thanked in turn, for rescuing you from that odious Mr. Darcy? What you must have been suffering, my poor girl! I see Jane is walking with Mr. Bingley, so that is very well. But after what that awful man said about you, I could not bear you to be so miserable, and miss out on seeing the officers!"

Elizabeth winced, and then made some little assurance of her gratitude, for her mother seemed still to expect it. "Very timely of you," Elizabeth said. "I am sure I was on the verge of saying something Mr. Darcy would have thought very foolish indeed."

***

As the day progressed, so too did Elizabeth's suspicion that she was going mad. What made her quite certain was the realization, upon arriving at her aunt's home in Meryton, that she had a greater hope of seeing Mr. Darcy there, than Mr. Wickham.

Her opinion of both men had been wavering a great deal recently, and if she was to continue repeating the same day over again, she feared her judgement would always be shifting. The only thing she knew was what she had told Jane – they could not *both* be good.

Perhaps it was only that Mr. Darcy's conversation had been more varied these last six days, while Mr. Wickham seemed only to alter his manners and comments very slightly. And of course, Mr. Darcy had now hinted three separate times at some sort of apology for his past offenses – she was not unmoved by his efforts. She was baffled by them.

She actually had to restrain a smile as Mr. Darcy entered the room with Mr. Bingley – they had arrived earlier on this occasion, and while Jane had every cause for delight, Elizabeth could not account for her own pleasure. She had resumed her listless attitude upon her return home from the market, and had in fact done very little to alter the course of the day – perhaps she was merely inspired to do so now.

Yes, that is it – I will speak to Mr. Darcy – I will provoke him if I can. Elizabeth smirked at her own musings, and once she had rationalized it enough to herself, she approached Mr. Darcy. "Good evening, sir." She bobbed into a curtsey and looked up at him with another wide smile.

He bowed. "Miss Elizabeth."

"I am glad you are come," she said. "I wondered whether such an invitation would tempt you."

"You promised some strangeness, which is not often an inducement for such gatherings – I confess my interest was more than a little piqued."

Elizabeth blushed. She had been very near to confessing her dilemma to him this morning, but had since then decided it was probably better that she had not. She now resolved to make a sort of study, as she had done with Mr. Wickham two nights past – she meant to figure Mr. Darcy out, if she could, and she would stand little chance of it if he believed her fit for Bedlam.

"I think I told you I was in an odd humor this morning – I should not have said such a thing, and you are in no position, sir, to judge me for regretting a thoughtless statement." She arched an eyebrow at him and watched her meaning land on him.

It seemed a curious sort of experiment, for things that amused her had often seemed to vex him in the past, but lately things that she was sure would offend his sensibilities only inspired mirth. Even now his eyes sparkled with amusement. "My own thoughtless statement I have every hope of contradicting, at the earliest possible opportunity. You may perhaps do likewise."

As his meaning struck her, Elizabeth gave a muffled sound of surprise, gaping at him for a moment before a smile tugged at her lips. "Do you mean to dance if some opportunity presents itself? Are you in humor to give consequence to ladies who are slighted by other men?"

He only nodded, his eyes smiling though his countenance betrayed nothing else.

Elizabeth laughed in spite of herself. "And I am to likewise contradict my thoughtless statement – that the evening would be a strange one. You make it very difficult, sir. And what, pray, is the opposite of strange?"

Mr. Darcy appeared to consider this a moment, though she suspected he was teasing her. "Perfect," he said.

Again she laughed, though there was a modicum of alarm in it this time. A perfect day – just what she had been striving for, though today she had all but abandoned her efforts. She had clearly gone mad, to be seeing such wisdom in Mr. Darcy – and even humor. "It is better than Bedlam, I suppose," she laughed, and shook her head as she realized she had voiced this thought aloud.

Mr. Darcy laughed with her, but his gaze was querulous. "Miss Elizabeth," he said, but then fell silent. Charlotte Lucas had arrived with her sister and was moving toward them;

behind her came several soldiers, Mr. Wickham among them.

Mr. Darcy's attitude changed abruptly. He seemed to go rigid, exhaled sharply, and stared at Mr. Wickham for a moment before looking back at Elizabeth. He seemed to be gauging her reaction now, and Elizabeth betrayed her sentiments only with a look of distaste and little shake of her head.

Charlotte came to greet them, and hers was a look of significance, too; clearly, she had not expected Elizabeth to be speaking with Mr. Darcy. "Lizzy, Mr. Darcy. How are you enjoying the party?"

"We have been speculating, Charlotte, on just how it will be," Elizabeth said, hoping Mr. Darcy's unaccountable affability would not vanish now that Mr. Wickham was amongst them. She gave him a teasing look before she explained to Charlotte, "I had predicted it would be very strange indeed, but Mr. Darcy recommends that I endeavor to make the evening quite perfect. He is happily qualified to speak on matters of perfection, for I once heard him called *a man without fault*."

Mr. Darcy recognized her allusion and gave a thin smile. "We have established Miss Bingley's authority on certain subjects as well."

Elizabeth was really beginning to enjoy herself with today's version of Mr. Darcy. "Such as accomplishment, surely."

He nodded his agreement; Charlotte looked on, glancing between the two of them with a wry smile and a twinkle in her eyes. Elizabeth relished the sensation of shocking her friend as much as her banter with Mr. Darcy – it was as if all their past disputes were now only a great private joke between them. How easy it might be to give them both a tremendous shock....

"Clairvoyance, too," Elizabeth said. "Another of her accomplishments, you recall." Again Mr. Darcy nodded; Charlotte only raised her eyebrows.

Elizabeth could not help herself. Her own delight at human folly was too great a temptation – it might all go wrong, but there would always be tomorrow. "And dancing, I am sure. But I believe I might display my own talent for both, and soon. Any moment now Mary will open the pianoforte, and then it will not be long before Lydia begins to demand a tune we can dance to – for Mr. Wickham has not danced in these three months. Mary will grumble, but ultimately relent."

"Much of that, I am sure," Charlotte laughed, "is easy conjecture for anyone who knows your sisters."

Elizabeth looked to Mr. Darcy, and was dismayed by what she saw in his face, for he was very pale indeed, and she imagined she had rather horrified him. She stammered but could think of nothing to say that would undo the awful moment as he gaped at her. And then Mary opened the pianoforte.

Charlotte laughed nervously. "She does love to exhibit."

She was cut off as Lydia loudly shouted at Mary from across the room. Mary made some little protest, but began to play a jig, and Lydia grabbed Mr. Wickham by the hand, leading him to the center of the room; Kitty and Denny followed, and Maria Lucas with Lieutenant Sanderson.

Charlotte coughed. "Lydia does love to dance," she muttered, eyeing Elizabeth nervously.

Mr. Darcy looked as though he was about to suggest they burn her for witchcraft, and his distress was greater still as Mr. Collins broke away from Mrs. Phillips and began to approach them. Elizabeth caught Mr. Darcy's eye, and with a wan smile she asked, "Should you prefer to hear your aunt praised at length, sir, or will you dance?"

He schooled his countenance and bowed before offering her his hand, but there was still a great confusion about him as he led her to join the dance, in a position as far away from Mr. Wickham as possible.

Elizabeth's anxiety surged as she began the movements of the dance – for a moment that was all she could think of. She should be relieved, she began to suppose, that he had still wished to dance with her, after her shocking display just now – she had seriously misjudged the situation. The only thing for it now was to get through this dance and the rest of the evening, and check her impulses better tomorrow. And yet…. something nagged at her.

She peered over at Mr. Collins and indulged in musing on what inanities he must be babbling to poor Charlotte, who was clearly wishing to dance. Mr. Darcy had regained some of his composure by now, and he finally spoke to her. "You are not repenting your choice to dance, I hope – should you rather be hearing of my aunt's genius, and Mr. Collins' shelves in the closet?"

Elizabeth laughed for a moment, but her breath caught in her throat, and she missed one of her steps. She had not attended to all of her cousin's lengthy speech that morning – had he known of Mr. Darcy's connection to Lady Catherine de Bourgh? Mr. Darcy was certainly aware of it, and seemed to presume that she was, for he had joked about it that morning. But had it actually been brought up by Mr. Collins?

"No indeed," Elizabeth said at last. "I have heard as much as I could ever wish to on that score."

Jane and Mr. Bingley had joined the reel, and Elizabeth smiled merrily as they came to dance beside her. Still, there was something off, some confusion that hung about her, giving her gooseflesh – perhaps it was only the intensity of Mr. Darcy's gaze.

"We must have some conversation," she said at last.

"Do you talk by rule when you are dancing?" Mr. Darcy smiled. "What think you of books?"

Elizabeth was startled for a moment. Though nearly everybody had been prone to repeat themselves from one day to the next, this was the first time Mr. Darcy had done so. Indeed, she had come to suppose her recent enjoyment in his conversation was because it had varied so much more than anybody else's. Again she felt dizzy, on the verge of – something.

"I suppose you wish to compare opinions," she said, deliberately repeating his own words back to him.

"Perhaps you cannot think of books while dancing at such a party," he replied likewise. "I daresay your head is always full of something else."

Jane and Mr. Bingley were very merry and animated at her side, and indeed all the dancers were lively, but the activity around her began to blur and fade away; Elizabeth muddled through the dance, her eyes locked on Mr. Darcy. "The *present* always occupies me in such scenes," she breathed. Mr. Darcy's eyes seemed to glow; Elizabeth felt dizzier.

Ill-timed as ever, Mr. Collins invaded the periphery of Elizabeth's vision – he was leading Charlotte to join the dance. Mrs. Phillips's drawing room was not small, but five couples reeling was quite enough. Still, Mr. Collins would push in anyhow, though there was little space. Elizabeth stumbled as the other dancers tried to make room for Mr. Collins and Charlotte; she could not break her gaze away from Mr. Darcy, and she did not see Mr. Collins' foot protruding as he took a wrong turn. She hit the ground hard and fast.

***

Something was damp. Elizabeth opened her eyes, understanding that she was now horizontal. There was a tremendous pounding in her head, and something more – she felt her brow, and found a wet cloth had been placed there. She opened her eyes for just a moment before the light assaulted her, and she was obliged to close them again. "Jane?"

Elizabeth heard the scrape of a dresser drawer, and then gentle footfalls. "Oh, Lizzy, thank God." She felt the mattress dip as Jane came to perch beside her. "We were all so worried for you – you cut your head very badly... so much bleeding.... Mr. Darcy is downstairs with Mamma and Papa, and they are all quite beside themselves. Papa threatens to forbid dancing forever."

Elizabeth managed a muffled laugh. "Perhaps that is best."

A little mirth crept into Jane's gentle voice. "Oh, Lizzy."

"Jane?"

"Yes?"

"May I have some water?" Elizabeth groaned as she adjusted herself in the bed; she still could not bear to open her eyes, but she managed to drink from the glass that Jane placed in her hand, spilling only a little on herself.

"I came to collect my nightgown – I think perhaps it is my turn to share with Mary. You must get some rest. I will let everybody know that you are sensible now – you were babbling very strangely when we brought you home."

"The present always occupies me," Elizabeth muttered. The image of Mr. Darcy floated before her for a moment, but connected to nothing and quickly vanished.

"Yes," Jane said skeptically. "That is very... well, at least you seem a little improved. I will let our parents know, and Mr. Darcy will be so relieved. He feels himself responsible for your fall, though I am sure Mr. Collins only insists you fainted because he is embarrassed."

"Punch him on the nose," Elizabeth muttered.

"I presume you mean our cousin," Jane laughed, "for you seemed to enjoy dancing with Mr. Darcy. Mamma insists you ought never to have done so – that you promised you would not."

Elizabeth groaned, her head still pounding. "Perhaps that is best," she repeated.

"I will bid you goodnight," Jane said gently. "There is a bell on the nightstand – ring it if you need anything at all." There had been a candle burning, and even with her eyes closed Elizabeth was sensible of it; Jane blew it out now, and the darkness that fell over Elizabeth was soothing. She heard the door close behind her sister, and though she endeavored to surrender to sleep once more, she lay in a state just shy of it, her thoughts unmoored and expansive.

Sometime later there were voices in the hall, several of them. She heard her name but had not the energy to focus her mind and make out anything else. Then the door opened. Candlelight again tinted the red darkness through her closed eyelids. The blankets were pulled closer about her shoulders, and Elizabeth murmured and hummed at the comforting feel of it. Her mother spoke. "Oh, my poor girl! I am sure that wretched man tripped her! Serves him right for standing up with Charlotte Lucas. I hope he is ashamed of himself!"

"Well, Fanny. She is not dying, you see – she only needs some rest. Come along now." This was her father, and Elizabeth's lips quirked up at the sound of humor in his voice.

A third voice spoke now, deep and familiar, stirring something in her that she had not the energy to examine. "May

I – may I ascertain that her injuries are not too severe?" Elizabeth hummed a little more, and still she smiled.

Neither of her parents replied aloud. More footsteps. Then, a warm hand on her face. She hummed and smiled. It was a large hand, the touch gentle. "Serves me right for tripping you last time," Elizabeth murmured. She tried to smile again, but it only came out a sigh. With the last shred of strength she could muster, she lifted her hand out from beneath her blanket and heaved it back against the pillow, her fingers twitching. She hummed.

"I will call again tomorrow, and if needed I can send for my physician from London."

The candle was abruptly extinguished, and then his hand wrapped around hers, their fingers briefly interlacing. Fading voices, fading footsteps, the scrape of a door. Blissful blackness. "Tomorrow," Elizabeth murmured. She laughed and drifted away.

***

This time Elizabeth fully screamed when Mary's elbow connected with her face. Her head pounded. She rolled over and groaned, and Mary sat up with alarm. "Lizzy! What is the matter?"

Elizabeth groaned. "A nightmare." It was not exactly a lie. "And a headache," she said a moment later. This was unfortunately true, and very severe. Laying on her side, she fumbled with one hand to feel around her head, but detected no evidence of her injury.

"I will bring you some water and ask Hill for powders." Mary slipped out of the bed, the motion of it dizzying for Elizabeth. Her footfalls were inconceivably loud as Mary hurried from the room.

She returned some time later with the promised powders and water, and after Elizabeth had consumed both, Mary gently laid a cool, damp cloth over Elizabeth's head.

"Mary, you are an angel," Elizabeth sighed, shifting into a more comfortable position on her back.

"You sound very ill, Lizzy."

"I am in agony," Elizabeth moaned. "I do not think I shall leave this bed today, Mary. Not for all the world."

"You will miss market day."

"Doubtful," Elizabeth grumbled. She could feel the frown radiating from her sister in the dark room, and burrowed further back into the pillows.

"I shall go and sleep with Jane," Mary said. "And make some excuse for you, with Mamma."

"Nothing matters, anyhow." Elizabeth groaned once more, or at least attempted to, and as the pain in her head receded, she let sleep reclaim her again.

She did not leave the house that day. She woke before her family had departed for her aunts' house, and though her headache was much improved, she had no wish to leave her bed. When the painful mist cleared away, she was overpowered by thoughts that she was not certain she could trust. Thoughts that made it impossible for her to face Mr. Darcy.

4

There was a clattering in the corridor, a maid dropping a tray on the marble floor. Darcy had come to despise this sound; it woke him thus every morning, and far earlier than he wished.

Today, however, he sprang out of bed, his heart brimming with a renewed sense of hope, after the increasingly agonizing week he had experienced. He began to dress, and the swelling of unusual optimism gave way to some little uncertainty. His first thought was for Elizabeth. The horror of watching her faint, of hearing her head hit the ground, and seeing blood pool around her thick brown curls, had been unbearable for him. He had abandoned all sense of decorum and insisted on accompanying the Bennets home, waiting with them until he could see for himself that Elizabeth would recover.

He was not sure even now if she was well – if, like everything else, her condition would revert to what it had been when the day faded into night and reset itself as they slept. She may even now be in some pain, or even danger. A chilling thought crossed his mind – what if the blow to her head had jarred her mind, had actually knocked her out of the repetition that he had only just discovered she was a part of?

The brief elation he had felt the night before, when she revealed that they shared this secret burden, had instantly become so dear to him that even now he felt his sanity depended upon it. He wished to believe she felt it, too – she had put her hand out for him to clasp, and he now felt bound to her in the most unimaginable way.

It was dawn, but he rang for his valet and dressed quickly despite the early hour. Surely by the time he reached Longbourn on horseback it would be a decent enough hour to inquire, and if she was not injured, her family may spend the day perplexed by his visit, but for no more than a day. It was worth it to brave the awkwardness; he departed in all haste.

His head was full of Elizabeth as the three-mile gallop brought him ever closer to her. How cleverly she had revealed herself to him, just as he had begun to suspect she had some part in this bizarre phenomenon. It was a mercy knowing that there was anybody else in a world seemingly gone mad that could understand what he was going through – that it was *her*, of all people, was sublime. *Better than Bedlam indeed.*

At Longbourn, Darcy was received by the housekeeper, Mrs. Hill, for none of the family had come downstairs yet. She did not conceal her surprise at seeing him there, and so early. Not wishing to arouse any suspicion if he could avoid it, he began, "I come on behalf of Mr. Bingley, to ask after Miss Bennet's health."

"Mr. Bingley cannot come himself?"

It was impertinent of her to ask, but Darcy had to admit his excuse was a little odd. "He is not an early riser – he will be awake, surely, when I return home, and glad for news of her. I awoke early and thought it might provide some advantage in summoning a London physician, if Miss Bennet's condition is not improved."

The housekeeper seemed to accept his reasoning. "That is kind of you, sir. Miss Bennet is much recovered, thank you."

"And all the family is in good health?"

"Well, Miss Elizabeth complains of a headache this

morning, the poor dear. But I do not think she has caught ill from Miss Bennet."

Darcy nodded evenly. "A headache? I hope she is not injured."

"Oh my, no. Poor girl just wants rest, that is all." Mrs. Hill, by taking a step back and easing her hand up to the door, began to signal that the visit was now ended, and Darcy took his leave with one final reassurance that he would be happy to fetch a doctor if needed.

He left Longbourn relieved indeed that Elizabeth's injury had not followed her into the next repetition of this day, but by the time he reached Netherfield he had begun to dwell on the disappointment of not seeing her. He had been gone but a half-hour; Bingley and his sisters had not yet woken. He had risen hours before them in every other version of this day, but today the time felt emptier, and he knew he must take his mind off Elizabeth.

Darcy returned to his chamber and began to pace. Before his discovery last night, it was Wickham that had occupied much of Darcy's thoughts. He had turned it over in his mind so much this last week that he feared it would drive him mad – he was sure it could not be by coincidence that the day he was doomed to repeat was one in which his former friend made an unexpected appearance.

He had struggled to make sense of it all; indeed, he felt he had no greater an understanding now than five days ago, when he had foolishly believed it had all been a dream. Darcy grew restless of pacing and rang for strong coffee. When it was brought a few minutes later, he seated himself at a large oak desk in the corner of the room. He even rolled up his sleeves, as if determined to do some manner of work on his situation.

He set a clean sheet of paper before him, dipped his pen in the inkwell, and after a moment of hesitation and a satisfying draught of the fine coffee, he wrote two words: *Wickham* and *Elizabeth*. He stared at the paper, unsure what should follow, and finally he threw down the pen in frustration. Ink splattered from the nib, and he reflexively wiped at it, brushing aside a stack of letters that had accumulated there since his arrival. One toppled over, and Darcy's eyes focused on it, a surge of feeling running through him. *Richard*. He had quite forgotten about his cousin. Darcy read over the letter he had received the day before all hell had broken loose.

In it, Richard expressed some concern at Darcy's state before his journey to Hertfordshire – he had met with Richard in London in September, and had still been greatly depressed over Georgiana's ordeal. Now Georgiana had come to London to stay with the Fitzwilliams, and by Richard's account her spirits were much improved. Richard closed by lamenting for himself – his father was suddenly fixated with some matrimonial scheme for him. It was a thing that would overtake him in spells from time to time – often of several months' duration before a heated argument between Richard and his father would put an end to it, for a time. It had ceased while the family went into mourning for the Countess, but now, it seemed, the Earl of Matlock was threatening to arrange a compromise between Richard and their cousin Anne, for the sake of seeing Richard married well.

Darcy had pitied his cousin when first he read the letter a week ago – twice he had even replied, but this he had abandoned after realized it would give his cousin no real relief. Now Darcy began to consider a new plan. He checked his pocket watch – it was only eight o'clock. A post sent express might arrive in an hour, perhaps less. Richard could depart the house before his father came down to breakfast, and be in Meryton by half past ten. He set out another sheet of paper, and composed a brief and pleading message, which he dispatched at once.

After this was done, a fresh sense of relief washed over Darcy. Richard could always be depended upon – he was the single person amongst all of Darcy's acquaintance that he would trust with his life. This madness must be conquered, and he knew Richard must be of some help.

He finished his coffee and rang for more, then returned to his first purpose, though he knew not just what that was.

Wickham. Elizabeth. Darcy stared at the words and picked up his pen once more. Beside Wickham's name he wrote his father's and Georgiana's, and then drew a line connecting Wickham to Elizabeth. Now he began to ponder. At first, they had shown a partiality for one another that had been excruciatingly painful for Darcy. But then something had altered. Elizabeth was aware of the repetition – presumably her feelings had changed – he noted this down beside her name. But what had caused it? He sipped his coffee and closed his eyes, trying to separate the many nights spent in so similar a fashion.

Darcy made notes below Elizabeth's name. The first two markets days, they had chatted amiably together. It was not until the third day that he realized her partiality for Wickham, first at the market, and then at the card party. She had jested merrily with Darcy and even danced with him, but when the subject had turned to Wickham, Elizabeth gave every indication of having heard *his* view of things – Darcy could only imagine what tales the blackguard had told her.

That was the night she had stomped on his foot. The little minx! Even then he had found it strangely enchanting. It had also been deeply disappointing upon later reflection, to see such a witty and intelligent woman fall prey to that scoundrel. The next night he had not the heart to attend the card party, for fear of witnessing the same spectacle.

Nor had he gone to the market the next day. The pleasant conversations they had had together, and the miserable guilt that he had felt when she challenged him over his insult – all this had ebbed away when she had flaunted her preference before him. Morbid curiosity, if nothing else, had brought him to the card party again on the fifth market day – but Elizabeth was not there. They were told she was ill, but Darcy had overheard the young Bennet girls laughing that their sister had been punished for her rudeness to the officers. That night, it had been Darcy giving Wickham all the smug looks, and though he did not understand the change, he had relished it.

And then, yesterday – it had been a miracle. She spoke with such animated candor to him at the market, even seeming a little disappointed to part with him as her mother carried her away. She had invited him to the card party – not Bingley, *him*.

He reflected on their morning conversation, and it struck him she had alluded to strangeness at the card party. She had wanted to tell him. Darcy's heart swelled, and he leaned back in his chair, sipping his coffee with a smile on his lips. She might have told him then and there, had her mother not prevented it. She sought him out at the card party, and after deftly turning his offense against her into the most tantalizing flirtation, she had summoned the courage to confide in him.

Darcy began to really appreciate her for such bravery – he had given her a few hints, but he had been too subtle, too afraid. Elizabeth had taken all the risk, for even Miss Lucas, her dearest friend, had seemed to think Elizabeth's clairvoyance a strain of credulity. Elizabeth's opinion of Darcy could not have been irrevocably tarnished by Wickham if she had taken such a chance – she alluded to Bedlam, but seemingly deemed it worth the gamble. She had placed a trust in him that, after a week of regretting his comments at the assembly, Darcy knew he did not deserve. He was uncharacteristically humbled by the notion.

The next task at hand, as he returned to taking his notes, was to determine what was next to be done. The paper that had originally contained only two names was now full of disorganized scrawls, lines and arrows connecting one thought to another, and over the next hour Darcy filled it with every detail of the plight he shared with Elizabeth. She was in his thoughts all the while, laughing, dancing, and reaching her hand out for his.

By the time he could fit not one word more on the paper, it resembled the scribbles of a madman. But there in the center of it all was one name, which he had traced repeatedly with his pen. *Elizabeth.*

***

Darcy had been so occupied with his notes, and had consumed such an inordinate amount of coffee, that he forgot about the argument. When he heard the first rumblings of the explosion, Darcy groaned – how could he have forgotten such a dreadful scene?

His room was at the end of the guest wing. Beside it, a wide and ostentatious staircase led down to the spacious front hall, and past the staircase was a long hallway, with a stately balustrade overlooking the front entry, and more guest rooms along the opposite side. At the far end of the hall was the family wing.

It was there, he had eventually discovered, that the argument would begin. Invariably, the shouts would come nearer, various vases on display in the corridor would be thrown down to the first floor hall with tremendous noise, and if Darcy had not yet emerged from his chamber, Joseph Hurst would begin to pound on his door.

He heard the first shattering of fine china – this, he knew, was Miss Bingley. Then came the second – Mrs. Hurst. Now Bingley would shout, "Pull yourself together, Louisa!" Darcy mouthed the words to himself even as he heard them ring out from across the house.

He had managed, by the third market day, to time his breakfast so as to avoid the argument, though he could always hear it from wherever in the house he fled to. Twice he had been made an unwilling participant in the family dispute; he had tarried too long upstairs, and now it would be a third. The shouting grew closer – he could hear Mrs. Hurst weeping now. Darcy glanced ruefully down at his notes; he had made little mention of anybody else at Netherfield. He sighed and began to adjust his sleeves before donning his waist coat.

Jos was at Darcy's door, poised to knock – or bang – when Darcy opened the door. His face was red with anger, anger that was about to be unleashed most unjustly, in Darcy's opinion. Today, it was a much sadder sight.

Darcy regarded his old friend – they were in fact distant cousins on his father's side, but had little connection in childhood. At Eton and later Cambridge, they had been inseparable – Jos had eased the sting of betrayal when Wickham's true character had become impossible to ignore. Jos Hurst had, at the time, been athletic, energetic, and quick-witted. The man standing before Darcy now was fat, lugubrious, and nearly always drunk.

Beyond him was his wife, her face streaked with tears. Louisa Bingley had once been a charming, diffident young lady, just the sort of sister Bingley could be expected to have by anyone that knew him. But she was still a tradesman's daughter, and she had endured three humiliating seasons without any success on the marriage mart – the family despaired that Miss Caroline's upcoming debut would be a dismal – and expensive – failure as well.

Darcy had depended on Bingley heavily while in mourning for his father, and afterward did what he could to assist his friend. He introduced Louisa Bingley to Jos Hurst, and even persuaded his relation, a gentleman of some means, to look past the pretty heiress's low connections. Their marriage was a celebrated success for Darcy, and for all the Bingleys – such a tie to gentry had opened nearly as many doors for them in society as the Darcy name. The next year, Caroline Bingley's coming out had been a vast improvement on her sister's experience – but with Mr. Darcy still single, it was not a complete victory for her.

Even now Caroline Bingley stood at the end of the hall beside her brother, her hair disheveled, her chest heaving with rage. She attempted to correct herself as Darcy's eyes alighted upon her; she could not know that he was already fully aware of the state of her family.

It had become clear over the six previous mornings that Caroline Bingley had started the family row – after two days of rain had confined the occupants of Netherfield to the house, tensions had been high. The night before market day, Bingley had brought up his intention of giving a ball at Netherfield, and Miss Bingley had spent the entire dinner attempting to dissuade him. She had not succeeded, but awoke every market day determined to carry her point. Her method was simple – she was invariably resolved to convince her brother of what a mésalliance his interest in Jane Bennet threatened to become.

Darcy felt the same, and indeed had cherished the same anxiety for himself, as his attraction to Elizabeth had grown – but he certainly knew better than to agree with Caroline Bingley at such a time. Bingley may need to hear some sense about the matter, but there were better, more civilized ways to achieve it.

Miss Bingley had chosen the path of most resistance, alienating the Hursts, who might have been her allies. When she could not bully her elder sister into complicity in her scheme, she assaulted the Hursts, and Bingley, with a barrage of aspersions that ended only when Jos brought Darcy into the matter. And every day, Darcy had come to resent them all a little more for involving him.

He stood up straight, allowing his full height to intimidate the four angry people who now stood frozen before him, like unruly children whose governess had caught them about some mischief. Slowly, Darcy fixed them each in turn with a quelling look. "Jos, what is the meaning of this?"

The answer was one Darcy had heard before. "I think you know damn well, Darcy – it has all been your own doing, and years in the making!"

It stung to hear this, even for the third time. "Have I given you all some cause to begin the day in such a state as this? What is my offense against you?"

He already knew the answer, and sighed with resignation as Jos waggled a finger at him. "The delusions of grandeur you have given the Bingleys! You have made this mess, Darcy, and I can bear it no longer. You pressed me to marry into this family, to ignore the stain of trade – well, as you can see, blood will out."

Jos waved his hand dismissively at the Bingleys. Tears streamed down Louisa Hurst's face and she looked down in shame. Bingley looked sheepish and genuinely remorseful, while beside him Caroline Bingley attempted the same, but with little sincerity. Darcy felt all the same frustration with them, but this morning there was something else. Some voice in the back of his mind telling him he *might* bear some shred of guilt – it was a voice that sounded remarkably like Elizabeth Bennet, bitter humor swelling around the word *tolerable*.

"I am an ass," Darcy sighed. "You would do better not to listen to me." This was unlike any response Darcy had made before in this situation – or any other. It was certainly not what Jos was expecting, and he only sputtered with indignation in response.

"Come, Darcy," Bingley said, trying to affect some cheer. "You know I shall always listen to you – but I should be grateful if you would take my side." He chuckled nervously. "I like it here, and I wish to stay at Netherfield. That alone proves I have no delusions of grandeur, eh?"

"None of your own, perhaps," Jos quipped. "No, you are merely led by *her* ambition." He pointed a stubby finger at his sister-in-law, and then looked at his wife. "And you are scarcely better."

"That is unfair, Jos," Miss Bingley said, holding her chin high. "I do not suffer from *delusions*, only ambition, a condition I daresay you have not experienced in quite some time."

"Aye," Jos snarled. "Not since I threw it away to marry Louisa."

Darcy had set the conversation on a slightly different trajectory, but to little improvement. Louisa Hurst began to weep again – she sent Darcy a pleading look before coloring red and fleeing to her chamber. Miss Bingley seemed not to notice her sister's hasty departure. Bingley had begun to speak, but she cut him off. "If that is how you feel, sir, you have no right to criticize *my* aspiration, or the hopes I cherish for Charles." She flared her nostrils at Jos, but began stalking toward Darcy with a look of absolute innocence.

"I am sure Mr. Darcy understands me – indeed, sir, we have been of one mind since arriving in Hertfordshire," she purred. "The society here is savage – Charles can do better, and if we do not remove ourselves from the area in haste, I am sure my poor brother is in danger of getting caught by some fortune-hunting social climber."

Jos harrumphed. "I know all about *that*."

"I have made no secret of my opinions, it is true," Darcy said sternly. "Indeed, Miss Bingley, I have given you every reason to believe I would agree with you – just as I have likewise given your brother every cause to expect my support. I cannot do both, and I should much prefer to recuse myself from the matter entirely. It seems a family concern, and I am not family."

"Not family," Miss Bingley cried, as if wounded. "Oh, Mr. Darcy, no indeed. You are dear to all of us, and we respect your superior judgement. Can you not see how we all rely on you?"

She moved closer to him, running her fingers down his sleeve.

Darcy drew his arm away and looked over at Jos, who shook his head. "You are family to me, Darcy, if distantly – and you are the reason they are my family now. Or perhaps you think you can go about arranging things to your liking, and then play the superior gentleman and *recuse* yourself when it all falls apart," he spat.

"Now just a minute, Jos," Bingley cried in alarm. "I always value Darcy's advice, but I may never enjoy it again if you are going to abuse him like this."

Jos' temper continued to rise. "That, young man, is just the point. If you want to stay here, stay here! Be a man and think for yourself, damn you." He turned and looked up at Darcy, heaved a great sigh, and then clapped him on the shoulder. "Sorry, old boy. I ought to have been open with you sooner, rather than waiting for it all to boil over – I have been wrong in this, but I stand by what I said, and only repent the how and the when. Think on it, Darcy, for my sake. I am going to get drunk until I no longer have cause to do so."

Darcy watched Jos walk away from them, his shoulders slumped; the daily argument had taken a much different turn this time, and Darcy really began to feel some culpability in the family fracas. He had often suggested Bingley take a firmer stance against his sisters, but perhaps he ought to have done more for his friend.

With the Hursts gone, only Charles and Caroline Bingley stood in the hall with Darcy, and a heavy silence fell on them as Darcy looked around at the various items that had been destroyed or disturbed in the wake of the quarrel. He briefly wondered if the Bennets had ever made such a scene at Longbourn, and looked up at Miss Bingley, briefly entertaining the idea of posing the question to her.

She spoke first, her tone much softer than it had been. She was not a nice person, nor particularly exceptional in any way – but she was not a fool. It was clear that after Jos' apology, she felt obliged to do likewise, if only to save face. "I hope you will both forgive me." She hung her head in contrition, but still spoke firmly. "I do not know what came over me – that is, ever since you offered to give a ball, Charles, I have been driven to distraction in worrying what folly may come of it. You are amiable and good, just what a gentleman ought to be, but it induces me to think practically when you will not. Mr. Darcy, I do owe you some apology. I am not proud of how you have seen me behave, but I hope you will at least understand what lengths I am willing to go to, for love of my brother, for our very family dignity. It is something I take quite seriously, and I mean to give it some further consideration – I hope we might speak of it again soon, in a more civilized fashion."

By the end of her speech, Miss Bingley appeared very well-satisfied with her own display, and was holding her head up high again, adopting an air of dignified dissent. Her apology scarcely merited the word, for she had twisted it to serve her true purpose – presenting herself to advantage, as always. Darcy had no wish to encourage her; he merely nodded and made a slight bow.

Bingley appeared perfectly satisfied with his sister's paltry defense, and took her hand warmly. "Well, no more about it, then. Let cooler heads prevail, eh Darcy? We shall speak on it later. I am ready to take some breakfast, and then perhaps I shall call on Miss Bennet, and ask after her health."

"I suppose it has been long enough that she is past the point of infecting you," Miss Bingley said placidly. "I shall join you for breakfast, Charles, and you shall find me perfectly agreeable."

Darcy betrayed no reaction, though it was clearly all for his benefit. He checked his watch – it was nearly ten o'clock. "I shall leave you to it, then," he told his friend. "I have an errand in the village – perhaps I shall meet you there, on your way to Longbourn."

"Very good," Bingley cried, and clapped Darcy on the shoulder. "Yes, indeed." He smiled brightly, his family's disharmony already forgotten.

"You are likely to meet a familiar face there – I expect my cousin, if you can spare him a room for the night. He wrote yesterday of wishing to be away from London, and as I woke early this morning, I took the liberty of writing him to come in all haste."

"Splendid!"

Miss Bingley's eyes sparkled. "The viscount?"

"No, the colonel," Darcy replied, to Miss Bingley's disappointment. "He will not stay long, perhaps a night or two."

"He must stay for the ball," Bingley said cheerfully.

Darcy could not help himself; he smiled calmly at Miss Bingley. "If that is *agreeable* to you, madam." His smile widened as he bid them good morning and departed for the village.

***

"You are a sight for sore eyes, Richard," Darcy said as they met in the high street in Meryton. Richard had just stabled his horse at the inn, as instructed, and the two men fell into step beside one another as they began to walk along the village square.

"I can see you are well – that is a welcome relief. I had not expected you to take all my lamentations so seriously, at least not until they had been followed with further complaints." Richard laughed. His problems could always be reduced to a lark; Darcy had never understood his cousin's devil-may-care attitude toward life.

Darcy knew not how to begin to explain himself. He wished to tell Richard everything, for he was sure his cousin would help him make sense of it all, but he could not fathom how such a thing was to be rendered believable. Still, he must get on with it, for Bingley was likely already on his way to the village.

Happily, Elizabeth was still ever-present in his mind, and he thought of how she had revealed herself the night before. Darcy clapped Richard on the back, now certain of what he must do. "Come with me, Richard."

"Where to, Darcy?"

"We must go and speak with a very silly woman," Darcy replied. "Mrs. Bennet of Longbourn."

Richard laughed. "And why should we want to do that?"

"Because something exceedingly strange and difficult to explain has happened – is happening – to me, and it pertains to the second of her five daughters, Elizabeth."

Richard guffawed at length. "Elizabeth, eh? Do not tell me you have fallen in love!" He howled with laughter now, eliciting several stares from passersby. Not that it would matter tomorrow.

"I would not say that, though I admire her. More to the point, I have come to believe she is an integral part of a curious dilemma – but I think you must see for yourself if you are to believe me."

Richard's look betrayed obvious intrigue. "And what, exactly, must I see? Your letter indicted a state of emergency, and I find you loitering about a village market."

"Market day is precisely the emergency – or part of it. But I shall tell you what you will see," Darcy said with confidence. "You will meet Mrs. Bennet, and no doubt your amiable manners will render her a degree or two more civil to me than she has ever been before. Her youngest daughters will flirt with you when they discover you are an officer, and Mrs. Bennet will do little about it but encourage their behavior, and praise them for your benefit."

Richard frowned. "Charming."

"This much is purely conjecture, but what follows is based on fact. Mrs. Bennet will tell us Elizabeth is at home with a headache. She will introduce us to her relation Mr. Collins, an exceedingly ignorant parson who will be astonished and almost repugnantly delighted to learn of our connection to his noble patroness, Lady Catherine de Bourgh. If Mrs. Bennet's sister, an almost equally vulgar woman called Mrs. Phillips is about, she will invite Bingley, and by extension ourselves, to a card party at her home this evening. Bingley is besotted with Miss Bennet, and will be gazing at her like an idiot while she shall be all blushes and mumbles and insipid acquiescence."

"I shall ignore all the malice, for the moment, and congratulate you," Richard quipped. "Bingley's Miss Bennet is your Elizabeth's sister – so you are to be brothers! Why, it is just what Miss Bingley has always wished."

"I knew it would be thus with you – from admiration to love, and from love to matrimony in a moment – but I have not forgotten my duty. To speak of Miss Elizabeth is crucial, however, to what I must tell you of my dilemma. It is far from what you may expect, far from the ordinary indeed. It is a very serious matter and may shock you – a familiar face will arrive in Meryton, though I cannot determine why."

Richard had raised his eyebrows higher and higher as Darcy went on, his face at first bemused, and now concerned. "Darcy, what are you on about? I can hardly imagine you have learned to tell fortunes – I wonder if you are part of some conspiracy."

"I hardly know what it is all about, but I will tell you more when we return to Netherfield. Bingley will put you up for the night, I am sure, and I should like you to attend the card party with us – trust me, you shall wish it, too."

Darcy led his cousin across the square, where Mrs. Bennet was gossiping noisily with her sister and two youngest daughters, as well as several officers – Miss Mary Bennet and Mr. Collins hovered nearby, whispering together.

Bingley was walking that way with Miss Bennet on his arm; he caught sight of them and waved. "There you are, Darcy – I have caught you up, you see. Colonel Fitzwilliam, welcome to Hertfordshire! May I present my – Miss Jane Bennet, of Longbourn. Miss Bennet, Colonel Fitzwilliam, Darcy's cousin."

Miss Bennet curtseyed and Richard bowed – then he gave Darcy a mischievous grin. "Longbourn? How quaint that sounds."

"It is, it is," Bingley said. "I have the highest regard for it."

Darcy could see the rest of the Bennet clan regarding them with open curiosity, which might have offended him, but that it suited his own purposes. "Miss Bennet, might I introduce my cousin to the rest of your family?"

She looked stunned, but quickly recovered herself. "Of course – that is very kind of you."

Richard was already aware of the younger Miss Bennets' interest in him, for they were hardly subtle, and he walked that way with such eager bemusement that Darcy suspected Richard meant to poke fun at him.

The introductions were made – Mr. Collins put himself forward before Mrs. Bennet and her two youngest had ceased to fawn over Richard. Darcy braced himself for the coming spectacle. The toady parson was determined to recommend himself to Richard as well, and happily managed to unwittingly prevent Miss Catherine and Miss Lydia from fully attaching themselves to the colonel, as he had seen them do so often.

Richard beheld Mr. Collins' obsequious verbosity with surprise, and Darcy knew his cousin well enough to detect some little amusement as well. Richard's sense of humor could be rather rubbish at times.

"Mr. Darcy of Pemberley – and his cousin Colonel Fitzwilliam," Mr. Collins cried with immediate recognition. He bowed again, and deeper this time. "There can be no mistake – you are the esteemed nephews of my most noble patroness, Lady Catherine de Bourgh of Rosings Park. I have the honor of serving as her parson at Hunsford, a duty as dear to my heart as the Almighty, I am sure. She could not have bestowed her kindness on a happier recipient, for I am so highly favored – I have several times been asked to dine at Rosings, and sometimes make up a whist party with Mrs. Jenkinson and your cousin, Miss de Bourgh. I flatter myself I am intimate with the family, and I am sure you will be pleased to hear I can assure you both of their good health as of three days ago."

Mr. Collins had spoken quickly and without taking breath, but now seemed winded by his own expostulation. He gave a simpering smile, both conveying and expecting inordinate deference.

"Excellent," Richard said with energy. "I can see my aunt must be perfectly content – I understand the parsonage is a near distance from the manor. Your company must delight her."

"A very near distance," Mr. Collins said haughtily. "My humble abode is separate from the park only by a lane."

"Only a lane, eh? Yes, I recall. It has been some time since I have visited." Richard looked at Darcy with wonder.

"It is a pleasure to meet you, Mr. Collins," Darcy said. Richard had seen one of his predictions come to pass, and he began to press for another. "My aunt is sure to be grateful for another whist player at her disposal; Richard and I are always pressed to play cards when we visit."

Richard eyed him with suspicious approbation, before apparently deciding to play along. "We are always happy to indulge her, eh Darcy?"

"I could never have doubted...." Mr. Collins appeared on the verge of another lengthy monologue, but happily Mrs. Phillips had the prescience to cut him off. "If you are fond of playing cards, you must come and play with us this evening, Colonel. I am to invite the girls, of course, and perhaps a few of the officers, but you must all come."

Mrs. Bennet had been whispering to Miss Bennet during Mr. Collins' tedium, but now she fluttered her handkerchief with excitement. "Oh, do you hear that, Jane? What a fine thing. Is that not kind of my sister? And you must attend, Mr. Bingley, and all your guests, of course." Here she gave Darcy a spiteful grimace.

Richard looked on, still managing astonishment and amusement at once. "I am happy to accept, madam, whether my friends here will or no. I look forward to it. But pray, forgive me – I must have misheard Darcy, for I had understood you to have five daughters, Mrs. Bennet."

"How very kind of you," she cried, as if the mere quantity were a compliment. "My second daughter Lizzy is at home this morning, in – she is practicing at the pianoforte, sir, and performing her other household duties."

At the same moment, Mr. Collins spoke, and much louder. "She complains of a headache, poor girl. It pains me, to know that my fair cousins are of such delicate constitutions."

"Sir," Mrs. Bennet cried, as her younger daughters giggled. "I am sure you are mistaken."

Bingley looked uncomfortable, and observed, "Well, I hope she will be among you all at the party tonight, feeling very well – I shall look forward to attending, of course." He gazed stupidly at Miss Bennet, who blushed and murmured some little agreement.

Lydia Bennet had now managed to attach herself to Richard's arm, and was trying to gain his attention, though he was chiefly occupied in giving Darcy some very odd looks. "I hope you are as fond of dancing as you are of cards, Colonel," she cooed at him, batting her eyelashes.

"Or fonder of it, at least, than your cousin," Mrs. Bennet said curtly. Bingley laughed, and Miss Bennet blushed.

"That is easily done," Richard bantered. "I am getting more eager for this evening by the moment, I assure you." He made a gallant, sweeping bow, and as he straightened he gave Darcy a roguish wink.

Miss Catherine was generally a little quieter than Miss Lydia, and at present she had been sulking at not having a share of Richard's attention, but she broke into a smile and exclaimed, "There is Captain Denny! And who is that handsome man with him?"

As she pointed that way with no discretion whatsoever, Richard looked over his shoulder, and Darcy knowingly awaited his cousin's reaction. Richard's face grew steely in an instant, and he barely recovered his composure before giving a parting bow to the ladies. "I have some business to attend to, but I will be eagerly anticipating your hospitality, Mrs. Phillips."

Darcy placed a hand on his cousin's shoulder to delay him a moment. "We have some little business and must return directly to Netherfield – forgive me."

"I shall catch you up," Bingley said. "Surely you can attend your business without me."

Darcy nodded. "Miss Bennet, Mrs. Bennet, please give Miss Elizabeth my best wishes for her speedy recovery."

Once they were some distance away, Darcy addressed his cousin, who had not taken his eyes off of Wickham at the end of the high street. "I know what you are thinking, Richard, but it is best not to act yet."

"Are you mad?"

"Possibly, yes," Darcy drawled. "You must trust me – I can well understand the temptation, believe me, but I fear it will accomplish nothing, unless we speak first."

Richard narrowed his eyes at Darcy. "Perhaps you are right. There is something you know – something you are not telling me."

"I have told you that I knew what was going to happen, and it all came to pass."

Richard had seemed all ease before, but he began to show some worry now. "Yes. That. You have made your point, I suppose, but I should thank you to explain. But first, there is something I must do."

They passed Mr. Wickham now, and Richard swiftly moved away from his cousin, toward Wickham and his companion. He greeted them very warmly, but Darcy knew the colonel was up to something. He hastily followed.

"Well, Wickham, you old dog! Imagine seeing you turn up here. I understand you are to join the regiment, and imagine my surprise! I would never have supposed you capable of it."

Wickham shifted his eyes between Richard, Darcy, and the other officers present. "When one has limited options," he stammered.

"Yes, yes," Richard merrily agreed. "One will be driven to extreme measures. But to think of you really *putting your life on the line*, good God! Have you any notion of the danger you face? You really ought to think on it. Colonel Forster is an old friend of mine, I shall have to tell him to keep an eye on you. Well! We must be going. Very good to see you, Wickham, truly most amusing!" He clapped Wickham hard on the back, smiled brightly, and began to move away.

"That was easily managed – and rather fun," Richard said as they walked along. "Of course, if you knew he was coming, you might have done the same."

"I have tried, but with less success," Darcy replied, earning him a quizzical look from Richard. "Let us get you to Netherfield, and I will tell you everything," Darcy promised, leading his cousin back to the stables.

***

Richard leaned back against the wide leather armchair in the Netherfield library, set aside the page of Darcy's frantically scribbled notes, and ran his hands slowly over his face. "I need a drink – Bingley always keeps his fine brandy well-stocked; let us have it then."

Darcy went over to the sideboard and poured then each a

generous drink before resuming his seat across from Richard. He had spared no detail in detailing his dilemma over the last few hours, even presenting the notes he had made, which he now had to admit were utterly ludicrous. "I need you to believe me, Richard."

Richard downed the glass of brandy. "Say that I do." He stood and went to refill his drink, slowly stalking back. "What do you intend to do about Wickham? And more importantly, what do you mean to do about Elizabeth Bennet?"

"I am seeking your advice."

Richard laughed. "Nothing so simple. Kill one, and marry the other, if she is pretty."

"Nothing about this is simple," Darcy said with some frustration. This was not the time for Richard to make light of serious matters.

"I can see that, from your...." Richard picked up Darcy's notes with two fingers and held the paper aloft. "Whatever this is. You have charted Miss Elizabeth's apparently increasing fondness for you – that cannot mean nothing at all."

"It means something, I am sure, but what I am more concerned with at present is whether it shall ever be Thursday!"

"Yes, obviously," Richard said with equal vexation. For a moment, the two cousins only glowered at one another, until Richard began to guffaw. "This must be, without a doubt, the strangest thing we have ever argued over, Darcy. I confess, I am bewildered by it all."

"As am I – and more bewildered still that I expected anything sensible or useful out of you."

"I stand by my advice," Richard insisted. "You must hear me out."

Darcy sighed heavily, but relented, and gestured for Richard to go on.

"I have listened to you at length Darcy, and even if you did not wish any counsel, I would give you mine anyhow, you know. I think I believe you – I wish to. It is not your nature to play some sort of prank, and indeed it would have been difficult indeed to orchestrate one such as this. No, it must be true. But you cannot go on like this, I sincerely fear it will drive you mad.

Likely your Miss Elizabeth must feel the same, if she is indeed experiencing the same phenomenon. Has she told you any of her experience?"

"No, she has not," Darcy said. "I only discovered it last night. But yes, I would wager she must be as frustrated as I have been, for it was a great risk on her part to tell me of something that would have made me think *her* mad, were I not suffering from the same madness myself."

"I do not see how. If she had no knowledge of your involvement, then she would have presumed she might say what she likes to you, and you will have forgotten it by morning. Is that not how this all works?"

"True."

"Aha, I have you there, Darcy," Richard chided him. "You give her too much credit, I think – because *you like her*."

"She is better company than nearly anybody else in the county – if it had to be anybody, at least it is she that I am suspended in time with."

"How very fortunate for you," Richard quipped. "But I do not disagree that her involvement is indeed significant. I only defy any distinction between this matter, and that of your obvious attachment to her. I think they are one and the same, Darcy – fate has brought you together."

"You cannot be serious," Darcy scoffed.

Richard rolled his eyes and began to read from Darcy's notes. "Days one and two, EB friendly and animated. Mentioned insult – apology attempted. Day three, EB witty jest about Miss CB – apology – dancing – defense of Wickham. Days four and five – did not meet, and then, day six. Market - EB lively and warm, nearly confided; card party – EB high spirits and fine looks, pleasant dance, obvious disgust with Wickham, she might have flirted with me. Our shared secret disclosed. You know it means something – we both know what."

"There will be time to think of that tomorrow, if tomorrow ever comes," Darcy sighed. "If you wish to advise me, tell me what I must do to make this all stop!"

Richard laughed ruefully and shrugged at Darcy. "I hardly

know, Cousin. I am sorry. Indeed, I am flattered you would apply to me for help, but I can hardly alter the passage of time. And it seems you do not need me; it is all written here. But I wonder – if Miss Elizabeth was to write out such a... thing... what would be written upon hers? You each, for *whatever reason*, hold a piece to the puzzle, and you must put them together, I think. Talk to her, Darcy."

Darcy nodded. "I would have done so already, were she not indisposed. I will approach her at the card party and contrive an opportunity to speak privately. Perhaps you might keep her sisters occupied?"

Richard winced. "You are certain I shall wake tomorrow and have no recollection of it?"

"Painfully so," Darcy sighed.

"I shall sacrifice myself for you, then, Darcy – but I must ask you something."

Darcy eyed Richard warily. "What?"

"Does Miss Elizabeth know you hold all her family in such high contempt?"

"Of course not – how dare you!"

"How dare *I*? Come, Darcy, you had nothing good to say about any of them. You called her mother silly and her aunt vulgar, and it was clear what you thought of her sisters."

Darcy felt his tempered rising. "And yet you wonder why I protest all your insinuations about my interest in her," he fairly shouted. "Can you not see it is a sort of torture for me to feel our attachment deepening, and know it is all in vain – it is a mere distraction, keeping me from my true purpose, to free myself from this endless cycle of repetition! It is true, I must acknowledge that she has some part to play in my dilemma, but I could never form any serious designs on her. She is beautiful and witty and kind, but she is... she is...." Darcy began to sputter with rage.

Richard only sipped another glass of brandy with irritating composure. "What is she?"

"Unsuitable," Darcy bellowed.

"Must you always be so stupid?"

Darcy leaned back into the chaise, in such a rage that he

could not make any reply. Everything was utterly wretched.

Richard took a few tentative steps toward him. "I am sorry, Darcy," he said gently. "You are only very stubborn, but clearly whatever you have been about this last week is not working for you. Forgive me if it seemed logical to try a new approach."

Darcy sat up, embarrassed at his little tantrum. "I am sorry, too, Richard."

"You could make it up to me. Let me have a go at Wickham, eh? The bruises will be gone tomorrow."

"No! That is out of the question."

"But why?"

"We ought to study him a little closer. You put him on notice today, but tomorrow may require more. Elizabeth must be my first priority tonight, but Wickham will be at the card party. Find out what he wants, and what it will take to be rid of him," Darcy said.

"It is fortunate he has not yet enlisted," Richard laughed. "I do not see *that* coming to pass." He turned serious. "He must be a part of this, too, Darcy. We could take care of it all tonight."

"I am not sure it is wise; indeed, I have no wish to know what you mean," Darcy said. "Tonight, what I desire is information. More pieces of the puzzle, as you say. I will send for you again in the morning, earlier this time. We can review what we learn tonight, and decide how to proceed."

"But I will not remember any of it," Richard reminded him.

"I convinced you this morning, and I can do it again. Whatever you learn of Wickham, tell me tonight, and I will tell you tomorrow." He picked up his page of illegible notes and laughed. "I will make a proper chart tomorrow, too."

"I hope this chart contains some little mention of possible violence against that blackguard, Darcy."

"First information, then plans," Darcy quipped.

Richard extended his hand for Darcy to shake and then asked, "And what shall we do until then? I know, let us drink."

***

Miss Bingley had been indisposed when Darcy and Richard

arrived at Netherfield, but she sauntered into the library now, running her hands up and down a folded piece of paper, in a gesture that was likely meant to appear graceful and alluring. Darcy heard Richard chortle beside him.

"Oh, there you are, Mr. Darcy. And Colonel Fitzwilliam, you are certainly an unexpected guest. What on earth could induce you to willingly leave the delights of London for Hertfordshire – most unaccountable," she drawled.

Richard offered her a dashing smile, ignoring her dislike of him as much as he had ever done, the few times they had met before. "It is a circumstance I am sure you can well understand, Miss Bingley. I find it a respite from the calamities of the marriage mart, and of course, my cousin Darcy is here."

Miss Bingley blanched for a moment, but quickly recovered and fanned herself with the letter in her hand. "You shall find us a house divided on the matter. I have found certain aspects of country life making me long for London, but it is likely you may have a different opinion of the place – officers are enjoying a surge in popularity here just presently – particularly among certain circles."

"So I have discovered," Richard replied, cheerfully defiant in the face of her thinly veiled disdain. "But I should never have doubted what a warm reception I would receive, particularly with the ladies."

"I wonder that Charles does not return," she said, again drawing attention to the letter – she handed it to Mr. Darcy with a smile. "He writes that he has gone to visit Longbourn and intends to dine with the family. Then he will go with them all to their aunt's house for an evening of dancing and whist. I cannot think what he is about, on a day when we receive *such* a guest."

Darcy examined the letter, written in Bingley's characteristically hasty hand. "As it says, Richard and I have consented to attend the party as well – he conveys Mrs. Bennet's warmest wishes, Richard, that we will join them for supper as well."

"Surely you will not." Miss Bingley gave an affected laugh. "What an idea!"

Richard took the letter from Darcy and glanced over it, then looked back up at Miss Bingley. "I could not refuse your gracious hospitality when you must be wishing us to dine here. Is that not so, Darcy? We can meet Bingley at the card party after. And what will you do, Miss Bingley? The invitation includes you, you see. What envy we should arouse, if I were to arrive at Mrs. Phillips' home in all my regimentals, and with you on my arm, in very fine looks? I am sure they should all be fainting away and swooning, ladies and officers alike. You must wear your blue dress, the one you wore to the opera, when you trod on the Duchess's train – you would look very well beside me in blue."

Darcy regarded his cousin with surprise, and then reproach. "Really, Richard."

"How you do go on, Colonel," Miss Bingley said, seeming at the limit of her patience – and false cordiality.

Richard laughed to himself. "What does it matter today, if there is no tomorrow, eh Darcy?"

"I beg your pardon, sir," Miss Bingley snapped.

"My dear Miss Bingley, you must forgive me, I beg you." Richard placed a hand on his heart. "It is an army expression – you could not have known."

"Perhaps it is best, then, that I do not attend this little party, for I clearly have no knowledge of military manners, and would be most out of place among such company."

"In that blue dress, Miss Bingley, you should never be out of place – or perhaps only your toes." He winked at her, and Miss Bingley began to seethe.

This unusual exchange had become rather entertaining for Darcy, but he decided he had better put a stop to it. "We ought to dress, too – I am sure they shall be ringing the gong soon."

"Yes, yes, Darcy," Richard laughed. "I shall see you at supper, Miss Bingley."

"The Hursts may be persuaded to join you," she replied. "I mean to take a tray in my room. I shall bid you good evening." Caroline Bingley swept out of the room, and Richard watched her go, then grinned stupidly at Darcy. "You must invite me to Netherfield every market day, Darcy, it is jolly good fun!"

***

Elizabeth did not attend the card party, and Wickham did not either. The latter, they soon discovered, had already reconsidered his enlistment, and fled the village.

5

Elizabeth was numb, this morning, to Mary's elbow hitting her face. She sat up in bed, gave a perfunctory sigh, and readied herself for a day she was not at all prepared to relive again. She had spent the previous day abed, alone with her thoughts, but was no better for it now; arguably, she was in much worse a state. Before, the consequences of one market day had never carried into the next, but all that, she suspected, was different now.

She knew she could not do nothing – she had to make whatever alteration to the day was necessary to end the absurd sequence of repetition – she would have to venture out, and likely face Mr. Darcy. Elizabeth groaned as she crept through the corridor to the room she shared with Jane. She began her preparations in silence, and managed to dress herself and brush out her hair before Jane awoke.

"Good morning, Lizzy," Jane said, chipper as ever. As she always did, Jane got out of bed, drew open the curtains, and opened her armoire. As she reached for her sprigged muslin,

Elizabeth turned about on her dressing stool and said, "I think there must still be mud – you should wear something dark."

"Of course, Mamma will be wanting us in very fine looks today." Jane blushed, then turned and peered out of the window. "At least it will not rain on us at the market. Oh! But who is that?"

Elizabeth jumped off the stool and joined her sister at the window. But of course it was Mr. Darcy. She felt her heart sink. She had been too bold when last they spoke – when she thought she might speak as she wished, with impunity. But he remembered – he had remembered the other markets days as none but she had, and the more Elizabeth began to think it almost a relief, the more she resented the revelation. Would that she had held her tongue!

"I wonder why he should be coming here, at such an hour," Jane breathed.

"Perhaps he conveys some message from Netherfield?"

Jane wrung her hands. "Oh! I hope Mr. Bingley is not in any distress!"

Elizabeth patted her sister on the back. "Surely not. Do not worry, Jane." She felt her own panic rising. "I had an idea – we might do something for Mary this morning – some improvement in her toilette, perhaps."

"What a lovely idea," Jane cried. "I am sure we need only suggest a few little things to her, and she might turn Mr. Collins' head, which I suspect is your motive."

"Indeed it is," Elizabeth said, glancing back at the window; Mr. Darcy was nearly to the front gate now. "Will you not go to her, Jane? I am sure you would do much better than I could."

"Oh. But I am not dressed – you are further along than me."

"Yes, exactly. Take your blue muslin, go and dress with Mary. You are so much kinder than me," Elizabeth insisted. "I should only give her some offense. Besides, I *am* further along, and I could go down and ascertain that all is well with Mr. Bingley."

"Oh, would you? Thank you, Lizzy."

Jane embraced her sister before collecting her things and hastening to Mary's room. As soon as the door closed, Elizabeth went into a frenzy. She threw open her armoire and retrieved her traveling bag, hastily shoving gowns and other garments into it. As she reached into her drawer and scooped up a handful of stockings, there was a clatter on the floor, and she glanced down. There was the pretty pendant necklace she had purchased on the first market day. "But how?" She picked it up and wondered at it for a moment, but her concentration was broken by the sound of Mr. Darcy entering the house.

Elizabeth slipped the necklace over her head and hastily braided her hair, then grabbed her bag. She opened the window and peered out, determining the safest route of escape. She was not going to repeat this day anymore – not in Meryton, at least, and not with Mr. Darcy. If she was to be suspended in such repetition, she would bear it better in London, with her aunt and uncle.

Her mother was in the hall now, her footsteps and shouts of excitement growing closer; Elizabeth barely had time to turn about, tossing her traveling bag out the window and blocking the view of it with her body, when her mother burst in.

"Lizzy, my dearest girl! Oh, what a vision you are, my dear, you are practically glowing! Perhaps you are not as surprised as I am – you sly thing! To be setting your cap at Mr. Darcy all along, and never tell your Mamma! Well, whatever you were about at Netherfield has worked, for he is here, child. Mr. Darcy is here – he is here for you, Lizzy!"

Elizabeth gaped at her mother. "He is here for me," she said flatly. Of course he was.

Mrs. Bennet, still grinning like the cat that caught the canary, narrowed her eyes at her daughter. "You are *not* surprised! Lizzy, you might have warned your Mamma! I thought you hated the man. Well, you had better come along and speak with him."

"I cannot – I am not ready."

"Not ready," Mrs. Bennet screeched.

"My... my hair," Elizabeth said, gesturing to her loose braid. "Give me just a few minutes – I will come presently."

"You will come now," Mrs. Bennet said, and grabbed her daughter by the wrist. "You look well enough, and if he can bear your constant impertinence, your hair shall hardly matter! He has asked for a private audience with you, Lizzy!"

Though she dug in her heels, Elizabeth was dragged from the room. Her mother brought her to the top of the stairs and fixed her with a firm look. "He is downstairs in the drawing room. Go."

Elizabeth sighed and did as she was bid, and her mother remained on her heels until she had reluctantly entered the drawing room – then Mrs. Bennet closed the door behind her, leaving her alone with Mr. Darcy.

***

Darcy waited calmly in the Longbourn drawing room, peering out the window, calmer than he had felt in a week. His salvation, he was sure, was nearly at hand. He would have a companion in all this madness, and they might even find some way in overcoming their shared dilemma.

There was some noise above him, heavy footfalls and the shrill voice of Mrs. Bennet, but Darcy ignored those and stared out at the garden, imagining what a pleasure it might be to walk there with Miss Bennet, to share their uncanny secret as they could with no one else. There was movement – something flew across the garden and landed in the shrubs – it was a suitcase. Then came more shouting upstairs.

Darcy could only shake his head; he was reminded of Richard's accusation, that he held the Bennets in high contempt. Throwing suitcases out of windows and shrieking in such a way were not dignified behaviors, but Darcy made some effort to overlook it. He had written to Richard already, and had no intention of earning such a rebuke again when his cousin arrived.

A few minutes later, Elizabeth entered, her hair hastily braided and coming loose about her face in a fetchingly tousled manner. The door slammed behind her and her eyes flashed as they did before a spell of bewitching impertinence. Darcy smiled at her in eager anticipation. "How is your head, Miss Elizabeth?"

She scowled at him, drawing closer as she hissed, "I rather wonder what is wrong with yours, coming here like this – have you any idea what my mother has assumed?"

Darcy was taken aback by her temper. "I am sorry, Elizabeth – but we both know it will not matter tomorrow."

She stepped closer and glared at him. "For Heaven's sake, keep your voice down. I can promise you, someone is probably listening at the door. It will not matter tomorrow, but there is still a lot of today to be got through – I had hoped to put it to better use."

"And so had I," Darcy snapped back. "I cannot account for your temper at such a time. You seemed to understand as well as I that we are a part of something, together, when you chose to reveal that fact to me two days ago."

"Indeed, you are mistaken," Elizabeth said softly; her voice was low, but painfully cold. "I believed it would be amusing to shock you, sir, as a means of making out your character, for you had been puzzling me exceedingly. I was not expecting to discover that – I was not expecting you to remember any of my actions that day."

This was a blow to Darcy, and he sat down heavily on the sofa. She had been warm and encouraging that day, so much so that he had begun to hope she had the same affection for him that he held for her. Darcy shook his head, pushing this thought away. The disappointment stung, but he had long been resolved to overcome his attraction to her, regardless of their strange bond. Her family was still most unsuitable.

He glanced out the window at the suitcase in the bushes, and the realization dawned on him. She had tried to flee. "You do not wish to talk to me, no matter the manner of my seeking you out," he said.

Elizabeth wavered for a moment, before finally coming to stand near him. "When you say it like that, you make me sound quite cruel, sir. It is only that I was not ready – and I was a little embarrassed of how it all came to pass. It was wrong of me to hide from you, and to try to run away, but – oh, come now, this is making me quite mad, surely you understand."

"I do," Darcy said softly. He reached out and tentatively

grasped her hand. "You and I understand each other in a way that nobody else can just now – do we not owe it to one another to speak about it, to try to make sense of the madness?"

She withdrew her hand, but sat down beside him, letting out a long sigh. "I suppose so. I have no other objections, at present, and I have tried everything else."

Darcy looked at her in some confusion. Bitterness swelled in his chest; he at once wanted to take her in his arms, and to flee, forgetting this mortifying conversation had ever taken place. He stood up abruptly, then stopped and looked down at her.

"Forgive me," he said. "I can see you repent your candor, despite what it meant to me. You thought only to amuse yourself at my expense, and have no wish to share this burden with me." He gave a slight, civil bow, and began to leave.

"Wait," she breathed. "Stay. Forgive me, I was only – I was not prepared, but I will speak with you."

Darcy turned back to face her, but he did not move. He heard some movement in the corridor and chose his words carefully. "Are you quite certain? I am asking more than that, you must know. Fate has drawn us both together in this, and I had thought if we are willing to work at it together, we might form an alliance of sorts – we might unite in our efforts, and be the happier for it."

Elizabeth chewed her lip as she considered. "I do not know if I would call it *fate* – it is simply madness to me," she laughed. "I am still in shock, but I cannot be so cruel, and let you suffer alone. We shall figure it out together."

Darcy smiled, and extended his hand for her to shake. "So, you accept?"

Elizabeth came toward him with a smile at last and shook his hand. "Yes, I accept."

The door burst open at once. Mrs. Bennet came through first, followed by the rest of her daughters, but the commotion was so great that it might have been a dozen people. Elizabeth instantly blanched at the misunderstanding in progress and moved to withdraw her hand from his.

Darcy held fast to her hand. She had been laughing at him all week, and though their truce was but moments old, he could not resist some little revenge. He pulled her closer and took her in his arms. "Elizabeth, you have made me the happiest of men!"

***

Elizabeth paced in the garden, fuming. At least, she was *trying* to be angry, but after the ludicrous nature of the last week, the whole thing now was incredibly funny. She walked along the boxwoods and saw her suitcase strewn across the shrubbery, and she gave into her laughter at last.

"Well played, Mr. Darcy," she muttered to herself. Their engagement would only last for the day, which was a relief, but it was still enough of a nuisance for her to be irritated. Even so, she rather admired him for playing such a trick, and she was satisfied that he was paying for it even now. Mrs. Bennet had, predictably, presumed them engaged at once, and now Mr. Darcy was obliged to pay a visit to Mr. Bennet's study.

Grateful that she would have some little time to collect herself, Elizabeth had begged Jane to occupy their sisters, claiming she was still quite overcome and required privacy. This was not untrue; Elizabeth was determined to gather her wits before her next conversation with Mr. Darcy.

She chided herself for spending the whole of the previous day sulking; she had done nothing useful, and had not even fully considered what it meant for Mr. Darcy to be in the same incredible situation as she was. Some congress between them, she ought to have realized, was inevitable.

And perhaps it might be a good thing. As he had observed, there was some consolation in knowing that somebody else shared in her problem, even if that someone was someone she despised. The sheer madness of it all had made him bearable, even enjoyable company.

After she had spent a half-hour alone with her thoughts, Elizabeth's good humor had returned, and she felt herself equal to returning to the house to face what must follow. Perhaps she might at least look forward to seeing Caroline Bingley absolutely lose her mind over the news of Mr. Darcy's engagement.

The man himself appeared before her now, on the garden path. "I hope this smile means you are not so very cross with me."

She arched an eyebrow. "Perhaps it means I am only thinking something wicked."

"Not plotting some retaliation, I hope."

"I hardly see any reason to limit my mischief to you, sir," Elizabeth replied. "You have made me optimistic – I see such endless possibilities before me."

Mr. Darcy had come to stand very close to her, and she saw the twinkle of mirth in his eyes. "I no longer puzzle you exceedingly?"

"No indeed. I have been provoking you this week, perhaps, with a greater candor than I might have shown, but I know you have been doing the same. *That* is what confounded me – that you should be so open, so amiable, and so determined to laugh at all my impertinence. But you, like me, thought yourself fully at liberty to say what you liked, without any real consequence."

Mr. Darcy looked crestfallen. "Is that really what you think? That my being amiable to you was so material a difference, and all because I thought it did not matter?"

Elizabeth hesitated, sensing it would be wrong to answer in the affirmative, but that was precisely what she had concluded. She remained silent, turning her face away from him.

His voice barely audible, Mr. Darcy said, "I was not enjoying myself at your expense, Miss Bennet. I was merely enjoying myself. I came to you this morning believing us to at least be friends."

"Oh." Elizabeth peered up at him. "I thought – I thought you were laughing at me."

He shook his head, studying her intently before he replied, "I would prefer to laugh *with* you, for there is so much of the ridiculous in this day."

Elizabeth smiled up at him. She had been unfair to him, and to ease her own conscience she had happily assumed he had been acting with the same motives. "Perhaps we better carry on, then," she said. "Absurdities do delight me, and there are sure to be a great many of them, today."

As if on cue, Elizabeth caught sight of her sisters watching them through the window. Mr. Darcy perceived it as well, and he laughed nervously before capturing her hand in his. "Let us, as you say, direct our mischief at others – at least for today. Tomorrow we may be rational again." He raised her hand to his mouth and kissed it, letting his lips linger for dramatic effect.

Elizabeth blushed. She could hear her sisters giggling from the window, and she pretended to be deeply affected by his gesture; there was some small part of her that really was, but she pushed that aside and allowed herself to just enjoy the moment. Taking him by the hand, she led Mr. Darcy back to the house. "I believe we must begin with some little competition between us, to see who can give Mr. Collins a fit of apoplexy first."

***

Mrs. Bennet nearly claimed that distinction herself, and Darcy was peculiarly grateful to her for being incapable of any discretion whatsoever. Darcy had underestimated Mr. Collins' foolishness – he knew of the parson's sycophantic devotion to Lady Catherine, but not that the man had actually had designs upon Elizabeth. Mr. Collins was convinced that Mr. Darcy's interference was the only reason his wishes would not come to pass, and had fled the house after venting his displeasure to an exceedingly unsympathetic Mrs. Bennet.

The whole house was in uproar, and as he and Elizabeth were drawn into the merry chaos, Darcy found himself the recipient of seemingly endless effusions from a woman who had gone from glaring contempt to extreme affection in no time at all.

"What a fine son-in-law you shall make," she cried. "Elizabeth Darcy, how well that sounds! But you must tell me all about Pemberley, sir, for I am sure it is quite the grandest house – we must visit at Christmas – no better time for a wedding – oh, when Lady Lucas hears of this!" She patted his cheek. "Oh, Mr. Darcy! Now we are only wanting dear Mr. Bingley to speak up, eh? Then how perfectly happy we shall be!"

Elizabeth's sisters had surrounded her as soon as she entered the house with Darcy, but now Miss Bennet looked over at her mother, her face red. Elizabeth perceived her older sister's distress and grimaced. "Mamma!"

Mrs. Bennet waved her handkerchief. "Oh! Well! I am so happy; I do not know what has come over me! Well, come along Lizzy, Jane, girls – dear Mr. Darcy, we must all go into the village and share the good news."

Darcy had been staring at Jane Bennet, studying her reaction. The poor girl clearly could not like the idea of her mother pushing her at Bingley. He turned his attention back to Mrs. Bennet, having forgotten already what she said. He cleared his throat and checked his pocket watch.

"Forgive me," said he. "I have forgotten the time – I must be wanted at Netherfield."

Elizabeth met his gaze from across the room and came toward him with her arm outstretched and a wicked gleam in her eye. "Darling," she said with malicious glee, "I am *sure* Mr. Bingley will be going to the market this morning. You must walk with us, and you can meet him there. Would that not please you, *my dear?*"

The minx! Even knowing that her regard for him was not what he had thought, Darcy wanted to kiss her, and struggled to keep his countenance serene. "Nothing would please me more, *my angel*. I have written to my cousin, the colonel, and I would like nothing better than to introduce him to you and your family. However, I must meet him at Netherfield and attend to some business...."

Elizabeth came closer, still smirking; she boldly took his hand in hers, clasping it so hard her fingernails dug into the top of his hand. "Surely you could not think of business on such a happy, *perfect day*." She looked meaningfully into his eyes – she meant to exact her revenge indeed.

Well, if she intended to bask in the absurdity of it all, she would find him no less willing to do so. Her parents were exchanging looks of incredulity while her sisters all looked on, affected by the sense of romance, and Darcy smiled down at Elizabeth. She had given him leave to take such liberties as he would likely never again be able to claim. If that was a punishment, he would bear it very well.

"Your candor does you credit," he said. He lifted her hand and kissed it again. "Of course, you are right." Now he cupped her cheek, savoring the look of chagrin she was obliged to quell. He gently stroked her face, and she smiled and blushed. "We must begin the wedding preparations at once, without delay."

Mrs. Bennet staggered backward against her husband and shouted for her smelling salts as Mr. Bennet helped her into a chair. In the commotion that followed, Elizabeth muttered some vague threats, almost lost on Darcy as Miss Catherine observed from the window that Bingley was approaching the house.

"There is another man with him – an officer," she cried, and Miss Lydia ran to the window, giggling wildly.

Darcy and Elizabeth had not broken eye contact – he was in a state of some confusion, while she looked positively wild. He feared he had pressed too hard, but at last a smile tugged at the corners of her mouth. "I shall set Mr. Collins on you."

"You wish us to duel for the honor of your hand?"

She leaned in close, placing her hand on his chest as she stood on her toes to whisper in his ear. "If anyone is to attack you with pistol or saber, it shall be me." She stroked his cheek, and then gave it a pat that was almost a slap before moving away to address her father. "Well, Papa, is this not very *tolerable* indeed?"

Darcy did not hear Mr. Bennet's reply; Bingley and Richard came into the room, each of them in a state of high humor. Darcy stared at them, stunned – he had told nobody of his intention to come to Longbourn, unless Richard recalled it from the day before. *Surely not....*

"What a fine joke, Darcy! We were nearly sending for Scotland Yard," Richard laughed, striding into the room so charismatically as to instantly command it. Mrs. Bennet and *all* her daughters beheld him with interest. "It is a lucky thing I stopped in the village, having no notion where to find Netherfield. A most curious little fellow importuned me, looking for the post office, and when I told him I had no idea, as I was searching for Netherfield and Mr. Darcy, he rudely informed me you were at another house, Longbourn, and directed me here."

"That is when I happened upon them both," Mr. Bingley added. "I directed the strange little angry man to the post office, and I have brought your cousin here, Darcy. I had wondered where you were gone off to."

Darcy could hear Miss Catherine and Miss Lydia giggling together, but he could not take his eyes off of Elizabeth; she watched him, smirking, and then mouthed *Mr. Collins* before closing her eyes and indulging in a moment of private mirth. It was a magnificent sight, until Darcy became aware of Mr. Bennet observing the interaction. And Richard.

"Well, cousin, I take it that odd fellow was correct – and you are to be congratulated? You had already quite surprised me with your letter this morning, and yet among your other curiosities you made no mention of an engagement!"

Darcy again looked over at Elizabeth, who seemed now deliberately attempting to distract him with her look of hilarity. Mr. Bennet finally came forward and extended his hand to Richard. "Thomas Bennet, sir. My cousin Mr. Collins, whom you encountered in the village, was quite right. As you can see, Mr. Darcy is besotted, apparently, with my Lizzy, and so you must allow *me* to introduce my family."

Mrs. Bennet was more subdued, having just roused herself from a swoon before their arrival, but she put her daughters forward with alacrity, saving Elizabeth for last.

Elizabeth bobbed into a curtsey, but she could not quite dismiss the merry smirk from her face as she greeted Richard, who seemed a little too well pleased with her. "What a pleasant surprise, Colonel Fitzwilliam. Mr. Darcy made no mention of your coming – no doubt he wished you to be his secret reinforcement, if I did not accept his offer." She looked at Darcy and grinned.

Darcy bowed. "I see I no longer puzzle you – you have me all figured out," he said, for she had guessed his exact reasoning.

"Perhaps I am clairvoyant," she laughed. Richard eyed her with momentary suspicion before returning his gaze to Darcy.

"Well done, Darcy," Richard said jovially. "Any lady who

can inspire you to make such stupid faces must be very worthy!"

Bingley clapped Darcy on the shoulder. "I had no idea – well, congratulations, Darcy! Miss Elizabeth, congratulations indeed! Absolutely marvelous! And of course, now, we must remain in Hertfordshire for quite some time!" He smiled and shook hands with Darcy, and then drifted toward Jane Bennet.

Richard was next in offering effusive well-wishes, but all the while he began to give Darcy imploring looks; Darcy had written him a much different kind of letter this morning, and he knew his cousin must have questions.

Darcy knew not how he might speak with any degree of privacy to his cousin, as they must do; out of desperation, he reminded Mrs. Bennet of their plan to walk to the market. This scheme was soon amended, for she declared they were too happily grouped to leave Longbourn. She suggested a luncheon, and then, despite Miss Mary's protest of the mud, and Miss Lydia's complaint at the lack of officers, Mrs. Bennet decreed they would have a picnic.

Richard seized the first chance he got to approach Darcy as they all milled outside together. "You astonish me, Darcy. You write to me, describing in detail *what I am wearing*, which you could not possibly have known. Your suggestion I wear my uniform was obviously made to arouse the attention of certain ladies.... And then the quarrel – I did not make it to Netherfield, but on the way here I wheedled the whole story out of Bingley, who was out of humor from the exact scenario you described – but you could not have known of it yet when you sent the letter, for it arrived very early in London. Even the odd fellow Collins figured into your letter, and Miss Elizabeth signaled his name to you in the drawing room. All this inexplicable intrigue – *and you are engaged to a woman who makes japes about being clairvoyant*. What is going on?"

Darcy looked around; Mr. Bingley was amusing the ladies by speaking of plans for a ball, and though the two youngest girls were looking every moment like they might seek Richard's notice, Mr. Bennet reprimanded them and gave Darcy a subtle nod. Darcy offered a slight smile of thanks. He knew he had but a few minutes to speak to his cousin before they must behave as gracious guests.

"I am not clairvoyant, cousin – it is only a private jest between Elizabeth and me. I knew what you were wearing, and what would transpire at Netherfield after I wrote the letter because I had already seen you, and the quarrel, the day before. I have been experiencing the same day over and over again, Richard, and unfortunately, as it is likely I will continue to do so, my engagement to Elizabeth is only for the day."

Richard was silent for a painfully long time, his eyes shifting in contemplation. "How is this possible? One of us is mad, and I hope it is you, Darcy."

"That is far likelier," Darcy grumbled. "I have repeated the twentieth of November seven times now – this is the eighth iteration. Nobody else seems much aware of it, and everybody goes about the same redundant activity over and over again. I did consider the possibility that I had gone insane – until two days ago, when I became certain that Elizabeth was experiencing the same phenomenon. She confirmed it this morning."

"And so you are going to marry her, and live the same day over together? That makes no sense at all," Richard scoffed.

"I came to Longbourn to speak to her about our dilemma – her mother presumed there was a proposal, and we sort of... got swept up in it." Darcy shrugged. "There is little to be done now but let it pass. Tomorrow, which will be another today – well, we shall find a more effective way of discussing what is to be done. You came to Netherfield yesterday, and it took me rather longer to convince you of my situation, but once I had, you assured me that Elizabeth held the key to it, although there is one other thing...." Darcy hesitated to mention Wickham; perhaps they might catch him by surprise at the card party.

Richard nodded slowly. "Just to be clear, Miss Bennet – she is also repeating the same day over again – and she understands that there is no real engagement?"

"I am sure the fact is as much a relief to her as it is to me, for she had very charmingly threatened me with violence, just before you and Bingley came in."

Richard roared with laughter.

***

Elizabeth was content to observe the growing affection between Jane and Mr. Bingley, but she sensed her younger sisters were getting impatient for their share of the colonel's attention. Mr. Bingley was speaking of giving a ball at Netherfield soon, but even this could scarcely keep Lydia and Kitty's notice – their father had been obliged to rebuke them once already.

"Mr. Darcy's cousin must be greatly surprised – the engagement gave us all a shock," he observed, fixing Lizzy with a pointed look.

Kitty giggled, and Lydia laughed until she snorted. "La! I have never been so surprised in all my life, Lizzy! What a fine joke, making us think you hated him! But now I wonder what you were getting up to at Netherfield."

"Lydia," Elizabeth gasped.

"Lydia Bennet, I will send you to your room without supper if you make any more comments of that nature," Mr. Bennet snapped; Elizabeth was astonished that he should be so harsh, until he looked over at her, as if fearing there *was* some truth in Lydia's implication.

Elizabeth was overcome with mortification, and abruptly stood. "I had better go and get better acquainted with my new cousin. Excuse me."

The colonel waved and called out to her as she approached them. "Miss Elizabeth, come and walk with us! You must tell me with what manner of eloquence my cousin attacked you this morning, for I cannot quite believe it."

Elizabeth was still in good humor from calling Mr. Darcy's bluff, and amusing herself while doing it. She took his hand in hers with a dramatic flourish. "I did not like him very well at all when first he came among us – I thought him very disagreeable, truly – but I have come to know an unexpected side of him." She grinned. "It was all exceedingly romantic – I shall never forget how he looked when he said...."

Mr. Darcy cleared his throat. "He knows."

Elizabeth dropped his hand at once and stuck her tongue out at Mr. Darcy. "If we are only to deceive my family, I hardly think it fair. Well, Colonel – do you think us both quite mad?"

The colonel laughed. "That my cousin should propose to such a charming and beautiful woman is the only thing that has not mystified me – and that is the part that is not real."

Elizabeth blushed. "He cannot have convinced you so quickly."

"I have learned some of your method," Mr. Darcy said, before his cousin could answer. "I observed your approach with Miss Lucas, and made one attempt at speaking thus with Richard yesterday, while you were occupied in avoiding me." He arched an eyebrow at her. "Today I improved on the approach, and simply wrote him a letter full of all the same sort of prophecy."

"Apparently," the colonel quipped, "I was in Meryton yesterday, and advised Darcy here that you were the key to his curious conundrum. Consider it an early wedding present." He waggled his eyebrows at Elizabeth.

She laughed him off. "I appreciate the vote of confidence, but I have not been getting on very well myself, since time has begun repeating itself."

"But it is only affecting the two of you, yes?"

Mr. Darcy gave his cousin a hard look. "When first you appeared at Longbourn, I could not account for it – I suspected you must have remembered our meeting yesterday."

"As I said, that bumbling – ahem, Mr. Collins, he told me your whereabouts, by some happy accident."

"And if you were repeating this day, you would tell me?"

The colonel guffawed, nudging his elbow into Mr. Darcy. "Probably not – not at first. You know I like a good jest."

Mr. Darcy shook his head at his cousin's antics. "He was quite helpful *yesterday*, Miss Bennet, I assure you."

Elizabeth clucked her tongue. "And now he has turned the tables, and is amusing himself at our expense."

Colonel Fitzwilliam pretended to pout. "Are you not also amused, Miss Bennet?"

"Oh yes, there is no tomorrow – I am excessively diverted,"

she replied.

Mr. Darcy laughed ruefully. "We are quite hopeless, are we not?"

The colonel screwed up his face, as if really mulling it over for the first time. "I do not know what I can do to help you. I hardly know how I would act in the situation you have described – you cannot force the hand of time itself."

"No, but...." Mr. Darcy furrowed his brow, and hesitated. "I cannot help but think there is something we must do, something we must figure out."

"Exactly," Elizabeth agreed. "I had thought that I might put a stop to the repetition by somehow altering the course of the day in some material way. As you said yourself, Mr. Darcy – a perfect day."

The colonel stroked his chin. "That is an interesting notion. But what exactly constitutes a perfect day – what would you change?"

"Nearly everything," Elizabeth said at once. "That is... every version of this day has just gone so horribly awry, in one way or another. But I do not know what change will put a stop to the repetition – there are many things, perhaps...." She trailed off, fidgeting with her necklace.

The colonel gave her a ponderous nod. "And what about you, Darcy?"

Mr. Darcy was also contemplative. "There is always room for improvement in anything," he said cautiously.

The colonel rolled his eyes. "This is no time to be fastidious, out with it. I suppose it has something to do with the row at Netherfield this morning, the one you expected to be embroiled in when I arrived – has this been a daily recurrence, too?"

Elizabeth looked at Mr. Darcy in some surprise. She had apparently guessed very near the truth, when she had supposed him to be so often out of humor for the same reason as she – his nearest and dearest. "I am in some suspense, Mr. Darcy – another key to the puzzle?"

"Hardly," he replied. "Though I have, regrettably, been drawn into the dispute on a few occasions, it is a *family* dispute – more Bingley's responsibility than mine." He paused and grimaced, as if trying to convince himself. "There is one matter that gives me concern – but I had better not mention it."

"Well, that is not helpful," Richard quipped.

"Perhaps not," Mr. Darcy replied. "I intend to make you aware of it, in the course of the day – it is inevitable, you know. But if I spoke of it now, you would wish to act at once, as you did yesterday – you rather muddied the water, but tonight I am hoping for more illumination."

Elizabeth could guess what he was referring to – Mr. Wickham. She arched an eyebrow at Mr. Darcy. "I suppose I can see the wisdom in that," she said evenly. "I have tried several approaches to that piece of the puzzle, with varying results – I think you may have discerned my unease in that quarter."

Though he had grown exceedingly serious, Mr. Darcy's countenance softened now. "I did, and it was a great relief. I imagine there must have been some falsehood or misrepresentation – but we shall discuss it this evening, for I imagine that when our engagement is talked of at the card party, the result will be quite different than anything we have previously seen."

The colonel glanced between them with confusion. "Well, keep your secrets if you like, but I can hardly help you that way!"

"No, indeed," Elizabeth assured him. "I can see your cousin giving us some very stern looks, which I believe means that he has a great deal to think upon, and we are resolved to think our way out of this mess."

"We are," Mr. Darcy agreed. "And you shall understand, later, how useful you might be in figuring out – but it must happen naturally."

"We cannot achieve perfection today, after such a beginning," Elizabeth laughed, "but perhaps our powers of observation will prevail, and we can find some more efficient means of discussing it at length tomorrow. And in the spirit of observation, we have an excellent study before us here; we should rejoin the picnic."

"A family of five daughters is always an excellent study,"

the colonel said with a grin.

"I am convinced the family dispute at Netherfield must be, as well," Elizabeth mused, suspecting that the colonel would enjoy seeing his cousin provoked. "I do hope Mr. Bingley will invite his sisters to the party at my aunt's house tonight."

"Oh, yes," the colonel cried, rubbing his hands together. "Miss Bingley despises me – I quite long to see her."

Elizabeth laughed and linked her arm through the colonel's as she steered them all back toward her family. "A kindred spirit at Netherfield, at last!"

***

Darcy and Richard joined Bingley in making themselves agreeable to the Bennet family for the better part of an hour when Mrs. Bennet began to say that the gentlemen must stay for dinner, and accompany them directly to the card party at Mrs. Phillips' house. Bingley accepted with alacrity, all smiles for Miss Bennet, who received his compliments with a placid blush that unnerved Darcy. He wished to separate his friend from the girl he suspected bore Bingley's attentions only to please her mother, and he wished to separate himself from Elizabeth, for the lively discussion of their fake engagement was beginning to wear down every reason he had to balk at the connection.

The drastic change in all the Bennets' behavior toward him had actually begun to please Darcy – the babbling affection of the mother and the sardonic wit of the father were almost endearing, in a setting where everyone was disposed to think well of him. It was only the youngest Bennet girls who tethered Darcy's mind in reality, for their antics reminded him that the parents who allowed such behavior as this could never be desirable in-laws, however much they might appreciate his attachment to Elizabeth.

Darcy had another object in mind when he declined the invitation to dine at Longbourn, for he also wished some time to speak privately with his cousin before attending the card party that night. Elizabeth eyed him with a wry smile as he made his excuses and offered to see him to the gate.

"Have your powers of observation been exhausted already?" She linked her arm through his, her countenance lit with mischief.

"I know you only mean to vex and punish me," Darcy replied, trying to meet her playful tone. "I am sure you shall have ample opportunity this evening."

Elizabeth scowled, and deepened her voice, mocking him as she threw his own words back at him. "Is that what you really think?" She shook her head, seeming genuinely bothered. "You said you came here this morning believing us to be friends – if that is the case, it could not be a punishment for you to accept the invitation from my family."

Darcy struggled to make any reply – she was right, and it pained him to face such a fact. He admired Elizabeth Bennet as he had never admired a woman before, but her family was intolerable, and he could not reconcile these two opposing impulses at all. Even if he could, he supposed it would matter little so long as there was no tomorrow.

Richard came to his rescue. "Perhaps your cousin Mr. Collins has mentioned our aunt, Lady Catherine. If she were among us, you would easily understand, Miss Elizabeth, the value of meeting your friends *away* from their relations – as our return to Netherfield will likely remind us."

Elizabeth arched an eyebrow and regarded them both with amusement. "I cannot argue that certain company at Netherfield *would* be a punishment, if that was my object. But as to Lady Catherine, I cannot agree. After hearing so much praise of her from my cousin, it is my dearest wish to someday set eyes upon her."

"As such an event could not possibly take place on the twentieth of November," Darcy replied, "I can only wish you success." He smiled at Elizabeth, and his attempt at banter was rewarded when she mirrored his expression before bidding them farewell until the evening festivities.

He was applied to at length by Richard, who had a great many questions about the madness that had afflicted both Darcy and Elizabeth, and the journey to Netherfield was insufficient for Darcy to relay all the same information it had taken him three hours to convey the day before.

Though he was grateful to his cousin for accepting such an implausible explanation, Darcy was not entirely pleased by Richard's enthusiasm for Elizabeth Bennet. He knew much of it was contrived – Richard again took delight in disobliging Miss Bingley, and praising Elizabeth was quickly revealed to be the surest way of doing so. Still, Darcy was so distressed by the end of his dinner at Netherfield that he began to wish they had remained at Longbourn – but no, this might have been a greater torment.

Richard seemed determined to vex Darcy at every turn – he insisted Miss Bingley join them for the card party, and hinted at his relishing the moment Miss Bingley's hopes would be dashed by the announcement of Darcy's betrothal to Elizabeth. Darcy bore it all as best he could, determined to remain committed to his original objective, observation. He only hoped that Richard could put his antics aside for long enough to be useful in discovering what George Wickham was up to.

Here, Darcy was not disappointed; he breathed a sigh of relief when their nemesis arrived, and Richard went rigid at his side. "I see," Richard muttered under his breath. "That is what you would not tell me before." He began to move away, but Darcy laid a hand on his cousin's shoulder to stay him.

"As I told you, Richard, you rather muddied the waters yesterday."

Richard turned to grimace at Darcy. "You will have to forgive me if I have no recollection of it – only the impulse to murder."

"You frightened him out of his wits yesterday," Darcy told his cousin. "All you did was speak to him on the street – well, you politely threatened him on the street – and it was enough for him to leave town. Surely this proves he is hiding something, some secret purpose in coming amongst us. We must show some restraint if we are to discover it."

"Discover his purpose?" Richard scoffed at Darcy. "Come now," he whispered. "You and your lovely betrothed agreed that your object is a *perfect day* – what could be more perfect than letting me gut the bastard?"

"It must be for me to decide. You will forget this tomorrow – I am the one who has to live with it," Darcy insisted, glancing around the room to make sure they could not be overheard. He stopped when his gaze landed on Elizabeth, who had been detained by Miss Bingley – the conversation did not seem especially pleasant for either of them. Elizabeth felt him watching her and looked over, giving him a pleading look. He nodded, betraying just a little smile, and Elizabeth abruptly walked away from Miss Bingley, who watched her go with a sneer.

Darcy moved away from his cousin and met Elizabeth at the center of the room, taking her hand in his. "I have a gift for you," he said, relishing the sensation of leaning down to whisper in her ear. "Only you must refrain from gazing at me in such ardent admiration; do not take your eyes off Miss Bingley."

When Darcy gave the signal, Mr. Bennet stepped forward to make the announcement, as they had agreed that morning. Raising his glass aloft, Mr. Bennet cleared his throat, gave a sardonic laugh as he gained the room's attention, and addressed them all with a look of bewildered mirth. "Yes, well, I have the great honor of informing you all tonight of the engagement of my daughter Lizzy to Mr. Darcy here. You may direct your congratulations to my wife, forthwith."

The room rippled with excitement; the other Bennets were all beset at once by the felicitations of the friends, while Darcy stood beside Elizabeth at the center of it all, their hands still entwined. Darcy instinctively found Wickham in the crowd, and watched his reaction closely. Wickham backed away from the youngest Bennet girls, and stared at Elizabeth with open interest.

Richard had perceived this as well, and moved that way with alacrity. He clapped Wickham on the back, just as he had on the last occasion. "Wickham, you wily bastard," Richard cried, laughing at such length that a few other officers were obliged to do the same. "I would never have imagined seeing you here – and you have enlisted! Well, my new brother in arms, you must introduce me to your colonel – at once!" Richard laughed again, nodding to the other officers as if they were old friends. "That is an order! Ha!" He merrily led a pale and miserable Wickham away.

All this happened very quickly, and at the same time Darcy heard another scene of equal interest unfolding. By the time he turned his attention from Wickham to Miss Bingley, she had already dropped her glass of wine on the rug, splashing it across her gown. She had also apparently stumbled backward into the pianoforte, knocking Mary Bennet from her stool and landing on top of her. Mrs. Hurst began to laugh as she moved away from her sister, and a moment later Mrs. Phillips flew to her niece's aid, with little care for Miss Bingley's dignity as she pushed the lady off of the quietly disobliged Bennet sister.

What amused Darcy the most was Elizabeth's mirth at the spectacle, and he watched her watching the ludicrous scene; he still did not let go of her hand. When she finally looked up at him, her eyes glistened with amusement, and something more – he began to suspect she was a little half-sprung. "Thank you for that, Mr. Darcy."

Darcy kept his countenance, but barely, and replied, "Consider it a peace offering – for you were so gracious as to refrain from drawing either pistol or saber on me, or the other weapon at your disposal, your cousin Collins."

Elizabeth laughed. "Lord, I forgot about Mr. Collins! But where did he go off to? I wonder at his absence – perhaps another key to our perfect day. We did set out to exert our powers of observation; this may be a monumental discovery." Her face twisted in a wry smile and her color heightened as she looked up at him; it was entirely bewitching.

Mrs. Phillips approached them, startling Elizabeth, whose hand slipped out of his. "Oh, my dear Lizzy – Mr. Darcy! Well! But how happy you look together here! Oh, Lizzy, you are the dearest girl in the world, I am so happy for you both, and your uncle and I are so honored you should announce it here – what an occasion!"

She stopped long enough to take a breath, and then patted Darcy on the cheek. "Oh, Mr. Darcy, you dear, dear man! He is so handsome, Lizzy – I see you blushing – I daresay you know all about it. Well! But I must hear what your mother says about the wedding preparations – I must be permitted to assist, before Madeline swoops in from London and – oh!" Looking very much like she required her sister's smelling salts, Mrs. Phillips swept away, and Darcy and Elizabeth gave way to laughter.

After a moment, Elizabeth said, "Thank you for that, sir. You could easily disregard my family entirely, and say that it will not matter tomorrow, but I hope you understand it means something to me. You are bearing it all very cheerfully, which I believe we must do, in our situation."

"Of course, Elizabeth. Our situation *is* a strange one, but we cannot abandon all decency and propriety."

She arched an eyebrow at him. "But so long as we are engaged you are permitted to hold my hand?"

"Yes." He took her hand again to prove his point, and she laughed gaily.

They were interrupted again – Mr. Phillips approached them now. "Well, Mr. Darcy, congratulations. My niece is truly the brightest jewel in the county – and quite her father's favorite, if you take my meaning. I understand the wedding is to be soon – well, good, good. It seems Thomas has accepted it, and perhaps in time you shall get on very well. Lizzy, my dear." Mr. Phillips only nodded to his niece, and then moved away.

Elizabeth let out a shaky breath. "That was odd." She glanced over at her father, who was studying them from some remove. "What did he say to you this morning?"

"He presumed – well, in his mind, your stay at Netherfield was but three days ago...."

As Darcy averted his gaze and shifted uncomfortably, Elizabeth gasped and ripped her hand away from his. "My father believes we – he thinks that I – you...."

"He was not angry, and it seemed more expedient to allow him to believe it, than to explain what would sound like madness." Darcy knew this was not enough, he could see it in her eyes. She had thanked him for considering her family's feelings, and he had not at all deserved it.

Her posture stiffened and she glared up at him. "You allowed my father to think such a thing? And he *accepted* it?"

She shook her head in disgust. "Forgive me, I must go and speak with Miss Bingley. I am sure the punch she handed me was spiked, but I should rather like some more." Without meeting his eye, she bobbed into a curtsey and stormed away.

***

Elizabeth felt her face flush with mortification as she hastened away from Mr. Darcy. She was too angry even to amuse herself by needling Miss Bingley – the notion had lost all appeal to her. She strode over to her father, her fists clenching in the folds of her dress.

"Well, Lizzy," he cried, the usual humor in his voice.

"No, Papa," she said. "It is not well." She glared at him, and then gestured to her younger sisters. Mary had resumed her performance, and Kitty and Lydia were dancing in the same brazenly flirtatious way as they had always done before. "Is that what you think of me, that I am worse than that? You permit them to throw themselves at the officers, and you think I would throw myself at Mr. Darcy in such a way, at Netherfield – that I would allow...."

Mr. Bennet laid a hand on Elizabeth's shoulder, and sighed with relief. "It is not true."

"Of course it is not!"

"But, Lizzy, he did not deny it."

Elizabeth gritted her teeth in frustration. "He did not deny it because he does not care enough to defend my honor, he merely thought it expedient for himself – he likes to have his own way, but he shall not with me."

"Now Lizzy," her father said, patting her shoulder again. "We shall sort it out, eh?"

Elizabeth felt a wave of unexpected resentment as she continued to watch her sisters merrily disgrace themselves. "You never sort out anything," she sighed. "But perhaps it does not matter. I shall not be engaged to Mr. Darcy come tomorrow, and there is nothing you can do about it." Tears pricked at Elizabeth's eyes and she hurried away from her father, hugging at herself to keep her composure with so many people around her.

Caroline Bingley chose this moment to approach Elizabeth and offer her congratulations, her voice dripping with disdain. "But what a charming sight, you dear girl, so overcome with feeling! Of course, when you are Mrs. Darcy you must learn to comport yourself. You shall have to learn quickly – I understand the wedding is to take place before Christmas – so soon after your staying at Netherfield! Well, Eliza, I congratulate your heartily on your success, it has clearly brought you great joy. Here, I have brought you another cup of punch."

Elizabeth accepted the proffered glass, her fingers gripping it tightly as she resisted the impulse to dump its contents over Miss Bingley's head. Fortunately, Colonel Fitzwilliam came to her rescue.

"Miss Elizabeth, Miss Bingley – but of course the two of you must wish to be better acquainted! I daresay one engagement may lead to another – your brother, Miss Bingley, certainly seems to be enjoying himself this evening! Well, but it is natural and right that you should be friends with the future Mrs. Darcy." The colonel smiled brightly, as if oblivious to the tension.

"Of course," Miss Bingley agreed, her tone icy.

"You always speak so fondly of your visits to Pemberley," Colonel Fitzwilliam said. "I am sure my new cousin would love to hear all your elegant compliments, for when next you are a guest there, Elizabeth Bennet will be mistress of the house."

Seething, Miss Bingley excused herself, and hastened to her brother's side, presumably to detach him from Jane. The colonel turned and regarded Elizabeth with some concern. "Are you well, Miss Bennet? You seemed to go from unabashed affection for my cousin, to something else entirely; I observed you as I was speaking with Mr. Wickham."

"Oh – I was a little overpowered by all the activity," Elizabeth said – it was not a complete falsehood. "And I suspect Miss Bingley has spiked my aunt's punch."

"Yes, I saw her do it just before the big announcement," Richard replied. "I meant to warn your aunt, but I have made the most of it getting that cad Wickham good and drunk, so we can get him talking. Forgive me – I presume you are familiar with the scoundrel in question? You and Darcy seemed to be making some secretive allusion to the matter this morning at Longbourn."

"Yes, I have encountered him several times before."

"May I ask what transpired?"

"For the first few days, it varied but little," Elizabeth said. "He would confide that Mr. Darcy had robbed him of his inheritance, on the basis of petty jealousy. He spoke of being denied a position in the church. And yet I wonder now that a man who would have liked the church could so often be very forward, to myself and even my younger sisters," Elizabeth observed, thinking aloud.

"At any rate, when I realized that Mr. Wickham had, through subtle measures, coaxed me into revealing the degree of my acquaintance with Mr. Darcy, and by – forgive me, I have had some reason to think ill of him – by my mentioning such a view, Mr. Wickham easily found me a willing listener. I determined to speak well of Mr. Darcy, on one occasion, and Mr. Wickham lost all interest in my company."

The colonel listened with interest, nodding thoughtfully. "Well, I see. He determined that you would be sympathetic to his contrived complaints. I cannot hold it against you, Miss Bennet – I can easily imagine Darcy does not always make the best first impression."

Elizabeth sipped at the punch Miss Bingley had given her. "You have no idea," she fairly growled.

"But this is quite perfect," Colonel Fitzwilliam said. "Forgive me if I now adopt a very stern look with you – Wickham is observing us from some remove – do not look. What you have told me is unsurprising, and happens to align perfectly with a seed I have planted in Wickham's mind. I could see I would get nowhere with the man myself, but he was watching you. When you appeared to become suddenly displeased with Darcy, I saw the look in Wickham's eye as he watched you storm away – and I made the most of it. I told him your father accepted Darcy's suit without your knowledge, and you were not happy. I thought he might be foolish enough to –

good God, Miss Elizabeth, you look as though you are going to cry." He hastily offered her a handkerchief.

Elizabeth accepted it and discreetly dabbed at her face. "He told you of it?"

The colonel was taken aback. "Seriously? I just made up whatever seemed expedient."

"Well, then you think just like your cousin," Elizabeth said bitterly. "Very well, I see you mean for me to go and speak with him; I am willing to present myself as an ally, if you think he may be more forthcoming."

"I am sure he will enjoy the challenge of trying to steal you away from Darcy." Colonel Fitzwilliam's expression turned very grim. "Do be careful, Miss Bennet. He is not a man to be trusted – he is dangerous."

"Thank you, sir. I will proceed with caution and see what I might discover. Anything that might help us put an end to this." She gestured broadly at what was passing around them. Steeling herself for what would likely be another distressing encounter, Elizabeth took a long draught of her punch and squared her shoulders back.

"You are ready for battle, Miss Elizabeth. Here, it will help if you look as though I have just seriously offended you."

Elizabeth gave the good colonel an apologetic smile and stomped on his foot before moving away from him – Mr. Wickham immediately put himself in her path, meeting her eyes with a warm smile.

***

Darcy looked on with dismay as Wickham charmed Elizabeth. "Richard, are you sure this is wise?"

"It was you who told me that I would get nowhere bullying and intimidating him – or killing him," Richard muttered. "Anyway, Miss Elizabeth said that on previous occasions he had sensed her dislike of you, and sought her out as a sympathetic ear for his own little tale of woe."

Darcy recoiled. "She said that to you?"

"Oh, right – sorry – you quarreled, I think?"

"We have had a few misunderstandings," Darcy said cautiously. He could not admit, even to Richard, how deeply it had wounded him to think that Elizabeth let Wickham pour his poison in her ear because she had already been so disposed against him – even after he had attempted to apologize for his comments at the assembly. And after his behavior today, he had given her more ammunition for the conversation he was watching this very moment.

Richard shifted uncomfortably. "Look, Darcy…. I still find this all very strange, but two things are clear to me. You have to figure out what Wickham is up to, and I hope Miss Elizabeth's conversation is fruitful – but I think you have some things to figure out where she is concerned, as well. I have seen how you look at her – and how you behaved together, before you somehow offended her. But I have also seen how you look at her family, and you can bet she has, too. Almost the first moment we met she was telling me she did not always like you. But you and she are trapped in this together; you summon me to help you sort through this madness because you cannot face the facts."

Darcy was too stunned to reply, and a moment later Richard moved away to speak with Bingley and Jane Bennet, his volume designed to vex Darcy further as he addressed them. "How happy you both look – do tell me more of your plans for the ball – Miss Bingley, I must claim your first set, and you must wear your blue velvet gown, the one you wore to the opera, the time you trod on the Duchess's train and tore it…."

The evening wore on, most of his companions relentlessly merry. Darcy resorted to lurking in the background as he was often wont to do at such gatherings, brooding over his annoyingly fluctuating feelings for Elizabeth Bennet, as he had also been prone to do in recent weeks. And all the while she sat on a sofa with George Wickham at the far end of the room, whispering.

***

Elizabeth was relieved when the night was over, and her

family prepared to take their leave. She was exhausted, if only from the mental exertions of the day, and a considerable part of her wished she had made it out the window in time that morning.

Still, she knew what she had to do. She could not like it, at present, though she hoped the prospect of collaborating with Mr. Darcy might soon seem palatable. She was simply too overwrought to see any other way out of her dilemma. As she took her leave of him that night, she managed to meet his eye and make some civil address, despite the tumult of her emotions.

"We need not endure such chaos for the sake of conversing tomorrow. I wake at dawn – I will depart the house immediately, and meet you at Purvis Lodge, in the copse of trees by the front gate." She kept her countenance guarded as she awaited his response.

"Thank you, Miss Bennet." Mr. Darcy gently clasped her hand and bowed, and Elizabeth was led by her father to the carriage.

Elizabeth was numb to her family's lively chatter as they returned home. When they arrived, she hastened upstairs and prepared for bed at once, eager for the day to be over. Jane sensed her unease, and slept in Mary's room, leaving Elizabeth alone to her wretchedness.

She laid in her bed for some time, but sleep did not come. Instead, someone came to Longbourn – Elizabeth was drawn from her miserable reverie by the sounds of a carriage arriving at Longbourn in the dead of night. There was commotion in the corridor – a servant waking her parents, Mrs. Bennet shrieking about robbers come to murder them – and then her father grumbling and shouting. She heard his step on the stairs, and Elizabeth could not resist following him.

She wrapped her dressing gown around herself and lit the candle at her bedside, quietly sneaking out of her room to find out what fresh absurdity this endless day had wrought. There was a pounding on the front door, and a woman shouting from the other side of it. Elizabeth crept down the stairs, listening as her father shouted back, and answered the door in open annoyance. "Well, what is it?"

Elizabeth lingered on the landing, holding her candle aloft. Looking down the stairwell, she could see her father standing in the corridor. He, too, held a candle, which illuminated the face of a stern and haughty woman in the doorway.

"Sir," she cried, her voice dripping with disdain. "Is this residence Longbourn – are you Mr. Thomas Bennet?"

"I am."

The woman sneered, the candlelight making her features almost sinister "And do you know who I am? My parson has told me enough of your family that I had understood to expect *some* degree of ill-breeding, but now I have discovered real treachery, and I have come to make my sentiments known."

"Ah," Mr. Bennet replied. He yawned. "Lady Catherine?"

"Indeed, sir – and I require a private audience with your daughter Elizabeth this instant!"

They had not yet perceived her, but Elizabeth instinctively drew back a little, holding her breath. Fortunately, her father was in no humor to entertain the great lady's demands. "No," he said flatly.

Lady Catherine assumed an imposing posture and thundered, "This is not to be borne! I have come all this way on behalf of my nephew Darcy, and I shall be heard! This shameful alliance cannot be permitted to take place!"

"Well, it is not going to," Mr. Bennet calmly observed. "My Lizzy has called it off – your nephew was not up to snuff, as it happens. So sorry you have wasted your journey, madam, but you are very welcome to carry your nephew off with you tonight if you wish, and nobody shall much lament it. Very good, off with you now." He yawned again, with greater exaggeration.

Lady Catherine looked aghast. "You dare insult my nephew? Where is Miss Elizabeth Bennet – I must have it from her lips that she will not disgrace my nephew; I will hear no more of your insolence."

"Then hear mine," Elizabeth called out from the landing. Her father and Lady Catherine looked up in surprise as Elizabeth stepped out of the shadows. "Your nephew is the last man in the world I could ever be prevailed upon to marry. I bid you a safe journey back to Kent, your Ladyship." Elizabeth curtseyed, fixing Lady Catherine with a look of contempt, and then she fled back upstairs.

6

Darcy waited for some time in the copse of trees Elizabeth had indicated, and breathed a sigh of relief when she finally appeared on the path to Purvis Lodge. Her hair was loose and her face was flushed from exercise, but her greeting was cold. "Good morning, sir."

His arms behind his back, Darcy stepped out of the trees, onto the road. Her posture tensed. "Miss Bennet. I began to fear you would not come."

Elizabeth spared him only a fleeting glance before turning her attention to the iron gate before them. She began tearing away at the vines that had grown over the lock on the gate. "I had some matters to discuss with my sisters, before I departed the house, as I will not be present at the market today – I still have some hope today may be a success. We are no longer engaged, so that is a good start," she laughed.

With the vines pulled back and the lock was wrested free, Elizabeth examined it. She let out a thoughtful hum, and then pulled a long, sharp pin out of her hair, which tumbled out from under her bonnet and splayed out around her shoulders. She shimmied the hairpin in the lock for a few seconds, and the mechanism yielded – she tossed the lock aside and pushed open the gate to Purvis Lodge, glancing over her shoulder at Darcy.

It was an enchanting sight, and for a moment Darcy could only take it all in. He knew Elizabeth was angry with him, and briefly wondered if she meant to punish him by heightening his nearly insurmountable attraction to her. His hands fell to his side, and he remembered his peace offering.

"I picked you these flowers, while I was waiting for you. To accompany my apology." He handed her a small bundle of wildflowers, bound with a ribbon he had brought along expressly for this purpose.

Her countenance softened as she accepted the flowers, and she smiled down at them for a moment before tucking the stems into the pocket of her pelisse. "We ought not be seen on the road together," she murmured, and turned to lead him through the gate.

Darcy followed her, and pushed the gate closed behind them. Elizabeth stopped and looked back at him, and Darcy once again drank in the sight of her with her hair loose and glowing in the vibrant light of sunrise. He gently took her hand. "I am sorry, Miss Bennet, for my boorish behavior yesterday. I wish us to be friends."

Elizabeth gave him the barest of smiles, and withdrew her hand from his. She removed her bonnet and handed it to him. "Hold this – please." Darcy instinctively did as he was bid, and watched Elizabeth as she gathered her hair at the back of her neck. She scowled. "Turn around."

Darcy obliged her, and gave way to a moment of mortification as his back was turned. He had pushed the bounds of propriety enough.

Elizabeth grumbled. "I cannot do this in gloves!" A moment later, she laid her gloves on his shoulder, her bare white hands flashing in his peripheral vision. He let out a heavy sigh.

After she reclaimed her gloves, she gave him leave to turn back around. Her hair was pinned back again, and she took her bonnet from him and put it on. "Shall we walk?"

"I believe so," Darcy replied. "You have made your point."

She looked up at him, her brow quizzical. "Have I?"

"Do you accept my apology, Miss Bennet?"

She smiled wryly at him. "Oh, very well. I shall not use you as a hat rack; it is beneath your dignity. From now on, we shall be friends, no more mischief."

"However much we may be tempted," Darcy mused.

Elizabeth did not look amused. "We must work together in this," she said firmly, her eyes fixed on the path that led through the park of Purvis Lodge.

Darcy nodded, feeling something cloud his heart. He had actually enjoyed the previous day a great deal – he had lost sight of his objective. It was good that Elizabeth remained focused on the task at hand; he was drowning in the feelings their feigned engagement had aroused in him, and she herself had thrown him a lifeline. He would conquer this. "Where shall we begin?"

Elizabeth hesitated. "Is – is your cousin not coming?"

"No, I did not see the need for it," Darcy replied. "Explaining the whole ordeal to him takes time, and he has had little success with Wickham. I thought that I might hear what you discovered – I understand you spoke with him last night."

"Yes." Elizabeth looked away, wringing her hands. "He was very drunk."

Darcy was instantly concerned. "I will not ask you to encounter him again, or allow Richard to suggest it." He offered her his arm, and when she accepted, he tentatively laid a hand on hers, and breathed a sigh of relief that she did not resist.

"I agreed to speak with him," Elizabeth replied. "I will do what I must to make this endless repetition stop."

"Yes, of course. Did he give you any indication why he has come to Meryton, or what he intends?"

"Mr. Wickham certainly feels that he has been wronged; he spoke with such bitterness," Elizabeth said, a sadness in her voice that Darcy feared might contain some pity. "He was especially riled by your cousin, who had called him both brother and... bastard. Mr. Wickham was livid. He said that you both have long held a grudge against him, and that your sister had done something to betray him as well. He said that you would all be very sorry one day, for treating him as an inferior."

Darcy nodded. This was unsurprising, and not entirely helpful. "Did he give you any specific information?"

"No," Elizabeth sighed. "I only know that he seems really to believe himself ill-used, and it seemed almost that he has some intention of gaining the upper hand in some way – a way that will disoblige all your family."

A groan escaped Darcy's lips. Of course Wickham was planning something. "It would not be the first time."

"Oh." Elizabeth knit her brow as if turning it over in her mind. "He was well in his cups, and for a man who has just enlisted in an obscure country militia, he certainly thinks himself destined for greatness. And bent on revenge."

"He has always had delusions of grandeur," Darcy replied, feeling the same tension in his body that always afflicted him when he thought of Wickham. "I will speak with him again, this afternoon."

Elizabeth peered up at him with alarm. "Will there not be some danger in it? I know there must be something that I am missing – but I can see that he is not to be trusted."

Darcy smiled down at her, grateful for her concern. "I have known Wickham all my life, Miss Bennet. I think I can manage a private conversation with him, and I will certainly have – some protection."

"Oh." She frowned. "You do not mean to...."

"Of course not. Not if I can help it."

"And you will not tell me why he harbors such resentment toward your family?"

"I have always supposed it to be jealousy."

"That is what he said of you," Elizabeth mused.

"And if you were me, Miss Bennet, the master of Pemberley, would you envy George Wickham? If you were raised alongside such a man, as Wickham was, would you resent the fortune of his birth, debauch yourself, and grow so twisted as to malign a fifteen year old girl to perfect strangers?"

Elizabeth let out a shaky breath and turned her face away from him. "You have made your point."

***

They walked in silence for several minutes, and Elizabeth grew uncomfortable. She and Mr. Darcy had been more at ease with one another the day before – perhaps too much so, but now the tension between them was a stark contrast. She knew there was more that he was not telling her about Mr. Wickham, though she had made some effort to show Mr. Darcy that she no longer held his rival in any esteem.

But she was just as guilty of holding something back; she had no intention of giving voice to all her plans for the day. He was the proud master of Pemberley, after all – he would not approve. She could well understand Mr. Wickham being the issue Mr. Darcy must resolve to end the repetition. Her conundrum must be her sisters, perhaps all of her family, and their problems were not something she wished to discuss with the man beside her.

Elizabeth had not been so lost in the intoxicating madness of the previous day that it had escaped her notice, how Mr. Darcy looked at her family. He was civil enough to her father, and seemed politely unaware of Mary, but her mother and youngest sisters clearly strained his patience. And poor Jane had fallen under Mr. Darcy's critical eye more than once, though happily she herself had been unaware of it.

It made Elizabeth angry all over again, to think that she had actually rather liked Mr. Darcy yesterday. She had certainly met her match in wits, and his remarkable sense of humor had been a wondrous surprise. They had crossed boundaries they perhaps ought not to have, had pushed each other and tested these boundaries, and it had seemed not to matter – until it did.

Today Elizabeth felt the loss of their unexpected camaraderie. She had genuinely enjoyed playing their strange little game; she was disappointed that it was over, and this made her quite cross with him, tearing open old wounds, in addition to the one she had claimed to forgive.

It was confusing, and the silence grew heavier, but they walked on anyhow. In time she relaxed, for they had moved to a side of Purvis Lodge she had not seen in quite some time, and it really was a lovely view. She let out a slow, calming breath as the clouds pulled back and lit the ivy-covered walls of the manor in sunshine.

Elizabeth looked up at Mr. Darcy. It struck her that she still almost liked him, despite his offenses against her. He had apologized for the ones he knew of – several times for the comment he made at the assembly. Even when he had no idea that she would remember, he apologized anyway. Though she could not quite determine whether that meant something or nothing, the notion brought a smile to her face.

Mr. Darcy looked back at her; it was clear that he too had been in his own private reverie, but his lips turned up as he met her eye. "Why do you smile?"

"Nay, why do you?"

"I smile because you do," he replied.

Elizabeth laughed. "I smile because...." she hesitated for a moment, but in the end she spoke her mind. "I like your company. It is soothing to know that this strange and horrible thing is not only happening to me."

Now he really smiled; his eyes seemed to glisten a little. "That is what I attempted to explain to you yesterday, and you would have none of it."

"Abominable reply! I accepted, did I not?"

Mr. Darcy's chest rumbled with laughter. "You hardly had a choice."

"And whose fault is that? You must promise never to do that again. Anyway, I like meeting here. I might almost forget the rest of the world is gone mad." Elizabeth blushed and looked away after such an admission, and then she began to fidget with her necklace. "Oh!"

"What is it?"

Elizabeth cupped the pendant in her hand. "I bought this on the first market day. I found it yesterday when I was – but how do I still have it?"

Mr. Darcy looked down at the pendant with curiosity, and tentatively ran his fingers over the filigreed locket, brushing the palm of her hand. "You are sure it is the same one?"

"Yes. I tucked it away in a drawer on the first market day,

and never thought to look for it again."

He arched an eyebrow at her. "Until you had to pack a suitcase?"

She smiled wryly at him. "Yes. But how is this possible?"

Mr. Darcy shook his head. "Can it mean something?"

"It must. I bought it from Baba Romilda – she is a gypsy, and a very dear old creature. You purchased something from her that day – do you still have it?"

"Like you, I had not thought to look. I bought a scarf for Georgiana – I will check my desk when I return to Netherfield."

"Good," Elizabeth said, her mind spinning with possibilities. "We have determined that you will speak with Wickham, and I will attend to my own... measures."

"Which are?"

"A few little hints and nudges to my sisters," Elizabeth said defensively. "Nothing to concern yourself with. I put some little plans into action this morning, and I think it will turn out well. With any luck, we might resolve the matter today."

"And if we do not?"

"Then we try again tomorrow, with the full day at our disposal. We might look for Baba Romilda at the market and ask her some questions."

Mr. Darcy nodded. "You seem confident."

"Hopeful, at least," Elizabeth replied. "If tomorrow is not a success... I do not know. Perhaps your cousin might come back to help with Mr. Wickham? But not in uniform, for my sake," she laughed; it would certainly make her sisters harder to manage.

Again he nodded, this time a little curt in his bearing. "If you think it wise. But if we are not successful soon, we must meet again, and perhaps alter our approach somehow."

"Very well, only let us not think of failure. I cannot. We will do our best today and tomorrow, and if necessary we can meet here the following morning, and convene with Colonel Fitzwilliam."

Mr. Darcy made no objection, though he did not look entirely satisfied with her plan. Elizabeth could not understand why he did not share her optimism, for he had been the first to insist that their collaboration would signify some improvement. He was silent again, and it made her restless.

"Will you go to the card party?"

"Perhaps," he said. "I suppose it will depend on Wickham. I thought to go see him this afternoon before he can enlist."

"Oh. Of course." Elizabeth silently chided herself for being disappointed. They had made a half circuit of the small park that surrounded Purvis Lodge, and Elizabeth was about to ask Mr. Darcy if he would like to go the rest of the way around, when he stopped abruptly.

"Forgive me – perhaps I ought to attend to that directly. It may increase our chances of success – and no doubt you have matters to attend to, whatever they may be."

"Of course," Elizabeth replied, looking away to conceal her disappointment. "We had better not be seen sneaking out of the gate together; we are near enough the village that there may be people passing to and from the market. You go; I will wait a few minutes."

She did not look back at him, and listened for his footsteps to fade away before she let out a shudder, and watched him disappear into the distance. She took the flowers he had given her out of her pocket, and brought them to her nose for a moment, enjoying the smell, and the soft petals brushing her face. She felt a surge of feelings, and in her effort to suppress them all, she suddenly hurled the flowers away from her.

***

Darcy would later reflect that it was unwise to go directly to see Wickham, in such a state as he was in when he parted from Elizabeth. He had known it would be difficult to conquer his attraction to her, while working with her to end their predicament; he had not anticipated her reaction to his cousin. She had been so insistent on his asking Richard back! He was now resolved to avoid it at all costs, and as he strode down the path at Purvis Lodge, his mind was plagued by every recollection of his cousin and Elizabeth laughing together the day before.

In the village, he took it out on Wickham. His rival was walking with some of the other officers, but Darcy strode up to him, intent on separating the man from his comrades. "My old friend," he said gruffly, slapping Wickham on the back. "What a surprise to see you here. Come and walk with me."

Wickham appeared surprised to see Darcy – he always did. He gave an odd look, as if he had been expecting Darcy to denounce him in front of his companions. Still, he acquiesced, and made some excuses to the officers before he followed Darcy down an alley with less traffic.

"Darcy, what are you doing here?"

"I might ask you the same question," Darcy said evenly.

Wickham smiled and gave an obliging nod. "Very well, I have nothing to hide, Darcy. I have sought some useful employment to keep myself occupied for a time."

Darcy allowed his disbelief to show. "Really?"

"What motive would you assign me," Wickham spat. "I had no intention of setting eyes on you again, after our last meeting. I had rather hoped to avoid it, until my circumstances are improved."

Darcy glared at him. "And might I suggest you improve them elsewhere?"

Wickham shifted nervously. "It is all the same to me. I only sought to be out of London for a time."

"To evade my notice?"

Now Wickham laughed. "What, were you looking for me? I cannot imagine I left much of a trace since last we parted."

This much was true. Darcy had been adept at keeping tabs on his erstwhile friend in the years since their final falling out, and had even purchased a great many of Wickham's debts along the way. Even these had been few in recent months; before Wickham had importuned Georgiana in Ramsgate that summer, Darcy had begun to hope Wickham might really be out of his life for good. Still he wished for it.

"I dare not hope you have been less debauched; you have grown better at concealing your activities."

Wickham laughed and clapped Darcy on the shoulder. "And conceal them I must. As ever, I cannot account for your obsession with me, Darcy – or perhaps I can. Perhaps you know more than you let on, old boy. At any rate, there is no reason you should wish me ill. Perhaps one day you will see that."

Darcy looked about; they were alone in the alley, and he shoved Wickham roughly against a wall. "No reason to wish you ill!"

Wickham schooled his countenance as he brushed himself off and smiled at Darcy. "And every reason to wish me well. And, as I have no wish to be thwarted by you again, I shall be happy to improve my circumstances elsewhere, as you say. You shall see, Darcy, just how well they improve, ere long." He bowed and made a hasty retreat.

Darcy watched him go and let out a heavy sigh. His temper had got the better of him, and his mind now swirled with questions. It was clear that Wickham was up to something and saw himself on the verge of some manner of success – but Darcy also believed that Wickham had genuinely not expected to encounter him. What mischief could he be about?

More to the point, did it matter? On the odd chance that Wickham was telling the truth, and merely sought employment, well, there was little else for Darcy to do but abide by his own desire to have no involvement in Wickham's life. Could it really be that simple?

Darcy pondered this throughout the card party at Mrs. Phillips' house. Though Elizabeth had professed a hope to see him, she spent the first half of the evening conversing with Miss Lucas. Left alone to his musings, Darcy had only just convinced himself he might have handled Wickham properly, when another problem began to disturb him. Bingley was looking very much like a man in love, and Jane Bennet remained, by all appearances, perfectly indifferent.

***

Elizabeth was actually pleased at the progress of the evening, and felt unusually relaxed. No Mr. Wickham, no overly alcoholic punch, and at least two of her sisters actually heeding her counsel.

Lydia and Kitty were much the same, and after expressing some disappointment at Mr. Wickham's absence, they amused themselves in their usual style with all the other officers.

But Mary and Jane were both doing very well. Mary declined to play the pianoforte, and her fine looks were coupled with fine spirits when Maria Lucas took to the instrument instead, and Mr. Collins asked Mary to dance with him.

Elizabeth had been conveniently occupied in conversing with Jane and Mr. Bingley when the dancing resumed, and once she had evaded her cousin, she endeavored to give Jane some privacy with Mr. Bingley. They did not dance, but Elizabeth thought it just as well that they were too engrossed in one another's conversation to join the reel.

Charlotte thought otherwise. She drew Elizabeth away from the others, to the same sitting area where Elizabeth had sometimes spoken to Mr. Wickham. "Tell me, Lizzy – what do you think of Jane and Mr. Bingley? You ought to have seen them together at the market this morning!"

"I needed a walk," Elizabeth replied.

"Trapped indoors for two days, I am sure you needed some solitude," Charlotte said with mirth in her voice.

Elizabeth laughed. "Oh yes – you have met my cousin Collins." She rolled her eyes for emphasis.

Charlotte swatted at her. "He is not so very bad, Eliza! Fortunately, Mary sees what you will not, which I suppose is just how you prefer it. But do not distract me. I know you were at Netherfield for several days, and I observed such intimacy between Jane and Mr. Bingley this morning. And just look at them now! Dare I hope you have passed my advice along to Jane?"

Elizabeth smirked back at her friend. She *had* encouraged Jane to invite Mr. Bingley to the card party, but beyond that Elizabeth had hesitated. She did not wish to press her sister too much, lest Jane shy away from the notion. "A little," Elizabeth said vaguely.

"That is hardly a satisfying reply," Charlotte chided her. "She looks well pleased with him, as she always does – to those of us that know her. But still, I think there is some disparity, for he is far more demonstrative. I had hoped to hear that she had given him encouragement at Netherfield, perhaps that they had reached some understanding."

"She was ill," Elizabeth cried, her amusement tinged with worry. Jane's serenity was indisputable, but that was just her way.

"She is not ill anymore," Charlotte replied. She sighed. "I do not wish to quarrel about it, really I do not. I only wish... that she does not end up like me," Charlotte said softly.

"Oh, Charlotte," Elizabeth breathed. "Do not be cruel to yourself."

Charlotte shook her head, attempting to laugh it off. "Forget I said that. I suppose I am only discomposed because Mr. Darcy has often been staring this way. What can he be about, do you think?"

Elizabeth suspected Charlotte only meant to change the subject, but she obliged her friend and looked over at Mr. Darcy. He *was* looking that way, and Elizabeth impulsively made a very droll face at him across the room. He cracked a smile, and then turned away, observing Mr. Bingley.

"Eliza!" Charlotte laughed and shook her head again.

But Elizabeth had been struck by an idea, and she clasped her friend's hand, her eyes wide with glee. "Charlotte, could you fancy an officer, do you think?"

Charlotte cast a dubious glance around the room. "At seven and twenty I ought to fancy any man who fancies *me*, but I am hardly expecting any of that here."

Elizabeth was fairly squirming with excitement. Though she had some hope that she was near to succeeding in ending the cycle of market day, she was in the beginnings of a contingency plan. "I would hardly recommend you give consequence to any of my sisters' followers," she whispered, smiling widely. "But what would you say to a young colonel – not quite handsome, exactly, but kind and amusing?"

"I would say a great many things, if indeed there was such a man," Charlotte replied. "Alas, I do not see him."

"Ah, but I know of such a man. And I might arrange for you to be introduced."

Charlotte rolled her eyes. "Do not tease me, Lizzy! If you wish to indulge any matchmaking impulses, let it be on Jane's behalf."

Elizabeth held her chin high, smirking at Charlotte. "Perhaps I might accomplish both. But you must excuse me – I really cannot abide Mr. Darcy's staring any longer, and I mean to ask him what he is about. And I will inquire as to whether he knows of any suitable colonels."

Elizabeth stood, eager to go and speak to Mr. Darcy, but Charlotte caught her by the arm. "Lizzy, do not do anything foolish – do not vex him, for Jane's sake. He is Mr. Bingley's friend."

Elizabeth registered her friend's advice and gave a little nod, before letting her bearing turn mysterious. She winked and moved away.

***

Darcy smiled as Elizabeth approached him at last. She was smirking at him, her eyes wide and bright. "You must indulge me, sir," she said. "I have told poor Charlotte that I intend to tease you mercilessly."

He suppressed his mirth, but leaned closer, dearly wishing she would tease him. "You are still of a mind for mischief?"

"I am, and I expected that you, of all people, would understand – and after all, I am sure your cousin is a man of odd humors and japes – you cannot be *so* unaccustomed to such larks."

Darcy only nodded, silently cursing Richard's charm and verbosity.

"Charlotte observed you staring at me," Elizabeth said.

"You know why I stare," Darcy replied.

Elizabeth arched an eyebrow. "I do *now* – before, I was never quite sure. I always supposed you disapproved of me. And that is what you must do now, Mr. Darcy. Do scowl as though I have just affronted you, and see how Charlotte shall cross her arms and shake her head."

Darcy did so, affecting a posture of disapprobation. "How is this?"

She grinned. "Very imposing! You look truly vexed. And if I come a little closer, and point my finger just so, she may think I am really giving you the business." Elizabeth moved near, her slender, gloved finger nearly jabbing his chest, and she twisted her face into a cheeky grimace.

Keeping his countenance stony, Darcy said, "If mischief were an accomplishment, Miss Bennet, you would have no rival."

She rolled her eyes. "You cannot flatter me while I pretend to be so very rude."

"Please advise me what you would most like to hear. After all, you did come to speak with me." A smile began to spread across Darcy's face, until a waggle of Elizabeth's finger reminded him to look stern.

He repressed the urge to grab her finger between his teeth, rip off the glove, and kiss her from her wrist to her lips. He cast a nervous glance around the room, thinking it odd that only last night it had been so different with her; he had held her hand, even drew her closer in unguarded moments. They had been lost together on a wave of chaos, and tonight was so drastically different. It was calmer, more sedate, and it made Darcy uncomfortable. He reflexively took a step back.

Elizabeth withdrew her hand and folded her arms. "Tell me about your day – have you had any success?"

Darcy considered before he answered, and here he was sure his face looked naturally grave. "I spoke with him, yes. He made similar allusions to some future scheme, as he did with you. But he left town very willingly. It has made me wonder."

"What?"

"Well, I wonder if he is as significant in all this madness as I had originally thought. Could it be so simple, to merely send him on his way? Is it necessary that I discover what he is up to?"

Elizabeth knit her brow as she mulled this over. "I have always supposed I had some purpose, something to alter and improve, in the course of the day, and I had believed you must, as well."

"And so I had thought," Darcy agreed. "But I begin to wonder if it is Wickham, or perhaps something else."

"Such as?"

Darcy involuntarily glanced over at Bingley, who was still sitting with Jane Bennet, conversing with animation as she smiled placidly at him. His heart raced. It could be that – but how could he tell her?

Elizabeth had followed his gaze, and something flashed in her eyes – hurt and anger and betrayal. And something very wild. Darcy shifted awkwardly and caught himself reaching for her hand as if it were the most natural response. He stilled himself, watching her face as so many emotions played out there.

"I am not sure about anything, anymore," he breathed. His fingertips twitched, brushing hers.

Elizabeth flinched, peering up at him curiously, almost fearfully. "Do not be too hasty, think it over," she whispered. Her hand brushed his again, and she drew in a sharp breath.

It was torture for Darcy. All evening it had nagged at him, that Bingley could not be allowed to seriously consider Jane Bennet, and yet Darcy himself was in way too deep with Elizabeth. The woman who would despise him forever if she knew what he was thinking, what he was growing quite convinced he must do.

Again his eyes drifted to Bingley. The man was falling for a woman who thought of him as merely an amiable acquaintance, nothing more, no little difference from Darcy's own situation. He would save Bingley to save himself, and if Elizabeth hated him tomorrow, at least there would *be* a tomorrow.

Several things happened in quick succession. Elizabeth's countenance went cold, and he knew she was not pretending anymore. He also knew she could see what he was thinking. She looked away suddenly; Miss Lucas had apparently perceived the tension between Darcy and Elizabeth, and was moving that way as if to intervene. The music had stopped, and Mr. Collins abandoned Mary Bennet once he had Darcy in his sights.

Elizabeth gave Miss Lucas a little shake of her head, and her eyes flicked over to Mr. Collins, whose lips were moving slightly, as if rehearsing the lavish praise of Lady Catherine that he would soon bestow on Darcy. Miss Lucas quickly changed her course and intercepted the parson.

Bingley came from the opposite direction, Jane Bennet on his arm. He clapped Darcy on the shoulder. "Darcy, how are you enjoying the card party? Not quarreling with Miss Elizabeth again, I hope?" He laughed nervously, and the Bennet sisters exchanged a silent, knowing look.

"We were speaking of you," Elizabeth replied, arching an eyebrow. She met Darcy's eye just long enough to land her point. "I was wondering why you were not dancing. You enjoy the amusement so much more than your friend, Mr. Bingley."

Bingley just smiled his affable, idiotic smile, nodded, and laughed. "Well," he cried after a moment, "we have been lost to all the world in conversation!"

Miss Bennet smiled as well, and said nothing. Quite the conversationalist indeed. Poor Bingley had probably been pouring his heart and soul out to her, in exchange for diffident smiles and wide eyes hooded with long, dark lashes.

Across the room, Miss Lydia appealed to her sister, Miss Mary, to take up the instrument where Maria Lucas had left off. Darcy tried not to flinch at the girl's grating voice, and he looked back to Elizabeth. "I fear Miss Elizabeth has not had as pleasant a partner in conversation as her sister," Darcy replied. "Though I am not fond of dancing, I am rather better at it than speaking, when words often fail me."

Again Elizabeth arched an eyebrow at him, her look so intent she could scarcely be aware of Bingley and her sister. There really was nothing he could say now, he knew. But he offered her his hand as the music resumed.

Bingley laughed. "Well, we shall not be outdone by Darcy here," he told Miss Bennet before turning to Darcy. "Well done, you know, turning the table on me – it is always me, urging you to dance." He guffawed again, "I shall not disappoint you, Jane." He grabbed Miss Bennet's hand and she gave a gentle laugh as he whisked her away to dance.

Darcy and Elizabeth had frozen at Bingley's use of Miss Bennet's christian name. Her hand hovered over his for a moment before she accepted it, and she kept her head downcast as he led her to join her sisters in the dance.

They began the movements in a heady silence before she finally looked up at him. He tried to smile, tried to convey some message of reassurance in his face, but something felt different now. Elizabeth glanced over at her sister, and then back at him. They turned in time to the music. "Will he?" They spun again. "Disappoint her?"

Darcy placed his hand against hers as they went down the dance. He observed Bingley as they moved past him. Elizabeth stared probingly at him. Miss Mary fumbled the keys of her instrument for a moment, and Miss Lydia laughed. The dancers all attempted to recover the rhythm; they spun again. Elizabeth's jaw tightened as he placed his hand on her back for the next movement of the dance. He knew he had not answered her, and she expected him to.

Darcy sighed. "I do not know yet." Elizabeth averted her eyes and did not speak for the rest of the dance.

***

The next morning, Elizabeth tried to remain optimistic when she awoke beside her sister Mary. She told herself she had done well the day before, but for missing the market. She would double down on her efforts, and really make the most of the day. She repeated the attempts she had made so many times already, encouraging Mary to put herself forward with Mr. Collins, encouraging Jane to do the same with Mr. Bingley, and encouraging Lydia and Kitty to do quite the reverse.

She did not confide in Jane – she had not, since discovering that Mr. Darcy shared in her secret. It seemed almost to belong to them – and perhaps Colonel Fitzwilliam, and unfortunately Mr. Wickham, too. But she no longer felt the need to unburden herself; Elizabeth only wanted to make things right.

She was less optimistic in the village – Mr. Bingley and Mr. Darcy were not at the market, and there was no sign of Baba Romilda, either. Of course, Baba Romilda had only been there the first day; it was Mr. Bingley's absence that disturbed

Elizabeth.

She had wanted to believe that perhaps she had misunderstood Mr. Darcy the night before. She might have made too great an assumption in supposing him to consider that his purpose was not Mr. Wickham but Mr. Bingley. But still the suspicion nagged at her, that he would separate his friend from her sister. If that is what he meant, surely his endeavors to thwart hers would only trap them in a vicious cycle forever.

She brooded in the village, certain that Mr. Darcy had kept Mr. Bingley away by design, to Jane's obvious disappointment. In such a state, she encountered Mr. Wickham with the other officers.

Elizabeth made a rash decision. Mr. Darcy might have come to think Mr. Wickham was not his concern, but Elizabeth still believed it was too great a coincidence that his nemesis should arrive the very day they were doomed to repeat. And she knew that expressing any displeasure with Mr. Darcy – which she felt in earnest at the time – would encourage Mr. Wickham to confide in her.

She began her campaign directly, and put herself forward, albeit with more decorum than Kitty and Lydia. Elizabeth knew what to say to catch his attention; it was easily done, though Lydia was making every effort to gain the upper hand.

Elizabeth detached Mr. Wickham from the others, and they agreed to walk together through the market. Though Elizabeth had come to find Mr. Wickham even more odious than she had ever believed Mr. Darcy to be, she smiled as she took his arm.

"You aunt was very kind to invite us all to her card party this evening," Mr. Wickham observed. "I was very glad of it."

"I hope you will be well pleased with the area," Elizabeth replied.

"I believe I shall, with such a beginning."

"And what has led you to joining the militia? A desire for society?" She forced a coquettish laugh.

Mr. Wickham smiled warmly. "I see you quite understand me – that was exactly my wish. I have been residing in London, and have been very content there with my mother. She is just out of mourning for her third husband and is reentering society.

I think she is on the lookout for number four," he laughed. "She is still rather young, at two-and-forty, and I wish her well, but cannot stand in her way."

Elizabeth nodded encouragingly. "She must have married very young indeed!"

His expression clouded, and Mr. Wickham changed his tack. "And so here I am, happily ensconced in such charming countryside, with every hope of being as delighted by the village as I am with my fellow officers. Tell me, shall I be disappointed?"

Elizabeth shuddered at his turn of phrase, but quickly recovered herself. "I have nothing but the highest praise for Meryton, but of course I am very biased," she replied.

"Well, but that says a lot – I take it you live nearby?"

"Yes, my father's estate is Longbourn, just over a mile from here."

"It must be a charming place, to have produced such lovely daughters. Tell me, are the other local families so agreeable? I am sure, if you are so biased, it must mean you have excellent neighbors."

"I do," Elizabeth said evenly, a plan beginning to form in her mind. "I am sure we dine with four and twenty families very regularly." She smiled to herself, recalling Mr. Darcy's reaction when her mother had made the same observation at Netherfield.

Mr. Wickham appeared much more interested and urged her to go on. "My nearest neighbors are the Lucases, of Lucas Lodge. Sir William Lucas is very affable and fond of entertaining, which will be a boon to the militia, I am sure. His eldest daughter Charlotte is my dearest friend, and you met her sister Maria, with my younger sisters."

He gave a sickening smile. "Miss Maria Lucas seems a lovely girl, and I am sure her sister must be a treasure, to have earned your friendship."

Elizabeth suppressed her mirth at recollecting what Charlotte had thought of him. "I shall look forward to introducing you," she said. And then she allowed herself a smile. "There is another great family in the area – recent arrivals, in fact."

"Oh?"

"Yes, Mr. Bingley came down from the north of England and took possession of Netherfield Park around Michaelmas and brought his sister Miss Bingley to keep house for him."

"You and your Miss Lucas must have been delighted to have another young lady in the area," Mr. Wickham mused. "Is Miss Bingley as pretty and amiable as every other young lady I have encountered?"

Elizabeth laughed. "I cannot deny that she is beautiful, externally. She is rather proud for my taste, as the very rich often are. They have a guest who is much the same, very above his company."

"I see," Mr. Wickham replied carefully.

Elizabeth had hoped he would inquire further, but resolved to press on, to provoke him if she could. "Mr. Bingley himself is very affable, and I understand he is expecting another guest at Netherfield, who is said to be excellent company. Colonel Fitzwilliam, I hear, is fond of japes and jests, and vastly different from his cousin, who is presently Mr. Bingley's guest."

Mr. Wickham's eyes betrayed him. "Colonel Richard Fitzwilliam?"

"I believe so, yes. He is Mr. Darcy's cousin, but I have heard him described as much more gentlemanly and open." And indeed she had, two days before, by nearly all her family. "Are you acquainted with him, sir? Shall he render Meryton more agreeable, do you think?"

Mr. Wickham laughed, but Elizabeth detected a nervous edge to it. "I suppose you really mean to ask if he is handsome," he drawled.

"Oh, no indeed." Elizabeth affected a laugh, in her best impressions of Lydia. "I daresay a man in uniform must always be very handsome." She batted her eyelashes, feeling a rising revulsion in her stomach as he drew her a little closer on his arm. She pressed on. "Likewise, I could never think a man handsome unless he was truly amiable. Humor and liveliness might make a plain man more pleasing, and lack of address might render a handsome man less so, in my experience."

Mr. Wickham smiled broadly at her. "And dare I ask if Mr.

Bingley's guest, Mr. Darcy, is handsome in your estimation?"

She had him; Elizabeth returned his smile with a calculating one of her own. "He is not at all liked in Meryton, if that is what you mean." She knew very well that it was.

"Is that so?"

"Forgive me – if you are acquainted with his cousin, you may perhaps know him yourself. I hope I am not too bold." Elizabeth forced herself to hold his gaze, though she knew he was capable of being far bolder.

"I am very intimately acquainted with both of the gentlemen, and have been all my life – we are practically family," Mr. Wickham replied smoothly. He proceeded to give her an abbreviated version of his usual communication, though Elizabeth noticed some little differences this time. He described the former Mr. Darcy as his godfather, and made no mention of his father being the steward at Pemberley. Neither did he mention any ill of Miss Darcy this time – instead his abuse was for Colonel Fitzwilliam.

Elizabeth listened attentively to his vitriol, and when he had concluded it, Mr. Wickham laughed ruefully and observed, "I begin to wonder – I should not bias you, before you have met the man."

"I imagine a first meeting with him must still prove enlightening," she said, arching her eyebrow. "Of course, I am not on such terms with Mr. Darcy as to expect he will introduce his cousin to me at all."

Mr. Wickham leaned closer. "Oh?"

"He insulted me on his first night amongst us, and did not dance at all at the assembly, though gentlemen were scarce, and more than one lady was in want of a partner. And he and Mr. Bingley have not deigned to attend the market this morning," Elizabeth said with real asperity.

Mr. Wickham made a droll face and nodded. "Then you shall have to find good company elsewhere – I shall be happy to entertain you, if the high and mighty fellows at Netherfield will not."

Elizabeth gave him the most flirtatious look she could muster. "I certainly shall. And I hope you will attend the party this evening, willing to dance if the opportunity arises."

He took her hand in his. "Depend upon it, Miss Elizabeth." He raised her hand nearly to his lips, a gesture only Mr. Darcy had ever made to her, and Elizabeth began to panic.

Elizabeth was relieved when Kitty and Lydia were upon them, trailed by a few of the officers. She instantly withdrew her hand from his, and when she saw his apprehension, she winked at him. She could not bear his touch, but had no wish to repel him yet. He had already confided a great deal, and she might uncover more information yet, at the party.

If Lydia did not interfere. The girl was putting herself forward, standing with her chest thrust outward, twirling a loose strand of hair as she clutched at Mr. Wickham – Elizabeth had never been more exasperated with her sister, or more resolved to curb her behavior.

At Longbourn that afternoon, Elizabeth sought out her father in his study. She had scarcely been able to face him that morning, or all of the previous day, after what he had believed of her at the time of her fake engagement to Mr. Darcy.

As she sat down in the comfortable chair by the window, Elizabeth looked at her father, reminding herself that this was not the same version of him, at least – he would have no memory of his offense against her, and she could not be angry with him for it.

Mr. Bennet smiled indulgently at her. "Well, Lizzy, how was the market? Did you buy as many fripperies as your sisters, or flirt with as many officers?"

"No, Papa."

"Well! None of them can compare with the illustrious Mr. Collins, eh?"

"None of them could tempt me," she replied, arching an eyebrow. Her father laughed at the jest, and she proceeded with cautious optimism. "The same cannot be said of my sisters – Papa, I wish you had seen them. They were very forward." She mimicked Lydia's posture and mannerisms, and her father shifted uncomfortably in his chair.

"Lydia is determined to put herself forward," Mr. Bennet observed.

"Can you not prevent it?"

He chuckled. "I am sure I would be obliged to lock them in their room to prevent them from exposing themselves every time they are in public."

"Then do that," Elizabeth cried. "At least for tonight, please Papa. I beg you would keep them at home, for Mrs. Phillips has invited a great many officers."

"Yes, and your sisters will mutiny if they are not permitted to be at the party."

"All the more reason they would do better to be restrained," Elizabeth retorted. "I am happy that Mr. Bingley was not at the market today, to observe their behavior, else it might have affected his esteem for Jane! But our aunt has sent an invitation to him, and if he is to attend the card party tonight, Jane would fare better without Lydia and Kitty's wild and unchecked behavior."

"Surely he is not bothered at all by it. He likes her very much."

"He likes her now, it is true, but he may not ever do more, if he is to always be reminded of what her sisters are like. Can you not see that Lydia and Kitty are materially damaging Jane's chances of marrying well, and that if Mr. Bingley cannot like the prospect of such in-laws, Mr. Collins may be the best prospect any of us girls may have? Is an evening of Lydia's tantrums and Kitty's weeping really so bad, worse than Jane's heart being broken, and one of your daughters bound to a pompous imbecile?"

Elizabeth had begun to pace the room, her hands gesturing wildly, her emotions high and unfettered. "I beg you, Papa, to keep them home tonight; let Mr. Bingley have one night of Jane's company, without her being burdened either by illness or her hoyden sisters. Please, give her a chance."

Mr. Bennet only laughed and shook his head. "I am sure it is not as dire as all that. I begin to wonder if your younger sisters might have frightened off one of your beaus!"

"And what if they had?" Elizabeth was fairly fuming at her father, who had again jumped to the exactly wrong conclusion. But perhaps....

Elizabeth swallowed back her pride and hugged at herself, still pacing. She could feel her breathing change and her heart quicken, and she met her father's eye with fire inside her. "What would you say if I told you something has happened between me and Mr. Darcy?"

Now she had his attention; her father leaned forward with concern. "Lizzy...."

She stopped and stared at him, her shoulders pulled back in defiance. She watched his face change as he silently speculated.

"Lizzy, *has* something occurred? What is it you want to tell me?"

She held back a moment longer, letting him squirm, letting the doubt seep in. "Of course not," she snapped. "But for a moment, you believed it possible. I saw it in your eyes. And if you can think it of me, your favorite, can you not acknowledge what Lydia and Kitty, whom you are often calling the silliest girls in England, are capable of?"

Mr. Bennet said nothing, but his face hardened. Elizabeth suspected she had wounded him, but she did not care. She reminded herself that Jane was an innocent, merely trying to do her best. The same could not be said of their father. Elizabeth pressed on. "We are prey to the officers and the Collinses of this world because we have little but our charms to recommend us. You cannot give us dowries – so be it. At least grant us some dignity."

At this, Elizabeth's reserve faltered. The image of Mr. Darcy, looking upon her family with such displeasure, pushed out every thought of Jane and Mr. Bingley, and Elizabeth burst into tears. She sank back down into her chair and wept, and in a moment her father had come around his desk to embrace her.

"Dear Lizzy, do not distress yourself. I suppose there is a reason the younger sisters do not come out until the elder are married. Your mother has a great care for you girls, though it is misplaced; she fears your younger sisters will miss some great opportunity."

Elizabeth shook her head emphatically, but could make no reply through her tears. She carried her point, in the end, though she had not intended to achieve it through such means. When she had collected herself, and thanked her father with a warm embrace, Elizabeth set about salvaging the day.

She spoke privately with Mary and then with Jane, encouraging each of them to be more demonstrative with the gentlemen they admired. All the while, Lydia and Kitty were carrying on at a tremendous volume, but even the lamentations of their mother could not daunt the optimism of the three eldest Bennets when they departed the house that evening with their cousin.

The mood at the Phillips' house that evening was far different without Lydia and Kitty's boisterous presence, but Elizabeth still felt a hum of excitement about her, for she was confident of her own success. Tonight would be the night, she was sure, that everything would be made right. She observed to Jane, "I have great hopes for this evening, Sister, if only for your sake."

Jane smiled diffidently at her. "Oh Lizzy, it was so brave of you to speak with Papa. But I feel awful for Lydia and Kitty - they will be terribly angry with us tomorrow."

"Tomorrow, perhaps," Elizabeth mused. "But it will be well worth it."

"I think I agree," Jane admitted. "I hope Mr. Bingley attends this evening. I am sure he will, but then I was certain of seeing him at the market, and I was wrong." She chewed her lip for a moment. "But tonight... oh Lizzy, I am sure it is very wrong of me to say, but I should like to spend some time with him, away from our sisters. The only time I have ever done so was when I was ill."

Elizabeth squeezed her sister's hand. "Believe me, I understand you perfectly, Jane."

As the self-assurance swelled within her, Elizabeth saw Mr. Wickham swagger into the room. She intended to extract more information from him this evening, and the way he met her eye made her sure she would discover a great deal. She felt a surge of resentment toward Mr. Darcy, who had done nothing helpful at all this day, and with such feelings as these, Elizabeth was quite ready to speak to Mr. Wickham.

***

Darcy watched Elizabeth speaking amiably with Wickham and felt sick at his stomach. He even began to wish he *had* summoned Richard again. Stalking the room, Darcy could not determine where to direct his ill-humor, but everyone around him had some little claim to it.

The obsequious toad who worshipped Lady Catherine was dancing with Mary Bennet, radiating self-importance, after having already accosted Mr. Darcy with his pompous nonsense. The youngest Bennet sisters were not present, but the stillness of their absence only highlighted their cousin's folly.

In the window seat, just where they had been the night before, and almost every night, Bingley sat with Jane Bennet in private conversation; they were sitting very close, and speaking with great animation, their hands nearly touching as they each gestured.

Darcy had done what he could for Bingley that morning, rescuing him from the worst of the argument by taking him out for a long ride. But Miss Bingley had said enough, by the time Darcy stepped in, to plant some doubt in Bingley's mind; Darcy had deliberately timed his interference so that Bingley might be disposed to confide in him.

Bingley had done just that, as they galloped the countryside together. A great deal of the conversation was spent on the surprising hostility Bingley had for his sisters, though he had never betrayed such feelings before. This, Darcy had not known what to make of, but he knew how to act when the subject turned to Jane Bennet.

Darcy could not, in good conscience, advise his friend outright against the connection. He had been very careful in his approach. He suggested Bingley examine his interactions with the lady more closely, to determine what *her* feelings may be, before he proceeded. Darcy had trusted that as long as Jane Bennet continued to be so reserved in company, Bingley would quickly come to understand that her feelings were not as strong as his.

Now he wondered. Darcy was surprised to see Miss Bennet

speaking with more animation; she was downright gregarious tonight, and Bingley was hanging on her every word.

The worst of Darcy's discomfort, however, was the agony of not knowing what Elizabeth and Wickham were talking of. He did have his suspicions, though. He had spoken with Wickham that afternoon and had utterly failed in convincing him to leave the area at once. Wickham was too pleased by the company to be had, and had hinted at some intention to catch himself an heiress. Darcy knew not what Wickham had heard of any of the local girls, and now he wondered if Elizabeth had made some deliberate misrepresentation.

Darcy felt a swell of anger. He had told her before that he needed only to convince Wickham to be gone, that he had other matters to attend to in the course of the day. And Wickham might very well have gone, but Elizabeth had plainly gone against his wishes and interfered.

Darcy could think of several reasons why, and none of them were good. Perhaps she wished to punish him for disapproving of Bingley's interest in her sister. And she had been eager for Richard to be needed in Meryton again – she might see this as a means to achieve it. He swallowed back the notion that Elizabeth might genuinely like Wickham.

He watched the villain charm her, eliciting the same laughter that Darcy had sometimes aroused. He was going to be sick.

But, no, Darcy decided – he was going to put a stop to it. He moved toward Elizabeth and Wickham, not knowing what he was going to say when he got there.

Elizabeth gave a gentle shake of her head at his approach, and Darcy tried not to betray any reaction. Wickham made no attempt to dissemble – he showed his disdain openly, which meant he and Elizabeth had been sharing confidences again.

"Miss Elizabeth," Wickham said, standing and bowing with great flourish. "I intend to acquaint myself with Sir William Lucas, upon your recommendation. I hope I might call upon you at Longbourn tomorrow."

"Tomorrow, yes." Elizabeth gave him one of her sister's diffident smiles. "Happy thought indeed."

As Mary Bennet began to play the pianoforte, and Mr. Collins took his place at her side, turning the pages, Mr. Darcy extended his hand to Elizabeth. "Do not disappoint me," he said, smile tugging at his lips.

Elizabeth did not look happy; she hesitated before taking his hand, and looked across the room with disappointment as Wickham began to dance with Maria Lucas. "I was making considerable progress," she hissed.

As Darcy and Elizabeth joined in the dancing, Bingley and Miss Bennet quickly followed suit. Darcy did his best to position them at the furthest possible remove from Wickham. "I told you I would attend to it."

"I cannot see that you have," she replied, watching his reaction as her sister and Bingley laughed together.

Darcy schooled his countenance into its usual mask, and went through the motions of the dance, aching for the intimacy that was usually imbued in the activity, when he partnered her. "I spoke with him this afternoon, Elizabeth. He is on the hunt for a wife, a wealthy one."

"That is not what he told me. He said that his mother is just out of mourning, and seeking a new husband in London – he had removed himself from Town to be out of her way."

Darcy rolled his eyes. "Mrs. Wickham died six months ago – he ought to be fresh out of mourning himself, not tainting her memory with his lies."

Elizabeth appeared thoughtful but made no reply. "He spoke of Longbourn with interest," Darcy observed. "And then he sought out another companion whose father has some property. Can you not see what he is about?"

"More and more you make it sound like my problem, and not your own," she replied. "But then, you must think everyone a fortune hunter."

"Wickham has long been a thorn in my side," Darcy said, realizing too late that he had been harsh with Elizabeth. He softened his tone. "I only seek to protect those I care about." Despite his frustration, he still included Elizabeth amongst that small number – far more than he ought to.

He glanced over at Bingley, who was dancing and speaking

with Jane Bennet with unmasked attraction, and even the lady was bolder tonight than she had ever been before. She was not indecorous, as her younger sisters invariably were, but she was merry and lively, and appeared to take greater pleasure in the evening tonight than she had before.

But she and Bingley began to dance too near the pianoforte. Mr. Collins drew back in an ungainly gesture and bumped into Mary Bennet. Her arm slid across the keys of the instrument, and the three couples halted in their dance as the music was interrupted. Bingley captured Miss Bennet's hands in his and laughed gaily; she grinned at him, her eyes bright, before she turned to reassure her embarrassed sister. Elizabeth turned away from Darcy and silently followed Miss Bennet away.

Perturbed by the disruption, Darcy took advantage of everyone's distraction to approach Wickham. He grabbed him and dragged the man out onto the balcony. He had noticed on previous evenings that one or two guests would occasionally come out and take the air, though who knows what the younger Bennet girls might have been getting up to with the officers, for the balcony was long and very dimly lit.

Darcy led Wickham as far from the door as they could go. "What is your purpose here tonight?"

Wickham tugged his arm free from Darcy's grasp. "As I told you before, I have come to amuse myself, and perhaps make some useful acquaintance. Is it to be thus, Darcy, every time I go anywhere? Truly, I had not expected to encounter you very much, as I understand many of the residents of Meryton are beneath your notice." He stepped closer, and Darcy could see the blackguard's mocking leer in the thin moonlight.

"I wonder you should attend an informal gathering such as this. You seemed to enjoy dancing rather more than usual, and what a pretty partner you had. She might have stood up with me, if you were not so bent on ruining my chances with her."

"Yes, and she might have informed you that Longbourn is entailed upon that great oaf who just fell into the piano," Darcy snapped.

Wickham chuckled. "She must have some fortune or connections, for you to pay her such attention. Or perhaps you really like her." He gave a hoot of amusement. "That would be rich, would it not? I know for a certainty she likes me better."

"She is not an heiress, but she is certainly too good for you and your lies," Darcy growled, grabbing Wickham by the scruff. "You will stay away from her, and from every respectable young lady in this village."

"Or what?"

Darcy stepped closer, towering several inches above his nemesis. "Or I shall stop telling Richard it would be a bad idea to kill you."

"And so every time our paths cross by chance, you will threaten my life?" Wickham scoffed, and shoved Darcy backward with a string of oaths. "Have it your way. I have too much at stake to lose everything because of your blind and bitter grudge. I am for London, sir, but surely we shall meet again."

Wickham stormed back into the house, and a moment later Darcy could see the man retreating down the street, into the darkness. He let out a sigh of relief, and leaned back against the side of the house, letting the cool, clear night air calm him. He tried not to wonder just what Wickham had at stake; he prayed it did not matter.

He heard the balcony door open again, and for a moment he dared to hope that it was Elizabeth, that she had seen Wickham go, and wished to make some amends. But it was Bingley – and he was not alone. Darcy drew further back into the dark corner of the balcony; Bingley was proposing to Jane Bennet.

***

The next time Elizabeth awoke beside Mary, she was not so accepting of it. Furious, she quietly dressed and went to walk in the garden, for she was not fit to encounter anybody. She could not account for why she was stuck in this endless charade – she had done everything right; she had been so sure of it the day before. Jane had actually become engaged – Elizabeth had felt a brief certainty in her triumph, and now it had slipped through her fingers, as if it had never been.

She began to wonder if Mr. Darcy was actively attempting

to sabotage her efforts. "Of course," she breathed. His reaction last night had been beyond mere surprise, and nothing at all like delight. And there had been other things – things she had hoped rather than believed to mean nothing. She recalled something Mr. Bingley had said, the day of the false engagement – something about staying longer at Netherfield. And the colonel had alluded to an argument at Netherfield....

Darcy's words rang in her ears: *I only seek to protect those I care about.* He sought to protect them from Jane, from her disgraceful sisters, from her whole family. She clenched her jaw as the pieces fell into place. Elizabeth knew she must have realized all along, on some level – this was why she had kept her plans to herself. Mr. Darcy did not want her to succeed in helping unite Jane with Mr. Bingley.

They were supposed to meet that morning, but Elizabeth could not bear to encounter Mr. Darcy. She could scarcely face her elder sister at breakfast, after such a revelation. She was lost in thought, and considering making some excuse to avoid going to the market entirely, when an interruption drew her out of her reverie. A note was delivered for Jane, from Netherfield.

"It is from Caroline Bingley," Jane said brightly.

"Open it, my dear, open it!"

Jane did as she was bid, silently reading it over to herself despite her mother reaching for it and demanding to know what it said. Elizabeth had not the same curiosity, only a sense of dread. She knew before Jane said a word, but still it was a dagger through her heart when her sister finally spoke.

"She says that by now they will have all gone away from Netherfield this morning, to London." Jane's voice trembled, and a tear slid down her cheek. "She writes that it is unlikely they will return."

Mrs. Bennet moaned as if the house was on fire; Jane instantly excused herself and fled to her room. Mr. Collins tried to bolster them all with some of Lady Catherine's wisdom on the nature of disappointment, but Elizabeth was spared his illumination as she followed her sister upstairs.

They spent the day locked away in their bedchamber together. Elizabeth comforted Jane as best she could, without having any real conviction that anything would ever really get better. It had all been so perfect, for a few brief hours, and yet it had somehow gone wrong. The sky darkened, and a heavy rain relentlessly battered the house.

***

On the eleventh market day, Darcy entered the fray at Netherfield before Hurst forced him to do so. The argument took a different turn, to Miss Bingley's sickening satisfaction. Darcy implored his friend to think sensibly before attaching himself to Jane Bennet, or raising any expectations.

Darcy had to say very little to turn Bingley's cheerful confidence into cautious doubt – Miss Bingley accomplished the rest, and even the Hursts put aside their domestic discord and agreed to return to London. They were gone from the house by half past nine, and though a wild sort of rain assaulted the carriage, Darcy insisted that they press on.

They were in London by noon, visiting with his sister Georgiana at Matlock House. Elizabeth was in Darcy's thoughts nearly every moment, and though it was likely that his companions could perceive his sullen distraction, he knew it equally likely that it would not matter on the morrow.

On the twelfth market day, he woke at Netherfield and again orchestrated a departure for London. This time his intentions were less clear in his mind. He was no longer sure that saving Bingley from the Bennets was necessary, or even wise. He was no clearer on what was to be done about Wickham, Richard, or Elizabeth. He was angry at all of them, but above all, at himself.

Darcy knew deep down that he simply couldn't face Elizabeth Bennet after abandoning her once, and so, fool that he was, he did it a second time with a conflicted, confused, and possibly breaking heart.

Darcy sat down at the desk in his bedchamber, sipping at his coffee as he composed another letter to Richard. It was the thirteenth market day, and though Darcy was not a superstitious man by nature, circumstances had taught him to expect the worst. He would not run away again – he could not bear it. Elizabeth was likely furious at him, and had every right to be, after he had chastised her for attempting to do the same.

And just as she had accused him once before, Darcy had called in Richard as reinforcement. He wrote to his cousin to ride like the devil to Meryton, that he was in a state of emergency. He very much was.

Beyond writing to Richard, Darcy knew not what was to be done. In summoning his cousin, Darcy had resigned himself to staying in Hertfordshire to solve his dilemma, and he knew not how to do it. It pricked at his pride that he had lost his self-reliance to all this madness.

And what was he going to do about Elizabeth? He had wanted her to be a comfort, in sharing this predicament.

Sometimes she had been. He drank more coffee and slouched in his chair, thinking over every moment in the last fortnight that she had looked at him with warmth and camaraderie, and something more besides. And then, when these happy recollections were exhausted, he dwelt upon the occasions when she had not liked him at all.

Darcy was roused from his reverie by the familiar sound of porcelain shattering in the corridor, as the raised voices of Bingley's sisters grew louder. Knowing he ought to intervene, and perhaps even try something new, Darcy threw on his coat and checked the time.

He recalled that Richard had stopped in Meryton, on previous market days. Darcy strode from the room, determined not only to extricate Bingley from the house, but convince Miss Bingley to accompany them to the market. Richard loved to tease her; it would keep him occupied, and while Bingley attached himself to Jane Bennet, Darcy would seek out Elizabeth. They were going to have to share this burden, because he could not bear it alone.

***

Darcy rallied his spirits as they met with Richard, who had arrived in the village already. He was carrying a parcel wrapped in brown paper tucked under his arms, and was eating a pastry he had just purchased from a street vendor, along with a small bag of candied fruits.

"Darcy, what a spot of luck – I have no idea where Netherfield is," Richard cried, approaching them all with a jaunty gait. "I had meant to stop and ask, but as you see I am grown distracted. I hope you are all well." He betrayed a brief moment of concern, for the tone of Darcy's note had been dire, but then Richard schooled his countenance as he addressed them.

"Bingley! I am glad to see you are forcing my cousin out into society – I have been rather worried for him. Miss Bingley, you are looking very rosy this morning – I trust the fine country air is agreeing with you." Richard gave the lady a ludicrous smile and began to eat his candied fruits; he offered her the bag, but Miss Bingley wrinkled her nose and recoiled.

Bingley shook hands warmly with Richard, and accepted a few pieces of candied fruit with a laugh that Darcy suspected was at Miss Bingley's expense – the two siblings had reached a very fragile accord before departing Netherfield. "I was delighted to hear you were expected this morning, Colonel. I hope you intend to stay with us a while – what fun! We have been shooting, and of course the society here is excellent – I have resolved to give a ball next week."

"For certain?" Miss Bingley looked up at her brother with annoyance, which she was obliged to conceal. She smoothed at her dress and smiled at Darcy. "It is no small thing, Brother."

Bingley appeared not to hear her. "Ah, here come the Bennets, excellent." His face lit up as he watched Jane Bennet approach with her family. Darcy groaned, for there was one Bennet notably missing.

Miss Bingley sighed and looked up at the sky. "Charles, it is beginning to cloud over – I think it will rain again. We ought to see the colonel back to Netherfield."

Bingley did not look away from his lady as he replied to his sister. "It is not going to rain – we only just got here."

Darcy could not speak, for thinking of Elizabeth. Richard voiced his agreement. "Indeed, I look forward to seeing the place." But then he glanced around and caught sight of the Bennets, who were still coming that way. "Of course, it is not going anywhere, and I am certain it will not rain."

Bingley greeted Miss Bennet eagerly; this was followed with several minutes of familiar chaos. The youngest daughters put themselves forward, even though Richard had not worn his regimentals, while their eldest sister quickly attached herself to Bingley – and all the while their mother praised and encouraged them. Mr. Collins made all his customary gestures of servility and devotion to Lady Catherine; Richard bore it with his usual bemusement, but Miss Bingley made no effort to conceal her disdain.

Darcy remained silent, for his mind was racing. He had become accustomed to orchestrating the events of the day, to some extent, and without Elizabeth at his side when she ought to have been, Darcy felt bereft.

Bingley wandered off with Jane and his sister, and Darcy was floundering. It was, by some miraculously cruel joke, Mrs. Bennet who threw him an unexpected lifeline, and she caught his attention by mentioning her second daughter to Richard. Darcy looked up at once. "Mrs. Bennet, I hope Miss Elizabeth is well this morning," he said.

She looked at him with some surprise but recovered herself and smiled again at Richard. "How kind of you, sir – I was just telling your cousin that Lizzy has gone for one of her long rambles – she loves society as much as any of us, but she is so fond of our lovely countryside here."

Darcy knew at once where Elizabeth was, and he smiled widely at her mother. "Indeed. There is an estate nearby, which I understand had been vacant for many years – I had wished to show my cousin. It is a short walk from where we stand."

"Purvis Lodge? Oh, the attics there are dreadful!" Mrs. Bennet stopped herself and regarded Richard with some interest. "Are you looking to settle in the area? Oh, well, it *is* a very fine house, I am sure...."

"Exactly," Darcy said before Richard could reply. "Come, let us go and take a look. Mrs. Bennet, it has been a pleasure – please convey my regards to Miss Elizabeth. I have enjoyed our recent conversations." This had exactly the impact he hoped, for Mrs. Bennet fluttered and smiled at him. Darcy bowed and led his cousin away.

He was vastly satisfied with himself as they walked down to lane toward Purvis Lodge. Of course Elizabeth would look for him there. He would beg her forgiveness, and together with Richard they would sort everything out. It was fine timing indeed, for Richard would know all, before setting eyes on Wickham, whom they had fortunately evaded.

Richard addressed him as soon as the village was behind him. "What the devil was that about, Darcy?"

"I needed some opportunity to speak with you, and Bingley did not wish to return to Netherfield just yet."

"So there is some emergency, then? I will admit, I am eager

indeed to speak of how you knew what I was wearing this morning. Is there some espionage afoot?"

Darcy rolled his eyes, knowing his cousin would be obliged to turn serious ere long – now was as good a time as any. He launched into his explanation, which had grown more concise with every retelling.

At the end of it, Richard nodded and gave a heavy sigh, taking it all in. "You know this sounds quite mad, and if I did not know you to be incapable of such jests, I would never believe it."

"Yes, I know," Darcy said drily. "But you have come to Netherfield twice before and been convinced."

"Which is how you knew what I was wearing," Richard muttered. He grew contemplative for a moment, and then gave way to some mirth. "There is one thing that must be different about me, for I made a purchase in the village." He gave Darcy a look of challenge.

Darcy studied his cousin intently. Richard had only come dressed this way once before – Darcy had urged him to wear regimentals the second time. *Incapable of jesting indeed!* "Your cufflinks," Darcy said.

Richard eyed him warily. "A lucky guess."

"Here is another," Darcy replied as they approached Purvis Lodge. "The vines will be torn away and the lock opened on the gate, and we will find Elizabeth Bennet walking the grounds here."

"And we are to join her in trespassing? Good God – is this an assignation? If she is as pretty as her sisters, perhaps you would prefer me to leave you alone," Richard chided.

Darcy bristled at him, for this was nearly the truth. "I had thought you may wish to meet her, for she is experiencing the same dilemma that I am."

Richard's incredulity returned. "Repeating the same day over again?"

"Yes."

"And nobody else is aware of this repetition? Only the two of you?"

"Yes. We tried to work together, to figure out what is

happening and why – to determine what must be done."

"And you need my help again?" Richard's eyes shifted with rapid thought, but Darcy had hope yet that his cousin would soon fully believe him.

They were at the gate now; the vines were pulled back and the lock removed. He gave his cousin a meaningful look. "More than you know."

"Well, well," Richard said thoughtfully, as they entered the park.

Darcy took care to close the gate behind them. Delighted as he was that Elizabeth was here, he began to doubt whether their meeting would be a pleasant one. "I should warn you, Richard – Elizabeth may be a little cross with me."

"Elizabeth, eh?" Richard waggled his eyebrows, then gazed at something over Darcy's shoulder. "Pray, is Miss Elizabeth a brunette, and uncommonly fetching when scowling?"

"That is oddly specific, but yes." Darcy had begun to turn about, and was instantly arrested by the sight of Elizabeth moving toward them in great haste, tugging at her gloves. She let them fall to the ground, stormed up to Darcy, and slapped him across the face with her bare hand.

Richard let out a cry of astonishment, and Darcy stepped backward from the force of her attack. Even Elizabeth was reeling from it, clutching at her reddened hand with pain in her eyes. She saw Darcy watching her in horror, and straightened her posture. She would not look back at him. "I am sorry you had to see that, Colonel."

Darcy rubbed at his face. "Elizabeth...."

Still addressing Richard, she said, "Fortunately, you will have no recollection of it tomorrow – until then you may rest assured that your cousin very much deserved that." Now she looked up at Darcy, hellfire in her eyes. "It apparently does not matter what pain one inflicts from one day to the next, so I suppose there are no consequences for anything anymore."

She bobbed into a curtsey, and began to walk away, but Darcy grabbed her and spun her around to face him. "Elizabeth, please." He held her shoulders, gazing into her eyes – they glistened with tears.

"Well?"

"I am sorry," he said softly. He could see that she expected more, and knew she deserved some explanation. He slid his hands down her arms and took her hands in his. "I...." There was a flash of lightning in the direction of the village, and Darcy felt his eyes go as wide as Elizabeth's.

A moment later a peal of thunder rolled across the sky. Her grip on his hands tightened, and Darcy unconsciously drew Elizabeth closer. He shivered, realizing that if Richard had not been present, pacing at some remove, he might very well take her in his arms and kiss her like there was no tomorrow. She shuddered, and he could see in her eyes that she felt the tension, too.

***

Elizabeth let out a shaky breath as she held Mr. Darcy's gaze. He had drawn her near, and she desperately wished he would give voice to the remorse written in his countenance. "Coward," she breathed.

He lowered his eyes and stroked her fingers with his thumbs. "It is not that simple, Elizabeth."

Rage swelled again in her breast. She ripped her hands away and shoved him. "You ran away! You begged and – and *tricked* me into this alliance, and as soon as I began to really enjoy it, you ran away."

Elizabeth glared at him, but the torture on Mr. Darcy's face was too much for her; she abruptly burst into tears. Mr. Darcy was there at once. He wrapped his arms around Elizabeth, breathing her name and stroking her hair. She brought her arms up, clutching at his coat with her hands, and for a minute Elizabeth could do nothing else but weep.

She felt him kiss the top of her head, and Elizabeth was suddenly warm all over. Her anger began to melt away, a calm familiarity holding her to him, but she grew embarrassed at how much she enjoyed his embrace, and the rage swelled once more. She pounded her fists against his chest, crying still. "I am so, so angry at you."

Mr. Darcy wrapped his arms tighter around her, and he laid his head against hers. "Can you forgive me?"

"I hardly know – I fear I must. We cannot go on working at cross-purposes."

"No," he said simply.

Mr. Darcy's tenderness was comforting and his contrition was sincere, but his reticence bothered Elizabeth. He would not speak of it, as they must do, to go forward. Her sobs grew heavier.

"Please, Elizabeth, please do not cry."

"Why should I not? This is a nightmare, and I cannot make it stop," she shouted, shoving him away again. "I have tried everything, only to discover that you have been working against me! You hold my family in contempt daily, and twice now you have caused my sister heartbreak of the acutest kind. Because of you I now know that my own father believes me capable of unspeakable things, and I have to live with that knowledge forever!"

Elizabeth covered her face and spent the rest of her tears. She knew she was making a great fool of herself, but in that moment she did not care. The madness of it all was unbearable, and she had never desired Mr. Darcy's good opinion, anyhow.

There was a hand on her shoulder, and Elizabeth looked up at Colonel Fitzwilliam. He handed her a handkerchief, and she dabbed her face with it.

"Upon my word," he said drily.

Elizabeth drew in a deep breath and slowly exhaled, glancing back at Mr. Darcy. "Did you tell him?"

"Nearly everything, yes. I wished to make some amends, before bringing the, ah, new recruit into it," Mr. Darcy replied.

She nodded – he wished not to speak of Mr. Wickham. "Make amends?" Elizabeth handed the colonel his handkerchief back and crossed her arms. "Go on, then."

"It was wrong of me to leave Netherfield yesterday, and the day before that."

"And?"

"And everything else you said before – I am guilty of it all, and thoroughly ashamed of myself." With a look of deep and gutting sadness, Mr. Darcy extended his hand to her.

"And Jane?"

Mr. Darcy hesitated, and finally he nodded to her. "Whatever is to be done, we will be as one." Elizabeth shook his hand and glanced back at Colonel Fitzwilliam.

The colonel raised his eyebrows with a look of exaggerated surprise. "Hertfordshire is vastly more entertaining than Town," he laughed.

A heavy breeze blew across them, laden with droplets. "It is going to rain," Elizabeth said. "My family will be leaving the market – I must return home."

Mr. Darcy looked between his cousin and Elizabeth as her fingers slid out of his. "Go. We will speak later."

Elizabeth nodded, and began to move away, when Mr. Darcy again captured her hand in his. "Elizabeth?"

She met his eye and understood his beseeching look. "Yes, I forgive you," she said softly. The damp wind picked up again and Elizabeth drew her shawl about her shoulders as she hurried away. She was still in a state of high emotion, but hope and relief were beginning to conquer the anxiety she had awoken with.

***

Darcy was obliged to answer a great many questions for his cousin when they returned to Netherfield. Once again they discussed the great dilemma over brandy in the library.

"I shall confess it, Darcy," Richard said, refilling his drink, "I would not have believed you if not for Miss Elizabeth. I think you both quite mad, but it seems your situation has driven you to madness."

"Which is why I have sought your help," Darcy retorted.

"Then let us discuss what you mean to do about Elizabeth Bennet."

"I have wronged her," Darcy admitted. "We had a sort of unspoken disagreement."

Richard raised his eyebrows. "An *unspoken disagreement?* Darcy, you are in love with her."

Darcy flinched. "I am not."

Richard leaned back in his chair, his posture full of challenge. "Liar. I am not blind, Darcy."

"Then perhaps you observed her strike me in the face?"

"Oh, right before she fell into your arms?" Richard mimicked Darcy's attempt to look imposing, then he idly swirled the brandy in his glass and took a sip. "What did you do to her sister Jane?"

Darcy groaned. "I have had some doubt as to the sincerity of her sister's attachment to Bingley. Her mother – well, you met her. The Bennets are entirely unsuitable, and I fear Bingley would repent the connection forever if he were to marry a woman and later realized her affection did not equal his own."

Richard guffawed. "And how do you reconcile such diametrically opposing views, Darcy? You cannot be in love with one sister and discourage Bingley from the other."

"Miss Bennet is not like Elizabeth. They are both vastly better than the rest of their family, but where Elizabeth is lively and witty and perfectly candid, her sister is diffident and reserved. I cannot read her at all."

"Well, who says it is for you to decide? You and Bingley have been in the area nearly two months now. Surely he must know his own mind, and hers, better than you. Miss Elizabeth said you had caused her sister some heartbreak, which suggests her feelings are more than you realize – what did you do to Jane Bennet?"

Darcy looked away to hide his shame. "Yesterday and the day before, our whole party left Netherfield and returned to London. I attempted to separate Bingley from Jane Bennet."

Richard shook his head and finished his drink. "For his own good, no doubt," he scoffed. "You shall not convince me that you are not in love with Elizabeth Bennet. It frightens you out of your wits, I think – you fear that if Bingley pursues one sister, the other will always be in your path, tempting you. But why should care that her family is – well, no less colorful than ours – and why should Bingley?"

Darcy pounded his fist on the table between them. "Of course I must care!" Richard rolled his eyes and poured them both another drink. Darcy sipped at the brandy, seething. "I cannot have her."

"That is ridiculous."

"What is ridiculous is that it has been the twentieth of November for nearly a fortnight. That is what I must apply myself to. Elizabeth is... a distraction. I must put an end to the repetition, but when life returns to normal, nothing will have changed between us. My intentions and wishes on the twenty-first of November will be just what they were on the nineteenth."

Richard shook his head. "I do not see how that is possible, when the interval has been full of secret meetings and embraces between you."

"You could not understand."

"I am sure I can – I have embraced a woman before, Darcy."

"Elizabeth and I share this unique dilemma – that is all that can ever exist between us. I am sure she will not lament the change when this is all over."

Richard stood, still shaking his head with cheerful frustration. "You are an idiot, Darcy. I am going to speak with Bingley, since you would have me solve your problems for you." He swaggered out of the room, whistling a tune.

***

A footman informed Richard that Bingley was in the drawing room with his sister; Richard heard his name spoken and lingered just outside the door.

"He might have warned us that he was coming to stay," Miss Bingley lamented. "I am sure it is not Mr. Darcy's fault – *his* sense of propriety has never faltered – but his cousin!" She groaned.

"Colonel Fitzwilliam is very welcome," Bingley admonished his sister. "I hope you will show him every kindness."

"Of course I will," she snapped. "How could you doubt it? I had hoped we might return to London, which is impossible now.

I had hoped that pathetic marketplace might show you how underwhelming and inconsequential this place is. Did you not see how the Bennets behaved? The younger girls ought to be locked in their room until the militia moves on, and the mother! And did you hear how the cousin carried on? All that was missing was Miss Eliza's willful insolence, and the picture would have been complete!"

If Bingley replied, Richard could not make it out; he was obliged to stifle his own laughter as he listened outside the open doorway. Caroline Bingley was in fine form indeed, and he was going to enjoy unsettling her.

"But really, Charles. One unexpected arrival is enough – and the Lucases can be nothing to us!"

"They are our neighbors, and I like them," Bingley said. "I am sure Lady Lucas wished to be included in Mrs. Phillips' invitation – she looked very disappointed this morning, which I can well understand. I was sure Mrs. Phillips was on the point of inviting *us* to her party before you asked me to help you find Darcy."

"We have avoided one vulgar entertainment, in favor of another," Miss Bingley drawled.

Richard strolled into the room, clapping his hands with glee. "Vulgar entertainment! I knew your abilities as hostess would surely dazzle me," he cried, seating himself obnoxiously close to Miss Bingley.

She instinctively moved a little away from him, a frigid smile pasted on her face. Her poor brother looked genuinely overwrought and appealed to Richard. "There is nothing vulgar about the Lucases," Bingley said. "I have invited them to dine with us tonight, Colonel."

"Excellent! If they are half as charming as the Bennets, I shall be very well pleased with the company," Richard replied, giving Bingley a pointed look. "If they were to be of the party as well, I should be vastly amused."

"The Bennets are already engaged for their aunt's card party tonight," Miss Bingley said.

Richard flashed her a bright smile. "A card party? That sounds like an after-dinner engagement. You had better invite them – at least allow them to accept or decline as they choose, but you cannot omit them. That is how things are done at Matlock – and Pemberley."

Miss Bingley glared at Richard, but her brother smiled widely. "I am sure you are right! Yes, very good."

Richard was surprised at how easy this was going to be. "I say, Bingley, I really do hope the Bennets can be tempted to attend. They seemed so very amiable, and there is one amongst them in particular that I am very curious about." He grinned wolfishly at Bingley.

"Oh," Bingley said, a nervous laugh catching in his throat.

Miss Bingley leaned forward with a vicious smirk. "Jane Bennet *is* a lovely girl. She would certainly suit... somebody. And I have it on good authority that her mother is very fond of officers."

Bingley scowled at his sister. "Caroline!" He turned and regarded Richard warily. "Miss... Lydia, perhaps?"

"No indeed," Richard laughed. "I thought the younger sisters too energetic, though they were very friendly." Bingley looked stricken, but Richard chuckled. "I am eager for a glimpse of the absent sister – Miss Elizabeth, I believe. Is she as lovely as your Miss Bennet?" He winked at Bingley.

"Nobody is as lovely as Jane Bennet, but Miss Elizabeth is very charming," Bingley replied, relief washing over his face.

Richard turned and fixed Miss Bingley with a teasing look. She had been after Darcy for years, and Richard wondered if Miss Bingley had detected any partiality between Darcy and Miss Elizabeth. "What do you say to that, Miss Bingley?"

She smiled brightly. "I would be delighted to introduce you."

"Excellent, Miss Bingley. Your sense of propriety never falters." He held her gaze as the barb landed, but she betrayed no remorse at all.

Oblivious, Bingley stood and went to the desk in the corner. "Well, I shall write them directly! Yes, I am sure an *early* dinner will do; surely they might stay two hours at least, before the card party – and they may invite us afterward, you know."

"Splendid," Richard replied. "You must tell Mrs. Bennet

that I was very pleased to meet her, and that I am eager to meet her other daughter."

Bingley looked up from his writing. "Capital! How very merry we shall all be, just capital!"

***

"Richard," Darcy grumbled. "There are other matters I would discuss with you."

Richard hardly stirred. He was leaning against the window casement, looking out on the park, watching Caroline Bingley in an unguarded moment. She had left the drawing room in quite a huff after Richard had wreaked some havoc on their dinner plans, and had apparently come outside to sulk. While he might have imagined her kicking at rose bushes or throwing stones, she had gone to a tree at the back of the garden and perched on a rope swing. The whimsy of it was unexpected, and strangely beguiling.

"Richard!"

"Yes, yes – I am listening," Richard said, turning to face his cousin. "Tell me more about your peculiar dilemma. But, no – tell me more about Elizabeth Bennet." Richard smiled, wondering if the same approach that had worked so well on Bingley might also give Darcy a nudge in the right direction.

"I have said all I wish to say about Elizabeth, for the time being," Darcy said stonily.

Richard raised his eyebrows. "Well, she has piqued my curiosity. I like her very well indeed, and if you truly have no intention of forming any designs on her...."

"I told you I do not – I cannot."

"Perhaps that is for the best," Richard replied.

Darcy sighed. "Unfortunately, it is. I mean to do better, for we are still bound by the same madness that traps us both in this day over and over – I will collaborate with her, as I must, and then I shall return to London and forget her."

"Right. Because her family is so unsuitable." Richard rolled his eyes.

"If you knew them as I do, you would understand. It is a

pity – if circumstances were different... but they are not. You met her mother for long enough to see what *she* is about – Mrs. Bennet is an artful, crass woman who lets her daughters run wild – encourages them to do so, to put themselves forward in a way that will end in scandal, mark my words. The father is too indolent to do anything about it but laugh at them, though there is nothing funny about it. A family such as theirs, with little fortune, is only as good as their breeding, their behavior. Even the cousin, who is to inherit, is a buffoon of the first order. The youngest girls are such silly, ignorant flirts, I cannot account for how Elizabeth could have come from the same house! You saw how they acted in the village – can you imagine such girls influencing Georgiana? I could go on – but I see you are determined to trivialize what ought to be the biggest decision of my life."

"No indeed," Richard quipped. "I find this all very illuminating. But of course, spending more time in their company will be ever so much better. Bingley has invited them to dine with us."

Darcy gave him a quizzical look. "That is not possible – the Bennets always attend a card party at their aunt's house this night."

"Bingley was not invited – I take it he has been, in the past? I understand Caroline maneuvered him away from the Bennets after you and I left the village. Anyhow, he has invited them here, and we shall see. Think of it as a test, perhaps. If they attend, instead of honoring the other engagement, it shall be a testament to Miss Bennet's affection for Bingley."

"Or a maneuver of her mother's," Darcy retorted.

Richard shrugged. "Or an opportunity for you to observe them better. It is clear that Miss Elizabeth takes her sister's feelings very seriously, and regardless of your feelings for *her*, you must, as you have admitted, endeavor to work with her to end your predicament."

"You are right," Darcy admitted. "We cannot work at cross-purposes. And there is another matter, too, where she and I have disagreed."

"I do not doubt it," Richard laughed. He glanced again out

the window, at Caroline Bingley – the wind had blown a tuft of her hair loose, but she ignored it. "Well, we shall work on that bit tomorrow, eh? I think you have a great deal to consider already – you must make things right with Miss Elizabeth, and you must do better toward Bingley and Miss Jane Bennet. Let that be your purpose, and if it is the twentieth of November again tomorrow, I shall come back again and help you through the rest – with Miss Elizabeth."

Darcy eyed Richard warily. "I suppose there is some merit in that idea."

"Of course there is! You have summoned me here for advice – you ought to take it. And I ought to take a walk – you have some thinking to do, old boy."

Darcy grumbled, and waved Richard away; grinning, Richard hastened out to the garden.

***

Caroline Bingley was still sitting on the swing when Richard snuck up on her from behind. He trod carefully on the grass, and when he was near enough he gave her a gentle push on the swing. She clutched at the ropes and spun awkwardly around, letting out a cry of alarm.

"Stay where you are, Miss Bingley," Richard said. "It is a most becoming attitude, to see a handsome young lady so at ease with country life." He began to smile at her, and stopped; her face was red, as if she had been crying. "Forgive me, Miss Bingley – I did not mean to upset you."

She spun around in the swing and looked up at him with her shoulders set in defiance. "Did you not?"

"You are displeased that I encouraged your brother to entertain his neighbors?"

"I might have thought it an honest mistake, but you have always enjoyed making jests at my expense," Miss Bingley snapped. "You cannot know what these people are – or perhaps you saw enough this morning to know they are unsuitable, and that just makes it all the more amusing for you."

"I thought they were very eager to be agreeable," Richard

said, giving her an innocent smile.

"Eager indeed," she huffed. "They are scheming fortune hunters, and it may be a lark to you – everything is – but I take life very seriously, sir. The fact of the matter is that Charles is in danger of arousing some *expectation* among our neighbors – he may even be compromised by this Miss Bennet. *She* seems sweet enough, but her mother is capable of anything! I must be sensible, where my brother is not. These Bennets are dangerous connections and will lead him to folly – and I am only punished for trying to protect him."

She stood now, and though Richard was broad and tall, Caroline Bingley became far more formidable in that moment. "I should not have to explain this to you, Colonel – I should not be obliged to explain my reasons at all, to anybody who seeks to arrive unexpectedly and then dictate what guests I entertain in my own home!"

It was windy, and Miss Bingley's hair had become disheveled. He had always thought her handsome, but she was distractingly so at present. At least she was not striking him, as Miss Elizabeth had done to Darcy. Richard smiled softly at her; he had pushed her further than he had meant to, and was actually a little sorry for it.

"Miss Bingley, you are quite right. I have taken a liberty I ought not to have."

She looked up at him, her eyes narrow. "Are you apologizing to me?"

Richard shrugged. "If you like. Tell me, Miss Bingley, are you always so remarkably high strung? You ought to relax, and try and enjoy life, like me. Let your hair down a little." He reached out and tucked a stray tuft of hair behind her ear.

She recoiled, but Richard thought she suppressed a brief smile before scowling at him. "I do enjoy my life – just not *here*. My family has risen, and may rise further, if my brother is not played for a fool in this awful backwater. I may not go through my life as you do, laughing at everything as if nothing matters, but I am capable of pleasure and pain just as much as anybody."

"Then I shall not laugh at you," Richard replied, giving a little bow. He considered what she had said – that he behaved as if nothing mattered. By Darcy's account of things, Richard's actions did not matter at all, presently – they would be forgotten by tomorrow. He could say anything – do anything – but there would be but fleeting joy in it, for he would not remember, either.

Miss Bingley had gone from a malevolent glower to open surprise at Richard's tender tone of voice. "Do whatever you like," she said. "I am sure it could be nothing to me."

She bobbed into a curtsey, but before she could move away, Richard took her in his arms and kissed her. Her body tensed up at once, but her lips yielded to his; she began to kiss him back in earnest, and her body relaxed against his. Richard grew bolder, his hands caressing her back as he kissed her deeply.

Caroline moaned throatily, and then her eyes opened wide and she drew away in horror. For an instant, Richard expected her to be furious – he was not prepared for the tears that burst forth.

Trembling, Caroline took a step back. "Why would you do such a thing? Do you really think so little of me?"

Richard could only gape at her. He was actually surprised she had not fled, or slapped him. He was not proud of making her cry, but her reaction confounded him. "I have kissed you, Caroline."

"Do not call me that," she snapped, wiping away her tears. "I do not trust you, and I do not like you."

"I like you," Richard said, tentatively reaching out to her.

She swatted his hand away. "Ugh!" Her bottom lip quivered, and her eyes filled with rage; suddenly Richard understood. He had sisters, and knew angry tears when he saw them. He had made a terrible miscalculation, and began to back away from her.

For a moment, Caroline stood frozen, rage and fear and confusion radiating from her wide eyes. Her breathing was ragged, and he longed for her to say something. The wind picked up, and she seemed to snap out of her high emotion. She drew her shawl around her shoulders, turned around, and ran back to the house, her loose hair swirling around her.

***

Richard did not see Caroline again until it was time for her to join her brother in receiving their guests. She did not meet Richard's eye, and he was relieved that at least his foolishness would soon be forgotten. She would forget what he had done, and even he would forget how much he had enjoyed it – and how much it had stung that she did not.

He was determined to make himself useful in the interval. Darcy was being an idiot, it was true, but he had done one thing right – he had asked for Richard's help.

When the Lucases and Bennets arrived for dinner at Netherfield, Richard stood at Darcy's side to greet them, hoping his own good cheer would render Darcy a little more agreeable. Their encounter with the Bennets at the market that morning had prepared Richard for a degree of chaos that was happily lacking as they were shown into the drawing room, for Mr. and Mrs. Bennet had brought only their two eldest daughters, and their cousin Mr. Collins.

As a guest himself, Richard was happily spared any further effusions from the loquacious parson; he directed his lengthy praise of the house to Miss Bingley, and Richard observed it with amusement as Caroline tried to remain calm and gracious.

Of course, as a single gentleman, he was still of considerable interest to Mrs. Bennet, and she attacked him directly. "Allow me to present my second daughter, Elizabeth," she said, and Richard reminded himself to behave as if this were indeed their first meeting. Darcy greeted her only with the barest of nods, but Richard took Miss Elizabeth's hand in his and gave her a wide smile.

"Miss Elizabeth, it is a pleasure to meet you at last. I have heard that all the Bennet sisters are charming and agreeable, and that you in particular are exceedingly... striking. It seems the rumors are true." He winked and kissed her hand; beside him, Darcy began to cough.

Miss Elizabeth grinned back at him, a faint blush spreading across her cheeks. "You are too kind, I am sure."

"Oh, my Lizzy is the dearest girl," Mrs. Bennet cried. "And

so kind of you to express a wish to meet her, Colonel! But I must apologize that my younger girls are not present – they have gone to my sister's – she is to host a card party, to entertain some of the officers quartered here."

"I am sure the colonel shall overcome the deprivation," Mr. Bennet said sardonically.

"Quite so," Richard replied. "I find the present company an exceptionally fine grouping indeed – though the gracious welcome I received from *all* your family this morning ought not be dismissed so easily. Such warm affability is often undervalued." He glanced over at Caroline, who had certainly heard him, and was now staring daggers at him.

"Not at Longbourn," Mr. Bennet laughed. He moved away, and Richard drifted again toward Caroline, if only to prevent her from disrupting her brother's conversation with the eldest Miss Bennet.

"I was sure you would be back at Netherfield very soon," Caroline was telling Jane Bennet, who seemed not to feel the barb.

"Perhaps you are clairvoyant, Miss Bingley," Miss Elizabeth observed. She took a protective step toward her sister but seemed to be looking across the room at Darcy. "Another accomplishment."

Richard looked back at his cousin, who was watching them all intently. Richard knew this look all too well – to the rest of the world, it looked haughty and cold, but Darcy merely had no idea how to join a conversation no matter how much it might interest him. Richard rolled his eyes in Darcy's direction – the poor blockhead needed way more help than either of them had realized.

"I only hope you will not be taken ill on this visit," Bingley told Miss Bennet.

"As do I," his sister purred.

Richard did not fully understand what was passing, but in an effort to move the subject – and perhaps even Caroline – along, he observed, "You ladies all seem to be the picture of health to me. I am sure your excursions this morning have brought on these rosy hues you wear so well."

Miss Elizabeth gave him an arch look, Caroline regarded him with all her usual contempt, and Jane Bennet, predictably, blushed even deeper. Bingley laughed merrily but moved a little closer to his lady. "Quite right – you look remarkably well this evening, Miss Bennet."

"Miss Elizabeth is looking very lovely, as well," Caroline observed, giving Richard another venomous sideward glance. The lady in question appeared startled but grinned with bemusement. "I understand you indulged in a long walk this morning, Miss Eliza – how refreshing to be so *at ease with country life*. You must find it so *relaxing*."

Miss Elizabeth only nodded, as if too astonished to reply. Bingley eyed his sister with nervous suspicion; it was Jane Bennet who attempted to turn the subject. "I am sure the country agrees with you, too, Miss Bingley. I see you are wearing the earrings you bought at the market this morning – how well they suit you. Oh! Lizzy, I forgot to tell you, but you missed Baba Romilda this morning – she was asking after you."

Miss Elizabeth blanched and began to fidget with her necklace. "Oh. How kind."

"Yes," Bingley said, "I thought everyone in the village uncommonly agreeable this morning!"

Caroline sneered with distaste, and silently moved away to attach herself to Darcy. Miss Elizabeth watched her go, and Richard could detect what he hoped was a degree of longing in her eyes as she regarded Darcy across the room.

In another moment, Miss Elizabeth seemed to recollect herself, and forced a smile. "Speaking of uncommonly agreeable – Colonel, have you met my friend Charlotte Lucas?"

They were approached by a plain but pleasant young woman, who appeared of an age with Darcy. Her presence seemed to put Miss Elizabeth more at ease, and so Richard made his escape once he had made all the appropriate remarks.

He moved through the room, watching and calculating. There was something strange in the air, for though these were the three most prominent families in the area, and their dining together must be perfectly natural – something was off. Darcy certainly seemed to feel it, for he was giving Richard many beseeching looks, and clearly hoping for some rescue from Caroline and Mr. Collins.

There was some amusement in Richard's choice to ignore this, though he told himself that it was only because he might find another means of assisting his cousin. At the first opportunity, he snuck out of the drawing room.

***

In the dining room, Richard strode down the length of the table in a state of high amusement. As he had suspected, Caroline Bingley had clearly planned the seating arrangements with a design to vex as many people as possible. He plucked a few of the place cards up and began to rearrange them to better suit his own purposes, when Miss Elizabeth entered the dining room.

"Forgive me, I...." She stopped, and as she perceived what he was about, she began to laugh. "Dear Colonel, I am very happy you are back in Hertfordshire again."

"Then I hope you will keep my secret," Richard said as he continued to rearrange the place cards.

"And I hope you will accept my apology," she said with a wry smile. "My outburst this morning must have been most alarming for you."

Richard schooled his expression. "I have never seen my cousin thus treated in all my life," he said evenly. He paused just long enough to watch Miss Elizabeth's eyes go wide, and then added, "It was a rare treat, and I ought to thank you."

Her surprise gave way to amusement, and she moved close enough to examine what he was about. "If you wish to thank me, please do not put me so near Miss Bingley!"

Richard laughed. "But you may say whatever you wish to her – which I suspect will be amusing for me – and she shall not remember tomorrow, is that not so?"

"True," she replied, tapping her finger to her chin as if considering the possibilities. "But I just chastised your cousin this morning for behaving as though his actions do not matter – cruelty and mischief are still wrong, even if nobody else but us shall remember it."

Richard was stricken with another pang of remorse for how he had treated Caroline, even as he placed his name beside hers at the table. "It is really true, then? You and Darcy are trapped together in this mad repetition of the day?"

"Yes," she sighed. "I am sure he was hoping you could help him make sense of it."

"Incredulous as I am, I still have a plan," Richard reassured her. "I like you, Miss Elizabeth."

"You may call me Lizzy," she replied, arching an eyebrow at him.

"Lizzy, if my cousin is to be frozen in time with anybody, I am glad it is a lady with a sense of humor, and no little gumption. We shall both hold him accountable, I daresay."

Richard moved to the other end of the dining room. Bingley would sit at the head of the table; Richard placed Miss Bennet and Darcy on either side of their host and gestured for Elizabeth to observe.

She ran her fingers idly over Darcy's name. "It is funny," she said quietly. "The last time Jane and Mr. Bingley spent an evening together, without my younger sisters present, he proposed to her. Of course, the next morning Mr. Darcy removed his friend from the area."

"He is very sorry, you know," Richard said gently. "I have scolded him for it, but I think he already felt some regret of his own. I cannot say why he has failed to see in two months what I have already observed between Bingley and your sister, but I hope you will give him another chance to do better."

Elizabeth shrugged, and began to walk back down the table, examining the other place cards. "It is not as though I have much choice."

"I suppose you do not, but if you wish to put an end to your troubles, it will do some good for Darcy to accept Bingley's attachment to your sister. I think she is shy, just as Darcy is, and does not show her feelings easily. It is prudent to be guarded – Darcy behaves this way himself, restricting his own feelings."

"Is that not hypocritical of him? I know he disdains my younger sisters for being too boisterous – and now you tell me that he distrusts Jane for her reserve – is there no pleasing him?"

Richard could see that he had incensed her and tried to undo some of the damage. "In Darcy's position...."

"In Mr. Darcy's position, all the world is offending every moment," Elizabeth spat. "Forgive me, I know he is your cousin. But it is not fair, sir, for my sister to be held to such impossible standards. Were she a woman of fortune, her feelings would be of no consequence at all, and Mr. Darcy would not feel obliged to counsel his friend on matters of the heart."

"I cannot agree," Richard replied. "Though I will say this, you and my cousin both rather overestimate his head, and underestimate his heart."

***

Richard was well pleased with his changes to the seating at dinner, though it was plain that Caroline was not. Mrs. Bennet, whom he had placed about halfway down the table, loudly remarked that it must be an *informal* gathering, as Caroline's seating arrangement had not given precedence to Sir William Lucas; Caroline seethed, while Richard shared a private laugh with Elizabeth.

The meal progressed just as he hoped. Caroline ignored him, at first, and even at times seemed to encourage Richard's interest in Elizabeth. This suited his purpose, for Richard was able to pass the first half of the meal in conversation with Elizabeth, even calling her Lizzy a few times, just to scandalize Caroline and Mr. Collins.

Though Elizabeth was reluctant to openly discuss her dilemma, Richard enjoyed her company, and was satisfied that he had aroused enough envy in Darcy to hopefully push him to examine his feelings.

Later in the meal, however, Caroline began to tire of her other dinner companion, Mr. Collins. This was also by design, for Richard had not been able to resist the urge to needle her a little more. He liked Caroline, even when she was angry with him, and if his company was only slightly more acceptable than that of the toady parson, at least she would speak to him.

They spoke of idle things, Richard and Caroline, and he could see that her patience was strained. Again he felt some remorse that he would have no memory of this day once it ended, for he would have liked to discover why she disliked him so much. As haughty and rude as she always was to him – which was usually amusing – she had not flown into a rage when he had kissed her; the tears were more human a response than he had ever expected. But before the tears, she *had* kissed him back – that, perhaps, it would be better to forget.

***

The next morning, Richard awoke with a start. He sat up in his bed, the disorientation of his fitful slumber washing away. And then he looked around at his bedroom in London, and as the inconceivable truth alighted on him, he burst out laughing.

8

Darcy awoke without any of the despair that normally clouded his mind as soon as he became conscious. He felt lighter, steadier, and he set about his day at once. He dressed, rang for breakfast in his chamber, and dispatched his usual letter to Richard. After this, he had only to wait – and to think.

There was some small part of him that balked at bringing Richard back again, though he knew it must be done, for they had done nothing yet about Wickham. The previous day *had* been fruitful, though Darcy had doubted for much of the afternoon that Richard would be of any use at all. But he had pushed Darcy to reexamine Bingley's attachment to Jane Bennet, and in doing so Darcy felt his fragile accord with Elizabeth might hold. She had forgiven him, but she had not shown him half the warmth and witty candor, last evening, as she had bestowed on Richard.

Of course, Richard had never hurt her. Darcy sighed; it was some relief to have Elizabeth's forgiveness, but she had essentially admitted that she had no choice but to cooperate with him. He wanted to earn it – he had, he now knew, been terribly wrong, and simply acknowledging his error was not enough.

He had once before prevented the daily domestic scuffle by going on an early morning ride with Bingley, and Darcy did the same this morning. He regarded his friend with shame as they trotted out of the stables together; he ought to have taken Bingley's side, every time. But then, he ought never have allowed Bingley to become so dependent on his opinions at all. Darcy, like every other man, was quite capable of being wrong.

"Which direction shall we ride?"

Bingley looked out at the horizon. "East, I think; the view is breathtaking."

Darcy urged his horse on, alongside his friend. "You like it here."

"Indeed I do! I was quite serious, the other day – I should be content to stay forever."

"Your sister will try to persuade you to leave the place," Darcy observed.

Bingley laughed ruefully. "Yes, she was not very pleasant last night, but I am sure it was only the rain."

"She has nothing good to say of the country, and she is trying to poison your mind against the place. I apologize if I am presumptuous, but I do not wish to see you bullied."

Bingley slowed his pace to a canter as they came up a low hill. "I was a little disappointed she did not like my notion of giving a ball – generally she likes to show off – and I thought she might wish to impress you."

Darcy winced. "Surely you understand that she could not – that her giving a ball would not materially alter my opinion – my intentions."

"Yes, I know – I cannot blame you," Bingley said. "I only meant that I did not expect her to protest."

"Well, I hope you intend to move forward with the scheme."

"I shall, if you think I ought to."

Darcy subdued his frustration. "I think you should do what *you* wish, that is my point. If you wish to give a ball, give a ball. If you wish to stay here, stay. And if there is *anything else* you wish, you should do that, too. You are your own man."

Bingley grinned back at him. "Well! Then I shall. Yes, I *will* stay here, and I *will* give a ball." His countenance turned reflective for a moment, but his smile did not waver. "As to the other matter – well, I think you know what I mean."

"Jane Bennet?"

"I love her, Darcy. I know it has been but two months, but I can think of nothing but her. She is the kindest, most angelic creature, Darcy!"

"You have been in love a great many times before," Darcy observed. "How can you be sure this is different?"

"Because *she* is so different," Bingley cried. "She is unlike any woman I have ever known. The girls I have admired in London were pretty enough to catch my interest and vapid enough to quickly lose it. They are all so… so like Caroline. Jane is not; she has substance, she says things that are real and pure and genuine; she does not simply repeat all the agreeable nothings women are taught in lieu of independent thought."

Darcy raised his eyebrows in surprise, struck by Bingley's rare poignance. It struck him perhaps a little too deeply. "That is incredibly insightful."

"So is Jane," Bingley said, spurred on by Darcy's approbation. "One time we just talked about leaves, and all the different shapes of them. It was marvelous! I thought to myself that I could never imagine any of the girls I have met in London having such a conversation, or even so much as looking at a leaf. But Jane thinks about things nobody does, and speaks in such a way that I want to think differently, too."

Darcy laughed indulgently at his friend's strangely endearing speech. "I did not realize that is what you spoke of. She is always so quiet."

"No, she is not. She and I talk about a great many things – real things, not meaningless, idle chatter. Anyhow, I would rather look at every leaf and tree in Hertfordshire with her than be in any London drawing room with a hundred copies of Caroline. I know it is wrong of me to speak so of my sister, but she is mean and angry, and perhaps a little frightened – certainly she thinks too much of society, and I do not wish for another such woman in my life."

"No," Darcy said. "No indeed." He shuddered. "You are in a fortunate position, my friend. You are your own man and need not be bound by your family's expectations. Miss Bennet is a gentleman's daughter, and though her fortune is small and her connections are not grand, she would not disgrace you."

Bingley rolled his eyes. "I have enough money for both of us, and her family is at least more affectionate than mine, which is not nothing, trust me."

"I do," Darcy conceded. "I only wonder what you are waiting for. Did you not like having her under your roof at Netherfield?"

"I did," Bingley cried. "That is – I did not like that she was ill, but I liked that she was *there*."

"And you might have her there always."

Bingley grinned widely. "You think so?"

Darcy nodded, his heart brimming with joy for his friend. Elizabeth was right – this felt right. "Go get her."

"I shall," Bingley declared, with his idiotic, besotted look. "I shall go to Longbourn directly."

"Go, then. I have an errand, and then I will join you there, to celebrate." Darcy began to bring his horse about and return to Netherfield, when he stopped. "Oh, and Bingley – please convey my regards to Miss Elizabeth. Tell her... tell her I hope she shall keep her gloves on."

***

Richard knew he had about an hour yet before he would receive Darcy's urgent letter, but he made ready to travel at once, as he would need to set out early this time. He was going to take the carriage.

Once he was dressed, Richard went downstairs to breakfast. As she had been the day before, Georgiana was seated beside the earl, speaking shyly. Richard considered this some progress – when she had first come to stay with them, she had said nothing at all.

"Good morning," Richard sang out to them, leaning back

indecorously in a chair across from his young cousin. She giggled at him.

"I hear you have ordered the carriage," the earl said. "I hope you are for Kent."

"Not a chance," Richard said, biting into a pastry. "I am for Hertfordshire, to see Darcy."

Georgiana's eyes lit up. "You are going to see William! Oh, can I go?"

"That is why I have ordered the carriage – your things are being packed even now, for we must set off at once."

The earl bristled at this. "What is this about? Why the hurry?"

Richard only shrugged. "Because we are eager to see him. Right, Georgie?"

"Oh, yes," she squealed.

"Now see here, Richard," his father sputtered. "You cannot be traipsing about the countryside at a moment's notice. Besides, Georgiana, did you not wish to call on Lady Carson with me?"

Richard guffawed. "The Merry Widow of Mayfair? Father, really."

"I like her," Georgiana said. "She is very nice – and so mysterious – I hear she has a tragic history."

"To lose one husband may be tragic," Richard mused, giving his father an arch look. "To lose three looks like carelessness."

The earl grimaced at Richard. "I know all too well you do not take anything seriously, Richard, least of all the tattle sheets!"

Richard let out a heavy sigh and shook his head. This was an argument for another time, though it began to bother him that everybody thought him so perpetually indifferent. He turned away from his father to address Georgiana. "We must leave at once – how soon can you be ready?"

***

The Fitzwilliam carriage was on the Great North Road within half an hour, and Richard began to formulate a plan at once. Darcy might be blind to why he was trapped in this day with a beautiful woman perfectly suited to him, but Richard had always known he was the clever one. He understood at once what his role must be – he would be the means of uniting them.

Including Georgiana had been an impulsive decision, but Richard instantly realized how it might work to his advantage. When Georgiana had concluded her lengthy and endearing effusions about being included in the Hertfordshire scheme, she paused and gave her cousin an assessing look. "Richard, why do you look like that?"

She swatted at him, and he laughed. Giggling, she pounced on him as she had done when she was a child. He tickled her for a moment, and she relaxed on the seat beside him. "Richard, you are far too merry – I like it, of course, but I wonder if you are up to something."

Richard tugged playfully at one of her pretty blond curls. "What if I am?"

Her face lit up with excitement. "Oh dear – William *does* know that we are coming, does he not?"

"He invited me, for I had been wishing to be out of London for a time, and his account of Netherfield sounds very pleasant. I have brought you along because I gather there is a particular lady in the neighborhood you may wish to meet." Richard smiled indulgently at the girl; she was going to adore Elizabeth Bennet, and Darcy would feel it.

Georgiana took his meaning and beamed. "Truly? Oh, Cousin! Who is she? What is she like? Oh, I ought to have worn my pretty blue dress to meet her – but did William really tell you this? He never tells me anything! What is her name?"

"Elizabeth Bennet," Richard replied. "She resides at a nearby estate, and I understand Bingley is fond of her older sister."

Georgiana nearly swooned. "That is so romantic! Oh, I have longed for a sister!"

Richard laughed indulgently. "Well now, let us not get ahead of ourselves. You know your brother – he is reticent about such personal matters, and I do not think Miss Elizabeth is yet aware of his feelings for her."

"Ah! I see what you are about – you wish to help him on."

Richard smiled, but held up a hand to still his cousin's youthful exuberance. "Yes, but... discreetly."

She screwed up her face with mock severity, a perfect imitation of their aunt, Lady Catherine. "I can be the soul of discretion."

"I hope so, or your brother will be very cross with us both. It is a case of some delicacy."

"Then tell me what I must do," she said earnestly.

Richard began to detail his plan. "To begin with, this conversation never happened – you must behave as though you have never heard of Miss Elizabeth when we are introduced. That is vital."

"So that she will not realize he has confided in you?"

He chuckled. It was, in fact, Darcy that Richard did not want to tip off. "Something like that," he said. "I expect you will like her very much. Her younger sisters are very exuberant – or so I hear. Your brother may have some apprehension about you befriending them, for their manners are bold and forward, but I think you ought to be civil to them – lead by example. Your brother would be much pleased."

"I see," Georgiana replied, with a tinge of hesitation.

"They are amiable girls, I only mean that you should urge them toward more propriety, rather than allow them to tempt you to less. Miss Mary, I understand, is fond of music, and is not so boisterous."

"And Miss Elizabeth?"

"I cannot say much more, but Darcy would not think so well of any lady who did not deserve his good opinion. I hope, however, that for today, at least, you might direct your focus to the other Bennet sisters."

Georgiana giggled again and gave him a knowing look. "You want William to be alone with her?"

He nodded. "I will take care of Miss Bingley if you manage the sisters."

"Oh, yes," she cried. "That is...."

Richard might have laughed, but he could not. "Come, you mustn't think too meanly of Miss Bingley. She is doing her best."

Georgiana gaped at him. "Oh. Well... so then shall I."

"I know I can count on you, Georgie." Richard gave her another playful nudge, and they passed the rest of their journey in pleasant camaraderie.

When they arrived in Meryton, Richard knew Darcy would likely be there to meet him, for Richard had stopped there for directions the day before. He did the same thing again, knowing it would be hard enough to explain why he had brought Georgiana this time.

When Richard spied his cousin from the carriage window, he instructed the driver to stop, and he hopped out of the equipage. "Darcy," he cried, and waved his cousin over. "What a spot of luck – I have no idea where Netherfield is – but here you are."

Behind him, Georgiana peeked out of the carriage. "William!"

Darcy went pale, and stood frozen, gawking at them. "Georgiana! Good God, is something the matter?"

"No indeed," Richard replied. "I thought it would be an excellent surprise – your sister heard of my plans this morning and wished to accompany me. Are you not pleased?"

"Of course," Darcy replied, though something in his eyes belied some concern. "Forgive me, I am only very surprised indeed."

Georgiana scrambled out of the carriage to embrace her brother, who received her warmly. But when he drew away, Darcy began to fidget. "We had better not tarry in the village," he said, glancing around nervously. "I expected you to come on horseback – I thought we might ride to Longbourn."

"Longbourn?" Richard smiled, playing his part well.

"It is a neighboring estate," Darcy replied. "Bingley has gone to visit there already, and I meant to join him."

So Darcy *had* seen reason – Richard was relieved, for this would make his own endeavors much easier. "Well, I shall not detain you, then."

"Certainly not – but we had better go at once," Darcy said.

"You say Bingley is already there? It is early yet – it must have to do with a lady." Richard winked at Georgiana, who giggled merrily.

Darcy nodded, and began to climb into the carriage. "Shall we be off? I shall ride with you, for I walked to the village from Netherfield."

Richard moved to deny his cousin entry into the barouche. "Pray, I should prefer to freshen up at Netherfield before I am introduced to any of Bingley's neighbors – Georgie must be wishing the same. Did Bingley's sisters accompany him, or are they at home?"

"They are at home," Darcy said. "Forgive me, of course you must wish a period of respite before going to Longbourn." Again Darcy looked nervously around; Richard began to wonder what his cousin was up to.

"I think you are eager to be off, Darcy. Go on then, we shall catch you up within the hour, I am sure, only direct us which way to Netherfield."

Darcy gave his instructions to the driver and waved them off before setting off the opposite way; Richard regarded Darcy through the window as the carriage converted them to Netherfield, and gave Georgiana a playful nudge. "What did I tell you, eh?"

She laughed ruefully. "You were right about Mr. Bingley, but did it not seem that William was acting strangely?"

Richard considered. It would probably be best to say nothing to Georgiana of the daily repetition; better to keep her occupied. "Bingley's lady is Elizabeth's sister – of course he must be eager to go there."

"Can we not go with him? I am sure I do not need to change my clothes at Netherfield first." Georgiana looked pleadingly at him.

"Let Darcy have a few minutes with her before he must share her with us," Richard said. "We shall be brief at Netherfield, but I do think we ought to give them some warning that you will be staying – only I was expected."

"Oh, right." Georgiana shifted anxiously in her seat. "I hope Miss Bingley will not be cross."

"Do not worry, my dear; I know she dotes on you," Richard

assured her. "Besides, I have already promised to handle her myself." He grinned, thinking what a fine thing it would be for Caroline to accompany them to Longbourn.

***

In the excitement of Mr. Bingley's unexpected visit, the market had been entirely forgotten at Longbourn. Mrs. Bennet made a loud and affectionate fuss over her eldest daughter, and captivated her youngest daughters at length as they began to speculate on flowers and wedding clothes.

Jane's face was streaked with tears of joy, but nobody's elation could surpass Elizabeth's. She knew that Mr. Darcy must be responsible for this, and that he had done it for her sake. But where was he?

Though Elizabeth was largely a spectator to the chaos in the drawing room, the rest of her family was swept up in the high emotion. Mr. Collins, in particular, seemed affected by the mood, and it began to make his attentions to Elizabeth more than usually disconcerting.

When Mr. Bingley had finished speaking with their father, he sought Jane out directly and asked her to walk in the garden with him. Eager to escape her cousin, Elizabeth offered to accompany them, with every intention of being a very negligent chaperone indeed.

"Of course you must come, Miss Elizabeth," Mr. Bingley cried. "I know you are fond of walking." He followed behind Jane and Elizabeth in the corridor; Jane donned her pelisse, and Elizabeth wrapped a warm shawl about herself. As the ladies both put on their gloves, Mr. Bingley began to laugh. "I almost forgot to mention it, Miss Elizabeth – Darcy told me to tell you something."

"Did he?" Elizabeth dodged Jane's inquisitive look, busying herself with the clasps at her wrists.

"Yes, he means to call here later this morning, and said...." Mr. Bingley furrowed his brow. "Well, something about keeping your gloves on."

Jane laughed nervously. "What can he mean, Lizzy?"

Elizabeth tried to suppress a smirk, and when she had schooled her countenance, she calmly met Mr. Bingley's eye. "Very true, I think. We would not want to be catching a chill; you have only just recovered, Jane."

She strode ahead, briskly leading them out the garden door, and only gave way to her mirth once Jane and Mr. Bingley had begun to stroll together at some remove. Elizabeth walked alone in the garden, keeping near the house, her gloved hands folded behind her back as she slowly moved along the rose bushes. For a few minutes she was content to watch Jane and Mr. Bingley walking arm in arm, their heads bent together in conversation.

Inevitably, her mind soon drifted back to Mr. Darcy, who had made this moment of bliss possible, and even imbued it with some private humor. She had not dared to hope that the colonel's plan would work so beautifully, that the proud Mr. Darcy would ever make such an effort to amend his error.

She began to wish he had accompanied his friend, and as she indulged her imagination, supposing what they might say to one another, she heard footfalls on the gravel path behind her. She closed her eyes for a moment, feeling a pleasant warmth creep into her chest. "I hoped you would come," she said softly.

But as Elizabeth turned around, her dreamy smile fell into dismay; it was Mr. Collins. He gave her an awkward, amorous look. "Cousin Elizabeth!"

Elizabeth instinctively recoiled, but her cousin approached her with his hands outstretched. "I am come – I must speak!" He moved closer, oblivious to her apprehension, and stopped to pluck a flower from one of the bushes. He held it out to her with one hand, his other coming to rest on his heart. She froze, gaping at him, and Mr. Collins lifted her hand and placed the flower there, closing his fingers over hers. She jerked her hand away at once, and he finally showed a modicum of hesitation.

"Sir," Elizabeth hissed. "I believe you mistake me – I did not know it was you there."

He smiled repellently. "Come now, fair cousin, there is no need to be coy; I believe we understand one another. The tears of joy you shed for your sister have made me understand that you must wish to be next, and I see no reason to delay what will complete your happiness, dear Elizabeth."

Mr. Collins lurched toward her, but Elizabeth quickly backed away. "Mr. Collins! Sir, I beg you would return to the house at once. I wish only to chaperone my sister."

Again he took Elizabeth's hand. "Believe me, Cousin – your modesty adds to your other perfections. But of course you wish to follow her to the altar ere long. I am ready to declare myself, for almost as soon as I entered the house, I singled you out as the companion of my future life!"

"Mr. Collins, that was but three days ago," Elizabeth replied, again backing away from him.

"Indeed it was! But before I am run away with my feelings, perhaps it would be advisable for me to state my reasons for marrying."

Mr. Collins clearly *was* overcome by feelings, though Elizabeth had never imagined such a ludicrous thing possible. She struggled to keep from laughing, and Mr. Collins continued his absurd address, detailing at length how Lady Catherine had compelled him to seek out a bride. "You will find her manners beyond anything I can describe," he said with a fatuous grin.

This time she could not restrain her laughter. "I am sure of *that*," she said.

Mr. Collins stammered, and gaped at her. "Your wit and vivacity must be acceptable to her, when tempered by the silence and respect her rank will inevitably excite."

Elizabeth shook her head. "I am sure you are mistaken, sir, I cannot imagine Lady Catherine receiving me with any measure of acceptance, nor should I ever wish it."

"Cousin Elizabeth! Think of what you are saying. You are a gentleman's daughter, and therefore a perfectly acceptable match for a man of my situation – particularly as I am to inherit this estate after the death of your honored father. But do not think I seek only to extend my charity in choosing amongst his daughters – I must now assure you, in the most animated language, of the violence of my affection. To fortune I am perfectly indifferent...."

Despite her attempts to stop him, Elizabeth began to fear her cousin would never cease. "Mr. Collins, please – you are too hasty, sir. I must thank you for the compliment of your proposal – but I must decline it."

Mr. Collins simpered and smirked at her. "I know it is the established custom of your sex to reject a man on the first application; I am by no means discouraged."

"Really, Mr. Collins. I am perfectly sincere in my refusal," Elizabeth insisted. She looked about the garden, but Jane and Mr. Bingley had snuck off together. She was happy for them, but what horrid timing!

Mr. Collins also perceived that they were alone, and he reached for her. "Cousin Elizabeth, you seek to increase my love by suspense, in the usual style of elegant females. You are uniformly charming!" He leaned in as if to kiss her, and Elizabeth was obliged to shove him away.

"Mr. Collins, I beg you would leave me alone this instant, or I will shout for Jane and Mr. Bingley."

"Cousin Elizabeth, I beg you would end my agony, and accept my suit," he said with gallantry, reaching for her again.

Elizabeth's patience was at an end. She recalled the occasion when she had driven him to accuse her of blasphemy by merely telling him the truth about her dilemma, and she was on the verge of doing just that when he seized her hand in his and began to pull at her. "Cousin Elizabeth, I beg you!"

"Sir, it is quite literally impossible for me to marry you!" His grip on her arm began to hurt, and Elizabeth struggled to wrest free. "Unhand me or I will scream!"

***

Darcy spotted Bingley walking with Jane Bennet in a pretty little wilderness beyond the garden, and moved that way to congratulate them, when he heard a scream. He took off running and reached the garden just as Elizabeth ripped her arm out of Mr. Collins' grasp and turned to flee. She stopped just short of colliding with Darcy, who instantly closed the gap between them and took her in his arms. "Elizabeth, Good God! Has he harmed you?"

"Mr. Darcy!" Elizabeth leaned into him, her breathing

ragged. After a moment she drew away from his embrace, but stood very near. "A little," she stammered. "That is, he has importuned me...."

"I think I see," he said gravely, staring down the toady parson, who cowered back, a wild look in his eyes. Darcy looked back at Elizabeth. "Do you require any assistance?"

She shook her head and laughed ruefully. "No indeed, I had everything perfectly under control – could you not tell?"

He laughed softly and took her hand in his. "You have kept your gloves on." She blushed, and he ran his thumb deliberately across her fingers.

Mr. Collins whimpered in indignation. "Mr. Darcy? Of Pemberley?"

Darcy drew himself up into an imposing posture. "Indeed I am, sir, and if you do not cease your unseemly addresses to Elizabeth at once, Lady Catherine will hear of it."

Mr. Collins gasped, and shrank back a little. "Lady Catherine," he sputtered. He looked down at Darcy and Elizabeth's hands entwined, and stomped his foot with a cry of horror. "No! I think I understand – but it is impossible! Oh dear – it must be true. I can think of no other reason my cousin should refuse me, but now I see, I see it all! She thinks to have you, Mr. Darcy – she has practiced her arts and allurements to draw you in! Think of your cousin, Miss de Bourgh!"

Elizabeth slipped her hand free and glared at her cousin. "Mr. Collins! I beg you would return to the house and allow Mr. Darcy and I to speak privately."

"I cannot allow that, Cousin Elizabeth – I cannot let you throw yourself at such a man as this! Can you not see the folly of putting yourself forward with a man so superior in every circumstance – and actually engaged to another?"

"That is a scandalous falsehood," Darcy thundered, taking another ominous step toward the dreadful parson. "Furthermore, it can be no concern of yours. If you know what is good for you, you will leave us at once, and you will henceforth cease to speak of what does not concern you."

Mr. Collins blanched and backed away from Darcy, but turned back to wag his finger at Elizabeth before he scurried away. "Your mother shall hear of this, Cousin."

As Mr. Collins retreated to the house, Elizabeth began to laugh hysterically, and again she leaned into Darcy. He knew he ought not be surprised that she could find the humor in such a shocking scene, and after a moment his own vexation gave way to a shared sense of mirth.

She looked up at him, her eyes sparkling, and she arched an eyebrow at him. "Perhaps I ought not have kept my gloves on."

Darcy laughed, and captured her hand once again. He gently tugged at one of her gloves, until it fell away. "Is that better? Perhaps you might catch him up, before he scampers off to tattle."

Elizabeth smirked, letting her hand rest in his. "I really ought to, before I end up in Mamma's black books for the remainder of the day – then again, she is so happy I doubt even *I* could vex her today." She clasped his hand a little tighter. "I have you to thank for that."

Darcy gazed down at her; he wished to say something eloquent, though his rapidly dwindling sense forestalled his from speaking. In the end, he only lifted her hand to his lips and kissed it.

She blushed and looked away, gently withdrawing her hand. "I am sorry for my behavior yesterday."

"It was natural and just," Darcy replied. "I realize I judged your sister unfairly; it is I who should apologize."

"I had already forgiven you," she said, looking back up at him. She chewed her lip for a moment, and Darcy hoped she might say more, but she only flinched as her mother called her name from somewhere in the distance. "I better go inside," she muttered. She hesitated, then stood up on her toes and kissed him softly on the cheek.

At that moment, there was another sound from the house – Mr. Bennet cleared his throat. Darcy and Elizabeth looked over at the window – it was open, and Mr. Bennet was standing behind it with his arms crossed. He did not look happy.

***

Caroline Bingley received Richard with a little more warmth today, though he knew it was only because Georgiana was present. What little civility she had mustered to welcome her guests soon vanished when Richard insisted she accompany them to Longbourn to congratulate Bingley and the eldest Miss Bennet.

Georgiana handled it all brilliantly; without expecting any explanation for why Richard was so desirous that Caroline should join them, Georgiana sweetly cajoled her into acquiescence.

"Perhaps I ought to go," Caroline finally agreed, eyeing Richard with suspicion. "You will find the Bennets quite shocking – there are a great many of them, and it can be overpowering."

Richard was certainly depending upon it. His primary objective was to afford Darcy some chance to speak privately with Elizabeth, and for all three of them to conspire in solving their shared dilemma. Georgiana could not manage it all; he was going to have to sow some discord. Caroline would do splendidly.

Happily, Longbourn was not far, for Caroline spent the duration of the ride thither insisting that Richard was mistaken – her brother could not possibly be engaged to Jane Bennet. Darcy had not actually said so, but Richard felt sure of it. Caroline's tantrum was going to be tremendous.

As the carriage stopped outside Longbourn and the passengers stepped down onto the gravel drive, Richard saw Charlotte Lucas approaching the house on foot. She perceived them as well and waved in their direction.

Georgiana smiled at Miss Lucas as she approached them. "Is that Miss Bennet?"

Richard looked over at Caroline. "Will you not introduce us?"

Caroline gave him a nasty look, but turned to address Miss Lucas; she was forestalled by the two youngest Miss Bennets running from the house, laughing. "Ugh," she sighed. Then she drew her shoulders back and led Richard and Georgiana toward the house, bidding the other ladies good morning. She performed the introductions, but made no effort to conceal her disdain, and Richard could scarcely contain his amusement. Georgiana, on the other hand, looked mortified.

The young Bennet sisters were oblivious to Caroline's incivility, and after they had admired Georgiana's gown and flirted with Richard, they began to gossip with Miss Lucas instead of showing their guests inside. Richard found it excessively diverting.

"We were just on our way to the village," Miss Lydia told Miss Lucas.

"I am just come from the market," Charlotte replied.

"The market," Caroline repeated, her voice shrill.

"A monthly tradition in Meryton, Miss Bingley," Miss Lucas replied. "I thought it strange the Bennets should be absent."

"You will never believe it," Miss Catherine cried.

"No Kitty, let me tell it," Miss Lydia said, giving her sister an indecorous shove. "Well, Charlotte, what do you think! Mr. Bingley came this morning to propose to Jane."

Miss Lucas smiled. "How wonderful!"

Richard glanced over at Caroline, who was clenching her jaw. She latched onto Richard's arm, her grip almost hurting him. "How perfectly delightful," he cried.

"And there is more," Miss Catherine giggled. "You will never, ever believe it."

"Mr. Collins – that is our cousin from Kent, odious fellow," Miss Lydia laughed, "Mr. Collins proposed to Lizzy, but she would not have him, and then Mr. Darcy came and threatened to fight Mr. Collins, and now he is quarreling with Mamma and Papa for letting Lizzy and Mr. Darcy get engaged. Lord, it was so amusing!"

Miss Lucas smiled, but did not appear to share the Bennet girls' surprise. "Lizzy and Mr. Darcy are engaged? Better and better."

Georgiana latched onto Richard and squealed with happiness. "It is true? Let us go to them at once!"

Richard looked over at Caroline, who still held his arm. She had gone white as a sheet. "Are you well, Miss Bingley?"

"No," she breathed. "I... I need to lie down." She promptly fainted.

***

Longbourn was in uproar, and Elizabeth was at the center of the tempest. Mr. Darcy was still in her father's study, and Mr. Collins was arguing his case to Mrs. Bennet, who began to profess a sudden esteem for Mr. Darcy – and a decided loss of interest in the wisdom of Lady Catherine de Bourgh. Elizabeth had heard quite enough from her mother on the matter of her cleverly catching Mr. Darcy, and when Mary began playing her instrument, Elizabeth resolved to flee the house.

Jane and Mr. Bingley had somehow evaded the madness and were still walking in the garden; Elizabeth did not have the heart to disturb them, and she went around to the front of the house.

There she was arrested by an unexpected and bizarre tableau. Colonel Fitzwilliam was standing near the door, inexplicably holding Caroline Bingley in his arms. Charlotte was there, speaking with a pretty young blonde Elizabeth did not recognize. Lydia and Kitty were scampering off, laughing between themselves as they headed toward the village. Elizabeth scarcely knew what was going on anymore, but half of Meryton would hear of it soon enough.

Charlotte waved and called out to Elizabeth, who hastened toward her guests. "Colonel, what has happened? Is Miss Bingley unwell?"

"Only in spirit, Lizzy," Colonel Fitzwilliam quipped.

Charlotte let out a strange sound, her eyes wide at the colonel's familiarity, while the young woman at his side looked over at Elizabeth in surprise. "You know my cousin?"

With mounting confusion, Elizabeth silently chided herself for the faux pas. "I...."

"We met at the last market day," the colonel said smoothly. "I was passing through the village – just for the day. Darcy introduced us; I remember it fondly."

Charlotte muttered some protestation, but Elizabeth

grabbed her hand and gave it a tight squeeze. She gaped at the colonel, the sudden comprehension stunning her into silence. Finally, Elizabeth broke into a wide smile. "I am so glad to see you again. Forgive me – do come into the house, all of you."

"Thank you," Colonel Fitzwilliam replied. "I should dearly love to set Miss Bingley down on a sofa somewhere."

"Of course." She led them inside, and into the drawing room. "What happened?"

The colonel gently lowered Miss Bingley onto a divan, and she began to rouse. "I believe she was carried away by her joy at the happy news."

Charlotte hovered at Elizabeth's side. "Is it true, Lizzy?"

The young blonde came forward and extended her hands, a shy smile on her face. "Are you Elizabeth Bennet?"

"I am."

"Forgive me," the colonel laughed. "May I present my cousin, Miss Georgiana Darcy. Georgie, meet your future sister."

Elizabeth had but a moment to look at the girl in shock, vaguely considering that she was nothing at all like the proud creature Mr. Wickham had described. A moment later, Miss Darcy wrapped her arms around Elizabeth in a tight embrace.

Miss Bingley sat upright and groaned. "This cannot be happening. I am dreaming, it is all a terrible dream."

The colonel crouched down beside her and took her hands in his. "Do you require a doctor, Miss Bingley? You are very pale – you look positively dreadful. Do you know where you are? How many fingers am I holding up?" He waved his hand in front of her face.

Elizabeth beheld all this with increasing bewilderment; beside her, Miss Darcy let out a sharp breath as if restraining laughter. Somehow, Mary was still playing at her instrument, though Elizabeth only became aware of it when her mother swept into the room, scolding Mary to stop.

Mr. Collins entered on Mrs. Bennet's heels, fussing in a shrill voice, his face red. "When my noble patroness hears of this, she will be most seriously displeased," he insisted.

Mrs. Bennet ignored him. "Oh, Charlotte! Have you come

to congratulate Jane and Lizzy? Two proposals in one morning, what a happy day!" She fluttered her handkerchief for a moment, before belatedly realizing that Caroline Bingley was sprawled across the sofa, and two unknown persons were staring at her with open incredulity.

"Mamma," Elizabeth said, a warning edge in her voice. "May I present Miss Georgiana Darcy, Mr. Darcy's sister, and their cousin, Colonel Fitzwilliam."

"Oh! Well, you are both very welcome! Mr. Darcy is speaking with Mr. Bennet, but you must make yourselves comfortable here. We are all in uproar, happy day!"

"Colonel Fitzwilliam?" Mr. Collins approached the colonel in a posture that was at once groveling and righteously indignant. "I am William Collins of Hunsford," he said.

The colonel grinned. "Hunsford! Not Hunsford, near Rosings, in Kent?"

"The very same, sir,"

"My dear fellow, I am very sorry for you," Colonel Fitzwilliam laughed. "My aunt is a dreadful tyrant."

Miss Bingley gasped, Miss Darcy snorted with laughter, Mrs. Bennet's jaw fell open, and Charlotte reached for Elizabeth with a questioning look. Mr. Collins sputtered stupidly. "I beg your pardon! Her ladyship has shown me the greatest condescension and civility – and I cannot permit my foolish cousin to defy her wishes, to ensnare Mr. Darcy in such a shameful alliance, which is so far beneath his dignity, and an embarrassment to his fair cousin Miss de Bourgh."

The colonel shook his head and tutted at Mr. Collins. "Then you have bet on the wrong horse."

"It is not true," Miss Darcy said, her voice trembling. She looked at Elizabeth in some panic. "William is not really engaged to Cousin Anne."

"Of course he is not," Mrs. Bennet huffed. "Dear Miss Darcy, what a lovely creature you are! I hope you will stay a while and visit – but we must have some refreshments. Hill, Hill! But you must meet my other girls – Lizzy, where are your sisters?"

"Mrs. Bennet," Mr. Collins cried, "I beg you to understand

me, this alliance cannot be permitted. Lady Catherine shall hear of this – she shall put a stop to it. I shall not stay another moment in this house if you do not talk some sense into your daughter, for she would be the ruin of such a great man!"

Miss Bingley roared with indecorous laughter. Elizabeth bristled with rage, and Charlotte clasped her hand tighter.

The colonel laughed again. "Mr. Collins, you really are an ass."

"Colonel Fitzwilliam," Miss Bingley cried, standing up shakily. "We must depart at once – I am not at all well. Mrs. Bennet, where is my brother?"

Again Mrs. Bennet looked at Elizabeth. "Lizzy? Where are Jane and Mr. Bingley?"

"They have gone off together?" Mr. Collins raised a hand to his chest and gasped. "Mrs. Bennet, I must insist you endeavor to control your daughters!"

As everyone continued to speak over one another in increasingly raised voices, Elizabeth cast an imploring glance at Charlotte, who still appeared very much in want of an explanation. Elizabeth could only shake her head in dismay at the scene unfolding around them; she could not begin to make sense of the chaos.

Charlotte eyed Elizabeth with concern and turned to address Mr. Collins. "Sir, I believe I must return home to Lucas Lodge. Would you care to walk with me? If you wish to remove yourself from the house, I am sure my family would be happy to entertain you."

Mrs. Hill came into the room with the tea things, and at last everybody fell silent. She smiled, oblivious to the tension, and on her way out of the room she stopped to offer Elizabeth her congratulations. Elizabeth could only whimper and nod her head.

"Mrs. Bennet," the colonel said, surveying the room as if nothing was amiss, "I believe you were asking after your eldest daughter, and Mr. Bingley – allow me to retrieve them for you." He made a very gallant bow. "Cousin Lizzy, you must walk with me, and we shall bring them back inside to celebrate with us all. No, Miss Bingley, you must stay here and rest, you are looking much fatigued – Georgiana?"

"Indeed, Miss Bingley – let me bring you some tea," Miss Darcy said. She met Elizabeth's eye and winked, and then Colonel Fitzwilliam offered Elizabeth his arm and swept her from the room.

***

Richard feared he had gone too far – Elizabeth was looking wild-eyed and frantic, and after witnessing her temper the day before, he suspected she was not far from another outburst. He could scarcely blame her.

They stopped in the corridor, and Richard offered Elizabeth a rueful smile. "Take a deep breath, Lizzy – we have much to discuss."

Her eyes were still wide, and she nodded absently, her breathing ragged. "You?"

"Yes," Richard laughed. "Most peculiar – but I am sorry for sowing such chaos. I thought to have a little fun with it."

She laughed. "I can well understand the impulse, but I beg you would not do that again. It is already gone so awry."

"It is not yet noon – we might salvage the day," he observed. "That is your object, is it not? A perfect day?"

"After such a beginning – I am engaged to Mr. Darcy – what a disaster!" She took another deep breath, exhaling slowly, and then looked up at him, one eyebrow arched with bemusement. "Does Mr. Darcy know?"

"Do I know what?" Mr. Darcy came around the corner, his expression unreadable.

"That I have brought Miss Bingley with me from Netherfield," Richard said quickly.

"We have been granted some respite from her congratulations," Elizabeth said drily, leading them out to the garden.

Richard studied her curiously, a thousand questions swirling around in his mind. What exactly had occurred between Darcy and Elizabeth this morning? And why should she call their engagement a disaster? He had seen Elizabeth's demeanor toward Darcy the day before; she was far from indifferent to the man.

It was enough, he supposed, that she had not exposed him to Darcy yet, for surely the secrecy would only help Richard ensure the success of his scheme. Feigning ignorance, he clapped Darcy warmly on the back. "Well, you sneaky old devil, I must congratulate you! And Miss Elizabeth, welcome to the family. Look, there are the other lovebirds." Ignoring the discomfort of his companions, he waved and called out to Bingley and Miss Bennet.

When they approached, Richard repeated his felicitations, and this time they were received with all the appropriate remarks. Bingley was nearly drunk on his own high emotion, and Miss Bennet, whose hair was looking very disheveled, blushed as she accepted his familiar praise.

The happy couple's felicity gave way to surprise, for Richard informed them of what they had missed during their walk in the garden. "Well, Bingley, you must congratulate your new brother – and the future Mrs. Darcy!"

Poor Bingley – the man actually began to look past Elizabeth. "Caroline?"

Richard guffawed. "No indeed – the incomparable Elizabeth Bennet has put my cousin out of his misery, is that not so?" He took Elizabeth by the hand, meeting her eye with a wag of his eyebrows as he drew her forward. "I do hope you made him suffer a little first, Cousin Elizabeth."

Her eyes flared wide, and she stomped on Richard's foot as she stumbled forward, before being embraced by her elder sister. "Oh, Lizzy! Can it be true?"

"Well!" Bingley looked flummoxed. "Well done, Darcy!"

Elizabeth grew redder as Bingley and Miss Bennet fussed over her, and all the while Darcy remained stoic. When he did speak, it was only to inform his friend that he and his betrothed were wanted in the house.

"Yes, Mamma was asking for you," Elizabeth agreed. "We shall join you in just a moment."

When Bingley and his lady had gone indoors, Richard prepared to appear surprised at their predicament. Somehow, they still managed to shock him.

Darcy cleared his throat and began directly. "Richard, there is something I must tell you." What followed was not only the same account as the day before, and all the lamentations about the baffling repetition of market day, but the complete shattering of Richard's hope for his cousin.

"You mean to tell me you are not really engaged at all?" He glanced between Darcy and Elizabeth, who were both doing their best not to look at each other. "Why does the whole Bennet family think otherwise?"

"It was an accident this time, I swear it," Darcy replied, more for Elizabeth's benefit than Richard's.

"This time?"

Elizabeth laughed. "Oh yes, it is not the first time I have been thus importuned, and if it happens again I may have to flee the county."

"I cannot see how that would be helpful," Richard observed, giving her an arch look.

"On the first occasion, I came to speak with Elizabeth about our dilemma, and her mother misunderstood the purpose of our private interview," Darcy said. "This morning, once again, I came only to talk, and things took a turn... we have rather lost control of the day now."

"We? Sir," Elizabeth said, "*I* had the situation well in hand this morning – and last time, you deliberately tricked me!"

"Darcy," Richard gasped, making an exaggerated display of astonishment.

"I tricked you because you tried to run away," Darcy said to Elizabeth.

She glared up at him. "*Tried* to. I did not really do it. Twice."

Darcy gestured with frustration at the house. "I have tried to make amends for that!"

"And I am sure I would thank you, if it mattered at all," Elizabeth huffed. "But now that we are tangled together again, it will not last. I really was going to handle Mr. Collins myself, before you came along – I may yet have to take my gloves off," she snarled.

Richard was very near to advising them both to shut up and kiss already, but it was all he could do not to betray any understanding of what Elizabeth meant by taking her gloves off. It *had* been amusing to watch her strike Darcy the previous day, but today he had every hope for progress. He cleared his throat and stepped between them.

"Let me understand – you did not propose to her, Darcy?"

"Her father saw us speaking in the garden, after I rescued her from Mr. Collins, and he presumed...."

Elizabeth gasped, her face suddenly white as a sheet.

"No, not *that* – but, well...." Darcy took a hesitant step toward Elizabeth. "We *were* getting along very well this morning."

"As you should," Richard cried, hoping to reconcile them. "After all – forgive me, but this notion of living the same day over again is difficult to believe – but what if tomorrow *is* Thursday? Would you really break off your engagement?"

"Of course," Darcy replied.

"Absolutely," Elizabeth said at the same time.

Richard did not believe either of them, not with the looks they were exchanging. Still, it became clear that this problem would not be as easy to solve as Richard hoped.

"It will not be Thursday tomorrow," Darcy said at last, after a long and heated gaze at Elizabeth. "Whatever it is that binds us together in this day, we believe it will continue to do so until certain matters are corrected."

"Such as the discord between you?"

"Colonel," Elizabeth said, a hint of warning in her voice, "Mr. Darcy has asked you here for some assistance."

Richard nodded; he would press no further, for he wished her to keep his secret a while yet. "Please tell me what it is you would like me to do."

Darcy appeared to consider. "Elizabeth and I have agreed that Bingley and Miss Bennet's engagement was the desired outcome – beyond that...."

"George Wickham," Elizabeth said flatly.

Richard instantly lost all semblance of composure. "*What?*"

***

Elizabeth led Mr. Darcy and his cousin back to the house; she had no wish to quarrel about Mr. Wickham's significance in their predicament. The two cousins were only agreed upon their wish to shield Miss Darcy from Mr. Wickham – hence their hasty retreat indoors.

At present, Miss Darcy was speaking with Mary near the pianoforte in the drawing room, but Mr. Darcy was eager to remove her to Netherfield. The colonel was hesitant. He had taken Elizabeth's part, and had wanted to discuss Mr. Wickham in further detail, but Mr. Darcy would hear none of it. Elizabeth was fuming, for Mr. Darcy had promised the day before that they would work *as one* to solve their temporal dilemma.

Elizabeth was still embarrassed to find herself in a room full of people who believed her to be engaged to Mr. Darcy, and she hung back as he and Miss Bingley tried to coax Mr. Bingley and Miss Darcy into taking their leave. Colonel Fitzwilliam was giving Elizabeth a great many furtive glances, and asked Mr. Bennet if they might play chess together – the two withdrew to the corner, and Miss Bingley seemed particularly delighted to leave him behind as the others prepared to depart.

When Mrs. Bennet urged her two eldest daughters to walk their guests out, Elizabeth took Mr. Darcy's arm, and they hung back from the others.

"Elizabeth...."

"Sir?"

"I hope we shall be friends today."

"And I hope you shall recollect your promise to me – that we shall make a unified effort to fix what is amiss."

"I have tried," he said with some frustration. "I will try again tomorrow – for your sister and my friend. I will endeavor to avoid that which is so distasteful to you."

"Distasteful!" Elizabeth laughed bitterly. "It is a disappointment that your efforts have been in vain today – and that is all your own doing. But I really think that Mr. Wickham has some role yet to play," she hissed. She looked up and gestured at the front gate to Longbourn; Lydia and Kitty were returning from the market, with several officers in tow. "Here he comes now."

Mr. Darcy made no reply, for his sister had let out a whimper of panic and latched onto him, her face paralyzed with fear. "Into the carriage, Georgiana – now." He did not look back at Elizabeth as he entered the carriage behind her, and she watched the equipage take off down the lane with a sense of dread.

***

Elizabeth was introduced to Mr. Wickham as the future Mrs. Darcy, and his interest was captured at once. Looking entirely discomposed, he tarried as Kitty and Lydia led the other officers into the house, and when they were alone Mr. Wickham grew more serious than she had ever seen him. "Miss Elizabeth, I wonder if we might take a turn in the garden together. There is a matter of great import I would discuss with you."

The colonel had warned her before that Mr. Wickham was dangerous – but knowing that her new co-conspirator was just within the house put Elizabeth more at ease. Concealing her revulsion, she nodded her agreement, but tucked her hands behind her back when he offered her his arm.

If he perceived her apprehension, he did not acknowledge it. "I understand you are to be congratulated- Mr. Darcy is a fine match indeed."

Elizabeth had no wish to delay the inevitable. "Are you much acquainted with him?"

Mr. Wickham smiled wistfully. "I have been connected to his family all my life."

She nodded, thinking carefully. She had already feigned a greater dismay than she felt at her engagement to Mr. Darcy; she would try a new approach, in the hope of gleaning some information to tell Colonel Fitzwilliam. "How fortunate for you," she said.

"It was, in happier times. Forgive me, Miss Elizabeth – I believe I must be perfectly candid with you, as you are soon to join the family."

She smiled wryly at him. "Of course – I should appreciate your honesty."

He nodded and mimicked her posture, his hands tucked behind his back as they strolled through the garden, near the house. "I suspect you observed what just transpired, as your new relations were making their departure."

"I did," Elizabeth said carefully. She waited for his reply with great curiosity, for he had often spoken unkindly of Miss Darcy in the past. Though Elizabeth had not much time to become acquainted with the girl, her impression of Miss Darcy was favorable, even protective, after witnessing her reaction to Mr. Wickham.

"I am sure you must be perplexed; I own myself to feel much the same," Mr. Wickham said at last. There was something very grave about him; either he was an excellent performer, or almost sincere. "I thank you for hearing me – I was too shaken by the unexpected sight of her and her brother to be in company."

Elizabeth considered what she knew of the man – he seemed always to flee after any confrontation with Mr. Darcy or the colonel. But Miss Darcy was just a girl – how could she have unsettled him?

Mr. Wickham continued to gaze earnestly at Elizabeth. "I hope I might confide in you, as you are to be her sister. You may have heard of our connection?"

"A little, yes."

"I can very well guess," he sighed. "I last saw the Darcys this summer, just after the death of my – of the woman who raised me. I sought some comfort from friends who had been like family to me in my youth. My efforts were repulsed in such terms as to leave me feeling myself to be the injured party. In short, I had always thought myself very ill-used by Georgiana, whom I held in my arms as a baby. She is dear to me, and our last parting wounded me, but until just a few minutes ago it had never occurred to me that she might be so dismayed. I would have been less surprised to see anger in her eyes – but the fear and sadness was another dagger in my heart."

Elizabeth studied Mr. Wickham in silence for a moment; he

did not seem to expect an immediate reply. He appeared lost in his own private reverie, and Elizabeth was filled with doubt. "What happened?"

He shook his head. "If she has not told you, I would not presume. Georgiana...." Mr. Wickham sighed. "She was very dear to me, as a girl. I do not like to think I might have pained her – I could sooner forgive her the trouble she has caused me."

Elizabeth could not help it; she was wild to discover the truth. "Sir, might I ask why you are telling me this?"

"I have never seen Darcy look at a woman but to find fault. If you have secured his good opinion, which is so rarely bestowed, you might speak to him – or better still, to Georgiana."

"On your behalf?"

"I only want to talk to her," Mr. Wickham said sadly. "Things were said – I only wish to know why. The history between my family and theirs is complicated, but I do not wish to be their enemy."

Elizabeth found this hard to believe, after the insinuations he had previously made. "I cannot promise to intercede on your behalf, without knowing any of the particulars," she said. If he did not give her some useful information, she would do better to end their strange conversation before her mind grew any more unsettled.

"All will be known in time, but until then, I only wish to speak to my – to my old friend. I suspect I may owe her some apology – there is much I wish to tell her."

This, Elizabeth knew, may prove useful. "I could arrange a meeting, perhaps. Miss Darcy does not mean to stay long in the area – tonight would be best. I assume my sisters have invited you to our aunt's card party this evening?"

"They have." Mr. Wickham looked away. "Thank you, Miss Elizabeth – truly. I am grateful you should even consider it. A few minutes is all I ask."

"I believe it would be best if I conceal this from Mr. Darcy," Elizabeth said carefully. "But I must warn you, it will go badly for you if you give me any cause to regret it."

***

Mr. Wickham did not accompany Elizabeth into the house, which was for the best. Colonel Fitzwilliam had just finished his game of chess with Mr. Bennet, and declared he must return to Netherfield. He and Elizabeth shared a significant look, and he asked her to walk him to the gate, just as she began to offer to do so.

"I must thank you for your discretion, before," he said as they stepped outside.

Elizabeth arched an eyebrow. "I thought I should at least discover your intentions before I expose you. But why should you wish to conceal it?"

"He is a difficult man to assist, do you not agree?"

She laughed ruefully. "Indeed he is. I think you share my opinion that Mr. Wickham must be connected to our predicament?"

"It is too uncanny a coincidence," Colonel Fitzwilliam agreed. "Why did Darcy not tell me yesterday? I would never have brought Georgiana here, had I known that villain was in the area!"

They had reached the gate, but the colonel stopped. "Will you tell me what he will not?"

Elizabeth gave him a brief account of all her interactions with Mr. Wickham in the last fortnight, and the colonel listened with increasing disdain. "He is a dangerous man, Lizzy."

"I have come to believe the same," she admitted. "But today was so vastly different – his seeing Miss Darcy seems to have evoked a drastic alteration in his demeanor. His style of candor today has been more honest than anything else I have heard from him. Mr. Darcy seems to think it sufficient to intimidate Mr. Wickham into leaving the area at once, but I feel that I am remarkably close to discovering what he is up to. Do you not wish to know?"

"Oh yes, I certainly do," Colonel Fitzwilliam said, his voice severe. "But I am not letting that blackguard anywhere near my cousin! Apologize indeed! He would compromise her in an instant, and Darcy would skin me alive."

Elizabeth considered – Miss Darcy had looked greatly upset by seeing Mr. Wickham, but his response had been so strange. "You did not see what I saw – I think she unsettled him, too. I will own, I have seen him bear you and Mr. Darcy a great deal of vague animosity, but I believe he was truly shocked to see Miss Darcy flee from him in such a way. I will not ask what happened – I am sure it is not my concern. But Mr. Darcy's inability to solve this Wickham problem has rather made it my concern – I am quite longing for it to be Thursday at last, you see."

Colonel Fitzwilliam laughed. "I am still rather bemused; it is but my second day. In two weeks I might very well run mad." He let out a heavy sigh. "I do think you are right, and Darcy is wrong – utterly pinheaded, really."

Elizabeth swatted at him. "If you are on my side, we must act."

"With caution," he replied, strumming his fingers on the gate. "Will the dinner at Netherfield happen again tonight?"

"No, that was new, yesterday. We usually all meet at my aunt's card party in the village. Mr. Wickham will be in attendance."

The colonel twisted his face with a look of great concentration. "Hmm. Well, if Darcy knows this, he will never allow Georgiana to attend."

"But he will expect Mr. Wickham to flee."

He nodded. "I cannot allow him to be alone with her – I will not put her at risk, or allow him to cause her any more pain."

"He wishes to apologize."

"He is a practiced deceiver, Lizzy, and will say anything."

"Yes, I know – what he has said to me has changed so much from one day to the next that I cannot make sense of it. Whatever he wishes to say to Miss Darcy must be a piece of the puzzle."

The colonel was silent, but Elizabeth was growing desperate. "She would not have to be alone with him – as long as he *thinks* they are alone. You could be there for her protection – please, ask her if she can do it, if she can get him talking. If he really wishes to apologize, it seems to me she deserves to hear it. What if there has been some terrible misunderstanding? His varying stories do not add up, for one day his mother is dead and the next she is on the hunt for her fourth husband – but I do not think he will lie to Miss Darcy."

"I will be present, with a pistol, and I will be ready to use it on the slightest provocation," the colonel replied.

"Of course."

"And this is all conditional upon Georgiana's agreement – I will not force her."

"I would not wish that," Elizabeth said.

Finally the colonel nodded. "One more thing, Lizzy – Darcy cannot know."

***

When Richard returned to Netherfield, he and Darcy spoke as they had done the day before about their dilemma, though Richard did not betray the true extent of his involvement. He taunted Darcy with feigned incredulity, needled him just a little about Elizabeth, and pressed for details about Wickham.

"I meant to speak to you about the matter," Darcy snapped at him. "I did not expect you to bring Georgiana here."

"How is she?"

"She was distressed to see him," Darcy said. "I did not expect him to appear at Longbourn, or I would have prevented their meeting. I have considered that he is somehow linked to my situation, though I know not how."

Richard scowled. "Elizabeth says you have always intimidated him into leaving the area."

"Sometimes you have done it – but clearly that is not working!"

"Yes, obviously," Richard drawled. "Lizzy thinks you ought to try something else."

"Do not call her that," Darcy growled.

Richard shrugged and poured himself a drink. "She gave me permission." He poured Darcy a drink as well, and sauntered back to the sofa. "Lizzy thinks your methods with Wickham are what has prevented Thursday from happening. Good God, I cannot believe I am entertaining such a notion as reality!"

"Yes, well, the reality is certainly *not* entertaining," Darcy quipped. "And I know Elizabeth is frustrated with me. I made a terrific mess of the last few days. Today was to be the day that put it all right, and I really thought I had achieved it, but...."

Richard laughed. "But you both believe that your false engagement will trigger another repetition, because it is not a part of the optimal conditions you are attempting to create."

"Well, that is true – but...."

"Not necessarily," Richard interjected. "But do go on."

Darcy grimaced at him. "Trust me, betrothal to Elizabeth would be delightful, in some respects, but certainly not *optimal*. But what I meant to say is that I intended to try some new approach to the Wickham problem today – that is the whole reason I asked you to come – but with Georgiana here, I think we must leave it for tomorrow."

Richard sipped at his brandy, considering carefully. He wished to explain to Darcy how very wrong he was, but to do so would jeopardize the plan already in place. "And tonight?"

Darcy's look grew even more severe. "We will attend the card party – it will be something of an engagement party, I suppose. Wickham is sometimes present – it varies, based on how much we threaten him early on in the day. But I cannot chance it – Georgiana must stay at Netherfield."

"No indeed," Richard cried. "If this is to be an engagement party, think how her absence would look. She has visited Longbourn – if she does not attend the party, the Bennets will think she disapproves of your choice. They will be insulted, and Lizzy will be embarrassed. With both of us present, Georgie will be safe." Richard grinned, enjoying the reaction he evoked in using Elizabeth's nickname.

"The Bennets will forget all about it tomorrow – and so will you," Darcy grumbled.

"Well, and by that logic, Georgiana will also forget, if there is any unpleasantness."

"Yes, but I would not subject her to it, even if her discomfort is only temporary," Darcy insisted.

Richard threw his hands up in frustration. Had Darcy learned nothing from the previous morning? "This reasoning must also be applied both ways, you great ponce! You cannot say that the Bennets' feelings do not matter because they will forget the day, and then protest the opposite about Georgiana! Perhaps you do not truly wish to be affianced to Elizabeth Bennet – which makes you a great fool – but I know you care about her feelings, at least. Did you not promise her you would do better?"

Darcy leaned back in his chair, deflated from the argument. "You are right," he said softly.

Richard leaned in, gesturing at his ear. "Pray, what was that?"

"You win – now leave me."

With a great guffaw, Richard clapped his cousin on the shoulder. "Yes, better get your brooding out of the way before the party, eh?" He sauntered out of the room, whistling a merry tune.

***

Richard knew he would need to prepare Georgiana for what was to occur that evening, but there was something else he wished to do first. It was probably folly, but he was like a moth to the flame.

Caroline was on the swing again, and he crept up behind her as he had done the day before – she was crying again, and this time he rather pitied her. "Miss Bingley?"

She spun around and looked up in alarm. "What do you want?"

He shrugged. "Pleasant company."

Caroline gave him a delightfully rude look. "If you are come to laugh at me, I beg you would go away."

"I am not," Richard replied, offering her a handkerchief. "I do not think so ill of you – perhaps you also need some pleasant company. May I sit with you?"

"I cannot think why you would wish to, but it does not matter," she said bitterly, dabbing at her eyes.

She had not actually said no, and the swing was wide enough to admit two, so Richard sat beside her, obliging her to slide over and make room for him. His feet planted on the ground, he gave the swing a gentle nudge, and for a moment they sat in silence, swaying together.

Caroline offered him his handkerchief back, but he pressed it into her hand. "Keep it. Every lady must have some memento of her admirer."

"Do not tease me."

Richard leaned closer as he looked at her. Her hair was even messier than it had been the last time, but he feared that if he reached out to touch it she would flee. Caroline Bingley was beautiful even when she was vexing – and very vexing when she was beautiful. Seeing her in such a state was disarming, but he could not let the moment pass. "Tell me why you are crying."

"I am not crying," she hissed.

He gave her a playful eye roll. "I have never understood why you dislike me – but I had not imagined you thought me stupid."

She laughed in spite of herself and shook her head. "Nobody ever does."

Richard smirked. He was daft indeed where she was concerned. "So, which of the two engagements are you *not crying* about? Does your brother's choice give you pain – or Darcy's?"

Caroline ignored him and leaned against the rope of the swing, staring out into the distance as tears slid down her cheeks. "We should never have come to this wretched place. What a horrid nightmare."

"Such an opinion of country life will hardly endear you to a man of property," Richard observed. Still she made no reply. "I wonder, Miss Bingley – you were so determined to have Darcy – what will you do now?"

She drew in a sharp breath and wiped at her face before turning to gaze at him, her head tipped sideways with a hint of challenge. "Colonel, I have no idea why you would say such things."

Richard leaned closer to her, wishing to affect the same magnetism upon her that she aroused in him. "Because, I wish to discover what is going on behind those pretty blue eyes."

His face was inches from hers, but Caroline did not recoil – she tipped her chin up, moving her mouth a little closer to his as she whispered, "If you kiss me, I will hit you very hard."

A sly smile crept across his face. "Worth it." He closed the distance between them, and gently brushed his lips against hers for a brief moment. Her body was very still, but her lips moved against his for just long enough to excite him – and then she sprang to her feet and slapped his face before running away. It stung a little worse than he had expected.

***

Elizabeth was tense as she stood at Mr. Darcy's side in the receiving line at her aunt's house, along with Jane, Mr. Bingley, and her parents. The two couples received congratulations from all of Mrs. Phillips' guests, though Elizabeth struggled to appear as joyful as her sister.

Poor Jane – all her joy would vanish tomorrow, Elizabeth was certain of it, for today was a massive failure. Again. She slipped one hand into Jane's, and her sister smiled widely. "Oh, Lizzy! What could be more felicitous?"

It was not the first such unanswerable question Jane had asked her since the chaos of the morning had given way to an uneasy calm. Elizabeth brushed her other hand against Mr. Darcy's, and he clasped it tightly. She looked up at him – more unanswerable questions, the foremost of which seemed to be how she was going to get through another night like this.

Mr. Darcy smiled. "I hope you have some cause for happiness, Elizabeth," he whispered.

"Some, yes." Elizabeth did her best to attend to the guests that filtered into her aunt's drawing room, wishing desperately to speak privately with Mr. Darcy, though she knew not what she would say.

When all the guests but one had arrived, Elizabeth moved about the room in a daze, sipping a glass of punch. The morning's events had spiraled beyond her control in so shocking a fashion that she felt as if she was just emerging from the mist of confusion. Her aunt's card party seemed strangely calm by comparison, and for a few minutes Elizabeth sat alone at the periphery of the room, taking it all in.

Her younger sisters were, predictably, speaking to the colonel with great animation, her mother was boasting loudly to all and sundry, and her father was speaking with Mr. Darcy, his face betraying no little amusement. Jane and Mr. Bingley were speaking together in their usual window seat again, while Mary played the pianoforte; Miss Darcy hovered nearby, turning the pages. Her cousin and Miss Bingley were happily absent again, and Elizabeth was only sorry that Charlotte had been obliged to stay at Lucas Lodge, to keep Mr. Collins contained.

As Elizabeth surveyed the room, Miss Darcy met her eye, and whispered something to Mary before moving away from the instrument. "Lizzy," she said with a happy sigh as she sat down on the sofa with Elizabeth. "Oh dear – that is what Richard calls you – I hope you do not mind."

"Of course not. Might I call you Georgiana?"

"Yes, or Georgie – we are to be sisters! Oh, I am so very happy. And I like your mother so much!"

Elizabeth laughed and raised her eyebrows in surprise. "Really?"

"She is so exceedingly kind. She told me that as I am to be your sister, and sister to all her dear girls, I must call her Mamma, since I have no mother."

"Oh!" Elizabeth winced; she could well imagine her mother making such an indelicate comment. "This pleases you?"

"Very much – your family is so warm and kind, and full of praise of you. I hope we are often together at Pemberley! It has been such a lonely place since... well, it has just been William and I for a long time, and we are so far apart in age."

"That must be difficult for you," Elizabeth said gently.

"And William, too. I have not always been the best sister. And then, I was so young, when – he has been more a father than a brother to me. I know I have been a burden. But I think he will like it, having such a lively family now." Georgiana beamed at Elizabeth, who had not the heart to contradict her.

"Mary and I mean to practice a duet to play together at

Christmas. And Lydia and I mean to secretly learn the waltz," she whispered, eyes gleaming with joy.

Elizabeth smiled feebly. Though Georgiana would forget it all tomorrow, it still pained her to see the sweet girl so invested in their lie.

"Have I said something wrong, Lizzy?"

"No! No indeed – I was only surprised. After hearing Miss Bingley's praise of you, I expected…. Forgive me." Elizabeth bit her lip.

Georgiana laughed. "That is what I like best about you and your sisters," she said quietly. "You are all nothing like her. I have long wished that William would marry, but I have feared it would be to – someone like that."

"I can well believe it. Mr. Darcy is so very grand." Elizabeth shuddered, recollecting his haste in assuring his cousin that morning that their engagement would be broken should Thursday finally come tomorrow. She had said the same, but she felt her reasons far more righteous – he was just a snob. A snob who had united her sister with his friend, at last. She sighed again.

"You do not call him William? He calls you Elizabeth."

"I suppose he does," Elizabeth replied. It had long ceased to bother her. "William," she said, trying it out – perhaps it *was* her turn to give him a shock….

"He is very grand," Georgina admitted. "But surely *you* know he is the very best of men."

"I know he is an affectionate brother," Elizabeth owned, remembering their conversations before the madness had escalated beyond all rational discussion. Georgiana knit her brow, her expression clouding. "You did not tell him of our plans?"

"No," Georgiana replied. "Richard said it would be best if I did not."

"He is right, dearest," Elizabeth assured the girl.

"I know. Richard said William will not be cross with me – if we tell him of it once it is past, and he sees that no harm has come to me…. and it is especially important, is it not?"

"It is. We must discover what Mr. Wickham is up to."

Georgiana gave a pensive nod. "If he means to apologize to me, I should very much like to hear it. It would make it so much easier to put the past behind me. William would only worry – he is very protective, Lizzy, of those he loves. And now you are among that number."

Elizabeth forced another smile and looked over at Mr. Darcy. He had assumed turning the pages for Mary when Georgiana had left the instrument, but he was watching Jane and Mr. Bingley closely. Protective indeed – but Elizabeth felt none of the same resentment.

Mr. Darcy looked up and caught Elizabeth watching him. He smiled, a strange expression on his face – she almost thought he seemed to approve of her budding friendship with Georgiana. Elizabeth returned his smile; Georgiana perceived it and let out a happy sigh. "I have never seen him look at anybody in such a way, Lizzy."

"Nor I," Elizabeth muttered, abruptly looking away in embarrassment. She finished her glass of punch and moved away on the pretense of refilling it.

Colonel Fitzwilliam joined her at the refreshment table, a look of high humor on his face. "Cousin Lizzy!"

She gave a playful roll of her eyes. "Richard. How are you enjoying the party?"

"I suppose you would not believe me if I told you I was pining over the absence of Caroline Bingley," he said with a guffaw. "How are *you* enjoying your engagement party?"

"Reminding myself that it might have been Mr. Collins, and not Mr. Darcy, has certainly made it an agreeable occasion," she muttered.

"Well, I am glad that my cousin rates higher than yours, in your estimation," he chuckled.

"I suppose I must give Mr. Darcy more credit than that," Elizabeth mused aloud, watching in wonder as Maria Lucas sat at the pianoforte, and Mr. Darcy stood up to dance a reel with Mary.

Lydia had already begun to drag Denny to the dance, and Kitty was coming toward the colonel, who downed his drink and made a droll face at Elizabeth. He leaned in toward her and whispered, "If you thought as well of him as he deserves – and as he thinks of you – your engagement would last until morning." He gave her no chance to reply and moved away to let Kitty claim him while Elizabeth stood frozen in shock.

Jane and Mr. Bingley had joined the dancing, and even Mr. Bennet had offered to stand up with Georgiana – things grew stranger still when Mrs. Bennet came to speak with her daughter.

"There you are, my dearest, loveliest girl! Oh, Lizzy! How proud you have made us – Mr. Darcy is such a dear man, and his sister – so elegant! She looks perfectly at ease with the girls – poor motherless creature! But now I see just how it shall be – for she will always be wanting to spend time with your sisters, and I daresay we will often be very merry together in London, and Jane and Mr. Bingley too! But I think I must speak with Lydia, you know. These officers here are nothing to the gentlemen she might meet in London, with two such brothers as your beau and Jane's. Oh, I am so happy I shall go distracted."

Without awaiting any reply, Mrs. Bennet refilled her punch and flitted away to speak with her sister. Elizabeth again wandered the room in an agitated reverie, drinking her punch. She watched the dance, her sisters laughing and spinning, and Mr. Darcy seeming to really enjoy being at the center of it.

She wanted to convince herself that he was only being agreeable because their dilemma had driven him to such madness – that he knew it would not matter tomorrow. But Elizabeth had consumed more punch than she ought to have, and the thoughts only swirled in her mind – whatever it was she was supposed to make sense of, it evaded her still.

Fortunately, she recollected herself in time for Mr. Wickham's arrival, just after the reel ended. Mr. Darcy did not perceive his entrance, but the colonel did, and he slipped out of the room. It was time.

Elizabeth caught Georgiana's gaze across the room and made a discreet gesture, signaling the girl that they must act at once. She, too, left the drawing room, letting Mr. Wickham see her go. Mr. Wickham looked at Elizabeth, but she gave a shake of her head as he approached her, and then subtly pointed toward the corridor that would take him to the library. He gave her a sad smile and moved that way.

All this had passed in the space of a moment, and Mr. Darcy's back had been turned while he conversed with Mr. Bennet. After all the praise she had heard of him, and after what he had done for Jane, she had quite literally gone behind his back – Elizabeth swallowed back her guilt and went to speak with him.

***

Darcy felt himself relax as Elizabeth approached him. "At last – it will make a great scandal if we do not dance together tonight," he teased her. "And Richard and Georgiana will be cross." He looked around for his sister and cousin but did not see them.

"I believe they are in the library," Elizabeth said. "You shall have to trust me to speak well of you when they return."

"And shall you?"

Her eyes glimmered with mirth. "Perhaps. It is what everyone else has done this evening. You have apparently charmed my whole family."

"Likewise," Darcy replied with a smile; he extended his hand to lead her to the small set forming in the center of the room. "Will you dance with me, Elizabeth?"

She gave him an arch look as she took his hand, and finally her rosy lips twisted into a merry smirk. "Yes, William."

Darcy drew in a sharp breath, his fingers brushing deliberately over hers as they began the movements of the dance. "You permit Richard to call you Lizzy."

Elizabeth spun with the other dancers, laughing gently. When she turned back to look at him, it was with amusement. "Yes, and Georgiana is calling my mother Mamma. These are strange times, are they not?"

"Would it be so strange, if we were friends?"

"Oh, I hope we are friends," she replied, waggling her eyebrows. "Tonight, at least, we are rather more than friends." Darcy laughed, but Elizabeth blushed and looked away. "Forgive me – I have had a little too much punch – and of course, we have both run quite mad."

"You are not angry with me?"

"No," she replied. "I believe your intentions do you credit, and I have heard such praise of you this evening as I never would have expected in Miss Bingley's absence." She giggled at her own jest, and Darcy chuckled.

"As to good intentions, we were both right. But I have considered the matter of Mr. Wickham, and I believe we might discuss it further tomorrow. I must only ensure that Richard comes alone."

Elizabeth's eyes went wide with alarm, but then she appeared to consider. "Yes, I think it best we speak openly at last. Tomorrow, I believe, much might be accomplished. I hope – I hope the day will begin as pleasantly as today has?"

Darcy took her meaning and nodded. "Of course. I would not wish it otherwise."

Again they spun together with the other dancers, and Elizabeth held his gaze, a gentle smile on her countenance. "Finally we are getting somewhere, William."

Darcy let his fingers caress hers as they went down the dance. "I have been doing some thinking, Lizzy...."

"Oh?"

The kind of thinking Darcy was doing at present was hardly helpful, as he watched Elizabeth's graceful movements. He pushed away the desire stirring in his chest, and replied, "Good things."

"What things?"

"Observations – perhaps a few theories about what would constitute a perfect day."

Elizabeth arched an eyebrow as their hands met for the next movement of the dance. "Such as me keeping my gloves on?"

Darcy ran his thumb deliberately over her fingers. "Not necessarily."

Her eyes flashed with surprise, and she laughed as she looked away. "What, then, would you have me do, sir?"

"I hope you would do as I have done, in accepting suggestions – learning and improving."

Elizabeth screwed up her face and giggled again. "Perhaps I shall do even better and listen the first time."

Darcy gave a significant glance in the direction of Bingley and Miss Bennet. "I hope I am not too proud to admit when I have been wrong."

"Of course not," Elizabeth replied, dropping her voice as she mocked what he had told her at Netherfield. "Where there is a real superiority of mind, pride will always be under good regulation."

Darcy grinned at her. "We are in agreement at last – I see you mean to join the rest of your relations in praising me."

"Ah, but shall you return the compliment?"

"Please advise me what you would most like to hear."

Elizabeth's face lit with mischief. "It may perhaps be difficult for your flattery to surpass Mr. Collins' eloquence. He has informed me that I am uniformly charming, even in my refusal of his addresses, and that my modesty adds to my other perfections."

Darcy knew better than to be surprised that she could make light of what would have been too dreadful for a lesser woman to mention. "I see you begin to regret your choice," he quipped.

They spun a final time as the dance came to an end, and then Elizabeth took a dizzy step toward him. "Do remind me, William, when exactly I made a *choice*."

Undaunted by her teasing, Darcy moved a little nearer, and took her hand in his. As he had done in the garden that morning, he brought her hand to his lips and kissed it, with a significant look. He relished the blush that spread across her cheeks.

"Oh, yes," she replied. And just as she had done that morning, she stood up on her toes and softly kissed his cheek. She let out a heady giggle, her face still flushed. "Tomorrow, William, we must be rational. Promise it."

Darcy was too struck by her gesture to respond directly. Just like every other time he had danced with her, Darcy had forgotten about everybody else present in the room; so, it seemed, had she. How easy it might be, to merely give in to his feelings, to take her in his arms. But he was not past reason, and neither was she. "Yes, Lizzy – I promise."

***

"Darcy, there is something I must tell you." Bingley had retired, and Darcy was on the point of doing the same, but Richard went to the sideboard and poured two glasses of brandy. "Sit."

Darcy did as he was bid, and sipped at the drink his cousin handed him "Why do I suspect I am not going to like this?"

"Because you will not."

"Well?"

"It is about Wickham."

Darcy swirled the brandy in his glass. He dearly wished to be in his bed, ending the day with happier thoughts. "Might we discuss it tomorrow?"

"Something has happened, and you ought to know."

Darcy regarded his cousin, who was shifting uncomfortably in his seat. "What?"

Richard averted his gaze, his face unusually serious. "I hardly know where to begin – you are going to be angry, but I would have you know I accept full responsibility for...."

"For *what*?"

"I wanted to know what he is up to, and it is beyond anything – Darcy, he is claiming to be my brother."

"How do you know this?"

Richard hesitated again. "He told Georgiana this."

"When?"

"Tonight at the card party."

Darcy shook his head in confusion. "That is impossible. He was not present – he must have fled, as he always does...."

"He was there, Darcy, for a little while at least. I allowed him to speak with Georgiana."

"You did what?" Darcy leapt to his feet and towered over his cousin. "How could you do something so reckless, and behind my back?"

Richard stood as well, glaring up at Darcy. "Would you sit down and listen? Surely you do not think me entirely out of my senses."

"Do not be so sure," Darcy growled, but he relented and resumed his seat.

"I was present for their conversation, though Wickham was not aware of it," Richard explained. "Georgiana was in no danger, and she consented to the plan."

"And what exactly was the plan?"

"Wickham claimed he wished to apologize to her for what transpired at Ramsgate."

Darcy was incredulous; Wickham had only ever fled from Richard on previous occasions. "He told you this?"

Richard shifted his gaze again. "He told Elizabeth, and she...."

"What?"

"Damn it all, Darcy, she wanted to help!"

As the realization dawned on him, Darcy recoiled as if he had been struck. Elizabeth had approached him, and said that Richard and Georgiana were in the library, and then she had danced with him, flirted with him - distracted him. "To help! I see. And how exactly is it helpful to allow that villain to spread more vicious lies, to expose Georgiana to any further distress at his hands?"

Richard glared at him. "As I understand it, Darcy, he has been more forthcoming with the ladies than he has been with either of us. Lizzy and I thought it could be useful to see what he might say. He claims to be my brother - is that not of any interest to you?"

"It is not! He saw an opportunity to manipulate the two women dearest to me, and you allowed it, knowing very well I would not approve. You have conspired with Elizabeth, with the deliberate intention of wounding me."

"No indeed, you great blockhead," Richard cried. "I am trying to help you - is that not why you asked me to come here? You might at least hear me out - I believe there must be some significance to what I have overheard this evening."

"Then you are a greater fool than I had imagined, and perhaps I do not need your help after all," Darcy snapped.

Richard strode to the door. "Very well, Darcy - I shall not

come back tomorrow."

"You will if I ask it of you," Darcy drawled, his temper fading into exhaustion. Tomorrow Richard would have no memory of their quarrel or the reason for it, but Darcy could not forget it so easily.

Richard shook his head in disgust. "Do not depend on it," he spat and stormed out of the room.

Darcy leaned back heavily in his seat, his head spinning from all that Richard had told him. He began to doubt his dismissal of Wickham's lies and to regret his anger with Richard. But this was nothing to what he felt about Elizabeth's involvement in the deceit. She had actually taunted him about his failure to solve the Wickham problem, and he had been vain and stupid enough to take it as flirtation. Everything, her use of his name, her kissing his cheek – all this had been a design to deceive him, because she thought him unfit to handle Wickham himself. He could scarcely fathom how he was to face her again tomorrow.

As wretched a state as he was in, things only got worse when Lady Catherine stormed into the house, despite the hour. She had received an express from her unctuous parson, and after failing to persuade "that obstinate, headstrong girl" to end their engagement, she had come to her nephew to make her sentiments known.

Lady Catherine could not have expected to find him in such a state of fury already, but she thoroughly deserved the dressing down he gave her for her unwarranted interference. Even so, it brought him no relief at all to spend his ire, for as Darcy retired for the night, all that was left was hurt, betrayal, and utter confusion.

9

Richard moved through the crowded theater, the hum of the haute ton like a symphony to him after six months of action in Portugal. He knew before Darcy told him – he knew as soon as he laid eyes on the bright-eyed redhead in the stunning blue dress. He wanted her.

The sea of people parted and he went to her directly, hoping to put a smile on her beautiful face, but he never got the chance. He drew her away from her companions – away from Darcy – but before he could speak things went horribly wrong. The Duchess of Cornwall moved that way, and Caroline made a momentous misstep. She fled amidst a peal of laughter, her breath shaky, her hair coming loose as she ran. He caught up to her, as he always did, and offered her a handkerchief to dry her tears. After all, he had seen a great deal worse.

But Richard bumbled through his attempts at reassurance, his humor failing him – and what a miserable failure it was. Every time he dreamt it, the result was the same – he could never find the right combination of words to soften her heart.

Richard sat up in his bed and groaned. He knew it would not do to stew in such thoughts, or he would be too tempted to go back on his word and ride to Hertfordshire. But Richard was in no humor to see Darcy today, despite the temptation of seeing Caroline Bingley. If the strange repetition continued, Richard knew he would have other opportunities to see her, to kiss her, and to perhaps discover if she could ever forgive him of the iniquitous crime of seeing her in a rare moment of vulnerability.

By the time he finished dressing, Richard had received the expected letter from Darcy, and he quickly penned a succinct response before going down to breakfast. Richard joined his father and Georgiana in a more speculative mood than he had done the day before. He was not often prone to such lengthy deliberations – he avoided such heavy thoughts at all costs, as a man who had seen the ravages of war. He preferred to jest and jape whenever he could, but this morning he could not.

Richard began to grow uncomfortable with his companions at breakfast. He caught himself several times searching his father's face for some trace of a resemblance to Wickham, an idea which did not seem as impossible as he wished. Toward Georgiana he felt an equal sense of dread, and he studied her for any hint of agitation, lest some recollection of the previous day dampen her spirits.

Georgiana was perfectly at ease, however; she smiled gently at him. "Are you well, Cousin? You have scarcely eaten anything."

"I am well enough; I slept fitfully, but perhaps fresh air and exercise will clear my head. I know – let us go to Hyde Park together, Georgie. It has been too long since we have spent the day together."

"That sounds lovely, Richard!"

The earl began to grumble. "You could have plenty of both in Kent – whenever you like, you know."

"Not a chance," Richard retorted. "For I should also like *pleasant company.*"

"I will go and get my bonnet and pelisse," Georgiana said, giving Richard a shy smile as she ignored her uncle.

"But we were to call upon Lady Carson," the earl sputtered.

Georgiana paused to consider. "I do like her very much, Uncle. Perhaps... might we not all go?"

Richard shook his head. "Good Heavens, no!"

"She is so kind and amiable – and she has asked after you a great deal."

"That is very gracious of her I am sure," Richard said, letting his father see his real opinion in the matter. "However, I am sure I could tolerate nobody's company but yours, Georgie."

She smiled brightly at him and went to fetch her things, and Richard followed before his father could make any further remarks on the matrimonial advantages of absolute harridans.

The two cousins chatted happily together as they walked to the park, and by the time they reached the Serpentine, Richard was convinced that none of Georgiana's high emotions the previous evening had carried over today. In a way, it was almost a pity – she had been upset, but in the end she had confessed that she was glad to have some closure on the matter.

Even if it was not true – which was a strong possibility, Richard had been glad to see Georgiana hear what she needed to hear, in order to move past the whole ordeal. Of course, that had all been stripped away now.

They strolled along her favorite part of the park, near the water, and after a moment of silently watching the swans, Richard cleared his throat to speak. "Georgie?"

"Yes?"

"I want to speak to you about something of no little importance. I fear it may distress you, but then you have grown up so much since this summer – it may pain you, but perhaps also do you some good."

Georgiana nodded, her countenance hardening. "You wish to talk about... Ramsgate?"

"Yes. About Wickham – his behavior toward you."

"I have already told William everything," she said softly. "What do you wish to know?"

Richard gave his cousin a reassuring pat on the arm and chose his words carefully for her sake. "Well, if you were to reflect back on all your interactions with him this summer, at the substance of his conversation, his intentions... do you think it possible that his behavior could have been borne from any other object, beyond what we presumed?"

"I do not understand," Georgiana said, shaking her head.

"The notion of seduction," he whispered. "You would not have known this to be Wickham's intention, if your brother had not informed you of the fact himself, is that right?"

"Of course! I had no idea – no reason to either fear or suspect – that is, such a scandalous thought would never have entered my head. It all seemed perfectly innocent, at the time. I thought George was pleased to see me, to spend time with me – well, in the way that you might be," Georgiana said, looking up at Richard with a nervous glance.

Richard nodded thoughtfully. "Perfectly innocent," he mused. "Did he give you no indication that he meant to – to woo you?"

"Truly, Cousin, I had no idea of it, until William told me so. I only thought he wished to reminisce on the happy times of our youth. If I had guessed any other purpose than that, it would only be some wish to reconcile with William."

This was not such a surprise, for he had heard as much the night before, hiding behind the screen. Wickham had rationalized every meeting to Georgiana, explained away every circumstance that she had later been told was predatory; she had not been able to think of anything, at the time, that could actually condemn his behavior. But Richard had to be sure.

"Forgive me, my dear, but I must know, beyond any shadow of doubt – was there anything in his actions at Ramsgate that could not be explained by some other motive – anything that irrefutably proves he meant to pursue you as a bride?"

Georgiana appeared to give his question all the consideration he would wish. "No," she said at last. "I do not know why he would seek to court me by acting so... brotherly. I did not understand at all what had happened, until William explained it to me – and I felt so stupid, so utterly naive! I am deeply sorry, really I am, and I shall never do it again!"

Richard stopped and laid a hand on his cousin's. "You mistake me, Georgie – I do not seek to lecture you or blame you. I begin to wonder if your perspective may indeed be nearer the truth than your brother's assumptions."

She let out a shaky breath and peered up at him, her eyes wide and hopeful. "You mean to say that William was wrong? That George was not only after my dowry – or worse?"

"Would it bring you some comfort?"

"It would, if this is true. Can it be possible?"

"I am not yet sure," Richard admitted. "You must tell nobody that we have spoken of this, Georgie, dear. It is only recently that I have begun to wonder."

Georgiana's delicate countenance was unusually pensive. "To wonder what, exactly?"

"If George Wickham might actually be an honest man."

***

Darcy began his day just as he had done yesterday, avoiding the family argument by riding out with Bingley, and he returned to Netherfield after encouraging Bingley to go to Longbourn and declare himself to Jane Bennet. He did not think this day would be the last repetition, but as angry as he was at Elizabeth, he could not allow her to say he had not kept his word.

He had not long to wait before Richard would arrive in the market, but Darcy was forestalled when an express arrived for him from London, almost as soon as he entered the house. It was written in Richard's hand; a sense of dread overtook him, and Darcy retreated to his room before opening it. The note contained but a single sentence, but the effect was devastating.

D –

As I told you yesterday, if you do not like my style of assistance, you can figure it out yourself.

–RF

Once Darcy recovered from the staggering shock of Richard's implication, he crumpled the letter and hurled it across the room. A hundred different questions began to nag at him, all of them at odds with a rage that could not be quelled by the how and why of things. He had to go to Elizabeth at once.

***

Elizabeth had been waiting at Purvis Lodge for more than an hour; alone with her thoughts, she had grown listless and maudlin. For a while she had walked the grounds, let her mind wander. She aimlessly traversed the events of the last two weeks, but it was the previous day that occupied her the most.

It was no small task, to look past the sheer madness of it all, and though Elizabeth tried to make sense of it all, her reflections left her with more questions than answers. The greatest enigma remained Mr. Darcy himself. He had finally seen reason regarding Mr. Bingley, but he was implacably opposed to exploring the mystery of Mr. Wickham. He regretted their false engagement as much as she did, and yet her father had told her before bed that Mr. Darcy had spoken with an almost reverential eloquence of her, that morning in the study. Elizabeth could not fathom why he would do such a thing.

Was his recent affability only performative, an unpleasant necessity of their dire situation, or merely the result of him running as mad as she had begun to do? Why did it feel like they were actually friends?

Elizabeth grew tired, if not physically then certainly in her mind, and after making a full circuit of the park she went to sit on the wide marble steps leading up to the manor house. She began to eat from the picnic basket she had brought along, feeling stupid for bringing enough for two.

It was just when she had begun to give up on seeing him that Mr. Darcy came through the gate. Elizabeth was too weary to walk out and meet him, but she went up the rest of the stairs and waved to Mr. Darcy from the front vestibule of the house.

He met her there, resting his hat on the ornate bricks at the top of the stairs. "Good morning, Elizabeth. I had looked for you at Longbourn first."

"Oh, that accounts for it – I was beginning to fear you would not see me."

"We have agreed we must work together," he said tersely.

Elizabeth was wounded by his tone, which was so different from his open cheer the night before. "Well, that would be easier to accomplish if we can avoid the dreadful charade of a feigned engagement, for we shall never solve our problems that way," she quipped.

Mr. Darcy was silent for a moment, regarding her stonily.

Elizabeth forced a smile. "I had meant to repel Mr. Collins, yesterday, you know. One market day I simply told him the truth of my dilemma, and he accused me of blasphemy. I thought to do the same again...."

"That is good to know," he said blandly; his countenance betrayed nothing, but he was so far from his previous demeanor that Elizabeth grew anxious.

"Well, here we are...."

He nodded. "Yes, I believe we must have some privacy, particularly this morning. We decided last night that we must have a candid conversation, and recent developments have... it will encompass a great deal."

"Yes," Elizabeth murmured. She dreaded telling him what she had done about Mr. Wickham, but she knew she must, if anything further was to be attempted. "Well, I brought a picnic breakfast, but I suppose you must have eaten."

"No," he replied, his countenance softening. "I went for a ride with Bingley, to repeat my endeavors there, as I had promised."

"I suppose it may not matter, but I thank you anyway," Elizabeth said. She had set the picnic basket on the wide marble ledge of the vestibule, and pulled herself up to perch beside it. She withdrew two chinked old teacups from the basket of provisions, and filled them from a canteen of coffee; she offered one to Mr. Darcy. "I hope you do not mind; I have already added milk and sugar. And there is some bacon, bread, cheese, and an apple."

He gave her a forced smile. "You are too kind."

This was hardly true – her offerings were borne, in some small part, out of guilt – and perhaps more affection that she wished to acknowledge. She sipped thoughtfully at her coffee. "I hardly know where to begin – I am dreadfully tired."

"My aunt?"

"Yes, she came again. Was she at Netherfield?"

Mr. Darcy's eyes went wide. "Again?"

Elizabeth winced. "Of course, she would not have come to you the first time, when I appeased her. I ought to have done so again, but...."

"But what?"

"But what you said to my father was... very lovely," Elizabeth said softly. "I had not the heart to abuse you to your aunt again. I did not realize I was only driving her to your doorstep."

"I do not blame you for that – her actions are her own. But there is something of greater import we must discuss."

Elizabeth nodded, and motioned for him to sit with her as she went through the picnic basket. Mr. Darcy hesitated, but finally seated himself beside her on the marble balustrade. "If it is the matter of Mr. Wickham...."

"It is," he said gruffly, and held up his hand. "Let me speak. I realize you may have been drawn in by my cousin – he has a mind for mischief, as I am sure you have seen, and we have both given in to some degree of nonsense since this all began, but I must warn you not to let him inveigle you in another such scheme. He *remembers it*. He remembers yesterday, and writes that he will not be back today. He had played us both for fools."

"He told you?"

Mr. Darcy beheld her with surprise, and then his countenance hardened. "You knew?"

"Yes," she breathed. "And he did not inveigle me in any scheme. If you are referring to what I think – if he confessed it to you, he must have meant to spare me your displeasure, but the idea was mine."

The teacup clattered to the ground as Mr. Darcy rose to his feet. He paced for a moment, anger radiating from his tense posture. "So you have deceived me twice over," he said at last. "I can easily believe it of Richard, treating even this dilemma as a lark, but... Elizabeth, how could you do it? How could you conspire with him behind my back, after berating me for not being more cooperative? I humbled myself, I promised to do better, to work as one with you."

Elizabeth was not unmoved by the pain in his eyes, but she had just as much reason to be upset. "Yes, you did promise it, but you have done nothing about Mr. Wickham. I am sorry for going behind your back, truly I am, but you left me no choice! If I had told you of our plan, you would never have agreed to it."

"Of course I would not," Mr. Darcy thundered.

"And that is precisely the problem!" Elizabeth launched herself off of the balustrade and stormed up to Mr. Darcy, letting her anger match his own. "It has been a struggle with you to accomplish anything – it has taken you two weeks to correct what we must with Jane and Mr. Bingley, after making such a mess of it!"

"And to what end? Twice now they have become engaged, and it has solved nothing!"

Elizabeth let out a snarl of frustration. "That is because the Wickham problem has not been addressed! Twice, and now, apparently, a third time, I will be subjected to seeing Jane's perfect happiness wasted and utterly shattered when the day repeats because you refuse to exert yourself in discovering what Mr. Wickham is about."

"You know nothing about Wickham," Mr. Darcy replied, nearly shouting.

"Then enlighten me, sir! Perhaps it was wrong of me to conceal Richard's involvement in our great mess, but you are clearly keeping something from me, too, so out with it!"

Mr. Darcy turned away, running his fingers through his hair in great agitation, and he began to pace again. "Very well, but I must warn you, what I have to say will be shocking, and I must have some assurance of your secrecy."

Elizabeth let out a sharp breath. "Can you doubt it?"

"No – I apologize, that was beneath me." He took a deep breath, checking his temper before he continued. "He has told you that his father was my father's steward?"

"Yes."

"My father was fond of Wickham, from the time we were boys. He supported him at school, and desired him to join the church."

"Yes. He said that you denied him this opportunity. I have long suspected it is a lie."

"It is. When my father died five years ago, Wickham asked for the value of the living, and I agreed, for I did not think him right for such a profession. He was given three thousand pounds, and I hoped then that this would be the end of our connection, for I knew him to be a man of many vices, not worthy of my father's esteem. That was not to be – when the money ran out, he wrote asking for more, and he was refused. Again, I hoped that would be the end of it. But this past summer, he sought out my sister while she was on holiday at Ramsgate. He recommended himself to her, for she was fond of him in childhood – he convinced her she was in love, and would have eloped with her had I not arrived unexpectedly to visit her. Georgiana confessed everything to me, and I sent Wickham away directly – he was perfectly willing to abandon her when I made it clear he would not receive a shilling of her dowry, which is thirty thousand pounds. This was undoubtedly his object, though injuring me must have been some inducement as well."

"Good God," Elizabeth cried. "That certainly explains her reaction when she saw him!" She took a few steps back from Mr. Darcy and leaned against the balustrade, her mind awhirl. She went over every interaction with Mr. Wickham in her mind, trying to fit the pieces together. But the previous day still made little sense to her. "I wonder, though – did you not perceive his reaction to her?"

Mr. Darcy glared at Elizabeth. "Forgive me, I was more concerned with my sister's safety at the time."

"Of course. But he was so surprised – so shocked at how

she acted, as if he had not expected to arouse such a panic. He told me he had long believed himself to be the wronged party."

"Of course he would say such a thing," Mr. Darcy cried. "He would say anything! He is a liar and a practiced manipulator. Nothing he says can be trusted, that is what I am trying to tell you."

"But we have to try! He is somehow connected to our problem, and we must figure him out. His story varies from one day to the next, but there must be some truth in there, somewhere, and if we do not figure it out, nothing we do shall matter. I am stuck in this ghastly repetition because *you* are not willing to do what needs to be done to fix it, and I cannot allow that! If you are determined to hold us back, I will not apologize for doing what I must to end this awful madness."

"Clearly," he scoffed. "It is always for me to apologize, when you have been just as wrong. You are being a hypocrite, Elizabeth. I have made amends for how I have wronged your sister, but you refuse to admit you have injured mine!"

"Injured her? She agreed to the plan! She wanted to do it, and I am not sorry, not at all, if it might put an end to all this. And you have no right to blame me for not basing my decision on information that you yourself withheld from me! I saw a chance to help and I took it, and even now your cousin might have been here with us, telling us if the scheme bore any fruit, but you have no doubt bullied him, too, and now another wretched day has been wasted."

Elizabeth had begun to pace as she spent her ire, but Mr. Darcy caught her roughly by the arm. "Yes, blame it all on me. Have you ever considered that there is more you might do to help our cause? Look to your own house, and let me tend to mine."

She wrested her arm free and shoved Mr. Darcy away. "Whatever do you mean? Go on, astonish me."

"Your sister Mary – I spoke to her last night, and I think there is something in it you have overlooked. I have seen your efforts to push her at Mr. Collins, over the past two weeks, and I do not think it is the right course. She told me last night that she had seen his true colors, and she was relieved he had not chosen her from amongst you all."

"Oh." Elizabeth was entirely disarmed by his observation. "Very well," she said at last, "I will not promote a match between them. I only thought, if he was determined to have one of us, and keep the estate in our family, that she would be the best suited to him. I will talk to her again, and if she really does not like it, I will let the matter rest."

Mr. Darcy nodded. "Good." He hesitated, and then moved closer and took her hand in his. "I want us to be fair to one another. Can you not understand that you have been blind about Mary in the same way I was blind about Bingley and Jane? I have endeavored to remedy my mistake, and I only ask that you do the same."

Elizabeth let out a shaky breath and peered up at Mr. Darcy. His anger had cooled, and the look in his eyes conveyed a different sort of intensity. She was sorry for deceiving him, sorry even for her own blind hypocrisy, and she longed to make it right. She squeezed his hand and moved a little nearer. "I have always thanked you, have I not, when you have done what is right?"

He raised his eyebrows in challenge, the trace of a smile playing over his lips. "You thanked me yesterday with a kiss, and then got angry when it obliged us to feign another engagement."

Elizabeth felt the heat spreading across her cheeks, but she refused to look away, despite her mortification. "You liked it," she whispered.

Mr. Darcy tipped his head toward her, and Elizabeth parted her lips, her neck craning back a little as she stared up at him. "Yes," he said, letting out a ragged breath.

She struggled not to smile, scarcely knowing what she was about as her hand reached up and rested on his chest. "You have flirted with me, too."

He held her by the shoulders, leaning in closer, until his forehead rested against hers. "Yes. You have been the only constant, the only one who has understood my struggle. A port in a storm. If I have shown you any affection it has been because of our peculiar alliance, but you... you flirted with me last night to fool me, to distract me from your duplicity."

Elizabeth gasped, and leaned into him. "Do not say that, please. You cannot know how it pained me to deceive you – after all the praise of you I heard, from your family and my own, it was like a dagger in my heart." She pursed her lips and whimpered as tears began to fall down her cheeks. "It broke my heart a little bit, when I had come to think so well of you – and you must know, I always meant to tell you, to come clean about it."

Mr. Darcy brushed his face against hers and then drew away just a little. He wiped at her tears, his fingers lingering on her face. "Was any of it real – your behavior?"

She nodded, sniffling miserably. "Yes, of course, William."

His eyes glistened, and he leaned his face toward her again. "Lizzy...."

She knew he was about to kiss her, and Elizabeth could not bear it; she wanted it – but she did not. It was all too much, and with a strangled sob she abruptly pulled away from him. "It does not matter, does it? We cannot even trust one another – and we had promised to be rational today."

Mr. Darcy closed his eyes and turned away from her, letting out a heavy sigh. "Yes, of course – forgive me. It is all getting to me, and I can bear it no longer. We must put an end to this madness."

Elizabeth hugged at herself, still overcome by what had almost happened. She could not bear to think of it, though it was tempting to give in to the insanity that drew them together like a magnetic force. "And what of Mr. Wickham?"

"Tomorrow. I will beg Richard to return; he is a part of this now, so he must come."

Elizabeth nodded. "I am sorry I did not tell you. I am sorry I did not trust you."

"You could not have known the pain he has caused," Mr. Darcy replied. "It pains me still, to see him every day; he delights in taunting me."

"There must be something – the sum of all his lies might hold some sort of truth...."

He came toward her again and extended his hand. "We will figure it out together, you and I – and Richard. We will examine everything, every problem, and we will keep no secrets."

"No secrets," Elizabeth repeated, taking his hand again. A sudden anxiety welled in her breast, and she looked up at him, bracing herself before she could give voice to what troubled him. "Everything is a disaster, is it not? Mr. Wickham, Mr. Bingley and Jane, Mary, and Mr. Collins – my whole family. And I think – Richard said there was trouble at Netherfield – something about a quarrel... I feel as if the world is crumbling around us, and I cannot begin to figure out how to fix it."

He stroked her hand, his face betraying the same sense of helplessness. "There will be another card party tonight, inevitably. We must simply apply ourselves to figuring it all out. We will observe as much as we can, since there is no point in exerting any influence. Tonight we must watch and listen, and tomorrow we will confer with Richard."

Elizabeth nodded feebly, but his words did little to diminish the agitation she felt. He cupped her cheek in his hand and tipped her face up until she would look at him. "We shall conquer this, Lizzy."

***

Darcy had gone to bed with his head full of Elizabeth, and he awoke the next morning exhausted in spirit. He had come dangerously close to giving in to his feelings, though thankfully she had prevented him from being a complete fool. Still, he had scarcely been able to get through the rest of the day, with such a turbulent battle taking place in his heart.

He had written the night before to Richard, assuring his cousin that all would be forgiven if only Richard would cooperate at last, but he had received no reply. Darcy had muddled through the evening in a blur, his mind occupied in worrying what Richard's involvement could portend, and in wondering what might have been if he had kissed Elizabeth. They had been so close; it was sheer torment, for he knew she had begun to desire him as well.

He had discovered little at the card party, as weak as his powers of observation had been, and Elizabeth had seemed just as dispirited. It seemed their hopes for the day hung upon Richard's contribution, and Darcy could only wait for Richard to appear.

Darcy did not go riding with Bingley, for he knew there was no reason to guide him to Jane Bennet today. He had forgotten about the argument, and was still lounging in his pyjamas, staring abstractedly out the window, when he heard the first shattering of porcelain in the corridor. He roused himself from such a stupor and quickly began to dress.

Darcy had managed to forestall the family fracas for several days now, and after his fractious encounter with Elizabeth the day before, this was the last thing Darcy needed.

"Pull yourself together, Louisa," Bingley cried in the corridor. Any moment now, Joseph Hurst would be pounding his door down; Darcy stepped into the hall, giving his friends a quelling look. "What is the meaning of this?"

Jos folded his arms and grimaced back at Darcy. "I think that must be clear, Darcy – it has all been your own doing, and years in the making!"

Darcy had heard Jos' accusations before, though the repetition of days had altered his reaction on this occasion. He hesitated, really beginning to consider what he knew Jos meant to say. "Whatever my offense against you, this is hardly how I would wish to discuss it. Let us go into the library and speak rationally."

Mrs. Hurst sniffled, and Darcy silently offered her a handkerchief. She offered him a feeble smile, her eyes filled with guilt and gratitude, and she hung back as Darcy led the other two men into the library. Miss Bingley did not remain in the corridor with her sister, but followed the gentlemen. Bingley regarded her warily. "I do hope you mean to take my side, Darcy."

"I am sure I shall, but I would like to know first what all this is about, and why Jos holds me responsible." Darcy looked at his old friend with what he hoped was reassurance, and then turned to address Jos. "Explain yourself."

Before Jos could reply, Miss Bingley put herself forward. "Dear Mr. Darcy, you should not have to listen to my brother-in-law's nonsense, this is a petty family squabble."

"Perhaps you are right," Darcy said with an edge to his voice. "But you forget, Jos is a blood relation to me, and if I have done him any ill, I should wish to remedy it."

"You have done us all ill," Jos retorted. "Particularly that one," he added, pointing at Miss Bingley. "Vanity working on a weak head produces the worst sort of mischief."

Darcy had every hope of receiving his cousin earlier than usual that morning, and wished this unfortunate scene at an end, so that he might go to Elizabeth directly. "I suppose this must have something to do with dinner last night," Darcy prompted him. It had been more than a fortnight, for him, since the evening in question, though he remembered it well. "I did not make my own opinions plain at the time, but perhaps I ought to have."

Miss Bingley beamed at him, fully expecting him to agree with her, for what little he *had* spoken on the subject of Hertfordshire was not very favorable. "I am sure," she purred, "Mr. Darcy can be trusted to be reasonable." She gave Jos a nasty look, and turned toward Bingley with impatience. "*He* would never select a wife from such grasping rustics without fortune or breeding, in a remote country backwater. Why should you, Brother? You can do much better than Jane Bennet – can you imagine living with such a family for the rest of your life? Tell him, Mr. Darcy."

Darcy bristled at being commanded about by a young woman who appeared half out of her mind, in such a state. "I believe I must, before you attribute any other opinions to me, which I do not actually hold, Miss Bingley," he said icily. She instantly drew back in surprise.

"I hope I am a reasonable man, Bingley," Darcy continued. "I know that you are. I have given you my advice about the estate – that I think it well suited to you in every practical aspect – but beyond that I cannot speak. I believe I am your superior in this regard, but certainly not in matters of the heart.

If your sister is correct in hinting that your desire to stay in the area is based on the eldest Miss Bennet, my opinion should be of little import to you."

Miss Bingley blanched, while her brother broke into a wide smile. "Well said, Darcy! Thank you for that."

Jos gave a slow, derisive clap. "Taking your high horse down the high road, eh Darcy? How liberal of you, to tell Bingley to be his own man, when you have spent years building his dependency on your almighty wisdom. And do not even start me on the expectations you have given *her*. You have made this mess, you know – but you think to prove your superiority by refusing to clean it up."

"Jos, you cannot speak to Mr. Darcy like that," Miss Bingley snarled.

"He is my relation and I shall say what I choose, Caroline. You can shut up and sit down, or I will remove you from the room and confine you to your chamber until you are grateful it is not Bedlam!"

"You have no right," she said, flying at him. She began to pound on his chest, but he shoved her away; she squawked loudly, but Jos continued to rail at Darcy. "You see what you have done? I know Bingley has been a loyal friend to you, but you have raised him too high, and it has given his sisters delusions of grandeur."

"Delusions," Miss Bingley shrieked.

"Enough," Darcy thundered. "I am perfectly willing to accept some responsibility – perhaps we *all* should – forgive me, not you, Bingley. Your intentions have always been what they ought to be."

"As have mine," Miss Bingley cried. "I only want what is best for my brother, and it is nothing that will be found here. We must depart this ghastly place at once, I beg you."

"I shall call you a carriage this instant," Jos spat.

"I am not leaving without Charles," Miss Bingley insisted. "I do accept responsibility, Mr. Darcy. I have not done my best to get my brother to see sense."

Jos rolled his eyes at her. "How can you, when you abandoned good sense years ago?"

"How dare you!"

Jos ignored her and turned to Bingley. "Why not send your sisters packing for London, eh? We can stay here a while, for the shooting, and if Caroline and Louisa have strangled each other by the time we return to London, so much the better."

"Now, Jos...." Bingley winced. "They *are* my sisters, even when they are cross – and really, I think Louisa is on my side."

"Yes, well, if she had taken your side more often to begin with, and not let Caroline bully you, the little harpy would not be so worked up now," Jos replied. He gave Darcy a dark look, drew a flask out of his coat, and took a long draught.

"When has Louisa ever taken *my* side? She is well-married and has little thought for what befalls Charles and I," Miss Bingley huffed.

Darcy had been waiting with mounting impatience for his companions to spend their wrath and tire of it, but they showed no signs of wearying. "Jos, Miss Bingley, I beg you...."

Jos scowled at him. "You may not want to hear it, Darcy, but you should. You pushed me to marry into this family, and you did not stop there. You have given Caroline laughably high hopes for herself and her brother."

"Charles," Miss Bingley screeched. "Tell him it is not fair – it is not wrong to be ambitious – think of what our father wished for us! Louisa has had the benefit of Mr. Darcy's friendship – and he has certainly introduced you to suitable matches, but I have been given no such advantage!" Miss Bingley now moved toward Darcy, her face red with anger, but her vehement speech was cut short when Richard sauntered into the room.

His countenance was animated and he laughed unabashedly in Miss Bingley's face; knowing Richard as he did, Darcy supposed his cousin must have been listening at the door for some time, waiting for the right moment to insert himself. The moment he had chosen was sure to end in an explosion.

"Come now, Caroline," Richard drawled. "I hope I do not hear that you are cross with my cousin. I am sure he has sent at least one very keen suitor your way. If you chose not to make the most of it, you can hardly begrudge him for not repeating his generosity."

Miss Bingley paled and peered up at Richard, who had moved near her and taken an imposing stance, though his bearing was still cheerful. Bingley laughed nervously and edged toward Darcy with a querulous look. "Colonel, I was not expecting you."

"Did Darcy not tell you? Ah, I suppose he had little chance, with all the excitement here! I hope you do not mind – I am just passing through, but I thought I might stay the night." Richard glanced over his shoulder and winked at Darcy.

"This is insupportable," Miss Bingley cried. "You cannot barge into my home and insult me with one breath and then ask for my hospitality in the next. You are intruding on a family concern, not that it matters."

"No, I do not believe it does," Richard rejoined. "More's the pity."

Miss Bingley balled her hands into fists and stepped toward Richard with a wild look in her eyes, and finally Darcy had reached his breaking point. "Enough of this," he barked. "You stirred this pot, Jos – get her out of here. Unless you wish to heed his advice, Bingley," he added, turning to level a gaze at Bingley. "You need to stand up to her – this is your house."

"Damn you all, I am going to my room, and you can all go to the devil," Miss Bingley cried. She gave them all a vicious glare and stormed away.

"Aye, well, I am going to go drink until I forget why I needed to get so drunk," Jos grumbled. He started to leave but stopped and looked over at Richard, "Our idiot cousin raised her hopes too high, but I should be very glad of it if you still wished to take her off our hands." He hastened from the library.

Bingley fell back against his chair. "Lord, I am damned sorry about all that, Darcy. You shut it down fast enough, Colonel, and I daresay you are welcome to stay as long as you like."

Richard laughed as he relaxed onto a sofa. "And woo your erstwhile sister? Poor Hurst; I daresay he is leg-shackled to both of them, and it is not what he bargained for, eh Darcy?"

Darcy glowered at his cousin. "How much of it did you

hear?"

"Enough!" Richard guffawed. "Forgive me, I have been on a little eavesdropping kick lately."

"Well, you might have rescued us sooner," Bingley said sullenly. "That was unpleasant. You were very quiet, Darcy – you are on my side, are you not?"

"I am, but I wish it did not matter so much. Jos is right, you need not depend on my opinion – and I accept the blame for it. You are your own man, Bingley. Do what you like, and if she gives you any trouble, send her away."

"She will go more quietly if she is made to understand she will not catch you, Darcy," Richard observed.

Darcy's patience was wearing thin, and Richard's cavalier attitude was hardly helping. He checked his pocket watch – Elizabeth must surely be waiting on them. He stood and cleared his throat. "Bingley, my old friend, I hope you know I shall always be on your side. But what matters more is that *you* are. Take some time, think it over. Richard and I have some business – perhaps a ride would do you some good, or a walk to the village. Clear your head and speak to your sisters."

Richard leapt off the sofa and clapped his hands. "Very good! Have some brandy, old chap, it helps in times of dire reflection. Well Darcy, on to more excitement I hope!"

Darcy took in a deep breath and slowly exhaled, trying to put this whole unseemly ordeal from his mind. He had other pressing matters, and after such a row he knew it would be an effort to return to any semblance of serenity. After the previous day's disaster, he would certainly need to check his temper and gather his wits for his next meeting with Elizabeth.

***

Though it was her sixteenth market day, Elizabeth was determined to be optimistic – and useful. The crisis had hit a low point the day before, but she was not so easily cowed, and after taking Mr. Darcy to task for not doing his part, she was resolved to do hers.

The morning began with setbacks, but Elizabeth refused to

be daunted. Mr. Collins was insufferable as ever, but Elizabeth decided to make a study of her ridiculous cousin, and improve him if she could. This same approach was applied to all her family, and though Jane was disappointed that Mr. Bingley was not at the market, Mary was in better cheer after some encouragement from Elizabeth.

The rest of her family was a puzzle to be worked on later in the day, for Elizabeth meant to find Baba Romilda – she had some questions to put to her eccentric old friend. Elizabeth wandered away from her family, searching the village, but Baba Romilda was nowhere to be found. It was enough to drive Elizabeth mad – she began to wonder if she had merely imagined seeing the affable gypsy on the very first market day. But, no – Jane had mentioned seeing Baba Romilda on the day that Elizabeth had spoken with Mr. Darcy and his cousin at Purvis Lodge. This had been the only other time that lightning had struck the village, and Elizabeth knew it must mean something. That Baba Romilda had been in the market when Elizabeth was not present was frustrating – it began to feel like a deliberate taunt.

Though her search did not bear fruit, Elizabeth met with the officers, and she took pains to be on good terms with Mr. Wickham from the moment of their introduction. She had not long to recommend herself to his particular notice before she spied Mr. Darcy and the colonel walking up the high street.

When they were near, it became evident that they meant to approach her, but she gave a subtle shake of her head. She suspected it would be better for her to remain on such terms that Mr. Wickham could be pressed to divulge his secrets, and receiving any notice from them would surely muddy the waters. They kept walking, and Elizabeth could guess where they were headed.

After flirting with Mr. Wickham as much as she could stomach, she made her excuses and discreetly followed Mr. Darcy and Colonel Fitzwilliam to Purvis Lodge. They were waiting for her, not far down the lane, in a place where a gentle slope concealed them from sight of the village.

"Lizzy," Colonel Fitzwilliam cried, giving her an

exaggerated kiss on the hand. Mr. Darcy eyed him warily, which the colonel appeared to enjoy. "We shall get on famously now, only do not mind Darcy – he has had a rough morning. A little domestic squabble at Netherfield, Lizzy, but I daresay we have more pressing matters to discuss." He offered Elizabeth his arm, and she accepted after a hesitant glance at Darcy.

"I am sorry if your day has already held some difficulty," Elizabeth said as they meandered down the lane together. "But I am glad you are come, Richard. I know we must discuss Mr. Wickham, but there is something else I must ask of you, for I have had my own little setback this morning."

"Oh dear, Lizzy," the colonel said. "Whatever is the matter?"

"I suspect it concerns you, too," she replied. "I made a purchase on the very first market day – and so did Mr. Darcy. We each bought an item from Baba Romilda, a very kind Romany woman who is often passing through the village. Right after that, there was a flash of lightning, which struck the great oak tree on the green. I still have the item I bought from her," she said, showing him the silver filigree pendant she wore around her neck. "If the day resets itself every night, why do I still have it? Do you still have your purchase from her, Mr. Darcy?"

"Yes," Darcy said thoughtfully. "I meant to tell you, but there is always so much else on my mind. I have not seen her since then, but – Richard, what is it?"

The colonel laughed as he displayed his cufflinks. "I made a purchase of my own – I wondered why I still had them."

"And lightning struck that day," Darcy mused.

"But he was with us when the lightning struck," Elizabeth replied.

Colonel Fitzwilliam grinned. "Perhaps there was another purchase made – we cannot have been her only customers."

Mr. Darcy did not respond to his cousin's attempt at provocation. Instead he approached the gate to Purvis Lodge, and drew a small knife from his pocket to cut away the vines and pick the lock.

The colonel hung back, and drew near Elizabeth to whisper,

"What a fine joke, if there are others who share in our predicament."

She instinctively suspected there was something in it, but she could not puzzle out what. "If you suspect anything, you ought to wait for Mr. Darcy. We have agreed to keep no more secrets," she hissed.

Colonel Fitzwilliam smiled broadly at her. "No secrets? So, does he know you are in love with him?"

Elizabeth recoiled, trying to look severe. "Please, Richard, do be serious." But the colonel was right. She did not know how he could be aware of it, for she scarcely was herself. Love was perhaps a stronger word than she was ready to use, even in moments of private reflection, but she was far from indifferent to Mr. Darcy. He had asked her the day before if any of her flirtation was sincere – and it was not until that moment that she realized it was. She had begun to like him very much, and without being aware of it amidst the chaos. But she knew that if he had kissed her on the stairs at Purvis Lodge, she would have let him – a small part of her had been wishing for it.

What little capacity she had for rational thought at such a moment gripped at her; now was scarcely the time to examine her mortifying feelings. She would have to guard herself, for as embarrassing as it was to be such a joke to the colonel, if Mr. Darcy were to realize how she felt, it would be so much worse.

"Richard," she said softly, "If we are to entertain conjectures, let them be about our great problem – for now, I daresay, nothing else matters."

Mr. Darcy had busted the lock off the gate, and beckoned for them to follow him into the park. Elizabeth slipped through the ivy-covered gate first, and accepted Mr. Darcy's proffered arm as they moved along the gravel path. She looked up at him, fearing he had heard what his cousin told her, but his expression was unreadable.

Richard took the lead. "Well then! Here we are – let us begin with Wickham. That devil might well be my brother, perish the thought!"

Elizabeth gasped. "Is *that* what he told Georgiana? Surely he cannot think that would justify their elopement – it makes it so much worse, if she is really his own family!"

Mr. Darcy smiled down at her with approbation. "Indeed," he said. "I see no reason to give credit to such assertions."

"Forgive me, Darcy, but you were not there," the colonel retorted. "As charming as it is to see the pair of you in perfect harmony, you ought to listen to what I have to say, for I was in the room with them that night. I should hate to think such first-rate espionage was all for naught."

Mr. Darcy sighed. "You are right – I will hear you. Please, continue."

Elizabeth looked up at him in wonder, and gave his arm a reassuring squeeze, for she could see the effort Mr. Darcy was exerting to check his temper.

The colonel had ceased to laugh at them and grew serious. "I believe I must begin by giving dear Lizzy my heartiest thanks. Your intuition about Wickham is much to your credit – and perhaps to our advantage. What he said to Georgiana that night – I cannot imagine any circumstances where he would have been so frank with us."

Elizabeth thanked the colonel for his kind words, but still she watched Mr. Darcy, for it was he whom Elizabeth wished might express such sentiments. He did not, but only made a silent gesture for his cousin to continue. Elizabeth looked away to conceal her disappointment.

"Your instincts were right, Lizzy," Colonel Fitzwilliam said. "He actually did apologize to her. He did not accept any responsibility – of course, this may be too much to expect from such a wastrel – but he claimed it all a misunderstanding."

A throaty laugh escaped Elizabeth's lips, for Jane had once supposed the same, but Elizabeth could not credit the possibility. "How? Mr. Darcy told me the truth, and if I had known before, I would never have trusted him!"

"Do not mistake me, Lizzy," the colonel said. "I do not trust him, but I do believe him. I spoke again with Georgiana yesterday – she had no memory of the encounter, of course, but I posed some questions to her about Ramsgate. Wickham denied having any romantic intentions toward her, and yesterday Georgiana conceded that it had not seemed that way to her, either, until you suggested it, Darcy."

"She was fifteen, of course she would not know his character as we did," Mr. Darcy replied. "Her naivety hardly absolves him."

"Yes, well, Wickham claimed to have thought she willfully misaligned him to you."

"Oh," Elizabeth cried. "That is what he said to me that morning – that he had thought himself the wronged party – that only seeing Georgiana's distress made him reconsider the matter."

"This is preposterous," Mr. Darcy groaned. "He seeks to malign me again, saying that I misunderstood his reasons for being in Ramsgate. It is a paltry defense – what other reason could he have had in going there?"

"That is where it gets curiouser," the colonel mused, grinning again. "He claims to have sought Georgiana out to reestablish the broken connection to our family. Though he did not confess it, no doubt he saw her as the most vulnerable target, if he meant to insinuate himself into our lives again. What surprises me is his motive. He claims to be my brother, and really seemed to believe his own words."

"Why not speak to *you* about it? I do not see why he would not be more direct about his intentions," Elizabeth said to the colonel.

"Because," he replied, "Wickham has always been a little weasel."

Mr. Darcy cleared his throat. "Did you not say, Lizzy, that he had often hinted he meant to make trouble for Richard and I, to show us up in some way, and triumph over us?"

"That is true," she replied. "And then he was so upset when Richard called him a bastard, and referred to him as a brother in arms. When I think of it now, it is almost as if he resented the connection – or that it was only acknowledged in such terms, and perhaps unwittingly."

"But surely he means to profit somehow from being my bastard half-brother," the colonel said with asperity.

Elizabeth strummed her fingers on Mr. Darcy's arm, thinking over all her conversations with Mr. Wickham – and about him. "Did you not say once that he was on the hunt for a rich wife, that he had misunderstood the situation of some lady in the neighborhood? If he is a fortune hunter, perhaps he means to make his descent public somehow, in the hope of attracting a wealthy wife. Forgive me for saying so, but I wonder he did *not* try to wed Georgiana – his familial claim might have made him think it possible."

Richard sighed. "Georgiana was humiliated, Lizzy. She believed him to be in love with her, willing to run away with her – and she would have done it. He told her he spoke only of future visits to Pemberley, of reestablishing old ties. But there must be more to it. Of course, this is all contingent upon whether or not it is true, and I cannot be so easily convinced that I share blood with that villain."

Mr. Darcy looked very grim. "Have you asked the earl?"

"God, no," the colonel replied with irreverent laughter. "Can you imagine how that conversation would go? I say, Father, did you ever take Mrs. Wickham as a lover in all your visits to Pemberley? It is no small thing, Darcy, to ask your father about his mistresses, though I am sure he has had some."

"It was no small thing to let Georgiana speak with Wickham," Mr. Darcy quipped. "That did not trouble you."

"Gentlemen," Elizabeth said firmly. "Please – we might finally be getting somewhere – do not spoil it with a quarrel."

Mr. Darcy gave her an appreciative smile. "You are right, Lizzy. That sordid business at Netherfield was quite enough discord for one day."

Elizabeth turned away to conceal how it had affected her when he used her nickname. He had called her Elizabeth for more than a week now, and she had grown used to it, but Lizzy felt different. The colonel said it – and she called him Richard in return – but that was nothing more than a joke. With Mr. Darcy, everything began to feel very different; again she struggled to push her mind back to the task at hand, for all she could think of was the embraces they had shared, the most recent one above all.

The colonel laughed again. "I could ask my father, but I daresay he would be offended at the idea of him and – well, Mrs.

Wickham was never much to look at. A kindly woman to be sure, but not handsome enough to tempt my father."

Mr. Darcy groaned, and drew Elizabeth nearer on his arm, his hand briefly resting on hers. Elizabeth had forgotten Mr. Darcy's insult, as if it was something from another life, but he had clearly spoken of it to his cousin. She would not allow herself to ponder what that might mean.

"I think you said she died," Elizabeth ventured. "Was Mrs. Wickham kindly enough to raise a child that was not her own?"

Mr. Darcy knit his brow as he considered. "She was a kind woman, yes. But again, we must think carefully before accepting anything Wickham says as fact."

"He has certainly contradicted himself at times," Elizabeth said, but then she began to reconsider. "On the other hand, it almost makes sense. He spoke of Georgiana as cold and proud, when first we met – but he believed she had falsely accused him of seduction to Mr. Darcy. And then, he did not say his mother died, he said *the woman who raised him*. He has spoken of his mother in different terms, for he told me she, not he, was of a mind for marriage. That she is only forty-two, and is in London setting her cap at a fourth husband. If it were a lie, I should call it not a very good one, for it is most incredible."

"Good God!" The colonel clapped a hand against the side of his head, his eyes wide and wild. "It cannot be!"

Mr. Darcy flinched. "Richard, what is it?"

"The Merry Widow of Mayfair – gossip sheet nonsense – but – oh no...."

Elizabeth looked up at Mr. Darcy in some alarm. "I have heard of her! One morning at Netherfield, do you not remember it? Miss Bingley wished to hear herself speak, and was reading the papers aloud. She read an item about her – Lady Cardew, I think?"

"Lady Carson," Mr. Darcy said, the hint of a smile on his face. "She is infamously lowborn – I have heard it said she was once a servant, in fact. She has been widowed three times, by increasingly wealthy men, and is reported to be a great beauty with raven black curls."

Elizabeth comprehended him. "Just like Mr. Wickham. But

I do not understand – if she is his mother, and so very rich, why would he join the regiment?"

"For many years I discreetly settled Wickham's debts in London," Mr. Darcy said. "I have continued to keep an eye on such matters, but it has been over a year since he has been up to any mischief of that kind. So perhaps he is enjoying some financial relief. But if Lady Carson is his mother, she could never acknowledge him – she had risen so improbably high."

The colonel went pale. "She could acknowledge him if – no, no, no. Darcy, my father is visiting her even now. He has been..." He broke off and groaned. "Courting her."

Mr. Darcy caught Elizabeth's hand in his and drew in a sharp breath; they were both too stunned to speak, and Richard was eerily quiet for a moment before shouting a string of oaths.

***

Richard and Darcy stayed at Purvis Lodge with Elizabeth long enough to contrive a plan, but she remained determined to do as little harm as possible despite the lack of consequences, and had no wish to worry her family by staying too long.

They had some time yet before the card party, and while Darcy went to cheer Bingley – a dismal thought indeed – Richard wandered the grounds of Netherfield. He knew better than to hope for any meeting with Caroline, as Bingley and Hurst had locked her in her room, but he still walked in the direction of her swing. As he moved past the back of the house, he caught sight of what appeared to be white linen sheets tied together, streaming from an upstairs window.

Richard laughed to himself, strangely proud of Caroline. "Intrepid little minx," he drawled, when he found her weeping in her usual place.

Caroline sniffled and glared up at him. "Why are you like this? Must everything be a joke to you?"

Richard deliberately handed her his handkerchief, just as he had done the day before – and the night they met. "Let me sit, and I will tell you," he replied, joining her on the swing as she begrudgingly made space for him. "I am simply doing my best, and that is the truth. I have seen horrible things, and not only at war. The world is a stupid place, I think – it is utterly ridiculous, and I cannot change that – so I laugh at it. I suppose that must be why you despise me."

"I despise you because you are unfeeling," she huffed, dabbing at her face with his handkerchief. "Not everyone finds humiliation and disappointment amusing."

"I am no good at comforting you – I never was. But I am doing my best," Richard said softly. "I think that is why you are crying – because you have only been doing your best."

"If you think so," she cried, "I wonder you did not speak up this morning, when nobody would defend me. You only teased me."

Richard began to fidget, and kicked his legs out to give them a little push on the swing. "I was trying to tell you the truth."

"What truth? When did Mr. Darcy ever introduce me to anyone?" Caroline began to weep in earnest, her face in her hands, and Richard could not bear her distress – or her willful ignorance.

He wrapped his arm around her and slowly drew her toward him, until she was leaning into him and weeping on his shoulder. He stroked her hair in silence, letting it grow disheveled, but the act seemed to soothe her. Finally she began to gasp and sniffle, and her tears died away. "I feel so stupid – I really thought that perhaps Mr. Darcy did not put anybody forward for me because he wanted... but it is too embarrassing."

"Caroline, that was never going to happen. If you think your brother's interest in Jane Bennet is a degradation, if you disapprove of such a thing, only think of the disparity between Darcy's station and yours."

"But it would not be such a degradation if Charles married well," Caroline said, sounding as though she wished to convince herself. Richard only looked at her and shook his head, and she collapsed against his chest in another burst of tears, clinging to his coat as her sobs grew more violent. "I know, I know," she wailed. "I have been such a fool. I have seen the way he looks at Eliza Bennet; I have done everything to make him look at me that way, and I know he never shall."

Richard embraced her and kissed the top of her head. "Are you in love with him?"

She drew back at once, her eyes wide and frightened. "I cannot think why I am even speaking with you. I suppose it does not matter, but you have no right to ask me that. I have the highest respect for Mr. Darcy."

"And so do I, but that is not quite the same thing," Richard said, his feelings churning in a hopeless tumult. "But if it does not matter anyway, I may as well tell you the truth. Only I think it does matter," he said softly, cupping her cheek in his hand as he brushed at her tears. "The truth is that Darcy did do you the same favor as he did your sister – he intended to introduce you to an excellent match, long before you ever thought of him."

"Oh." Caroline's countenance changed, betraying comprehension, astonishment, and perhaps a trace of pleasure.

"That night at the opera...." Richard smiled and wrapped his arms around her again. He ran his fingers over her shimmering diamond earrings, the ones he had heard the Bennet sisters say that Caroline had purchased from Baba Romilda.

"You," she breathed.

Richard let his fingers tangle through her hair as he pulled her face toward his. He brushed his lips gently against hers, savoring the feeling while waiting for her to give in. She kissed him back, her arms wrapping around his neck; she let out a little whimper, and he pulled her into his lap. For a minute they both lost themselves to what had been years in the making; Richard had never known such ecstasy.

When they both drew away, their breathing ragged, Richard smiled widely at her, dizzy with delight. "Darcy would never have done a thing like that," he whispered, and she looked up at him with heady mirth. "I hope to God you remember this tomorrow, for when I come back, we are going to have a talk. Your secret is safe with me, but you had better get back to your room." He kissed her cheek, and then nibbled at her ear. "You have much to consider, I daresay."

He sauntered away, his confidence entirely contrived, for inside he was still reeling.

***

Elizabeth knew what she was about, and smiled to herself as she moved through her aunt's drawing room. Her younger sisters were all dancing with officers – even Mary – and Jane was partnered with Mr. Bingley. She saw her moment to act; tonight she intended to take a lesson from Miss Bingley, and make some improvements to the punch. She drew near the refreshment table and looked about to ensure that nobody was watching as she emptied the contents of Richard's flask into the large crystal bowl.

She discarded the flask, hiding it just under the tablecloth, as there was no reason to bother returning it – for their plan to work, both Mr. Darcy and the colonel could not speak to her this evening. She was just in time, for the reel was over, and Mr. Wickham met her eye. Elizabeth summoned her best seductive look, beckoning him with her eyes.

"Miss Elizabeth," Mr. Wickham said with a gallant bow. "I was hoping to meet with you again." He filled a glass of punch for himself and began to offer her one, but Elizabeth lifted her glass, which she had filled before pouring in the whisky. She meant to keep her wits about her.

"I am glad to hear it," she said. "I began to grow rather envious of my younger sister."

"That may be easily remedied," he said. "Will you dance with me?"

Mary had taken Maria Lucas's place at the pianoforte, and Elizabeth smiled in spite of her contempt as she gave him her hand. "I shall have to make the most of such happy company while I can," she said as they began to dance together.

"I can easily agree," Mr. Wickham replied. He had not taken the bait, but Elizabeth supposed she could not speak as she wished with her sisters so near. She was obliged to make merry with him, sustaining idle chatter even as her anxiety mounted over the course of the dance. He was friendly and open, but Elizabeth would not let her guard down. She wondered what sort of man he really was, beneath the lies – but there had been too many lies for her to really enjoy his company, despite his charm.

After the dance, she got another glass of punch in him, while still avoiding the consumption of any herself. "You are a fine dancer, Mr. Wickham. I knew you would be. I only hope I have another opportunity to stand up with you sometime – perhaps at a ball."

"I hear Mr. Bingley is to give a ball," he replied. "Your sister Lydia told me."

"Yes, I believe so. I only hope it is soon, for I am to go to London next month, to stay with a relation. My mother does not like the plan, for my cousin is rather notorious in Town, but she and Sir Robert were always fond of me."

Elizabeth felt an uneasy fluttering in her chest, for she knew she had raised his interest. There was no turning back now – her courage rose, and she abruptly turned away and sneezed. She glanced up while her head was turned, making sure Mr. Darcy had seen her signal. He gave a slight nod and began to discreetly make his way to the corridor. Elizabeth feigned another sneeze to be sure Mr. Wickham kept his eyes on her and not Mr. Darcy, and then looked back with a nervous smile. "My goodness, I hope I will not get ill before I travel. I so long to see Lady Carson."

He inched closer to her. "Lady Carson? Not Lady Amelia Carson, of Mayfair?"

Elizabeth gave an affected laugh. "The very same." She glanced deliberately at Colonel Fitzwilliam, who was glaring at her as well as Mr. Darcy ever had. "Forgive me, George, but I cannot quite bear the way your brother looks at me," she said softly. She met his gaze and held it, then stood up on her toes to slowly whisper in his ear. "*I know who you are.*"

She let her breath linger on his neck in the way that Colonel Fitzwilliam had scandalously informed her could be quite exciting, saying what she had practiced with far less trepidation than she felt before. The moment was upon her, and now that she was quite sure she was in control, Elizabeth felt she might enjoy what would follow.

She heard him draw in a sharp breath as she lowered herself

back onto her heels, her eyes still locked on his. Elizabeth smiled, pursing her lips just slightly, and then winked at him and moved away. He watched her go, and she paused in the doorway to give him a significant look over her shoulder, and then she hurried into the corridor, knowing he would soon follow.

***

Darcy was crouched in a frightfully undignified position behind the screen at the back of the Phillips' library, which was surprisingly impressive for the home of a country solicitor. He waited and worried, until at last Elizabeth entered the room. "Are you here?"

"Yes," he whispered.

She laughed softly. "This is madness."

"You rehearsed it beautifully," he said, but then fell silent. It would not be long now.

He could hear Elizabeth pace for a moment, and then there were heavier footfalls. "Miss Elizabeth?"

"You must call me Eliza, as my dear friends Charlotte and Caroline do," she replied. There was a trace of mirth in her dulcet tone, and Darcy let out a silent sigh of relief. She was going to catch him out very well.

"Eliza, I have brought you a drink; your aunt's punch is quite delicious. I think we are destined to be great friends."

Her tinkling laughter tore at Darcy's heart as it mingled with Wickham's raspy, provocative chuckle. "Your mother seems to think so. I wrote her that Mamma did not want me to go to London, and I see she has sent you to carry me off! You have my thanks," she purred, laughter bubbling in her voice.

"I fear I must disappoint you, Cousin Eliza. My mother knows of my plans to enlist in the militia, and suggested Hertfordshire for its proximity to Town – she has not mentioned any plan to abscond with a beautiful woman. Indeed, I was not aware that she was expecting a guest in Wimpole Street." Wickham sounded cautious; Darcy closed his eyes, willing himself not to burst out of hiding and call it off at once.

Elizabeth was the cleverest woman – cleverest person of his acquaintance; she would pull it off.

"Oh, you are far from a disappointment," she fairly purred. "She told me you were handsome, but I supposed it a mother's bias. It seems we are both to have a surprise." There were soft footfalls, and Darcy pushed away the repugnant image of Elizabeth standing so near Wickham to speak. "*Surprise*."

There was a pregnant pause, and then Wickham began to laugh seductively. "My mother is a sly creature indeed."

"I suppose she wished us to meet on our own – she ought to have known we would figure her out, for we know her wicked ways," Elizabeth said, her voice like honey. "But a mother does know best, and I am very glad to meet you. Of course, I am sure I shall tease her vigorously when we are together in London, now that I know what she is about."

Wickham's rumbling laughter mingled again with Elizabeth's coquettish giggle. "And what is that, Eliza? Say I fulfill your desire, and carry you off – what then?"

Darcy's stomach turned at Wickham's breathy flirtation; things had begun to go off script. Elizabeth only laughed. "Did you not know that Sir Robert left a generous portion of his fortune to the favorite daughter of his favorite cousin? Dear Aunt Amelia is so devoted to me – and I have had quite the accounting of you! Can you guess what she is up to? I have."

"Yes, I think I see," Wickham replied, a low growl in his throat.

There was more tinkling laughter. "I am rich and you are handsome. It is a combination with such *tempting* possibilities."

Darcy bit back a laugh, his heart swelling to know that Elizabeth could think of him at such a moment – what agonies she must be suffering!

"I am beginning to see that."

"I do hope so. Imagine the pair of us, coming out of obscurity and taking London by storm when Aunt Amelia weds the earl. They have been seeing a great deal of one another, it cannot be long now."

"I do know how much longer I can wait, Cousin Eliza...."

"I am glad to hear it. But, tell me, what is to be done about your brother? We have crossed paths once or twice in London this summer, but I cannot think what he is about, coming here and being so abominably rude to everyone. He is worse than his cousin, Mr. Darcy, who is at least handsome when he is out of humor."

Darcy's breath caught in his throat. He wanted to end this now, and take Elizabeth in his arms, but they were very close to discovering what they needed to know.

"I did not expect to see Richard – if he learned of my plans, he might be following me."

"Surely it cannot be coincidence," Elizabeth replied. "I am worried for you – for us. If he knows your secret, I fear he will prevent it being made public."

"What matters is that it is made known to my father. I should not object to a measure of acceptance from the *ton*, and I begin to fancy taking a bewitching heiress for a wife, indeed – but I shall be happy with less."

Elizabeth began to struggle. "I do not understand – I thought that was the whole point."

"For my mother – she wants the best for me, of course, but on her own terms. I am glad she has thought to put you in my path, very glad – but I would not have you believe that I agree with all her plans. She has been in love with the earl for most of her life – this, and her affection for me, has made her believe the earl will accept me with open arms. I am under no such delusion. The Fitzwilliams think the worst of me – it will be enough to feel acknowledged, when he and my mother marry."

"I see," Elizabeth said, her voice shaking. "That is rather noble of you."

Wickham scoffed. "Hardly. It has crossed my mind that a wealthy wife might make the earl more amenable to a relationship, but I do not expect there will be much money until... God willing, for many years."

"And the colonel?"

"He and our cousin Darcy have some reason for their hostility – the consequence of my wild youth, I suppose. I mean them no harm, though truthfully I shall savor some little triumph when the truth comes out. But they are my blood; I have been jealous, but I mean them no mischief." Wickham sighed. "I do not blame you for disliking them, and once I did wish some revenge on them, but since I have learned the truth – what is the point?"

"I hardly know what to say," Elizabeth muttered.

Darcy silently agreed – he was bewildered by all that he had heard, and the mirth in Elizabeth's voice had given way to gentle wonder. This was far from what they had expected.

"Say it is not about the money for you either. I like you very well, Cousin Eliza, and if we were not both so well in our cups I might kiss you. But I will carry you off to London tonight if you still wish it."

They had got what they came for, and Darcy's unexpected compassion gave way to alarm as he heard a momentary scuffle. He darted out from behind the screen and grabbed Wickham by the shoulder. There was a moment of absolute astonishment on Wickham's part, and then Darcy shoved him away from Elizabeth. "Damn you!"

Wickham staggered backward, his eyes wide with disbelief. "Darcy? What is this?"

"Go," Darcy barked. "Leave, now."

Wickham gaped at them a moment more, then turned and fled. Darcy looked over at Elizabeth, whose face had twisted in dismay. He instantly moved to her side and embraced her. "Good God, Lizzy. Do not distress yourself, he is gone."

He ran his hands down her back, trying to calm her sobs, but Elizabeth drew back just enough to look up at him, her eyes sparkling. She sputtered with mirth, and a moment later threw back her head and roared with laughter. Her empty glass slipped from her hand and shattered, and her laughter increased. "Come, William, do not look so serious!"

Darcy was stunned, but he broke into a wide smile and gazed down at her in wonder, relishing the feel of this bright, beautiful woman in his arms. "You are not upset?"

She shook her head, still giggling softly. "We have heard happy news – and that was the most fun I have had in ages. Do you think me a proper spy?"

"I think you are magnificent," Darcy breathed.

"I wish I knew what to think of you," she murmured.

She brushed her hand against his face in an endearingly sloppy manner, and he captured her hand in his. He slowly moved it toward his lips, and closed his eyes as he softly kissed the inside of her wrist. He heard her let out a shaky sigh, and Darcy looked down at her. She smiled serenely, but her chest heaved with anticipation. Darcy could resist no longer, and he kissed her eagerly.

Elizabeth leaned against him, her hands fumbling in his hair as his lips parted hers and the kiss deepened. Darcy gave in, for a few blissful minutes, before his senses took over. He withdrew and released Elizabeth, but she let out a shaky breath and clung to the lapels of his coat. "Oh," she said. She took another shaky breath, but a slow smile spread across her face. "I am sorry – I think I am a little drunk."

Darcy felt his heart sink in his chest. "I had no idea!"

"Nor I," she laughed. "But I suppose I must have dosed the punch very heavily, for one glass to affect me." Her hands lingered on his chest, and she did not look the least bit repentant.

Darcy was on the brink of throwing all caution to the wind, when his cousin sauntered into the library. "Well, how did it go?"

Elizabeth looked over at Richard with bewilderment, and then back at Darcy. "It was not at all what I expected – but... wonderful."

Richard raised his eyebrows as he took in what he had interrupted. "Is that so, eh?"

"I hardly know what to say," Elizabeth giggled.

"Lizzy," Richard cried. "Saucy girl, you were not supposed to drink the punch. We will discuss it all tomorrow, you had better get home and lie down."

"That sounds lovely," she agreed, her eyes still lingering on Darcy.

Richard gave him a look of annoyance and rolled his eyes. "I am glad you have seen sense, but this is hardly the time," he whispered, and ushered Elizabeth out of the room.

10

The seventeenth market day dawned as dismally as it ever had, and Elizabeth tarried in bed with Mary, her head throbbing. By the time she crept back into her own room, Jane was already stirring, and Elizabeth hurled herself onto the bed. "Oh, Jane," she groaned.

"Lizzy, whatever is the matter?"

It had been nearly a fortnight since Elizabeth had taken her sister into her confidence, and she had not the spirit to do so now. "I am only out of sorts," she replied. "I hope you will not be terribly disappointed if I do not come to the market with you."

"No, but are you sure you wish to stay home? You love market day, and after being cooped up inside for two days, I am sure a walk would do you such good."

"My enthusiasm for the market is not what it once was," Elizabeth said archly. "I may take a walk later, but for now I want only to languish here in this bed. I cannot tell you how much I have missed waking up here."

Jane smiled warmly. "Dear Lizzy, I have missed you, too – but I am feeling so much better."

"I am glad to hear it," Elizabeth replied. She leaned back against the pillows and closed her eyes; though she was far too agitated to sleep any more, she had not the will to do anything but wallow in her wretchedness.

She knew she must walk to Purvis Lodge and face Mr. Darcy and his cousin, but first she must overcome her mortification; her behavior the night before had been unpardonable. She had been so very anxious about speaking privately with Mr. Wickham, and had scarcely been able to eat a bite of her dinner. Then, when the moment was upon her, she had foolishly accepted the highly alcoholic punch he had brought her, and her nerves were in such a state that it had been a comfort to drink it all. This must be why she had actually felt some compassion for the villain – and why she had done what she did next.

Once the rest of her family had gone off to the market, Elizabeth sat up in bed, her knees curled into her chest, and she took the liberty of dwelling on the kiss. Her memory of it was muddled, for she had been quite drunk – but she had liked it very much, and she could not say which fact disturbed her more.

What must Mr. Darcy think of her? He had been against the whole plan, though the colonel had brought him around. She hoped they would not consider it a complete failure, for Elizabeth had rather indulged her own mirth, in speaking with Mr. Wickham, and had not been prepared for the turn their conversation had taken.

Elizabeth had certainly not been prepared for what had followed, but perhaps she ought to have been, as often as she had found herself in Mr. Darcy's arms of late. They had been playing a dangerous sort of game, letting the madness supersede all prudence and propriety, and Elizabeth feared she was in too deep.

She gave into the pleasant recollection until she grew quite flustered, and forced the thought away, else she would never be able to face Mr. Darcy. No, she already had some amends to make for being so half-sprung, for they might have discussed Mr. Wickham at the end of the night and put some plan into action. Another day was to be wasted, for which she had recently scolded Mr. Darcy, but this time it was all her fault.

Elizabeth let out a heavy sigh, threw aside the blankets in a cantankerous heap, and prepared to make her walk of shame.

***

"The twentieth of November."

Caroline let out a sigh of resignation, her teacup clattering against the saucer. "Of course it is. Forgive me, Abigail, I fear that after having unexpected houseguests, and all the rain, time has grown rather muddled for me."

The maid put the finishing touches on Caroline's hair and took a step back. "Of course. Will that be all, ma'am?"

"Yes, thank you." Caroline studied herself in the mirror a moment longer, comforted at least that she did not *look* like a madwoman, and then she willed herself to get up from her dressing table and do what she had resolved to after the shocking events of the day before.

It was still quite early. Caroline liked to put it about that she kept fashionable Town hours – in truth she preferred to draw her morning routine out, taking some private tea as she dressed for the day. She had been coerced into coming to the country, but at least she still had something of her own.

She took a deep breath as she moved through the corridor, smoothing out her favorite day dress before she perched on the top stair and leaned against the bannister. Now she had only to wait, for she knew not when Mr. Darcy would leave his room – it always seemed to vary. Happily, she had come prepared, and she began to read a novel while she listened for the sound of Mr. Darcy's door.

A dozen pages later, she heard the sound of him emerging from his bedchamber and she hastily set her book aside; she was pretending to fasten the lace of her walking boot when he appeared in the corridor.

"Good morning, Miss Bingley. Do you require some

assistance?"

"No, thank you. Just a loose bootlace." She smiled up at him, pulling her foot back under her dress, waiting for him to offer her his hand.

He belatedly recollected himself and helped her to her feet, and she displayed her book. "I meant to take a walk after breakfast and find some scenic place to read."

He seemed surprised. "Really?"

"I should like nothing better," she replied. "And after all, is it not a sort of accomplishment?" She smiled again, recollecting how he had praised Elizabeth Bennet for such nonsense. But for Caroline, he only grimaced. Things were not looking good, but she was determined to press on.

"I am happy to have met with you," she said sweetly as they walked down the stairs together. "I hope you might take a turn in the garden with me before your repast, for there is something I must speak to you about."

"Forgive me, Miss Bingley – I have some business in the village. I am expecting my cousin, Colonel Fitzwilliam. I hope he might be permitted to stay the night, if it is not too much trouble."

"It is a pleasure," she replied, a little more truthfully than ever before. "I am happy to accommodate him – but I would be most obliged if you would speak with me – I do not think it will take so long."

She could see his good manners taking over, and he nodded. "Of course, if you wish it." He offered her his arm and led her out into the garden.

"As you know, Charles and I are not of one mind about Hertfordshire, and I am reluctant to remain in the area. In short, I fear for my brother, and throwing a ball for such people may be construed as a dangerous degree of interest in a particular lady of the neighborhood. I should like to know your opinion on the matter."

Mr. Darcy was quiet for a moment, as if giving the matter serious consideration, and she felt a mounting anxiety in the pit of her stomach. "I can understand why you would be cautious," he began, choosing his words carefully. "I was once rather skeptical about Jane Bennet myself, but I have recently come to believe she is a fine match for Charles. It would be a true love match, I think, and she *is* a gentleman's daughter."

"That is true," Caroline said, trying to remain calm. "But her family is most unsuitable."

"That may be, but how can it affect you? Bingley is only renting here, and he may choose to settle elsewhere. We have often spoken of him finding a house near Pemberley, if ever one would come available. He might see the Bennets but once or twice a year, if he wished it."

"Yes, but if he married a girl with better connections, we might see *them* much oftener, and it could be to our advantage."

"It would be advantageous, I suppose, if he fell in love with such a girl, but he has not," Mr. Darcy replied.

"He has fallen in love before – I cannot let him be taken in! As often as his affection has faded with other beauties, we would be left with nothing once the attraction passed, if he married Jane Bennet. Surely *you* would never be caught by a pair of fine eyes – not when you have such a reputation to consider."

Mr. Darcy shook his head. "You must know that it is not the same for your brother."

Caroline frowned. She *had* hoped to sway him, but that was not her primary object – she knew she had better get on with it. "And could you – be taken in?"

He drew in a sharp breath and halted his steps; Caroline feared she had been too bold. But then he looked back at her, and his countenance seemed to soften a little. "Miss Bingley, I think I see what you mean. I am sorry to disappoint you – but then perhaps it is time we speak of this, and then it may be forgotten."

Her breath caught in her throat, and she gave a curt nod. "I see. You do not mean to offer for me – perhaps you never thought of me."

"No, I never did. I wish you well – you deserve every happiness, but it could never be with me. I, too, desire a love match, although unlike your brother I *must* take care to fall in love with an appropriate woman."

Caroline swallowed back the pain of his rejection and gave a shaky nod of her head. It was what she had feared, but now that the worst was over, she might put it behind her and think of no more – perhaps there may be peace in that, eventually. "Well, thank you for being honest with me. Just to clarify – there was nothing I could have done...?"

He shook his head and offered her a handkerchief, but she waved it away. "I am truly sorry to have pained you."

"Think no more of it," she murmured. "I shall not." She took a step back, trying to keep her composure. "I am sure you must be about your business – good morning, sir." She gave a half-hearted curtsey, and then hastened to her swing.

There she sat and wept, wondering whether the wrong man was interested in her, or if she had simply pursued the wrong man.

***

Darcy set out for Purvis Lodge in a strange mood after his encounter with Miss Bingley. His mind dwelt on what he had told her – that unlike Bingley, he must marry well. He had Pemberley to think of, and Georgiana's future prospects; he could not, unfortunately, make such a decision based on a pair of *fine eyes.*

He very much wished that he could, and under ordinary circumstances he might even consider himself honor-bound after last night. Of course, they had twice now been engaged, and it had been happily forgotten the next day, as if it had never been – and in the eyes of all the world, it had not. But this... this was something else entirely.

He felt no better than Wickham for taking advantage of Elizabeth at such a moment, after everything she had endured in speaking with the blackguard. He had not known she was inebriated, but he knew his behavior was still beyond justification – what must she think of him?

Elizabeth was already at Purvis Lodge when Darcy arrived, laughing and chatting with Richard, who waved and called out to him.

"About time! We were beginning to despair over you," Richard chided as Darcy approached them.

Darcy gave his cousin a dubious look – they seemed to be getting on very well indeed, and he felt awkward at coming amongst them in such a heavy mood. "Forgive me, I was detained. As a matter of fact, it was an odd business."

"Oh?" Richard grinned. "Odder than what we are here to speak of?"

"In a way, perhaps just as strange."

Elizabeth had not yet met his eye, but now she looked up with trepidation. "What has happened?"

"I spoke with Miss Bingley, and I wonder – she was very forthright with me, almost recklessly so. It rather made me think of how we have all behaved in the past, as if there were no consequences for our actions."

Elizabeth looked away and shifted uncomfortably, though Darcy was not sure which part of his speech had disconcerted her. He very much feared that there would indeed be consequences for *his* reckless actions, though he could scarcely ask her forgiveness with Richard present – he was lucky she did not give him a slap.

"Well," Richard laughed. "What a harrowing notion! But you must leave her to me – I ought to make some contribution to our efforts. I will speak to her this afternoon. Hopefully there is nothing in it, beyond her usual presumption."

Darcy nodded. "Good, thank you." He certainly could not bear another conversation with Miss Bingley today.

"Right, then," Richard said, clapping his hands and rubbing them together eagerly. "Let us discuss last night! I am all eager anticipation. Lizzy?"

Elizabeth flinched, a pretty blush spreading across her cheeks, and she lowered her eyes for a moment before looking up at them. "Very well, but I must begin by apologizing for my failure last night – I behaved most irresponsibly. I meant to be so careful, and not drink any of the punch after I tampered with it. Mr. Wickham brought me a glass of it in the library, and I feared it would be suspicious if I did not drink it. I thought it might calm my nerves – I did not realize its potency."

Richard guffawed. "Poor Lizzy! But we can always try again, eh? But surely *some* good came of the affair?"

Darcy gave his cousin a warning glare, and then looked down at Elizabeth, willing himself not to draw closer to her. Finally she met his eye, the trace of a smile on her lips, but not in her eyes. "I ought to behave better – I acted stupidly, at the end, and I am heartily ashamed – indeed, I find myself wishing you both had woken like everybody else, with no memory of my boorishness. I hope you will forgive me for not accomplishing as much as I ought to have."

Though she had squared her shoulders back and held Darcy's eye for much of her speech, he hesitated in formulating a reply, and she looked to Richard for some relief.

"Lizzy, you are an absolute marvel," Richard said; Darcy was sure his cousin had guessed what happened between them, but was relieved that for once Richard would not be so facetious about such a serious matter.

"There is nothing to forgive," Darcy said at last, hoping to give Elizabeth the same reassurance that Richard had. "I am sure I would have intervened much sooner if I had known you were affected by the punch – I would never have... allowed things to have taken such a turn. But at least, I think your conversation with Wickham was not unproductive."

It was the best Darcy could do, but Elizabeth appeared to understand him. "Thank you – I suppose it was quite a revelation. I hope you will not be angry with me when I tell you that I felt rather sorry for him."

Darcy knit his brow, struggling with the same uncomfortable sentiment. This had not been the first time Darcy had heard Wickham make such an emotional appeal – he had tried at Ramsgate, but Darcy had not been willing to believe, or even hear it.

Richard was not at all receptive to Elizabeth's sympathies. "Then I daresay you have not gleaned any useful information, only more lies," he said, his voice harsher than Elizabeth deserved.

Darcy bristled at his cousin. "Let her speak, would you? I

will own I have given it all a lot of thought – you did insist that Wickham would have no reason to lie if Elizabeth presented herself as a powerful ally, and she did an admirable job of it."

"Thank you, William," Elizabeth said, her eyes flashing wide with surprise.

Richard grumbled, but finally relented. "Go on, then."

Elizabeth let out a shaky breath and began to recount the events of the previous evening. Darcy had heard it all, though he had not seen what she had, and the picture she painted for them was a generous one. "I did not like his manners," she admitted when she finished recounting the substance of her exchange with Wickham. "He was forward and leering at times, but I cannot accuse him of being guilty of anything worse. Much of what he said, if true, casts him in a more favorable light than before, for he actually warned me that he was not after the earl's money, and said that he would not wish to, ah... recommend himself to me under false pretenses of wealth. He also claimed to have no wish to harm you, though I might have pulled a little more at that thread, just to be sure. But it seemed as though he really does wish only to be recognized and accepted by his Fitzwilliam relations."

Richard was taking it all in, a look of dread on his face, and he turned to Darcy for affirmation. "Well? What is your opinion of all this? I am far too biased – I have always despised him."

"I can well understand," Darcy replied. "In truth, when he said that we had just cause for our hostility – when he alluded to his misspent youth – it is true that his behavior at Cambridge was often idle, even salacious – but there is more to it. We have resented him all our lives as an outsider. I confess there were times, in my youth, when I feared he might be – but I knew my father loved my mother too much to stray."

Richard gave him a look of pity. "Darcy, I did not know you thought that."

Darcy nodded and looked back to Elizabeth. "You cannot deny that you have done well. I am only sorry that he...." Darcy could not bring himself to say it, for he instantly realized his own shameful hypocrisy. "I heard you scuffling, before I came out from behind the screen. What he said was defensible enough, but that... I am sorry you had to endure such shameful behavior."

Elizabeth looked at him in confusion. "Scuffling? Oh! Oh dear, no – it is most embarrassing. I drank more of the punch than I meant to – all of it, in fact. I stumbled, and he caught me – it was not... it was not he who behaved badly."

Darcy recoiled, stung by her words. He was worse than Wickham – he knew it, and she must think the same. Elizabeth looked away in embarrassment, and Darcy cleared his throat. "Yes – well, let us think upon what we have heard. Wickham did not refute any of Elizabeth's assertions about Lady Carson, so they must be true. He seemed confident that his mother and the earl will marry, though he claims he does not seek profit or public acknowledgement from it. As to his hints that he wished to triumph over us, it seems he means only to force us to acknowledge him as family. I cannot like it, but I had feared far worse."

Elizabeth offered him a weak smile. "I am glad I was not completely taken in – he did have the mark of sincerity about him. You said once that he was a fortune hunter; he did acknowledge that taking a rich wife might make him a more palatable connection for the Fitzwilliams, but if he believed me to be an heiress, as I claimed, he might have deceived me. Would it not have been to his advantage to suggest there was some windfall in his future, when I implied that was what I was after?"

With a heavy sigh, Richard nodded, his shoulders slumping. "I hate to admit it, but it must be true. If this is what was said – and after what I heard that night with Georgiana, and again from her the next day... I am only having some difficulty in reconciling this version of Wickham with the cad we grew up with."

"He admitted to some delinquency in his past," Elizabeth said. "And some jealousy of you both."

"Wickham – my brother. And his mother to wed my father!" Richard shook his head emphatically. "This is madness."

Darcy laughed bitterly. "Everything is."

"So, what next? Tell me what I am to do about this horrid business," Richard said numbly.

Elizabeth tapped her chin thoughtfully. "You wake in London every morning?"

"Yes."

"That could prove useful, if that is where your father and Lady Carson are," Elizabeth said. "You might speak with them, gather information. It sounds as though your father is unaware that Wickham is his son – but that seems improbable. Would he not recognize Lady Carson as a former mistress?"

Richard shrugged. "Perhaps not. There have been many. As to the rumor that Lady Carson is a former servant, I can scarcely credit it – my mother learned after her second lying in that it was not practical to hire pretty housemaids."

"Oh." Elizabeth blushed.

Darcy made a speculative sound. "Since Wickham was raised by the steward of Pemberley, it may well have been a servant there. I think one or two of our staff were relations of Mrs. Wickham, when I was a child. She was warm and friendly with many of the servants."

"I do not know what might be discovered there," Richard replied. "Pemberley is three days' journey – it is out of reach."

"Perhaps – but no!" Darcy broke into a smile as he realized their good fortune. "My father's younger sister did not marry until she was five and twenty – for most of the years before I went away to school, we spent more time in London than at Pemberley – I am sure my mother chaperoned Aunt Violet through six or seven seasons. My father kept a set of ledgers at the London house for convenience, and I believe they are there still. I have never removed them. There may be some records of servants employed by my family twenty-six years ago. If the books go back to eighty-six, there may be some record of a servant called Amelia, who might have been about sixteen. Mrs. Wickham's maiden name was... Thorne? Thornton? I recall it was a common name in Lambton."

"If I find anything, I can take a look in my father's books. I suspect there might be a payoff sum from around that time."

Richard tucked his arms behind his back and began to pace. "And when I review the records of servants, perhaps I might discern if there are any former staff who currently reside in London, that I might speak with – see what they know of any dalliance. For now we have only Wickham's word, and for me it is not enough."

Elizabeth was listening intently to Richard's plan, when suddenly she exclaimed, "Oh! Thorne – yes. Forgive me, my favorite aunt, Mrs. Gardiner, was once a Thorne– and I believe she grew up in Lambton. If it is a common name in the area, she may be a cousin of the late Mrs. Wickham – perhaps she may know whom they adopted their child from. Indeed, my aunt would have been about the same age, perhaps sixteen or seventeen – she was apparently quite popular in the village, as the parson's daughter and an absolute angel. She might even have been friends with Lady Carson, or at least acquainted with her. Whoever she was at the time."

Darcy fairly gaped at Elizabeth. "Not Madeline Thorne? The apple tart queen!"

Elizabeth laughed. "She does not do much baking in London anymore, for my uncle keeps a cook, but yes, she knows what she is about with pastries."

"They were my favorite part of summer as a boy, for we were always at Pemberley for the annual village fair – those apple tarts won the prize every year."

"I have heard this many times," Elizabeth said, betraying genuine mirth for the first time that morning.

Darcy could feel some of the tension in his body release. "I recall you saying they lived in London."

"Tell me where, and I shall visit her," Richard said. "If not for information, for the tarts – I remember them well. One year, Darcy, you got such a scolding for spoiling your dinner!"

Elizabeth held her chin up high. "Gracechurch Street, number fifty-seven."

"Capital! Shall I convey your regards?"

"Please do! Oh, I long to see her, for if time had passed as it ought to have, my aunt and uncle and their children would all be soon to arrive for their Christmas visit."

Darcy was struck by the odd notion – it ought to be well into December by now. "Surely we are near the end of this awful business now – I think we are really getting somewhere."

"Yes, but I may have to spend several days in London," Richard replied. "To review your father's records, speak with my father and Lady Carson, and perhaps track down some other former servants, and then call on the Gardiners – it will take time, and I would rather spare myself the daily journey with so much to do in London."

"Begin tomorrow," Darcy replied. "We must have done with this whole sordid mess."

Richard nodded, laughing ruefully. "I shall. Still, it is a pity, as I suspect I shall be leaving some unfinished business here, but I cannot be in two places at once."

***

There was one place in particular Richard wished to be, and he went there directly when he returned to Netherfield with Darcy. He sought out Caroline on the swing behind the garden, for he had promised Darcy to speak to her, and Richard hoped to discover that his cousin's suspicion was true. The earrings had been a small thing, but her behavior was certainly suspect. And of course, there was a great deal more he might say to her if she remembered their last encounter.

She was just where he expected to find her, but her face was red from weeping, and she looked half-mad. "Caroline, what has happened?"

She looked up at him in torment. "I have been waiting for you. I... I... oh, it is too awful!"

Richard sat down beside her and took her hand in his. "Yesterday?"

The color drained from her face. "How? How is this happening? You – you know of it?"

Richard chuckled. "Yes."

Tears slid down her cheeks. "Why is this happening? Oh God, I have been afraid for days that I had gone truly insane. Is it all – real?"

He entwined his fingers with hers and smiled sadly. "It is, I think. It has been, what, five days?"

"Yes. The morning that the lightning struck."

"Ah, yes," Richard replied, recollecting Darcy and Elizabeth's strange reaction at the time. "That accounts for it. Did you not suspect me before yesterday?"

"No, not at all. I have been so preoccupied with my own circumstances – I had never considered that anyone else was repeating the day. Everyone has varied so much from one day to the next, and I scarcely know what to make of it."

"True," Richard said, delighted that she still allowed him to hold her hand. It was a small miracle. "I did notice your earrings, which Jane Bennet observed on the first day – that you had bought that day. How do you still have them?"

"I had wondered about it," she admitted. "It is so odd, for the lightning struck just after I purchased them from that bizarre gypsy Miss Bennet was so keen to dote upon."

"I purchased these cufflinks from her that same morning," Richard said. "She must have something to do with it."

"What? Do you mean to suggest she put some sort of spell on us?" She wrinkled her nose with disdain.

Richard laughed at her indignation. "It is just what I like – romantic, in a way – yet frightening. Perhaps there is some sort of enchantment being worked upon us."

Caroline withdrew her hand and swatted at him. "Must you always talk nonsense? This is quite serious!"

"I agree – and as fate would have it, we must puzzle it all out together. Perhaps you might track the old woman down in the village again. I must go to London – or rather, I must remain there, for a few days."

She actually looked a little disappointed. "Why?"

"Business – well, family business – it is complicated. But I have come to believe that this is happening for some reason; one reason, I believe, has to do with my brother, and therefore I must attend to certain matters at home."

She nodded thoughtfully. "But there are other reasons?"

"I think you know there are," Richard said softly, reaching up to brush at her disheveled hair. "We cannot pretend that yesterday did not happen – and the day before that, and the day before that...." He leaned in close to her, their lips nearly touching, but then he tipped his chin up and gently kissed her forehead, his hands cupping her face. "Can you not see some reason we should be trapped in this predicament together?"

Caroline let out a shaky breath, averting her gaze. "Colonel...."

"Richard."

"Richard, I... I did something rather foolish this morning."

"Astonishing."

She frowned. "Do not tease me."

He shook his head and laughed. "When will I ever learn?" He wrapped his arm around her, and she leaned in to rest her head on his shoulder. "Go on, then. I will be good, I swear it."

Caroline drew in a deep breath and slowly released it. "I *had* considered that I had some purpose to accomplish – only mine, I thought, was to be gone from Hertfordshire. I had thought to convince Charles to leave Netherfield, to abandon Jane Bennet. I had also thought – oh, it is too embarrassing." Caroline began to cry again, and Richard offered her the same handkerchief he had given her the past three days.

"I think I can guess the rest. The way you spoke yesterday of Darcy...."

"Yes," Caroline groaned. "I asked him all about it – about Charles and Jane, and him and I, and he is entirely wrong about all of it, but there is nothing I can do."

"I see," Richard replied – he could well understand, now, why Darcy had been suspicious. But it was a fine thing that Richard had offered to speak with her himself – better that Darcy and Elizabeth remain in ignorance until he returned from London. "I hope you will not do anything like that again. You ought to try and accept it."

"How can I? How can I let go of hopes I have cherished for so long, for Charles and for myself? How can I ever face Mr. Darcy again? It is so humiliating!"

"Will he remember it tomorrow?" Richard gave her a sly smile.

"I supposed that is a relief," Caroline muttered. "It is the only reason I had the courage to ask – to risk...."

Richard stroked her cheek. "I shall ask you again, because you would not give me a straight answer yesterday. Are you in love with Darcy?"

Caroline drew her shoulders back and pulled away from him. "I could never really love any man who preferred another."

"Could you love a man who has admired you from the moment he laid eyes upon you? A man who has seen you at your worst and still found you utterly beguiling?" Richard gazed at her, half hoping that if she could not, she would at least finally say something cruel enough to end his attraction to her once and for all.

She peered over at him, her eyes searching his. "Is that really true?"

Richard gave her the surest answer he could; he wrapped his arms around her and kissed her more passionately than he had done in the days before, wildly tugging every last pin from her hair, until he could wind his fingers freely through it as she arched her body into his.

He drew back at last, fairly gasping for breath, and slowly whispered her name. She leaned into him, her arms still around his neck as she rested her head on his chest. "This makes no sense. I do not like you."

"Yes, you do."

"Perhaps," she huffed. "I will concede that I never felt such passion for Mr. Darcy – I never thought of anything like this, not with him."

"I thought not."

"It is a small relief, at least, that Eliza Bennet will not have him. I do not know how they came to be engaged three days past, but I suspect there was some mischief in it, for he told me this morning that she is beneath him, and he will not stoop so low in marriage."

Richard recoiled in dismay. "He said this?"

"Yes. I told you, I was quite impertinent."

"That is disappointing, for I quite like her – I thought them very well matched. And if Bingley does marry her sister –

well, we might all be one big, happy family."

Caroline screwed up her face. "Ugh."

"Well, you ought to think upon it while I am away," Richard said.

"Must you really stay away for several days?"

He laughed, delighted at the hint of sadness in her voice. "Dare I hope you will miss me?"

She shrugged, pursing her lips in a very fetching pout, and Richard kissed her again. She was responsive, but drew back after a moment. "Perhaps it is best – this is so… sudden. And everything is completely mad – I really must think about it."

Richard was impressed. "I think it right. Indeed, I should like it if you think a great deal upon the times we have spent here on this charming swing. I know I will – and I shall be hoping for more."

Caroline met his gaze with a saucy smirk. "Good, I think." She blushed. "Damn and blast, I do not like you! But do I?"

Richard threw back his head and laughed. "I am growing on you – excellent!"

She gave him a gentle shove. "I am rather stuck with you, I suppose."

"Tease me all you like, you vexing minx – I will not complain."

Caroline rolled her eyes and stuck out her tongue at him. "When will you come back?"

"Three or four days. Shall I write you? Your reputation will survive it."

"That is hardly necessary," she quipped. "I am sure I shall endure the separation."

"I hope it passes quickly," Richard replied, taking her hand and giving it a gentle kiss. "And productively. I daresay you have a great deal to think upon – just as I have certain matters to attend to, I believe you do as well. Truly, my dear, I must urge you to reconsider your thinking."

She looked dubiously at him. "About…?"

"This, for one thing," Richard replied, kissing her again. "You must consider this." He brushed her lips once more, and then his mouth traveled down her neck. "And this." She leaned in, her lips brushing his ear, her breathing ragged.

Richard pulled away, and this time Caroline was reluctant to release him. He grinned. "But you must also think very seriously about what you might accomplish here at Netherfield. You must give up this scheme of convincing your brother to abandon this place. Try to do some good, with him and with your sister – I think there was something in that quarrel yesterday, and you ought to make peace with them. Perhaps you might put forth some effort with Jane Bennet, for if she is to be your sister, you ought to start on good terms with her. Would you do this, for my sake?"

"You really think these things matter?"

"I do. I think we ought to be better versions of ourselves tomorrow than we have been today, and so on – and we must draw some good out of others. Promise me, at least, that you will not say anything untoward to poor Darcy again."

Caroline knit her brow, and for a moment Richard feared she meant to be difficult. "I do not know how much change I can affect in one day's time, but I will try. Nothing matters anyway, so why not?"

***

Caroline sighed and sipped at her tea as Abigail finished arranging her hair. The maid took a step back to look over her work. "It's awful simple – but are you sure you like it that way, ma'am?"

"Quite sure, thank you. I doubt I shall leave the house today, and if I do, who cares? Nothing matters anyhow, and I have greater concerns." Caroline groaned, and looked back at her maid through the mirror, regretting her ill humor. "It is perfect, just what I had wished, Abigail."

The maid looked bewildered – she bobbed into a curtsey and scurried away. Caroline only made a droll face at her reflection and shrugged; she was probably going mad, but what did that signify?

She had spent the last two days doing just what Richard had suggested: thinking. It had not been an enjoyable enterprise at first, for she had begun with anger. But on the second day, locked away in her room, she started to doubt whether it was anger at all. Perhaps it was only disappointed hopes, and a sort of fear deeply rooted in the things she had been taught, things she now questioned the wisdom of.

Caroline could not abide spending a third day confined to her bedchamber, though she had little hope of seeing Richard yet. She very much wished to – now that her eyes had been opened, it was almost funny. He had liked her all along, and in ways she had never even thought to hope that Mr. Darcy might.

She missed Richard, and had not the spirit to fight the sentiments that had been growing in her heart since the first time he kissed her. Whatever it was between them could not be resisted, for it was new and exciting, and without such private musings to secretly indulge in, she would almost certainly lose her mind.

Today she meant to do better. As pleasant as it was to dwell upon thoughts of Richard, she was determined to face the feelings that made her uncomfortable. She would be a finer woman than any of them had ever given her credit for – perhaps almost as good as the Caroline Bingley that Richard seemed to believe in.

This resolution led her to knock on her sister's door. Louisa did not share a bedchamber with her husband, and so Caroline walked in without waiting for an answer. Louisa was still at her dressing table, and she spun around with irritation. "Caroline, it is too early."

Of course – this was just how the argument had begun on the first market day, and again on the fourth, when Caroline had escalated things beyond what she ought to have. She sighed heavily; though she must do it, it still chafed at Caroline to humble herself before the sister she had grown up in constant competition with. "Louisa," she said softly, wringing her hands. "Might we speak as we did when we were girls?"

Louisa rolled her eyes at Caroline through her mirror, and waved the maid away. "Leave us."

Caroline sat down on the bed. "Louisa, do you think I

ought to apologize to Charles?"

"What for?"

"That quarrel – last night – and some other occasions, which you may not remember."

Louisa swept across the room and put her hand on Caroline's forehead. "You do not have a fever...."

Caroline swatted her sister's hand away and held onto it, peering up with an earnest look. "I mean it."

"This is not a trick?"

"No! I know I must sound... unusual...."

"You never apologize for anything, Caroline."

"Well, perhaps I ought to begin – do you think I should?"

Louisa let out a deep breath and sat down beside her sister. "What brought on this change? Has something happened since dinner last night?"

"A great deal," Caroline said, laughing bitterly. "I have been thinking – reflecting, I suppose – things have gone so very differently than how I wished, and I begin to wonder if there is any point in fighting it."

"You refer to our being in Hertfordshire?"

"That, yes, and.... Just, everything. I cannot make Charles see sense, I cannot make Mr. Darcy admire me – what is the point of it all, anyway?"

Louisa gave her a sad smile. "I have not seen you so low in many years, Caroline. I wonder if this rain has been getting to you."

"I have been low these past two days," Caroline admitted. "In truth, I feel like I have undergone such a material change that I now question everything I once believed about the world. I have been such a fool, chasing after Mr. Darcy, professing opinions which are not my own, and all for what? Do you know, I have never really imagined what it would be like to actually be his wife. I had fancied myself as Mistress of Pemberley, but that is not at all the same thing. I cannot even fathom what it would be like to kiss him – I daresay he would just stand stock still like a statue – I do not know how we should ever go about making heirs."

"Caroline!" Louisa tried to look severe, but she quickly

gave in to laughter. "Oh my! I wish I had not thought of it. But you know, it may just be that neither of you feels any passion for the other."

"I had never really thought of it. I only thought that no other man so rich would ever be so... within my grasp. I felt it my duty to catch him, if I could."

"That is what we have been taught to do," Louisa said morosely. "See how well it worked for me – I assure you, if Joseph owned ten Pemberleys he would be just as unbearable."

"Why? You liked him so much when you married."

"Do not ask me – the answer would only make you cross, and I like pensive Caroline much better."

Caroline gave her sister a half-hearted laugh. "Me too. I am in no mood to be angry today, so I will say no more about Jos."

Louisa held her sister by the shoulders, smiling affectionately. "Who are you, and what have you done with my sister?"

"Do not tease me," Caroline groaned.

"So, no sudden sense of humor? Well, at least you mean to give up Mr. Darcy. I have been waiting a long time for you to come to your senses in that quarter."

"Have I? Have I come to my senses? Or taken leave of them? I cannot tell the difference anymore." Caroline slumped back against her sister, who gave her a tender embrace.

"My goodness, Caroline. You are in some crisis! But as you rarely desire to hear my opinion, I believe I must say what I like while I can."

Caroline only nodded, enjoying her sister's embrace. Why had they always felt so distant?

Louisa took another deep breath and let it out slowly, tightening her arms around her sister. "You spoke last night of wishing to make Charles see sense, but I think he does, while *you* have not. I am sorry that things are not different, that it is not Charles trying to make you see reason. If you have begun to do so on your own, I am proud of you. We have all rather been at our wits' end about it."

Tears began to slide silently down Caroline's cheeks.

"Have I been so horrible?"

"So horrible," Louisa agreed. "I know it is not your fault – you were not taught any better. Nor was I, and look at me."

"But what about Charles? He was raised just the same as us, constantly criticized by our mother, held up to such impossible standards – how is he always so happy?"

"He has been more in the world, had more freedom. In truth, I hardly know. But if he were not as relentlessly cheerful, I daresay our lot would be vastly different."

"You think he is right?"

Louisa shrugged. "He is better liked than we are, if such things matter. Certainly he is happier."

"Do you think I should be more like Charles, and not the reverse?"

"It is worth attempting – I think what you have been doing since you came out has not worked."

Caroline sat in silence for a moment, considering what her sister had said. "So... you think he and I should marry for love?"

"I cannot recommend the alternative," Louisa said gravely.

"Things are that bad? Surely that is not... irreversible?"

Louisa smiled enigmatically. "Perhaps not."

***

Elizabeth passed the two days of Colonel Fitzwilliam's absence in relative tranquility. She stayed home, telling herself at intervals that it was not to avoid Mr. Darcy, but because she needed peace and respite. Nothing could be done about Mr. Wickham until the colonel returned from London, and there were other matters that she might attend to without any involvement from Mr. Darcy; if she saw him now, it would be because she *wanted* to, and not because she needed to. This she simply could not allow.

Instead, Elizabeth spent two cheerful days at Longbourn with Mary, who had been easily persuaded to stay home from the market and the card party. Mr. Darcy's advice had been on

Elizabeth's mind, and when she applied herself to puzzling her sister out, Elizabeth easily discovered that he was quite right.

"I think well of Mr. Collins," Mary conceded, as she sat in the drawing room with Elizabeth, who had made the excuse of illness for the second evening in a row. "But I am sensible of his indifference to me. Jane was his first object, but he transferred his attention to you so quickly that nobody could believe him sincere – which I really think a clergyman ought to be."

Elizabeth was relieved to hear her sister say such things. "I am glad you know what you are about," she replied.

"Will you refuse him?"

"I rather hope to prevent it from coming to that – but yes, I will, if I have to."

Mary nodded thoughtfully. "I cannot imagine you a clergyman's wife at all, Lizzy, not even with a more sensible man."

Elizabeth laughed. "And you? Could you fancy a *more sensible* clergyman?"

"I have always supposed that is just what I should like best. But now I wonder," Mary mused. "I suppose it would depend on the man, and his situation. Do you think that there are other such Lady Catherines in the world, dominating their vicars with relentless wisdom?"

Elizabeth nearly doubled over with astonished laughter. "Mary!"

Mary gave a hesitant chuckle. "I did not mean to be facetious – I suppose it *is* funny – but I am perfectly serious. I am sure you have noticed that he speaks of her a great deal."

"Oh yes, I am aware of it," Elizabeth agreed.

"It is an odd sort of recommendation, is it not? For him to speak to a prospective bride about a great lady interfering in his life – as if we should like to look forward to such a thing."

Elizabeth bubbled with mirth. "I suppose he believes that her notice grants him some degree of importance in the world."

Mary knit her brow as she considered. "Is this the normal way of things? I hardly know, for I have seen so little of the world. Perhaps a clergyman's wife must always endure the great lady of the neighborhood, but I think – well...." Mary sighed, and looked sheepishly at her sister. "It would be no different than living with Mamma forever," she said softly.

"Oh, Mary!" Elizabeth embraced her. "You need not fret about it, dearest. I daresay you will have your chance – I do believe Jane will marry Mr. Bingley, and Mamma is not wrong about what that will lead to."

"It will throw us in the path of other rich men," Mary said, mimicking their mother.

Elizabeth grinned and waggled her eyebrows. "Surely you cannot dislike such a prospect as that."

Mary smiled weakly. "I do not know, Lizzy. I am sure I will not marry before Kitty and Lydia – and you, of course. If we had a brother, I might be the spinster sister who stays at home to care for Mamma and Papa so that his wife can attend the children, and I am sure I would be a wonderful aunt."

"You do not wish to marry? I can well imagine Mr. Collins putting you off the entire clergy, but surely not all of mankind?"

"No, that is not it at all – I hardly know what I mean to say. It is only that I do not know what I should like. As the plainest sister, I have never had to think about it. Meryton is a small village, and I have only seen what I do *not* like. And – I know it is a dreadful thing to say, forgive me – I do not like gentlemen who like my sisters – who prefer them. You understand? I have no right to such vanity, but I should like to be first amongst us in the eyes of one person in this world, which will likely not happen so long as my four sisters are all unmarried."

Mary had spoken with feeling, but maintained a composure of strong resolve. It was not an idle notion, but clearly a matter she had given considerable thought. Elizabeth was heartened by her sister's conviction. "Mary, I cannot tell you how glad I am to hear you say such things, when the alternative would be so unhappy."

"Really? You do not think it is rather pathetic?"

"No indeed, Mary! I think it shows an excellent strength of character and self-respect that I wished our younger sisters possess – either of them, I am sure, would happily take a man who had first preferred the other. But it is not wrong that you wish to be special, to be understood and cherished. I would not wish you to settle for anything less."

Mary smiled brightly, but Elizabeth suddenly jumped to her feet, struck with sudden genius. "I have had an idea – but what if you go to London? You could stay with our aunt and uncle after Christmas. You say you have seen too little of the world to know what you want – and in London there would be no sisters to compete with – is it not a perfect plan?"

"Oh – yes," Mary said, her eyes going wide as she considered it. "I think I should like that very much. But would Mamma agree?"

"Mamma will soon be busy planning Jane's wedding, that I can promise you," Elizabeth replied. "And then we might ask her anything."

But Elizabeth had no intention of waiting. She wrote her aunt the first thing after waking up the next morning, her twentieth market day. She hoped that if she sent the express early enough she might expect some reply that same day, and then she might feel she had accomplished *something*.

With this done, Elizabeth decided she might venture into the market, even if the colonel was not expected back yet. She had done Mary a good turn – far better than uniting her with Mr. Collins – and now Elizabeth longed to make more of the day.

Elizabeth walked with Jane, whom she had seen little of in the two days she had spent at home with Mary, and the sisters talked of idle things as they made their way to the village. It was a relaxing change of pace for Elizabeth, after the chaos of the last few weeks, and for a time she was able to put Mr. Darcy from her mind entirely.

This brief respite was shattered, however, when she and Jane encountered Mr. Bingley and his sister, and Mr. Darcy was not with them. It chafed Elizabeth to realize that she missed him, and she was rather wounded by the notion that he might be avoiding her, just as she had done to him.

Once Mr. Bingley had made all his usual address to Jane,

Miss Bingley began some unusually civil greetings of her own. "How well you look, Miss Bennet – I am delighted to see you so recovered. My brother is to give a ball next week, and you shall have no excuse for not dancing every set!"

Jane made a typically gracious reply, but Elizabeth could only gaze at Miss Bingley in wonder. As she stared, something caught the light – Miss Bingley's sparkling diamond earrings. They were the same ones Jane had complimented the night they dined at Netherfield – had not Jane mentioned Baba Romilda in the next breath?

With equal measures of horror and curiosity, Elizabeth inched closer to Miss Bingley, who had glanced over her shoulder with a look of disdain. Elizabeth followed her gaze – Mr. Collins was approaching, and Miss Bingley seemed to disapprove of him already. "Come and walk with Charles and I, Miss Bennet."

Mr. Bingley offered Jane his arm; while Jane was sharing a sweet look of longing with him, Elizabeth swiftly arched herself to Miss Bingley. "I hope I may join you. I wish to have a look around, for I cherish a secret hope that I shall see my old friend Baba Romilda here today. She is not always at the market, but on the occasions when she is, it is always quite *memorable*."

"Baba Romilda," Miss Bingley repeated, tugging idly at one of her earrings. Elizabeth fairly gaped, studying Miss Bingley's reaction as Jane innocently explained who the woman was.

"I should very much like to meet her," Miss Bingley replied with interest.

Elizabeth grinned. "Let us go and look for her at once." She had not much hope of finding her, but she was beginning to suspect that their failure to locate Baba Romilda might just disappoint Miss Bingley as much as it did her.

It was actually a surprise to Elizabeth that Baba Romilda was out with her cart in front of Mr. Miller's shop once again, and the four of them approached eagerly. It was certainly a relief, for Elizabeth had some questions for the mysterious old lady.

But Baba Romilda forestalled her by making a great fuss over her new customers. "Dear Lizzy, dear Jane! Oh, it feels like *ages* since I saw you last!"

"It certainly does," Elizabeth quipped.

Baba Romilda smiled and winked at her, and then turned to exclaim over Jane. "How lovely you look, my dear! And who is this handsome young man here?"

"This is Mr. Bingley," Jane said with a blush.

"Mr. Bingley, I like the look of you – you know what you are about," Baba Romilda said with a laugh. "And what about you, Lizzy, Miss Bingley – where are your *beaux* this morning?"

Elizabeth arched an eyebrow as she watched Miss Bingley's reaction. "Have you met before?"

Baba Romilda made no answer, but took a few steps away to speak to another customer who had come to peruse her wares. Miss Bingley was looking pale, and Elizabeth very much wished to question her and Baba Romilda, but hesitated to do so with Jane and Mr. Bingley present.

"Oh, look, Jane – there is our Aunt Phillips. You must go and bid her good morning, for I think she was wishing some opportunity to invite Mr. Bingley to her card party tonight."

"A card party," Mr. Bingley cried. "What fun! Come, Miss Bennet, let us go and speak with your aunt."

When he and Jane moved away, Elizabeth looked back at Miss Bingley, who was visibly panicked. Baba Romilda's customer had gone away, and the old woman looked at them with a slow grin and a twinkle in her eye. "You must have some questions – but you have not answered mine. Where are the other two?"

Miss Bingley's dismay turned to confusion as she knit her brow, and she looked querulously at Baba Romilda. She turned to Elizabeth next, and for a moment she began to speak, but then turned on her heel and stalked away. Elizabeth stood frozen in shock for a moment, watching Miss Bingley retreat.

She eyed Baba Romilda, who still smiled serenely at her, then Elizabeth groaned and went after Miss Bingley. She had gone half a block from Mr. Miller's shop when Elizabeth hesitated. Caroline Bingley could be easily tracked down later, but Baba Romilda had been elusive – this might be her only chance. But when she turned back around, Baba Romilda and her cart were gone. "What in the world?" Elizabeth sighed and rolled her eyes before pursuing Miss Bingley toward the village square.

Miss Bingley was standing with her back turned, staring at the ancient oak tree, when Elizabeth caught up to her. Just around the corner, Elizabeth could see Mr. Darcy – he was speaking with Mr. Wickham. She made another impulsive decision, and hastened toward them.

"Good morning, Mr. Darcy," she said, daring to meet his eye, despite her embarrassment.

"Good morning, Miss Elizabeth," he replied, giving her an odd look. "May I present my old friend, Mr. George Wickham? Wickham, this is my friend Elizabeth Bennet of Longbourn."

Elizabeth managed to make an appropriate greeting, though she could scarcely contain her shock and yet another odd turn of events. "Mr. Darcy, I hate to interrupt, but I believe Miss Bingley is unwell and needs an escort back to Netherfield – might I ask you to come with me?"

"Of course. Wickham, I shall look forward to seeing you at the card party this evening," Mr. Darcy said. He offered Elizabeth his arm and began to lead her across the green.

Elizabeth accepted his arm, but slowed their pace and leaned in to whisper, "While whatever that was must surely be fascinating, there is something more pressing. I begin to share your suspicions about Miss Bingley. Did Richard ever...?"

"I forgot to ask him, with so much else going on. But surely you do not think...."

"Indeed I do, and I shall prove it to you," Elizabeth said, throwing her shoulder back with confidence. "And when I am proved right, we must go to Purvis Lodge, I think."

They reached the place where Miss Bingley was standing, still staring at the oak. Elizabeth moved to her side, and likewise looked out at the tree. "The rains have cleared, Miss Bingley, and yet there is still such a stormy look about things. I feel as though lightning might strike at any moment."

"I believe that same thing happened but a week ago," Mr. Darcy replied, a trace of humor in his voice.

Miss Bingley's eyes flashed with recognition, and she looked at them with utter astonishment. "No, it cannot be," she whimpered. She latched onto Elizabeth as if suddenly dizzy, and her face twisted for a moment as tears began to spill down her cheeks.

Elizabeth reacted at once, moving around to the other side of Miss Bingley so that she and Mr. Darcy could support her from both sides. "Walk with us," she said softly, giving Miss Bingley a reassuring look.

Together they made their way from the village square to the lane that led to Purvis Lodge, and only then did Miss Bingley speak. "Am I to understand that – that you have experienced market day before?"

Elizabeth had never thought well of Miss Bingley, but to see the haughty woman humbled by the same dilemma inspired no little compassion. "It was a surprise for us too, when Mr. Darcy and I found each other out – but once you have got over the shock, it may be a relief to you."

"When did you…?" Miss Bingley stumbled again, but quickly recovered herself.

Elizabeth glanced up at Mr. Darcy, but he nodded for her to speak. "About a fortnight ago; we had both been repeating market day for a week, each of us thinking we had gone mad, until we figured each other out. The lightning struck then, too – just after we made a purchase from Baba Romilda."

"Yes," Miss Bingley said with a heavy breath. "The same thing happened when I bought the earrings – which I obviously still have, though it ought to be impossible. Eliza, did you not hear the gypsy – she said *where are the other two* – she meant Mr. Darcy and…."

"Richard," Elizabeth replied, realizing with bemusement that Miss Bingley had said his name as well. For a moment the two women only stared at one another, and Mr. Darcy gave a gentle chuckle.

"We ought not to have trusted Richard to confirm my suspicions," Mr. Darcy observed.

Elizabeth met his eye and laughed, at ease with him amidst a crisis once more. "I suppose you are right – we ought to repay his mischief."

Miss Bingley whimpered again. "How can you find any humor in this ghastly mess?"

They had arrived at the gates of Purvis Lodge, and Elizabeth asked Mr. Darcy, "Have you got that little knife?"

"No, I did not bring it – I did not expect to see you, for you have not been at the market or the card party these two days."

"You *have* been?" Elizabeth could not conceal her surprise – and some little hope that he had wanted to see her.

"I have, oddly enough, been rather enjoying the company of George Wickham, in a reminiscent way," he said with a smile.

"Oh, well that is good, too," Elizabeth replied, before recollecting Miss Bingley, who was watching them in agitated confusion. "Will you see to the gate?" She quickly pulled the sharp pin out of her hair and handed it to him.

When Mr. Darcy went to tear away the vines and pick the lock, Elizabeth gave Miss Bingley a comforting pat on the shoulder. "We have been meeting here, sometimes, to discuss our peculiar dilemma. We were not keen on cooperating, at first, but a burden shared is a burden halved."

"And Richard? He has been conspiring with you, too?"

"Yes, although at first it amused him to conceal his intentions. That day, when the lightning struck, he heard Mr. Darcy's account of our predicament, and when he awoke the next morning and realized he had also begun to repeat the day – well, you may recall his mischief at Longbourn."

Caroline nodded, and then suddenly groaned. "Oh dear – Mr. Darcy must remember – but it is too horrible – I am going to wring Richard's neck, for he might have prevented this!"

Elizabeth did her best to conceal the amusement this inspired. "Please, Caroline, do not leave – you must have a thousand questions, and I wish to take you into our confidence. We have all agreed that are things we must do if it is ever to be Thursday again, and we must all work together."

Miss Bingley had begun to withdraw, but now she

hesitated. "You – you wish to include me?"

Elizabeth extended her hand. "Come, we shall be friends. I did not much like Mr. Darcy when this all began, but we have made some little progress at least."

Miss Bingley snorted with laughter, but followed Elizabeth through the gate as Mr. Darcy held it open for them. "This is all very strange, but *you* may really be mad."

***

Richard smiled warmly at Mrs. Gardiner as he took a seat in her drawing room. "I am sorry my husband is not here to greet you," she said. "He is usually home by this hour, but occasionally his business detains him."

"Think nothing of it," Richard replied. "I was pleased to make his acquaintance this morning, but it is actually you I came to see."

He could tell the lady was surprised, but her manners were flawless. She schooled her countenance and resumed her genial smile. "If it is about the apple tarts, I fear I must disappoint you."

Richard laughed. "Only temporarily, I am sure. I hope I shall still be at Netherfield for Christmas, and Miss Elizabeth has said that she expects a visit from you then." He waggled his eyebrows.

"I am still astonished at the coincidence," she replied. "My sister has been seeing a great deal of the earl in recent months, and now his son is acquainted with my niece. I had a letter from her this morning, but she made no mention of it."

"No, but I daresay she had a few choice words for my cousin Darcy."

Mrs. Gardiner betrayed a little smirk. "Not on this occasion – though I see you know my Lizzy well."

Richard arched an eyebrow. "There is another of her recent acquaintance you might find coincidental – did her letter mention that George Wickham has come to Meryton to join the regiment quartered there?"

Mrs. Gardiner went pale. "Of course – you know him well,

I daresay."

"How long have you known he was your nephew? And more to the point, how does a parson's youngest daughter end up a kitchen maid at Darcy House, and then Pemberley?"

"It is not an easy thing to speak of," she replied with a heavy sigh. "I hope it is not hard for you, after losing your mother, but surely you must have seen this morning that there is real affection between your father and my sister. She might not have been good enough for him twenty-seven years ago, but she has come up in the world, she has her own money, and he has his heirs. Surely you would not begrudge him this happiness?"

Richard leaned forward pensively stroking his chin. "I have observed them together on several occasions, Mrs. Gardiner. I can see that her attachment is genuine – I do not accuse her of anything, Mrs. Gardiner, nor do I ask you to speak against your own sister. I have my reasons for wishing to know the particulars – and some right to, as well. I only wish to fully understand, before I make any overtures of support."

She nodded appreciatively. "If you know about George already, I suppose there is no betrayal in my filling in the gaps, not if it will help you accept him and Amelia into the family."

"Thank you, Mrs. Gardiner, that is all that I ask."

Mrs. Gardiner sipped at her tea. "It is difficult to know where to begin. I have not spoken much on the matter in twenty years, and lately it has only been with my sister. As to George being in Meryton, I think I may be responsible for that. Amelia wished him out of the way awhile; she was a little embarrassed about her courtship with your father. I hardly know why, for she has been married three times before, but with the earl it is as if she is fifteen again. And of course, she wants to be sure of him before she brings George into it. I had mentioned the regiment in Meryton, for she was here when I read of it in a letter from Fanny Bennet."

"Would she have known also that Darcy was in the area?"

"No, not from me. Lizzy has mentioned him, as you say, but my sister-in-law is more preoccupied with Mr. Bingley and the regiment; there was nothing in her letter about Mr. Darcy, so Amelia would not have known."

"I see," Richard replied. "And am I to understand that my father is unaware of the child they share?"

"No - he has known for many years."

This revelation stung. "He has?"

Mrs. Gardiner let out another shaky sigh. "I ought to start at the beginning - to answer your question from before. Amelia was always a wild creature - far too wild for a parson's daughter. You know my nieces - Lydia rather reminds me of Amelia as a girl, and she was about that age when she met your father. Our cousin Sarah had just married Mr. Wickham, the steward at Pemberley, and Amelia managed to convince Sarah to sneak her into the Twelfth Night ball. I do not think she knew what she was getting herself into - she said later it was just a lark, that she had wagered with some friends whether or not she could pull it off. But she did, and it was a masked ball, so nobody knew her. But she caught your father's eye that night - to hear her tell it, it was love at first sight on both sides."

Richard laughed bitterly. "Poor girl - my father was twice her age."

Mrs. Gardiner averted her eyes, her teacup clattering against the saucer.

"There is more," Richard pressed her.

"There is, but I am afraid that I cannot defend your father without impugning your mother, and I have no wish to offend you," Mrs. Gardiner said cautiously.

"I have never believed my father to have been a faithful husband - though in truth I have endeavored to think of it as little as possible. I know my mother was a difficult creature. Theirs was not a love match; she was a cold woman," Richard said with feeling.

"It was no great secret then. They came to Lambton sometimes, when they visited Pemberley - the whole village knew of the earl's misery. I - I even spoke to him about it once, just after he met Amelia. He asked me to assist in arranging an assignation, and I agreed - I am ashamed to say it, but I accepted a bribe, after he had convinced me of the joy my sister brought him. Amelia did not name me as an accomplice when my father found out about – about the baby," Mrs. Gardiner said, her voice shaking.

Richard offered her a handkerchief, and she dabbed at her eyes before continuing her story. "My father cast her off, cast her out of the house that day. I gave her the money I had saved, the money the Earl had given me, and every other penny I had. It was enough to get her to London, for the Darcys had already gone to Town to give old Mr. Darcy's sister another season. Lady Anne was such a kind woman; she took an interest in all the servants and their families, and had always been on good terms with my father. Amelia could think of no other option, in the face of certain ruin, and she was too frightened of the countess to go to the earl. So, she went to Darcy House and threw herself on Lady Anne's mercy."

"Thinking that Lady Anne would help for the sake of the babe, her own nephew."

"And she did," Mrs. Gardiner replied. "I do not know the particulars – that is, I cannot guess if she thought of her brother, or only the plight of a frightened young woman. But she acted with great generosity, and Amelia was always so grateful to her. She gave Amelia a job in the kitchens, where none of the family would recognize her, and passed her off as a recent widow. Amelia worked there for six months, until the baby came."

"And Lady Anne actually allowed the baby to be brought to Pemberley?" This was what shocked Richard the most – surely his aunt would not have wanted the earl's bastard so close.

"No, not exactly. Lady Anne, bless her, found a childless couple in Cornwall, and arranged for them to take the baby. The plan was for Amelia to travel there and nurse little George, and then she would have work at Pemberley, once she was recovered. But Amelia could not go through with it, once she had given birth. Our cousin Sarah had just suffered another stillbirth, her third one, and she was heartbroken. Amelia saw her chance, and Sarah was just weak enough to agree. So Amelia told the couple in Cornwall that *she* had had a stillborn, and Sarah Wickham's stillbirth was concealed – the world was told she had delivered a healthy baby boy."

"So the Darcys never knew the truth about Wickham?"

"I doubt Lady Anne would have allowed Amelia to work at Pemberley if she knew the child was so near. She was a gracious woman, but there are limits," Mrs. Gardiner ruefully observed.

"Surely at some point there must have been suspicion," Richard replied. "Your sister could not have been so near her son without betraying too much interest."

"She played the part of an indulgent aunt very well, but Sarah loved little George, and begged Amelia to keep the secret. She did not even tell the earl for nearly a decade, just before she married."

The sound of a carriage outside signaled that Mr. Gardiner was home, and Richard could see that Mrs. Gardiner would not like to speak of the matter in front of her husband. It is just as well, for Richard had discovered what he had come to. He began to stand, and Mrs. Gardiner rose as well.

"I hope I have been helpful, Colonel Fitzwilliam. If I have made you think less of my sister, I will heartily regret what I have told you. I will only say one thing more – the affair between your father and my sister was not a passing dalliance. It continued until the time of her first marriage, and I believe there is real and genuine affection between them, even now. He has told her that if he had not already been married when they met.... I am sorry if this pains you, but I hope you will consider giving them your blessing. Amelia tells me your father delays only for fear of what his children will say. There are rumors about my sister and her husbands, but she can hardly be blamed for drowning, old age, or Sir Robert's duel."

"Of course," Richard said with a bow. "You have given me a great deal to think of, and I believe you have put an end to my qualms about Lady Carson. It is George Wickham that concerns me." Richard Bowes and took his leave.

His mind was in great turmoil over all that he had heard, though it was easily reconciled with all that he had observed over the last four days. Mrs. Gardiner had been far more informed than he had expected, and Richard felt confident that he had uncovered enough information to return to Meryton in the morning.

Indeed, he was so well pleased with his own efforts that he indulged in a nightcap before retiring, savoring his father's fine brandy and a great many pleasant recollections of Caroline Bingley.

11

Darcy broke away from Bingley and his sister when he spied the Bennets approaching from Longbourn. He stood at some remove and held Elizabeth's gaze; as the rest of her family greeted the Bingleys, she hung back and moved in his direction, a slow smile spreading across her face.

He let out a sigh of relief – they were to be friends again. "Good morning, William – at least, I have every reason to believe it shall. But where is Richard?"

"I expect him any moment. You are sure we have not made a mistake, taking Miss Bingley so fully into our confidence?"

Elizabeth arched an eyebrow at him. "She was very cross yesterday, but not at *us*."

Us. Darcy smiled warmly at her. "It will certainly be amusing, when he arrives and finds her with us."

"Shall I walk there with her first, and perhaps remind her how angry she is with him?"

He laughed, delighted that she could be easy with him

again, even mischievous, after how he had behaved at the last card party with her. "I would by no means suspend any pleasure of yours," he replied. "And I daresay he deserves her wrath."

Elizabeth winked and gave his hand a brief squeeze before moving away. "I ought to be going, then."

Darcy watched her go, his hand twitching from her touch. She had avoided him for two days after the unpardonable liberty he had taken, but it appeared she had forgiven him, without his having done anything to deserve it. He did not mean to question his good fortune, for they were facing an imminent explosion; he hoped they might revel in it together.

He watched Elizabeth lead Miss Bingley in the direction of Purvis Lodge, and a few minutes later, Richard approached from the other end of the village. He met his cousin at the square, and clapped him on the shoulder. "How was London? I trust you have discovered enough that we may proceed?"

"Yes," Richard replied, "I was perfectly satisfied with the information I uncovered, though it is still difficult to accept. But I should rather save my breath and only tell it once. Shall we?"

Darcy nodded, but kept his pace slow as they made their way to Purvis Lodge, hoping they would not see the ladies from the lane as they made their approach. He knew not how Miss Bingley would react to Richard, but he had every hope of it being akin to the morning Elizabeth had taken her gloves off – and he looked forward to sharing the amusement with Elizabeth.

***

Caroline was hardly aware of what she said; Charles and Miss Bennet exchanged a look of confusion as she made her excuses and hastened away with Eliza Bennet. She had always despised the chit, but at present Caroline was determined that they must be allies, if only to end her nightmare – and revenge herself on Richard Fitzwilliam.

Like the previous morning, Caroline kept silent until the

village was behind them, and then she grinned at her companion. "This is rather fun, is it not, Eliza? Being a part of some little intrigue is far superior to believing I had gone insane."

"Call me Lizzy, please. But yes, it has been amusing, most of the time. Of course, we have not always agreed amongst ourselves." She arched an eyebrow at Caroline.

"I suppose it is a relief that I am not the only one of us who is fed up with Richard's nonsense – I ought to give him a piece of my mind!"

"I am sure he has done us all a disservice," Elizabeth agreed.

Caroline narrowed her eyes. "Why are you being kind to me? We do not like one another."

Elizabeth chortled with laughter. "My opinion of you has ever been based on your treatment of Jane – mostly. But you were kinder to her yesterday, and as long as that continues, I see no obstacle to our being friends. At any rate, you were in such distress, and I understood what you were feeling – I thought it only right to behave as I would want to be treated at such a time. And of course, if you are to be a part of this, it hardly seems helpful to exclude you."

"As Richard would have done," Caroline quipped, anger swelling in her chest again.

"I cannot think what his motives would be, when he knows how eager Mr. Darcy and I are to break this awful cycle."

"Well, perhaps we shall inquire," Caroline laughed, exaggerating her indignation to elicit more humor from Elizabeth.

"I give you leave to abuse him as much as you like," Elizabeth replied. "A dressing down might make him more willing to cooperate; if it does not, we may have to resort to a blow to the head."

Caroline sputtered with astonished laughter at Elizabeth's cheek. "I have already tried hitting him."

Elizabeth blushed and bit her lip for a moment, giving Caroline a shifty look. "I struck Mr. Darcy, the day of the lightning. I was very cross with him. But then he apologized. I imagine Richard would probably just laugh."

"He did, and then committed the same offense again the next day," Caroline said, leaning in and really enjoying the exchange of confidences.

"We all have some little grievance against him," Elizabeth said. "But yours seems the greatest, and you ought to speak first."

They reached the gate to Purvis Lodge, and Elizabeth was on the point of pulling out her hair pin, but Caroline laid a hand on her arm. "Oh, might I try? It looks like such fun!"

Elizabeth stepped back and made way for Caroline, who tore away at the vines with destructive glee, and then pulled a pin from her hair to pick the lock. It was harder than she had imagined, but Elizabeth waited patiently, and finally it gave way. "Ah! I am a real burglar now, Lizzy."

"It is a great accomplishment," Elizabeth said archly. She led Caroline up the front path of the small park, and the two ladies sat down on the marble stairs that led to the front vestibule of the manor.

Caroline glanced curiously at Elizabeth. "You have positioned us so that Richard shall not see me until a moment of my choosing." Elizabeth only smirked and shrugged her shoulders. "You and Mr. Darcy are cross with him, too, and you think it amusing that I intend to give him a lashing." Now Elizabeth laughed, and Caroline seized her hand with enthusiasm. "Perhaps we *shall* get on, Lizzy."

The gentlemen were not long behind them, and as their voices grew nearer, Elizabeth stood and waved them over.

"Lizzy, you are looking merry this morning," Richard called out; he and his cousin were very near now. "You might at least pretend to have missed me."

Elizabeth glanced down at her, and Caroline stood up and glared at Richard. "Should I pretend to have missed you? Or should one of us be honest?"

Richard stopped on the gravel path leading to the front drive of the manor. "Caroline! How wonderful you are here – you shall never believe it! Darcy is actually experiencing the same strange phenomenon as you and I – Miss Elizabeth, are you repeating the day as well?"

Elizabeth crossed her arms and gave him a hard look. "She knows everything, Richard."

Mr. Darcy cleared his throat. "We thought it only right."

"I see," Richard said, beginning to shift nervously. "I did not anticipate an ambush."

"Ambush? *You* did not...?" Caroline stammered as she fairly bellowed at him. In a moment she forgot everything except her fury; she was scarcely aware of how she got down the stairs, but she shouted every vulgar word she had ever heard as she flew at Richard.

She collided with him, obliging him to stagger backward as she screamed and pounded at his chest. "You tricked me, you vile, sneaky, lying, greasy rat! I trusted you! I *kissed* you!"

Richard tried to grab at her wrists but she was too quick for him, and hammered away at his broad chest as the two of them careened backward.

"Caroline, stop – let me explain...." When he could not capture her wrists he grabbed her by the waist and threw them both to the ground, deviously maneuvering for her to land on top of him. "Now will you listen?"

Caroline struggled against his hold, and a sudden jerking upward of her knee accomplished her freedom; Richard cried out in pain and curled his knees up as Elizabeth rushed forward to help Caroline to her feet.

"No, you listen, Richard," Caroline spat as she kicked some loose gravel at him. "That nasty trick you played has cost you. I would have believed everything else you said – I wanted to believe it all, I think, but you have ruined everything. I will never trust you again." Caroline moved to kick at him again, but Elizabeth held her back and began to pull her away.

Richard sat up, having the nerve to look confused by her anger, and he dabbed at his lip – his fingers came away bloody. Caroline had brought a handkerchief along, expecting a confrontation with Richard might end in tears – she had seriously underestimated herself. She threw the handkerchief down at him and moved away.

Mr. Darcy had positioned himself with his back turned during the scuffle, but he turned around now and helped Richard collect himself. Caroline let out a shaky breath to still her nerves after her outburst, and held Elizabeth's hand for support.

Richard brushed himself off and drew himself up to his full height. He glared at each of them in turn, his face red with what Caroline hoped was shame. She held his gaze with her shoulders back and her chin high. Despite everything, Mr. Darcy and Elizabeth wanted her here; they wished her to participate in their plans and schemes. It was Richard who had done wrong, and Caroline felt entirely vindicated as she silently stood her ground.

"Well," Richard said in a low growl. "I see. Perhaps I should take my leave until we can all speak calmly." He started to go, but Mr. Darcy grabbed him by the elbow to stay him.

"No, we will speak now," Mr. Darcy thundered. "No more deception, no more mischief. We all have some part to play in ending this redundancy, and we will work together, whether you like it or not. I had every hope of finding you more cooperative."

Richard looked down and ran his hands through his hair as he kicked at the gravel. He gave a heavy sigh before he looked up at them all. "I am sorry, truly I am. I meant to tell you all when I finished everything in London."

Caroline bristled at him, but tried to check her temper. She squeezed Elizabeth's hand until her new friend began to whimper, and Caroline released her with an apologetic glance. "So you deliberately left me in ignorance for nearly a week? I might have retained some modicum of dignity – of sanity, had you seen fit to be honest with me. Instead you... you took advantage of me, of my ignorance and my panic. I did not think well of you before, and if you were trying to change that, you have accomplished the reverse."

"I know," he replied softly. Richard turned and looked at Mr. Darcy. "I have some business with Wickham – I will speak with you later." The two men exchanged a long, tense look before Mr. Darcy finally let Richard go, and he hastened down the path and out the gate.

There was a long and unpleasant silence, and nobody would make eye contact. Finally Caroline spoke up. "I am sorry for my uncouth behavior. I will try to make amends with him, if we must all work together."

"We have all had our lapses in judgement," Elizabeth said. "Perhaps we may yet salvage the day."

Mr. Darcy shifted uncomfortably. "Yes, my cousin is merely frustrated, I think – he does not like the idea of Wickham being his brother."

"Well, I think *that* ought to be Mr. Wickham's problem, and not ours," Caroline replied.

"I fear it is about to be," Elizabeth said, giving Mr. Darcy a questioning look.

"He wrote last evening that he had discovered a great deal in London – that it is essentially confirmed," Mr. Darcy explained. "We know everything but Wickham's intentions. If he can make any discovery there, that may put an end to our crisis."

Caroline mostly followed this, for her companions had filled her in on a great deal of shocking information the previous day. "So Mr. Wickham is the key to this? But I thought there was more – other changes that must be made."

"We have tried a great deal of improvements to nearly everyone," Elizabeth replied. "I think the trick is getting everything right all in one day – finding the right combination of events."

Caroline nodded slowly. "The days that Charles proposed to Jane – was that one of your improvements?"

"Yes," Elizabeth said, her eyes flashing with defiance.

Caroline affected a defensive posture. "I might have once protested, but I will not. I have been thinking – Richard did actually give me *some* good advice when he was spinning his lies. Jane makes Charles happy. So what else must happen to make things right? I assume I have little to do with the Wickham affair, but I should like to be of use." She braved a glance at Mr. Darcy, still mortified that he must remember her presumptuous questioning.

"By all means," he replied.

"Well, I have thought over the argument. On the first market day, it was not so awfully bad, but the next time was very dreadful. I had no idea Jos was so resentful – and I have learned that things are not well between him and Louisa. I should like to remedy that if I can. Perhaps some trial and error, until I can discover what works best."

"That sounds like an excellent notion." Mr. Darcy smiled at her – it was the most genuine smile she had ever got from him. There was nothing like *that* in it, but Caroline found that she did not mind. She was bolstered by the confidence his appreciation inspired. Perhaps Richard was going to make a muddle of their plans, but Caroline resolved to make an effort. *She* would not be a disappointment – quite the reverse. She would be the best at… whatever this was.

"And, Lizzy – forgive me, but have you any plans for your younger sisters?"

"I had thought that Mary might suit my cousin Collins, but she confided in me at last that she does not think very well of him. My new scheme is for her to go to London and stay with my aunt and uncle. She wishes to see more of the world without so many sisters about," Elizabeth said with mirth.

"An excellent notion," Mr. Darcy replied.

Caroline nodded her agreement. "And what of the younger girls?"

Elizabeth rolled her eyes with a smirk. "I suppose I had not yet tried tying them up for the day and leaving them in their room."

"I will think on it," Caroline said decisively. "I had better be going, but I will think upon a great many solutions."

"Thank you, Caroline," Elizabeth said in some surprise. "I hope you will come to the card party tonight. It will be an excellent opportunity for observation."

"Of course."

Elizabeth glanced over at Mr. Darcy, her smile wavering, and then she turned back to Caroline. "Shall I walk back to the village with you?"

"Please do," Caroline said, astonished by how pleased she

was with the prospect of such company.

***

Richard had freshened up and was waiting for Caroline when she entered her bedroom. She closed the door and took a few steps into the room, kicking off her shoes and she approached her bed and threw herself down on it with a heavy sigh. He stepped out of the corner and revealed himself, and Caroline sat up with a start. "What are you doing? Who let you in here?"

"I bribed a servant – I had to speak with you."

"Get out this instant or I will scream," she hissed.

"Please," he begged her, taking a hesitant step closer. "I want to apologize – to speak as I dared not in front of Darcy and Lizzy."

Caroline drew her legs into her chest as she recoiled against her pillows. "What explanation can possibly justify how you have acted?"

"I love you," Richard said simply.

Her blue eyes went wide. "You lied to me!"

"I withheld the truth, a little," he admitted. "I did mean to tell you when I came back from London, truly Caroline."

"You left me to anguish alone, when I might have had the comfort of knowing that I was not the only one suspended in time – and if you had told me the truth when your first realized what I was experiencing, you might have spared me the acutest humiliation – but I suppose you delight in that as well," she spat.

"No, Caroline, I do not delight in the knowledge that even after I kissed you and bore my heart to you, you threw yourself at Darcy anyway," Richard cried, taking another step toward the bed. Angry as he was at being thoroughly lambasted after four days of life-altering discoveries in London, Richard still wanted her desperately. The sight of her on the bed, her stockinged feet poking out from under her dress, was almost too much for him. "I want to marry you, Caroline."

"What?"

Richard's fingers fumbled in his coat pocket as he withdrew the tiny black box he had brought with him from London. "This was my mother's, and I cannot bear the idea of my father giving it to Lady Carson. Caroline, I love you, and I have loved you since the moment I laid eyes on you."

She leapt to her feet and railed at him. "Are you mad? Did I damage your brain when I attacked you before, or shall I be obliged to hit you again? How dare you insult me like this!"

"Insult you?" Richard still held the box, but his hand began to shake. "Are you refusing me?"

"What do you think?"

"Are you... are you laughing at me?"

Caroline's anger began to subside, and he realized that what was left was pain. She made no answer, but only shook her head.

"I am sorry I hurt you," he said softly. "I did not want to bring you into our group until I came back – I thought it would be easier."

"You wanted me to be excluded because you did not trust me to behave well to them," Caroline said, her voice cracking. "You know I have wanted Darcy, that I have envied Lizzy in the past."

"You have clearly done well with them," Richard said with feeling. "I am proud of you."

"Well, that means exactly nothing, when you have underestimated me," Caroline said flatly. "I have been willing to put my feelings aside and do what is best for all of us, and you have only been selfish and manipulative. Now I must ask you to leave."

Richard could not will himself to move. "Caroline, please. We are meant to be together, you and I, just like Darcy and Lizzy. That is why we are all trapped in this day together. Can you not see it?"

Caroline looked at him in absolute horror. "Get out!"

***

Richard was still reeling from the bitter sting of Caroline's rejection, and he was propelled to the village by the sheer force of his anger. Just as well, he supposed, that he should encounter George Wickham in such a state.

His plan was just what it had been with Caroline – but with Wickham the possibility of failure did not matter. He strolled into the inn and paid a hefty bribe for access to Wickham's room there, and then he waited. He was seated at the little desk by the bed when Wickham sauntered him.

Wickham froze, then reluctantly stepped into the room and closed the door behind him. "Colonel, what an unexpected pleasure," he said, visibly nervous.

"Is it? Are you delighted to see your brother? Are you overcome with familial affection?"

Wickham strode over to the bed and sat down heavily, forcing a smile to cover his surprise. "They told you?"

"One way or another, I have discovered everything," Richard replied neutrally. He pulled out his pistol and set it deliberately down on the desk beside him, letting his hand linger over it for a moment before folding his hands in his lap and looking calmly at Wickham. "Everything, that is, except *your* intentions."

Wickham could not conceal his fear, and he sat up straighter, his eyes on the gun. "Now, listen, Richard," he said slowly, holding up his hands. "It is not like that."

"Oh? Tell me, what is it like, then?"

Wickham lowered his hands and let out a shaky breath. "I just want my mother to be happy. She loves our father very much, and has since she was a girl."

"You want nothing for yourself? I cannot imagine you would be content with a soldier's life while your mother is parading around the parlors and ballrooms of the first circles in London."

"I wish to return to London, yes, when they marry. I should only be in the way of their courtship," Wickham replied.

"You mean to lie in wait while your mother works her wiles and convinces my father to recognize you. You are waiting for your payoff," Richard retorted. "It has always been about money for you. You gambled away what Darcy gave you, and had the nerve to come back asking for more."

"It was wrong of me," Wickham said evenly. "I regret it all the more because apparently my past behavior led you all to believe the worst of me when I approached Georgiana at Ramsgate."

Richard had heard Wickham's justifications to Georgiana, but some part of him still resisted believing. "Have you been terribly misunderstood?" He mocked the man.

Wickham's eyes flared with anger, but he checked his temper. "I do not know whether Georgiana really believed my intentions were romantic, or if it was Darcy who supposed something more sinister, but I can see that is what you believe."

"And what would you have me believe?"

"The truth," Wickham replied. "I never meant her any harm, Richard, I swear it. I only wanted to make some progress, to reconcile with you all. She seemed the surest start – she was always fond of me as a girl. I never imagined she would get the wrong idea."

"So, what, you thought a visit with Georgiana could turn the tide and assure you some welcome into the family?" Richard frowned.

"I thought it a fine beginning. I had just found out the truth – my mother swore to keep the secret, and only told me after Mrs. Wickham died in May. But she has been supporting me in secret – ask Darcy, for I know he was always purchasing might debts, and he could not have done so in at least a year, for there have been none. Lady Carson has been supporting me."

Richard nodded begrudgingly, for Darcy had already told him this. "And you are content with such an allowance?"

Wickham shrugged. "Obviously."

"You see, I think you do want some of my father's money. I believe you want to be acknowledged, but you are not sentimental enough to settle for that, when there is real profit to be had."

"Then why would I come here? What secret explanation

can you expect to threaten out of me? If I wanted our father's money, why should I not be wooing him alongside my mother?"

"That is what you are going to tell me," Richard insisted.

"There is nothing to tell," Wickham said, standing up and glaring down at Richard. "I do not want a single damn thing from our father except the acknowledgement he has denied me my whole life. For as long as I can remember, there were whispers about me. I always knew there was something, but I had it quite wrong. I thought it was Mr. Darcy, for all the interest he showed in me."

Richard let out a heavy sigh and grunted with some little agreement. "He said the same, you know. He was sometimes afraid that you were *his* brother."

Wickham's posture relaxed. "I suppose we know now why we always hated each other."

"Jealousy?"

"Yes," Wickham sighed. "Can we not just put it behind us? I am not the same angry, idle wastrel I was at university, or the years after. I am just a man who wants to be a part of a family."

Richard let his hand linger on the pistol for a second before he tucked it back into his coat. He could see Wickham breathe a sigh of relief, and Richard began to feel ashamed of his aggression. He turned around in his chair, and picked up a pen from the desk. "So you would swear it? In writing?"

"If that is what you wish," Wickham said. "I do not believe our father will need such convincing, but if you require it, I will sign whatever you like. I have more than enough from my mother, and every reason to expect to marry well. I want nothing from our father but some sort of relationship – and the same with you, someday, if you were not so damned angry."

Richard dipped the pen into the inkwell and then hesitated. He closed his eyes for a minute and took a deep breath, then put the pen down and stood to face his brother. He extended his hand, and though Wickham wavered for a moment, he finally shook it. "I hope I will not regret this."

Wickham smiled ruefully at him. "My word may mean

little to you at present, but I give it anyway, with a hope someday it will be worth something."

***

Darcy had been brooding in the library for some time when Richard returned to Netherfield, and he called out as his cousin strode past in the corridor.

"Oh, Darcy! I was going to speak with you. I have seen Wickham."

"And?"

Richard poured himself a drink and then sat back on the sofa. "I have decided to accept the truth and give the whole damned mess my blessing."

Darcy raised his eyebrows, wary of his cousin's recent antics. "That is quite the reversal."

"He offered to sign away any financial claims, and after everything I have heard these past five days, I can see no other mischief in it, beyond my own stubborn refusal to accept that a man I have always loathed is my own flesh and blood."

This sentiment was not unlike what Darcy himself had been struggling with since Wickham's parentage had been confirmed. "I think it will be a relief just to have it all out," Darcy sighed. "I spoke with him yesterday and the day before – I have made my peace with it, and as long as his debauchery is behind him, I think I can accept him."

In truth, Darcy had been rather moved by all that he had read in the express Richard sent the previous evening. His last concern was for his sister. "I only hope we can get it all over with quickly – and quietly. I would not want any lingering tittle-tattle to taint Georgiana's coming out."

"No, of course," Richard said, leaning back heavily. He looked preoccupied, and Darcy could guess why.

"I ought to speak to you about this morning."

Richard took a long draught of his brandy. "For the love of God, Darcy."

"It was badly done, on both sides. I will admit it was wrong for Elizabeth and me to encourage Miss Bingley's wrath, but we were disappointed that you would deceive us a second time."

"I am in love with her, Darcy, and now she hates me."

Darcy was surprised to find that he was not at all surprised by his cousin's revelation. "Can you not try to reconcile with her?"

"I can always try again," Richard signed. "But I have really stepped in it. It is strange – I love her fire and her ferocity, but I had no idea that I was invoking such ire."

"You hoped to keep her in ignorance until you returned from London?"

"It might have worked," Richard lamented. "I thought it would serve you and Lizzy better, for you have some things yet to resolve between yourselves. Caroline would have been in the way. And I wanted to be a little surer of her affection for me, but then I ought to have known better."

"Elizabeth and I have resolved our differences; we are on friendly enough terms to work through the crisis, and you and Miss Bingley must do the same," Darcy replied, his thoughts drifting back to Elizabeth.

"You are an idiot, Darcy," Richard groaned. "You ought to leave me. I will do better tomorrow, I will make some sort of plan – but tonight let me wallow in it all, would you?"

Darcy felt enough pity that he resisted the urge to lecture his cousin, and silently left the room, letting Richard sulk in peace. In the corridor, he spied Miss Bingley peek out of her bedroom, and she waved him over with a frenzied look.

He approached with some little curiosity. "Are you well, Miss Bingley?"

"I have had an idea, Mr. Darcy. I have thought of a way to help."

"I would be happy to hear it."

"Well, I recalled the things Jos said to you that one awful morning – you must understand, Mr. Darcy, I did not yet understand why I was repeating the day, and I was quite at my wits' end." Miss Bingley blushed and looked away.

Darcy felt he owed her some little sympathy. "Of course."

"Well, I think that you must make amends with Jos. In a

few minutes, he and Charles will come out of the billiard room, as they always do at this hour. I will say something unpleasant, and you must reproach me." Caroline met his eye nervously. "Tell Charles that he must insist I go to the card party and accept Jane as his choice – something like that. That is what Jos wants from you, to encourage Charles to defy me and do as he pleases. I will support my brother, but it must appear as though Charles has stood up for himself."

Darcy was impressed. "That is very insightful."

"I have had a great deal to consider and reconsider," Miss Bingley admitted demurely.

There were voices in the hall, and Miss Bingley gave him a significant look; Darcy nodded his silent agreement. As Bingley and Jos came around the corner together, Miss Bingley affected a look of disdain. "I will certainly not attend such a gathering, Mr. Darcy, and I wish my brother would not, either," she said haughtily.

Darcy was still astonished by her transformation, but managed some reply. "That is disappointing. Bingley, you will attend the card party tonight, will you not?"

"Of course! Will you go?"

"I will. If Jane Bennet is really your choice, you have my support, though I know you do not need it."

"No, but I should like to have it anyway," Bingley replied. "And I hope you will come round to the idea, Caroline."

Miss Bingley crossed her arms and stomped her foot. "You can do so much better, Charles."

Jos bristled at her. "Must you be such a shrew, Caroline? Bingley, you ought not to put up with her constant complaining."

Darcy edged a glance at Miss Bingley, and then addressed his friend. "Jos is right, you know. You are your own man, Bingley. Nobody's opinion need matter but your own; I should never allow Georgiana to protest my choice of bride."

"Georgiana is too well-bred to ever do such a thing," Miss Bingley gasped.

"Clearly you are not," Jos snapped at her, and Caroline sputtered with performative rage.

"Charles, do not let him bully me."

"It is you bullying him," Jos thundered.

Darcy gave Bingley a hard look, awaited his shoulders, and nodded encouragingly. "If you are ever to take a stand, now is the time."

Bingley knit his brow for a moment, then mimicked Darcy's posture. "Caroline, you will not speak to Jos like that – or me." he glanced at Darcy for reassurance, then smiled. "And I wish you would come to the card party tonight. Jane Bennet is an angel, and I wish you to be friends. You have only complained since we have come to Netherfield, when I am sure you would like it if you tried."

"Bravo, Bingley," Darcy said, while Miss Bingley looked contrite.

"Charles, if you tell me I am to love Jane Bennet as my sister, I am sure I will accept what I must," Miss Bingley said softly. "But are you quite sure?"

Bingley nodded, grinning widely. "I am sure! I love her, Caroline, and I am going to marry her. If you do not like it, you may return to London, or go and stay in Scarborough with our aunt."

Miss Bingley pouted. "Charles...."

Bingley looked to Jos, and then to Darcy; both gentlemen nodded approvingly at him. "That is my decision, Caroline."

"Very well, Charles. I will attend the card party and make the best of it, if it is what you wish." Miss Bingley retreated into her bedchamber and slammed the door.

Jos broke into laughter. "About damn time, my good man."

***

Elizabeth and Jane greeted the party from Netherfield very merrily that evening, but Elizabeth did her best to focus her attention on Caroline; she still could not meet Mr. Darcy's eye, though it had been nearly a week since she had drunkenly kissed him. She had thought about it more than she could admit, even to herself, and she was fearful that she would betray her thoughts the moment she met his eye.

Jane and Mr. Bingley had quickly drifted away, lost in each other already, and now Mr. Collins was moving toward them. Caroline snorted with laughter and looked up at Mr. Darcy. "I have solved one puzzle, and here comes another. Now it is your turn, sir. Lizzy, come and walk with me."

Elizabeth linked her arm through Caroline's and glanced back over her shoulder at Mr. Darcy as they abandoned him to Mr. Collins' exaltations about Lady Catherine de Bourgh. She had played such a joke on him before, but it was odd that she should now be sharing the joke with the suddenly amiable Caroline Bingley. And Caroline had been rather familiar with Mr. Darcy – Elizabeth began to feel the sting of jealousy.

"What puzzle have you and Mr. Darcy solved?"

"It was a small triumph, but I have made some progress in settling a family dispute," Miss Bingley replied. "I allowed Charles to give me a little dressing down, and Mr. Darcy facilitated it."

Elizabeth arched an eyebrow. "That was brave of you, although I suppose I ought not be surprised, after this morning."

Caroline actually blushed. "I had no idea I would act in such a way, but we had better not speak of it."

They were silent a moment, strolling around the perimeter of the room, and Elizabeth laughed at the recollection of another occasion when they had done the same. "Do you remember when we took a turn about the room at Netherfield, and teased Mr. Darcy?"

Caroline laughed. "*You* teased him; I had only paltry praise. But he is watching again – what did he say then? Our figures appear to best advantage when walking. Well, I can guess which of us he is admiring."

For a moment Elizabeth assumed that Caroline was referring to herself, but she looked pointedly at Elizabeth. She had not let herself look in that direction, but now Elizabeth braved a glance at Mr. Darcy; he was staring intently at her, as he had often been wont to do. She shivered, and smiled softly at him, then looked back at Caroline.

"Lizzy, can I ask you something?"

"Of course."

Caroline looked at Elizabeth with some trepidation. "When Baba Romilda asked us about our *beaux* – when she expected to see the four of us together...." She wrung her hands. "Do you think there is some particular reason why it is the four of us all trapped in this together?"

Elizabeth was surprised by the question, but she wished to give it due consideration. "I have no idea. We ought to try and ask her. I have not seen her since my first market day, and I intended to question her, but then I realized you were – I ought to have spoken to her first."

"We should look for her tomorrow," Caroline said, fidgeting still.

Elizabeth was quiet for a moment as she pondered Baba Romilda's words. She had thought her friend was merely taunting them, but could there be something in it? Elizabeth could not convince herself that she did not have feelings for Mr. Darcy, not when that kiss, and every other embrace, had consumed her thoughts constantly. But that would mean....

"You like Richard," Elizabeth breathed.

Caroline glanced down, and dropped Elizabeth's arm. "There are many other angles to our dilemma that I must consider – I mean to speak to everyone, in the hope of some second stroke of genius – and I promised Charles I would talk with Jane." She abruptly moved away, and Elizabeth laughed to herself as she considered how Caroline had accosted Richard that morning.

Mary began to play a jolly tune, and in another moment Lydia and Kitty were dragging their favorite officers by the hand to make up a dance. Hoping he was still staring, Elizabeth glanced again at Mr. Darcy; she broke into a wide, irrepressible smile as he met her eye with a look of emotions just as tumultuous as her own.

Every strange turn of events in the last three weeks swirled in her mind, stirring her heart. She had begun to revel in the madness of it all, the strange and exciting sensation of clinging to him in the eye of a storm, laughing at the world and making merry as if there were no tomorrow. Could it not be what it was a week ago? But this small hope quickly grew into something bigger. *Could it not be more?*

She willed him to come to her, her face flushing with warmth as they stared at one another from across the room, and after a breathless moment, he did. He took her hand in his, and she could see in his eyes that he felt what she did.

"Will you dance, Lizzy?"

She was utterly gone, and she knew it. She did not care. She wanted to laugh and spin and lose herself; she knew it could not last forever, but she would savor every blissful moment with him. "I would like nothing better, William."

***

Under other circumstances, Caroline might have followed Charles and Mr. Darcy into the library for a glass of brandy after they returned from the card party, but tonight she had not the heart for it. She had exerted herself to be more amiable than ever before to the people of Meryton, though she did not especially care for most of them.

The two eldest Miss Bennets she could tolerate, even like – she had been getting on very well with Elizabeth, until her new friend asked about Richard. Caroline had been very near confiding, but in the end, cowardice had got the better of her.

Just as it had with Richard. Scarcely a minute had passed all evening that she did not think of him, and berate herself for refusing him with such vehemence. If only he had waited until she was ready to accept! She had begun to think they could do well, once she had set her hopes of Mr. Darcy aside. She had Mr. Darcy to thank for that, and Elizabeth as well, in some small part.

Though Caroline had set out to prove her value to their unlikely group by solving all the puzzles that plagued them, she had done nothing of the kind. Instead she only watched Elizabeth and Mr. Darcy together, in a state of awe and jealousy. She was no longer jealous of Mr. Darcy, for as Louisa had said, she could never have had any passion with him. But she might have, with Richard, if only he had not spoiled it – and had she not then doubly ruined everything.

Mr. Darcy and Elizabeth had been utterly lost in one another, oblivious to everything around them; they had looked so blissfully happy. Caroline finally understood. That was it, the thing that Charles and Louisa thought was more important than fortune and status. Charles had it with Jane Bennet, and perhaps even Louisa and Jos might find it again – but Caroline had thrown it away when her pride was wounded – more than once now. "I am my own worst enemy," she muttered as she stalked through the corridor to her bedchamber.

There was gentle laughter from the end of the hall. "I know the feeling," Richard said as he stepped out of the shadows.

Caroline was at once excited and irritated that he should intrude on such a reverie. "Well, at least I can be sure you are not lurking hidden in my *boudoir*."

"As much as I should like to be," he whispered, moving toward her.

"You have some nerve," Caroline hissed.

"Not really," he replied. "I had to get very drunk to approach you again."

"Charming."

"Not enough for you, though, darling." Richard was very close now, and he slowly raised his hands to hold her by the shoulders.

Caroline was not unaffected by the torturous look in his eyes. "I was cross with you today, and I had every right to be. But I did not mean no forever."

Richard laughed and tugged at a stray wisp of her hair. "I do not suppose I ought to ask again at such a moment."

Caroline tipped her face up toward his. She would not say yes – not yet – but she would not object to a kiss. "Not now, Richard. For Heaven's sake, let me think on it."

"You will?"

"I have been thinking of it the whole time you were away. I might have told you had you behaved in a more gentlemanlike manner," she chided him. Richard grinned stupidly at her, and Caroline's eyes went wide. "You love it, you awful man. Every attempt to put you off only makes you want more. Well, I might have some fun with that."

Richard moved quickly, and before she knew what she was about, Caroline was pressed up against her bedroom door, kissing him deeply. She gave in to the thrill of it – they might be caught at any moment, not that it mattered. For another moment all that mattered was the way their bodies felt together, and the places where his lips travelled.

Caroline let out a throaty gasp as he kissed along her neck, and he responded with a moan and a laugh as he ran his hands through her hair. "Please, Caroline, end my suffering," he whispered.

She smiled as he looked into her eyes, and when her hand finally found the doorknob, she turned it and stepped backward into her room. "I am sure I shall – but not tonight." She slammed the door in his face and threw herself down on the bed with a dizzy grin.

12

Caroline and Elizabeth met early and scoured the market for Baba Romilda, but to no avail. The streets were growing more crowded, and Caroline was in no humor to linger. "Lizzy, shall we keep looking – or might we go to Purvis Lodge?"

"I doubt we would find her," Elizabeth conceded. "Shall we locate Mr. Darcy?"

"I think not," Caroline said, leading her friend toward the lane to Purvis Lodge. "I meant to ask your advice, if you do not object."

"No, not at all. I believe I can guess the subject," Elizabeth said with an arch look.

"Is it that obvious?"

"Well, you did say – or shout – that you had kissed him – when you were beating Richard yesterday."

"Right." Caroline blushed. "I wonder – do you think I ought to forgive him?"

"Oh dear, I could not tell you – you must be the judge of your own feelings."

Caroline laughed ruefully. "That sounds like advice I might have got from Jane."

Elizabeth screwed up her face. "You must understand, I consider you both my friends, though you have both done me some mischief before."

"Well, surely there must be some code of sisterhood I might invoke," Caroline said with mirth. "In my position, what would you do?"

Elizabeth tipped her head to one side as she considered. "Mr. Darcy played a little trick on me when we first found out about each other – I had some revenge, which was amusing – for both of us, I think. But then we made amends since we must collaborate to solve our dilemma."

Caroline made a droll face. "Is that all?"

"We are talking about *your* problem," Elizabeth said, nudging her shoulder against Caroline's. "But for what it is worth, I think we are very near to the end of our troubles – at least, I hope we are. We have discovered a great deal, surely."

"So you think I should forgive him?"

"At least enough for us to get on as we must. A little needling would not go amiss, but then I think he might enjoy it," Elizabeth said with a twinkle of mirth in her eye.

Caroline blushed again as she recalled their encounter last night. She could forgive him just enough, as Elizabeth said, but a little mischief would not go amiss.

The two ladies spent almost an hour together at Purvis Lodge, speaking mostly of Charles and Jane, until the gentlemen finally arrived. Caroline had grown quite at ease with Elizabeth Bennet, who was all the things Caroline had previously assumed she only *pretended* to be. Indeed, Caroline was beginning to feel optimistic that this day was going to turn out much better than the one before it.

Richard and Mr. Darcy arrived together, stunned to find Caroline and Elizabeth sitting together on a low-hanging tree branch at the back of the park. Caroline was almost embarrassed, but decided at the last to affect the same unabashed bemusement as Elizabeth.

"You are in no state to receive an earl this evening,

Caroline," Richard called out to her, laughing.

Mr. Darcy had come forward to help Elizabeth down, but she jumped off the branch and landed gracefully on her own before taking his arm with a grin; Caroline attempted to do the same, but her landing was not as sure. Richard was at her side the moment she began to stumble, his arm encircling her waist so naturally that for a moment she could only stare and smile stupidly at him.

She rested her hands on his chest to steady herself, and Richard laid his free hand atop one of hers, guiding it down his jacket so that she could feel the shape of what was in his pocket – he had brought the little black box from London again. "Wicked man," she drawled, shoving him away.

Elizabeth was swatting at Mr. Darcy for something he had said with shocking mirth. "What is this about receiving an earl?"

"Richard has invited his father and Lady Carson to Netherfield," Mr. Darcy replied. "Lady Carson will bring her sister and brother-in-law as well. You were gone early this morning, but I informed Charles that we would need extra rooms, and that we will have a large party for the engagement dinner."

Caroline stiffened and moved away from Richard before she rounded on him. "Engagement dinner? For whom?"

"Did you not receive my letter this morning? I wrote to you and Darcy explaining my plan," Richard said.

"I did not get any letter," Caroline hissed. "Is this another trick?"

"I swear it is not. I had to give my father and the others some good reason to travel on short notice, for I think we ought to have everybody here – I mean to bring Wickham into it tonight, but I could not tell them that."

"I see – more lies," Caroline huffed. "Well, if I am to receive guests, I better return home to assist with the preparations – but if there is no letter from you, I am going to wring your neck."

Richard caught her hand as she moved to leave. "But you will go along with it?"

"It need only be for tonight, you know," Elizabeth interjected. "Mr. Darcy and I have had to do the same before."

"But that is just it," Mr. Darcy contradicted. "If Richard's plan succeeds, tomorrow will be Thursday after all."

Richard glared at his cousin, and looked imploringly at Caroline. "Surely you mean to accept me eventually – I know you only wish to make me squirm a little."

Caroline glowered at him and jerked her hand away. "Since, as usual, I do not even know your plan, I cannot be sure it will work. But yes, I will go along with it – but you *will* squirm." She turned on her heel and stormed away.

***

Wickham arrived at Netherfield while the earl and his party were still settling into their rooms and preparing for dinner. It had been impossible to exclude Georgiana from the scheme; Darcy was upstairs with her now, explaining that the mistake at Ramsgate had been his.

Meanwhile, Richard received his guest in the parlor. "I was not sure you would come."

Wickham's look was skeptical. "And I am not sure why I did – or why I was invited."

Richard motioned for him to sit, and offered Wickham a drink before pouring one for himself. They moved to the sofas, though Wickham still looked about as if suspecting to find some hidden enemy. "I cannot imagine you merely want to have a pleasant chat."

"Can you not?" Richard swirled the drink on his glass before he took a sip. He was here and the moment was upon him, and though Richard had faced far worse, his resolve began to falter – he was at a loss for words. This lasted but a moment; Richard downed the drink and laughed, and the whole story came spilling out of him.

Wickham listened with incredulity, and even indignation at times, as Richard explained what he and his companions had been through. When Richard was done, Wickham finished his own drink and stared blankly at him. "How is this possible?"

"Does it matter?"

"I should think so," Wickham retorted. "It begins to sound to me as though this is some sort of prank. You summon me here, tell me things I have no memory of, though you *do* possess certain facts that you could not have known...."

"But I have never been kind to you before," Richard supplied. "At least, not in many years. This is true, but you are my brother, and now that I know it, I shall just have to accept it."

"Because you think you have no other choice," Wickham edged.

"Well, that is the rub – as it happens, I have come to believe you less the villain than I had thought, and I have no objection to whatever my father decides to do with you – clearly your mother holds considerable sway. But you cannot know for sure that I support you, any more than I can be sure that you have pure intentions. So it is a matter of trust both ways."

Wickham nodded. "And Darcy?"

"He was more easily persuaded than I," Richard replied. "He is upstairs with Georgiana, for she must be prepared for the shock of meeting with you."

"I see." Wickham looked away for a moment. "And you say there was a day that I spoke privately with her, explained my side of things?"

"Not quite privately – I was hidden behind a screen."

"Ah. Well, I suppose I would have done the same in your position," Wickham sighed, hanging his head. "Would Darcy allow it again? That is, I presume Georgie would have no memory of it either, and if I truly brought her any peace on that occasion...."

"Darcy is already explaining his error in judgement," Richard replied, and he watched Wickham's eyes go wide with shock. "But I am sure it can be arranged."

Wickham leaned back against the sofa. "This is quite a shock. I had no notion of Darcy being in the area when I came here – I did not expect to encounter either of you until after things were settled. I certainly did not imagine you would make it so easy."

Richard smiled sadly at him. "That must be a failing on my part, and on Darcy's – though of course you have given us some little grief in the past."

"I have," Wickham admitted. "It has been many years, but yes, I was rather a reckless youth. I envied you both a great deal."

"And now?"

"I seek no profit in this," Wickham said. "Five years ago, I might have done, but since I have come to know my mother, to understand what she has been through, I just want us to be a family. She deserves that much."

"Well, then." Richard extended his hand. "I suppose I ought to start calling you George."

***

The Bennets arrived at Netherfield just after the Lucases, and the large party spent a quarter hour exchanging pleasantries in the drawing room. Georgiana was looking more serene after her conversation with George Wickham, and when Darcy introduced her to the Bennet sisters, she took to them at once.

Darcy hung back, as he tended to do in crowds, but he was filled with a tremendous sense of peace and calm. Everything was going well – splendidly, in fact. For the first time in three weeks, he dared to hope this might be the end of his troubles.

His eyes landed on Elizabeth across the room. She was speaking to the Gardiners, who were her aunt and uncle, as well as sister and brother-in-law to Lady Carson; the merry widow greeted Elizabeth affectionately as she presented her to the earl.

Elizabeth was magnificent, so warm and easy in company, so natural. As he watched her, Darcy struggled against the sense of duty that had been bred into him, that he had been reminded of all his life. He was so near to freeing himself from the redundant nightmare – could he really risk it all? Surely whatever force bound them in this cycle would not allow him to jeopardize such a weighty decision.

He had Georgiana to consider – her prospects might already suffer if the earl decided to publicly recognize Wickham. And then, he could not be sure that Elizabeth would even have him – he could not risk so much on so little, for what had there been between them but madness that increased daily?

***

Elizabeth and Darcy had been seated across from one another at dinner – a deliberate choice on Caroline's part, Elizabeth suspected from the looks their hostesses had been giving them. However, Georgiana was as eager to be acquainted with Elizabeth as she had been on the last occasion – and perhaps eager to distract herself from George Wickham at the other end of the table – and so Elizabeth had not much opportunity to speak with Mr. Darcy himself. Not in the way that she wished to, at least.

They were a large party – two dozen, as the Lucases had been included – and there was no separation of the sexes after dinner. Elizabeth was one of the last to go through to the drawing room, and faced the difficult task of deciding whom she wished to speak with first.

The presence of her aunt and uncle Gardiner had been a delightful surprise, for she had not realized Lady Carson was her aunt's sister – she had met the charming woman many years ago, when she was still Mrs. Bentham. Still, the draw of sharing a private jest with Mr. Darcy was too great, and Elizabeth began to move that way.

Caroline intercepted her and linked her arm through Elizabeth's. "Well, Lizzy, I have been up to some scheming tonight, and I still think I do a better job of it than my unfortunate fiancé," she said with a roll of her eyes.

"Oh?"

"Oh, yes," Caroline replied with satisfaction. "You have done well to recommend Mary to your aunt and uncle for a London trip – especially as she will be moving in the finest circles when the earl and Lady Carson marry. But what of your youngest sisters? They may be wishing they were at the card party with all the officers, but look at the company they might keep. I think your mother is beginning to understand, for I have observed her scold your sisters on their behavior, and I have never seen such a thing happen before."

"It is a rarity," Elizabeth said wryly.

"And I have some thoughts about Mr. Collins, too," Caroline continued. "You need not marry him for the sake of Longbourn, not with Jane to marry Charles, and you know he is too ridiculous for any of your sisters – only observe him there with your friend Miss Lucas. I sat them near me at dinner on purpose to spy, when I was not provoking my intended. Miss Lucas almost renders your cousin sensible, and I think she would take him."

"I would not wish her to suffer such a fate," Elizabeth cried.

Caroline set her mouth in a pragmatic expression. "Does she appear to be suffering now?"

A glance in that direction told Elizabeth the truth – Charlotte looked content, even happy speaking with Mr. Collins, and her posture suggested that she was actively trying to hold his attention. Elizabeth pushed away her revulsion. "Ugh," she muttered.

"Well, just think on it," Caroline replied. "I am determined to put an end to this repetition by any means necessary, and if improvement is called for, we must rise to the occasion."

Elizabeth was struck by the notion that this might really be it – everything had gone so well that evening. Mr. Bingley had been glued to Jane's side since the moment they arrived, and seemed every moment to be on the verge of declaring himself. Richard and Mr. Darcy appeared satisfied with the outcome of their efforts with Mr. Wickham. It finally began to seem that everything was falling into place.

"Tomorrow might really be Thursday," Elizabeth breathed, daring to hope.

Caroline's eyes suddenly lit up. "You must stay the night, Lizzy!"

"What? Why? I have not brought my things – and as far as my family knows, I just stayed several nights only a few days ago."

"Yes, and we have come to form a very dear bond," Caroline said, giggling. "Do not be daft, you must know I wish to celebrate if you are still here in the morning. You shall wake to me jumping up on the bed and positively dousing you in champagne!"

Elizabeth arched an eyebrow. "A tempting offer indeed."

Caroline steered them across the large drawing room, to where Georgiana was speaking with Lady Carson and Mrs. Gardiner. "You must all convince Lizzy to stay the night. She would be most agreeable company at breakfast, and then we might spend the day tomorrow together – can you think of anything better?"

"No indeed," Georgiana cried, clapping her hands.

"And what say you, Mrs. Gardiner? Lizzy has been making great claims of being your favorite, though Miss Mary has been the lucky winner of the prize trip to London."

"Do stay, Lizzy," Mrs. Gardiner entreated, squeezing Elizabeth's hand. "I think it would please *everyone* here at Netherfield a great deal." She cast a significant glance in the direction of Mr. Darcy, who was watching her from across the room as he spoke with Mr. Gardiner.

Elizabeth smiled at what was a happy sight for her; she felt flustered from the rush of tender sentiments the moment aroused in her. Still, she attempted to resist – in a small way she scarcely trusted herself. "I have not brought any clothes," she repeated, the only objection Caroline had not rebuffed.

"We are a near size," Georgiana said. "I will loan you something. Oh please, I am sure we can stay up all night talking – is that not what you do with all your sisters?"

The look on the girl's face was so eager, and even Caroline seemed beyond any degree of affability Elizabeth might have expected from her. "I shall have to ask Mamma," she said weakly.

Georgiana bounced with excitement. "Let me," she cried. "I am so very fond of her – she is terribly kind, and so full of praise for everyone."

Elizabeth laughed at the notion that her mother had once again unwittingly charmed Georgiana Darcy. "Go on, then," she laughed, and Georgiana scampered away to speak with Mrs. Bennet.

Elizabeth could not resist teasing her new friend, and gave Caroline an arch look. "Mamma is rather wonderful, is she not?"

Caroline coughed, then broke into a smile. "A woman who dines with four and twenty families is perfectly capable of making fine friends – I think she is very fortunate in her new devotee," she replied diplomatically.

"And as I am not to go to London, I shall take Mamma's part and say the country is a great deal pleasanter than town," Elizabeth chided her.

There was a squeal across the room that indicated Mrs. Bennet had given her permission; Georgiana was grinning and nodding at Elizabeth, while her mother fluttered her handkerchief. Elizabeth blushed, and Lady Carson came to the rescue by calling for some music. "Why are the young people not dancing? I am not too old for the activity, and I suspect some others are willing."

Mary quickly obliged them by opening the pianoforte. Elizabeth instinctively looked to Mr. Darcy – she knew he would come to her, and so he did. Richard followed, and Caroline eyed him with a wide grin. But just as the gentlemen approached, Caroline turned to the side and solicited Mr. Wickham as her partner.

Elizabeth watched in horror as Richard's shoulders sagged and his face fell into a gape of dismay. She gave Mr. Darcy an apologetic look and slipped her hand into Richard's, determined to rescue the poor man.

They danced alongside Jane and Mr. Bingley, while the earl partnered Lady Carson. Elizabeth glanced at Caroline with a stern look, but her friend only smiled and gestured to where Mr. Collins was leading Charlotte to join the dance. Elizabeth rolled her eyes and turned her attention to Richard.

"You are kind to stand up with me, Lizzy," he said, casting

a wary glance at Caroline. "She is determined to punish me."

"She was ready to forgive you," Elizabeth said. "You *have* made it rather difficult. I still do not understand why you have been so dishonest with her – and all of us."

Richard turned and spun Elizabeth with the other dancers. "I only deceived her once. I really did send her a letter this morning to warn her of my intentions – I bore my heart and soul, truth be told. And she gave me encouragement when we spoke last evening. She is a very stubborn woman, which I usually find charming, but at present it is immeasurably frustrating."

"But why did you not tell her about Mr. Darcy and me?"

"I thought she would get in the way while I was in London."

"What do you mean?"

"I mean you and Darcy," Richard whispered with a wag of his eyebrows.

"Richard, please," Elizabeth cried. "You must not say such things!"

"Why not? I know what I walked in on that night at your aunt's house, and every time the two of you are together you look like you want to devour one another."

Elizabeth felt a sudden heat spread across her cheeks; she could not bring herself to deny it. "Caroline and I saw Baba Romilda, and she said something about the four of us – Caroline thinks it means...."

"Of course it does," Richard said. "You and Darcy began to repeat on the same day, as did Caroline and me. It is blisteringly obvious. I am not being as uncooperative as you all think – I believe I am the only one taking the correct approach."

Elizabeth's eyes landed again on Mr. Darcy as she and Richard went down the dance. He was watching her, and he offered the trace of a smile. "Could it really be that simple?"

"Perhaps the other things are a part of it, all the improvements, and Wickham – the perfect day. But in the most important part of our dilemma, Darcy and Caroline are being incredibly pigheaded."

It was all too much for Elizabeth. "Forgive me – may we sit down?"

"Of course." Richard led Elizabeth to a quiet corner of the room. Mr. Darcy perceived them and began to move that way, but Mary ended her song and quickly began another, and Caroline detached herself from Mr. Wickham in favor of Mr. Darcy.

Elizabeth felt her heart sink as Mr. Darcy looked helplessly at her before beginning the dance with Caroline. "What am I to do?"

Richard sat at her side to commiserate with her. "You must see that he cares for you very much."

"I... I am not sure," Elizabeth replied. "Sometimes I think I am being terribly foolish."

"I know what you mean exactly," Richard sighed. "You and I are clever, Lizzy, and we know what we want – but we have the misfortune of loving two people who are both their own worst enemy. They will cut off their nose to spite their face, and I think we must be the ones to do something about it."

She let out a long, shaky sigh. "You are not suggesting I...."

"It would be not as strange as all this madness," Richard replied, gesturing broadly. "He is stubborn, but he is not without feeling. But I suspect you are braver."

"Then you suspect wrongly," Elizabeth teased him half-heartedly. "I could never...."

"Just say it?"

Elizabeth considered, really giving the notion some thought. But she could not imagine the prospect without a tremendous sense of trepidation that battled the pleasant recollection of what it had been like to kiss Mr. Darcy. "That night at my aunt's house, you may recall I was quite drunk."

Richard grinned at her and produced a flask from his coat pocket. "We must all do what need be done, Lizzy. Do you not long for Thursday?"

Elizabeth seized the flask before anyone could see what they were about. He waved over a footman with a glass of wine and handed it to her. "Drink that, and then fill it from the flask. Well – half should do."

"I should say so," Elizabeth laughed, sipping at the wine. "I cannot believe I am taking your advice."

"My advice was to drink that, not sip it."

Elizabeth laughed, and then downed the glass, the strong claret overpowering her. She let out a shaky breath; Richard took the flask and poured a small measure into Elizabeth's empty wine glass. "In for a penny, in for a pound," he whispered, tucking the flask back into his pocket.

This time it burned, but afterward the taste was pleasant. Elizabeth chuckled at her own folly. "I am really going to do this."

"Just the spirit!" Richard clapped his hands. "Fear not, Lizzy. All will be well, and perhaps we shall really wake up to Thursday."

Elizabeth drew her shoulders back and nodded. "I do think you are right – but if you are not, I swear I shall not leave my house tomorrow."

The dance ended, but Richard stood and called for another, and Mary relinquished her place at the instrument to Maria Lucas. Richard extended his hand and helped Elizabeth to her feet, and she smiled brightly as Mr. Darcy moved that way with Caroline on his arm. She cast a sideward glance at Richard and whispered, "Shall you be brave, too, Colonel?"

"I have faced down many a foe, but none so frightening. Perhaps you had better lead the charge, General," Richard chided her.

Mr. Darcy came to claim Elizabeth, Richard grinned at Caroline before moving away to ask Georgiana to join the dance. Caroline blanched, but Elizabeth was only peripherally aware of it. Her eyes had locked on Mr. Darcy's, and again Elizabeth felt a strange heat as he led her to the dance.

She could hardly declare herself right here in the drawing room with two dozen people present, but Elizabeth was determined to work up the nerve to find her chance. In the meantime, all she could do was enjoy being with him, freely and openly as she had never allowed herself before.

This was easy. She did not feel the need to speak to him, she simply let herself *be*. Everything faded away but Mr. Darcy, and the look in his eyes told her more than could be said with words. They danced together afloat on a sea of strange and wonderful memories, of other evenings spent in a similar manner, happy and easy together despite the madness.

Elizabeth was surprised to see the party begin to break up just after the dance ended. She and Mr. Darcy lingered near one another as the other dancers began to move away and say their goodbyes. Amidst the chaos, Elizabeth slipped her hand into Mr. Darcy's. "I might be cross with you, you know, but I suppose there is enough of that going around."

He smiled wryly at her. "How have I offended you, Lizzy?"

"I think you know," she said, scrunching her face. "That night you refused to dance with me – I have forgiven the insult, but now that I know what I was missing – every time we dance, I think of how it might have been, if we had begun on better terms, if we had not always quarrelled." She met his eye boldly, not caring who saw as the room swirled with activity around her. "Could it have always felt like this?"

"Elizabeth," he breathed, but his voice was nearly drowned out by his sister; Georgiana bounced over to them, smiling brightly as she called their names. They instantly drew apart.

"Uncle says I must go to bed, so I will say good night, William," Georgiana said. "If you wish to borrow something, Lizzy, you had better come upstairs with me."

"Let me say goodbye to Mamma and Papa," Elizabeth told her as Georgiana began to lead her away. "I will come up with you, and then perhaps I might go find something to read in the library." She looked back over her shoulder, hoping Mr. Darcy had heard her, but she could not be sure.

***

Caroline had been punishing Richard all evening; she ought to have expected that he would not let her get away with it. As her guests departed and everyone else went up to their rooms, Richard drew her into an alcove by the stairs. "I had hoped you would stop fighting this."

"Then you have hoped in vain," Caroline hissed. "I told you I was not ready. Instead of respecting my wishes, you inveigled me in another scheme without my consent, and I will not have it!"

"I wrote you this morning, I swear it! I sent two notes – one to you and one to Darcy. He clearly received his."

"That hardly makes a difference – I cannot imagine you were giving me a choice – only a little advance notice, so that you would not have to bear my wrath in person. But I never received this note and I wonder if you only mean to lie your way out of things. Again."

Richard began to look remorseful. "I am sorry if you did not get my letter; I think if you had, you might understand me a little better. I have not wooed you well, but I love you, Caroline. Even after tonight, after all your antics."

"Antics!"

"Petty revenge," he snarled. "You flirted with George all through dinner, refused to dance with me – and I heard you tell Lady Lucas, an infamous gossip, that I had coerced you into a compromise."

"Well, *good*," Caroline spat. "I hope it was quite humiliating for you, after what you have done to me."

There was a low rumble in Richard's throat as he edged closer to her. "After you embarrassed yourself, making a play for Darcy? That was not pleasant for either of us."

Caroline glared up at him. "You stupid man! I did not mean to – of course not! I only wanted to understand why – I wanted some way to accept it. Or would you have preferred me to always wonder?"

Richard looked deflated, and he began to stroke her shoulder. "Is that really why you did it? I thought you still wanted a chance to catch him."

Caroline leaned into his touch for a moment, but she was not quite ready to relent. "You must stop assuming the worst of me. It makes it exceedingly difficult to have any faith in your declarations of love."

He leaned in, but Caroline pushed him away. "Kissing will not solve anything, you brute! I told you I need time to think, and maybe you should do the same, because nothing you have said has convinced me."

Caroline turned and fled upstairs. As she dressed for bed, Abigail produced a small white envelope from her pocket. "Forgive me, ma'am, there was a letter for you this morning. You were already gone to the market, and Jimmy was supposed to give it to you when you got home, but the colonel who sent it had arrived and so Jimmy set the note aside, thinking it did not matter. I only just found out it had not been delivered, but I thought I had better bring it up."

Caroline took the note delicately in her hands, a feeling of dread in her stomach. "You were right to bring it to me – and I give you leave to box Jimmy's ears for his dereliction," she said with half-hearted humor. She reached for the hairbrush Abigail was running through her hair. "You may leave me."

Caroline slowly went through the motions of preparing for bed, staring at the note on her dressing table all the while. Sometimes she took a small glass of brandy before bed; tonight, it was a rather larger one. She sipped for a few minutes, steeling herself to read what she knew was likely to soften her heart.

Finally she read the letter, and a beautiful one it was. It was too much, and Caroline could only feel what a fool she had been. She crumpled the letter and threw it at the fire, sobbing, and then she threw her glass of brandy; the crystal smashed against the marble fireplace and the fire hissed. Caroline hurled herself onto her bed and wept until she fell asleep.

***

Elizabeth wrapped the borrowed dressing gown around herself as she crept into the library. The fire was still lit, so she set her candle down on the mantle and made herself cozy in the window seat. She had not the chance to speak to Mr. Darcy, and she did not know if she would see him again tonight, but she had to hope – she was certainly still too tipsy to sleep, for she had not known the party would end so soon.

She selected a book and attempted to read it, but she did not seriously attempt to focus on the words; laughing at herself, Elizabeth leaned back and indulged herself in reliving some of the more exhilarating moments from that night.

There were footsteps, and Elizabeth knew it was him before she opened her eyes. She looked up at Mr. Darcy and smiled. "You came," she breathed.

He had not seen her before, but now Mr. Darcy looked over at her. He, too, was dressed for bed, his muscular form accented as the fire lit him from behind. "Elizabeth," he said, halting beside one of the shelves. "I could not sleep."

"Oh." Elizabeth stared at him; she was hoping he had taken her hint from before. She let out a shaky breath, equally afraid of speaking, and of losing the chance – but she could not determine which would be worse.

Mr. Darcy picked a book off the shelf and began to move away, then hesitated. "You said – were you expecting me?"

In for a penny, in for a pound. Elizabeth nodded slowly and stood. "Yes, William."

He took a few more steps toward her. "Why?"

"You know why," she breathed, looking at him with a wild intensity that she no longer wished to repress. She had never been afraid of him, and in this moment she was not afraid of anything. "I love you; you must know it."

His face twisted with emotion. "I did not – not until tonight. I saw it, and it made me want to weep because – because I love you, too."

Tears pricked at Elizabeth's eyes, and she felt her entire being light up with excitement. She closed the space between them and wrapped her arms around him, but he drew back. "Elizabeth, no."

The air rushed out of her lungs; Elizabeth rested her hands on his chest and looked up in some confusion. "No? I do not understand."

He covered her hands with his and shook his head, his expression clouded with grief. "We cannot do this, Lizzy. Not now, not when we are so close."

Tears streamed down her face. "What are you saying?"

Mr. Darcy turned away from her, pacing toward the fireplace. He leaned against the mantle, but Elizabeth pursued him. "William, if you have felt what I have...."

"Of course I have," he breathed. "But I cannot – I cannot speak of it now. Do you not see? How could I promise you anything, when we do not even know when tomorrow may ever come?"

Elizabeth recoiled from him, her heart searing with the pain from his unexpected rejection. "I was so sure...."

"How? How can you be so sure?"

"Because we have been through hell and back together," she said, her face twisting as she wept.

"Yes, exactly."

Mr. Darcy's voice trembled, and Elizabeth moved closer; in the light of the fire she could see that his face was streaked with tears. Her own began to flow again, and she covered her face with her hands. Mr. Darcy drew her into an embrace, and it was sheer torture for her. She clung to him anyway, savoring the feel of his arms around her; she had ruined everything, and may never have such another opportunity. She buried her face in his chest, her hands clutching at the thin fabric of his shirt. "I love you," she whispered.

He drew her closer. "I love you, too. I am so sorry, Elizabeth. After everything we have been through...."

"I know," she moaned.

"What if it is only the madness?" His voice cracked with emotion. "You have been so brave, so remarkable through all of this, even when we have quarreled. And we have quarreled so much – I cannot say how it will be when all this is over."

Elizabeth scrunched her face to still the tears, but she was still gasping from the force of her sobs. "Must it be so different?"

"Can we not find our way out of this mess – can we not be as we were? You have been so perfect and right, and that is just what you must be until this is all over." He spoke soothingly, stroking her hair as Elizabeth wept. "You have been my dearest friend in this impossible situation, and I cannot lose that – we cannot risk it."

"Your friend," Elizabeth repeated with a sniffle. She lifted her head from his chest, but she still could not look up at him. How wrong she had been! Richard had convinced her that this was the way out of their dilemma, but Mr. Darcy only wanted her help, and not her heart – he did not see this as a solution, but a complication. An unwanted complication.

Elizabeth struggled to understand him. He loved her, and he felt what she did – everything that had passed between them had been real, and not a fancy of her own. She tried to cling to that, even if he could neither acknowledge nor offer anything else. She held fast to him, the tears now rolling gently from her eyes, and she could hear that he was still softly weeping as well.

They held each other in silence for several minutes, but it could never be enough for Elizabeth. She had no intention of begging him – her pride would not allow it – but neither could she will herself to break away from him. Her hands roamed up his back, and she shifted in his arms. He moved with her, and as she began to lift her head, he lowered his. She stopped as her forehead came to rest against his cheek, moving just slightly enough to brush her skin against his.

Elizabeth let out a shaky breath and stilled herself. She had only to turn her face just a little, and her lips would find his – she already knew how delightful a sensation it could be, and she wanted it again so badly it hurt. She tightened her grip on his shirt, desperately wishing he would be the one to do it, and for a moment they were utterly still, breathing raggedly.

Would he kiss her back? What stilled her was not a fear that he would reject her again, but that he would give in, and regret it afterward. This thought tore at her heart so brutally that she suddenly stepped several paces backward and let out a strange, guttural groan. She loved him too much to cause him any pain by taking such a liberty, but he had wounded her, and some small part of her seethed with a wild and desperate resentment.

She met his eye, and instantly wished she had not; but she could not look away. He appeared just as tormented as she was, and she could not bear it. "I am going to bed," she said, and then she fled the room. Her chamber was not far, and once she was within, Elizabeth threw herself against the plush pillows of the bed and cried herself to sleep.

***

My Dearest Caroline,

I have been a fool, once again – my passion for you has always rendered me thus, though I should happily devote myself to amending my wicked ways, if you could find it in your heart to forgive me. I love you, though I must not let it make me stupid.

But there is one thing that holds perfect clarity for me, and that is that we belong together. I have known it since the moment I saw you, saw the tender heart you always try to hide from the world. Though you were mortified that night at the opera, it was a small miracle to me; your distress was the most genuine thing in the room, and you the most beautiful woman in it. I have never looked at you without seeing that night; the memory of it has made you, in my eyes, the finest woman I have ever seen, or ever wish to.

I have made a joke of what I knew not how to express to you – even now I am writing the seventh draft of this letter already, having discarded six other abysmally inadequate attempts to convince you of the depth of my affections. I wish I could have done so when I wounded you last week – how I wish I could crumble up my actions and throw them away until I can manage better.

But you have given me hope for the first time ever, and I cannot let go of it. Though I am not an eloquent man, and am prone to as many odd humors as yourself, we are right together. Holding you in my arms is right; kissing you is the only way I can express what I have failed with words to convey, and I beg you to understand me, for I have never been so honest as when my lips meet yours.

I have loved you too long in suffering, dearest, loveliest Caroline, and I beg you to let this letter serve as the declaration I ought to have made so many times since this madness began – since I have known you. I must have some excuse to bring my father and Lady Carson from London on such short notice, that I might unite them with George Wickham. I can think of no better way than the dearest wish of my heart, that I might introduce them to the finest woman walking this earth – as my fiancée.

I throw myself upon your mercy, and beg you soften your defiant heart at last.

Yours in body and soul, forever,
Richard Fitzwilliam

The crumpled letter landed just short of the fireplace, at the base of the escritoire. A moment later, a crystal glass of brandy shattered against the fireplace. The fire roared, and sparks flew. An ember ignited the corner of the paper, and a small flame began to burn, blue and white at first, and then a brilliant orange.

The flame spread slowly, but eventually it engulfed the entire ball of paper, unnoticed by the woman who had thrown it. As her sobs stilled and she gave in to a fitful sleep, the flame blazed brighter. The burning paper shifted as the fire consumed it, and brushed against a leg of the heavily varnished desk.

The desk went up in flame much faster, with a great whooshing of air as the fire spread across it. A tapestry hung above it, and soon the flames licked up at it, until it, too, was consumed.

The wallpaper began to peel and pop; at last Caroline sat up in her bed. She opened her eyes just in time to see the heavy tapestry fall from the wall. The desk chair toppled backward, spreading more flames across the carpet. Caroline roused herself from the wretchedness of her slumber, gripped with fear. The fire had spread between her bed and the door – there was no way out.

The heat was unbearable, and the smoke stung her eyes; she recoiled, gripping at the sheets from fear. And then it struck her – a way out. She moved quickly, ripping the sheets from the bed and rushed toward the window, pulling it open and hanging her head out into the cold night to breathe some fresh air.

She worked quickly, knotting the sheets together and tugging to make sure they were secure. Choking on the smoke, Caroline quickly threw back her weight and tugged at the heavy wooden bed frame. When she had pulled it nearer the window, Caroline carefully tied one end of the bedsheets to the bedpost, and then threw her makeshift rope out the window into the darkness. Fear was just as strong an impulse as fury, and she climbed into the window casement and slowly rappelled down the side of the house.

Caroline took off running as soon as her feet hit the cold ground. She went around the side of the house, stopping at the window to the kitchens, which was at the ground level. There was a light still on within, and Caroline dropped to her hands and knees beside it. It was too dark for her to make out the mechanism to open it, so Caroline wrapped her fist in her nightgown and punched out the glass. The cook was just finishing up her duties, and stared at Caroline in astonishment through the jagged hole in the windowpane.

"There is a fire upstairs," Caroline shouted. "Get everyone out of the house."

The cook turned and fled toward the servants' hall, shouting imperceptibly; Caroline scrambled to her feet, stumbling in the darkness and shivering against the cold as she ran around to the front of the house.

The front doors were locked, but Caroline shouted and pounded against them, and it was not long before they opened for her by a footman. There was already some panic and scrambling of servants in the foyer – the butler came up from below with a silver candelabra in his hands, his look stern. "Is there fire, Miss Bingley?"

"Upstairs in my room," she replied. She took one of the candles from its place and held it aloft as they rushed upstairs. "Go into the family wing – I will go the other way. Get everyone up, out of bed."

Caroline went straight to Richard's door and began pounding on it. "Fire, fire," she shouted. She went across the hall, shouting still, and banged on Mr. Darcy's door.

Richard's door flew open and he rushed to her side. "Caroline, what is the matter?"

She hurled herself into his arms, finally giving in to her terror. "There is a fire in my room."

"My God, are you hurt?"

"No, but we have to go, we have to get out!"

Mr. Darcy emerged into the corridor next. "What is going on?"

"There is a fire," Richard said, wrapping his arm protectively around Caroline.

"Good God," Mr. Darcy cried. "Where is Elizabeth?"

Caroline groaned. "The guest wing was full – I put her in the room next to mine."

"Take me to her," he said. "Richard, wake the others, and look after Georgiana."

Mr. Darcy took off running down the dark corridor, and Caroline followed as quickly as she could without extinguishing her candle. Flames burned at the base of her bedroom door and thick black smoke billowed out into the hall of the family wing, curling into sinister shapes in the cloudy candlelight. Caroline coughed and froze in terror, pointing to Elizabeth's room.

Mr. Darcy kicked down the door and charged into Elizabeth's smoke-filled bedchamber, and Caroline forced herself to follow him – if any harm came to her new friend, she would never forgive herself.

Flames lapped at the bedclothes, and Elizabeth sat up, coughing and sputtering. She let out a cry as she saw them burst into her room and apprehended the reason for it. Mr. Darcy moved quickly, drenching himself with a pitcher of water from Elizabeth's nightstand. He leaned over the flickering flames and scooped Elizabeth into his arms.

"We have to get you out of here," he said, both to Elizabeth and to Caroline. Thick, dark smoke poured into the room where the wall joined with the ceiling, and the wallpaper had peeled off, curling as it burned. Desperate to be useful, Caroline picked a glass of water off the nightstand as she followed Mr. Darcy out of the room. She took a long sip of it to ease her burning throat, and then hurried after Mr. Darcy to offer the water to Elizabeth.

Charles, Louisa, and Jos were hastening from their rooms, and there were shouts from the other side of their house as all their guests and servants made their way through the corridors, toward the stairs.

Caroline latched onto Elizabeth, who was barely conscious. "Lizzy, drink this," she said, pressing the glass into her friend's hands and helping Elizabeth raise it to her lips.

Mr. Darcy slowed his steps so that Elizabeth could drink, and she finished the water before letting the glass fall to the ground. Then she coughed and buried her face in Mr. Darcy's chest, her fingers gripping his wet nightshirt. "I am so frightened," she wheezed.

"I will get you out of here," Mr. Darcy said, hurrying toward the stairs.

"My aunt and uncle?"

"I will bring them," Caroline said.

"Hurry," Mr. Darcy called over his shoulder as he started down the stairs with Elizabeth in his arms. "Find them as fast as you can – you cannot remain long. I will be back once she is safe."

Caroline gave a frantic nod and took off running into the guest wing, where all was pandemonium. Maids and valets were rushing out the door that led to the servants' stairs, some of them carrying armfuls of possessions.

The smoke had reached here from the other side of the house, and the flames were not far off. Somewhere behind her there was a loud crashing sound; something collapsing in the family wing. More screams as servants rushed past her to safety. In the confusion, she collided with Richard.

The earl moved past them with Lady Carson and Georgiana – they hesitated, looking expectantly at Richard. "Go," he cried, again wrapping one arm protectively around Caroline. The earl led the women away, and the Gardiners appeared in the hall. "Elizabeth is outside," Caroline shouted, pointing toward the stairs. "She was asking for you."

The Gardiners also hastened downstairs, and Caroline clung to Richard, sobbing and choking on smoke. Like Mr. Darcy, he had drenched himself with water, and though it was a strange sensation, Caroline felt safe in Richard's embrace. "Is everybody out?"

"You are not," he chided her. He lifted her in his arms and began to carry her downstairs. "Let it not be said that I am not as gallant as my cousin."

The commotion in the foyer was greater now, and the smoke had pooled here. Footmen were carrying sofas and other furniture out of the house; Caroline tried to tell them not to bother, but her voice was too hoarse.

"Hush, my love," Richard said, kissing her on the top of her head.

The night air was cold and shocking as they exited the house, and Caroline held Richard closer. He carried her across the lawn, to where the servants had begun to pile furniture. He laid her down on a sofa, beside Elizabeth, who was coughing and weeping. Mrs. Gardiner knelt at Elizabeth's feet, comforting her.

"Sir, my niece needs a doctor," the woman told Richard.

"Good God, Lizzy! I am so sorry," Caroline cried at the sight of her friend. Elizabeth's eyes were red, her hair was wildly disheveled, and her nightgown was stained from smoke and singed on one side. Caroline burst into tears. "Are you burned?"

"No," Elizabeth wheezed. Her whole face twisted in pain and she grasped at her throat.

"Do not try to speak, Lizzy," Mrs. Gardiner said softly.

"I will fetch help," Richard said. "I must leave you now, but I will be back."

Caroline leapt up from the sofa and threw her arms around his neck. "Please be careful," she said softly. "I found your letter – I read it – I am sorry for everything, I am so, so sorry."

Richard held her close, his wet shirt soaking her thin nightgown. "You... you did not set the fire, did you?"

She laughed through her tears. "Not on purpose, I swear it. Now promise me you will be careful, Richard."

"I will, my love, but I must go and be useful." He drew away, but Caroline tugged at his hand.

"I love you," she breathed.

Richard grinned and shook his head. "Not tonight, my darling." He turned and ran back to the house.

Caroline watched him go, sniffling back her tears, and then turned her attention back to Elizabeth. "Oh, Lizzy, I am so very sorry!"

Elizabeth was inclined back on the sofa, and Mrs. Gardiner shifted her so that she could sit beside her niece on the sofa, for the ground was so very cold. Elizabeth moved awkwardly, her eyes glassy, and she slumped against Mrs. Gardiner once her aunt was settled.

Caroline sat down on the other side of her friend, rubbing Elizabeth's back as she shivered. Elizabeth coughed, her whole body shaking, and then she reached her hand out to Caroline. Even her fingers were smudged from the smoke, and Caroline took her friend's hand with a terrible sinking feeling. "Do not be afraid, Lizzy."

Elizabeth nodded feebly, her voice raspy as she croaked one word. "William?"

Caroline looked over at the house, which was now engulfed in massive flames that burst from all the upstairs windows. She could see a great many people running about, but they were all black silhouettes against the roaring blaze. She could not discern anybody, not even Richard. "He is safe," she said, huddling next to her friend for warmth.

There were more shouts from elsewhere on the lawn, and in a few minutes they were joined by Georgiana and Lady Carson. Caroline looked up with alacrity. "What is happening?"

"They have found the fire mark and summoned the fire brigade," Lady Carson said, cradling her weeping young charge. "Hush dear, your brother will be well; he has taken charge with Mr. Bingley. "They sent for the doctor, and to the neighboring families, for they shall need help manning the pumps. Mr. Bingley has asked the butler to make sure all the servants are accounted for."

Caroline had seen Louisa and Jos make it out, and Mr. Gardiner and the earl as well. She was glad they were safe, but she longed for Richard to return to her.

It felt like an eternity before he came back to her, with Mr. Darcy at his side. A servant followed with a pitcher of water and an armful of blankets, which she began distributing to the other women all huddled together. Caroline made way for Mr. Darcy, who perched on the edge of the sofa and wrapped a blanket around Elizabeth. Mr. Gardiner approached and called out to his wife; she shifted her barely conscious niece into Mr. Darcy's embrace before rushing to her husband.

Richard covered Caroline's shoulders in a heavy blanket, and draped it over himself as well, embracing her beneath it as they clung to one another for warmth. She laid her head against his chest and wept, struggling against her exhaustion, for she feared what she would wake to if she fell asleep now. She and Richard held fast to one another in silence with their companions as they watched Netherfield burn.

13

Caroline opened her eyes and took in a deep breath. "It is a miracle," she breathed, slowly sitting up. Though she felt a little worse for wear, her nightgown was clean and her bedchamber was immaculate. She climbed out of bed and paced the room, marveling at it all. They had been offered shelter at Lucas Lodge at the end of the harrowing night before, and their guests had taken lodgings at an inn in the village. But here she was, safe in her room.

She had been given a second chance, and she was determined that she would not waste it. She was going to be good, today – perfect, if possible.

After she dressed, Caroline again waited for Mr. Darcy on the stairs. This time she did not occupy herself with a novel, but simply drank in the sight of the house, whole and unburned. She had never been so delighted by the place. When Mr. Darcy came out of his room, she leapt to her feet at once and hurried to meet with him.

"Good morning, sir. I hope you are well after... the

ordeal?"

"I am tired and a little sore, but I am glad that is all," he replied.

"Are you not also filled with a brimming optimism? I awoke with such a lightness in my heart," Caroline mused, suddenly feeling quite silly.

"That is certainly understandable," he said. "I have received a note from Richard, and he shares your enthusiasm. He thinks today shall be the day."

"Oh." Caroline had received nothing from him, and it tore at her heart to think that his beautiful letter was now lost. "Did he... mention me in his plans?"

"We spoke last night at the inn – we shall take a different approach today."

"Oh. Well, shall we begin directly?"

"I am expecting Charles any moment."

"Good. Shall I put up some resistance again, and let him bring me round?"

Mr. Darcy knit his brow. "No. Say what you told me just now, that you have woken with a fresh perspective – better willingness than coercion."

She gave him a wry smirk. "I suppose your cousin has come to the same conclusion."

He responded with a faint smile. "Yes – but, as I said, he is just as optimistic as you are."

***

Half an hour later, Darcy and Bingley were on their horses, riding to Longbourn. "You really did not need to accompany me," Bingley said. "I have a particular reason for visiting."

"And so do I," Darcy replied.

"You will not be uncomfortable with Mrs. Bennet and the other ladies, while I am speaking to Jane? I shall have to go to her father after, you know. You will only stare out the window or quarrel with Miss Elizabeth," Bingley chided him.

"I have quarreled with her," Darcy admitted. "I am eager

to make amends."

"You had a few arguments with her at Netherfield," Bingley observed. "You will have to be more specific."

"I rebuffed her declaration of love," Darcy said stonily, meeting his friend's gaze.

Bingley roared with laughter. "Are you really not going to tell me the truth?"

"I daresay you would not believe the truth," Darcy quipped.

"I can scarcely believe anything, at such a moment," Bingley replied. "Can you believe Caroline? I ought to have the doctor examine her for a head injury, but then I should not question my good fortune. I wonder what could have brought about such a change!"

"I think her time at Netherfield has been good for her. And she has had some opportunity recently to see how much you care for Miss Bennet – she had such high hopes for you – out of affection, I am sure, but of course she wants you to be happy, just as she said."

Bingley guffawed again. "Well, she has certainly taken a new view of what happiness entails!"

"It is possible," Darcy said. "After the way she spoke this morning, I almost wonder if she has some romance of her own to give her such cheer."

Bingley narrowed his eyes at Darcy with no little incredulity. "Surely not – I never thought...."

"No," Darcy said quickly. "I do not speak of myself – I am sure she knows that was never going to happen. But perhaps there is somebody. She sounded very much like a woman in love." Darcy gave his friend an appraising look, for surely Bingley would be astonished at the sudden change in Caroline's attitude toward Richard.

"Caroline in love," Bingley mused, and chortled with laughter. "You are funny this morning, Darcy."

***

Elizabeth awoke with a start and grasped at her throat. Her

eyes adjusted to the dim light creeping through a gap in the curtains; she slowly realized there was no pain in her lungs, though she had expected it. She was only terribly, desperately exhausted.

Mary sat up in the bed beside her, and Elizabeth yelped. "Lizzy, what is the matter?"

"What happened last night?" Elizabeth was a little hoarse, and her eyes felt dry, but she ought to have been so much worse.

"Nothing," Mary grumbled. "Have you had a bad dream?"

"I... I do not know." Elizabeth let out a shaky breath, flushed with what might have been relief, had she the energy. She had dreamt of falling asleep in Mr. Darcy's arms, but that could not be – not after how she had humiliated herself.

Elizabeth dragged herself out of bed and moved slowly through the corridor, back to her own room. Jane was just waking, and Elizabeth crawled into the bed before Jane could leave it.

"Lizzy, are you well?"

Elizabeth burrowed down beneath the heavy covers. "No," she moaned.

Jane rolled over and embraced her. "Whatever is the matter?"

"Oh, Jane, it is too horrible," Elizabeth groaned. "I do not know how you bear it, for being in love is utterly miserable."

"What?" Jane's eyes lit with astonishment. "Lizzy, tell me!"

Elizabeth might have wept had her eyes not been so fearfully sore. She turned around on the bed and splashed some cool water on her face from the basin on their nightstand.

Jane pursued her, scooting playfully across the bed until her head came to lay in Elizabeth's lap. "Lizzy, you cannot mean to leave me in suspense, for you provoke me to venture a guess that it is Mr. Darcy."

Looking down at her sister, Elizabeth sighed. "Oh, Jane, I have been such a massive idiot."

Jane's eyes flared wide for a moment. "Something happened at Netherfield, and you did not tell me!"

"It was the last night I was there," Elizabeth said. "Mr. Darcy came into the library, and I was there... I told him what I have begun to feel."

"And what did he say?"

Elizabeth let out another shaky breath. "He made it clear that he desires only friendship."

"Oh, no!" Jane sat up and embraced Elizabeth. "But this is incredible – I had no idea that you liked him – but I had rather suspected that he admired you."

"He does," Elizabeth murmured. "He loves me, but he thinks it a risk."

"Oh," Jane gasped.

"So, you see, it is a hopeless case."

"I am so sorry, Sister," Jane said, rocking Elizabeth gently in her embrace.

There was a knock on the door, and a moment later Mrs. Hill came into the room. "There is a post just come for you, Miss Elizabeth."

"Who is it from?" Jane looked on with curiosity as Elizabeth took the letter and opened it.

General Bennet,

Assuming Netherfield is still standing, I will report for duty with my battalion at the appointed hour. Victory shall prevail – commence Operation Perfect Day. Proceed with established protocols and maneuvers. Reinforcements are on their way.

Colonel R Fitzwilliam

"It is from Caroline Bingley," Elizabeth lied. "She writes that they are expecting some additional guests to arrive at Netherfield today, and we are invited to dine with them. We discussed the possibility on my last night at Netherfield; I am sure that is why she writes me and not you."

"Oh, of course – but how wonderful. Who are the other guests?"

"Relations of Mr. Darcy's," Elizabeth said. "But I do not know if I can face him today." She had told Richard in no uncertain terms how she would act if his plan failed, and after the horrific fire, she did not know if she could ever set foot at Netherfield again.

"No, of course not," Jane said sadly. "I am so deeply sorry for you, Lizzy. You look as though your heart is breaking."

"I will get over, in time," Elizabeth sighed.

"I hope you will still come to the market," Jane replied with forced cheer.

Elizabeth considered it. She had half a mind to find Baba Romilda and give her a dressing down that would make Caroline's wrath look like a primer on propriety.

Jane rose and opened the armoire to begin dressing, but then she went over to the window with a gasp. "Oh, Lizzy!" She extended her hand to Elizabeth, beckoning her with a wide smile. "It is a miracle!"

***

Darcy and Bingley were informed that none of the family were downstairs yet, and Darcy asked Mrs. Hill if they might wait in the garden until the two eldest Misses Bennet could join them.

"I fear you will give Mrs. Bennet the wrong impression, if you only mean to apologize to Miss Elizabeth."

Darcy gave his friend a slow, enigmatic smile. "I never said I was *only* going to apologize."

Bingley exaggerated his surprise with a wild look. "Darcy, you sly devil – but surely what you said before cannot be true!"

"It was not the whole truth," Darcy admitted. He had not the chance to say more, despite his friend's obvious interest. The back door opened and Jane Bennet stepped out into the garden, smiling brightly. Her mother poked her head out the door and waved at them, insisting they must stay for breakfast, and then she disappeared back into the house, shoving Elizabeth out the door before hastily closing it.

Darcy was reminded of a morning two weeks past, when she had similarly been thrust into the parlor to speak with him – this occasion, he hoped, would come to a happier conclusion.

He smiled at her, relief washing over him when he recalled

her condition only the night before. She was safe, but for a moment she wavered apprehensively before she would meet his eye. Darcy could only hope that his intentions were plain; after a moment her countenance softened. Yes, she understood him.

Bingley greeted them cheerfully and suggested they walk. He chose to go in the direction of a pretty little wilderness beyond the house, where the path conveniently only allowed for two. He led Miss Bennet away, and Elizabeth came to stand beside Darcy.

By unspoken agreement they waited until their companions were well out of sight before they began to walk down the path, and only then did Elizabeth look up at him. Her eyes searched his, and Darcy smiled warmly at her. "You have no idea how happy I am to see you, Elizabeth – to see that you are safe and well."

"I am a little hoarse," she said softly. She accepted his arm with a shy smile as they slowly meandered down the path. "Thank you for rescuing me last night."

"Of course."

"I remember little after sitting with Caroline – I think there was a sofa on the lawn?"

"Yes."

She furrowed her brow, her eyes moist and anxious. "Was it very horrid?"

Darcy could scarcely bring himself to describe it. "Nobody was harmed. Wickham came from the inn, and your father and Sir William Lucas came to help man the pumps. It went on for hours, and Bingley was a wreck. But my thoughts were only for you, the whole time. You passed out, and the doctor never came – your father took you home, but I feared... I hardly know."

Elizabeth shivered and Darcy drew her near. She looked up at him with tears in her eyes. "You are too generous to trifle with me," she said, her voice trembling. "My affections and wishes have not changed from last night, but one word from you will silence me forever."

Darcy felt too much to speak. She had been so brave already, and even in the face of his colossal failings, she was not afraid. She was magnificent. He stepped closer to her, his arms slowly circling around her, and she instantly surrendered to the embrace. He held her gaze, and he was utterly lost. He brushed his lips against hers for just a moment, but when he drew away, her hand slid around his neck and she pulled him back to her, kissing him with total abandon.

Darcy felt as though his heart might explode. When Elizabeth finally drew away, gasping with the intense emotion of the moment, Darcy leaned his forehead against hers. "My feelings have not changed, Lizzy," he said, gently cupping her face in his hands. "But I did not fully accept them until – I think the moment I kicked down your door last night."

She laughed softly. "That is one way to woo a lady."

"It was not my first choice," he said. "But I think it taught me what you mean to me, when I had been refusing to see it. I could not trust the madness that brought us together, but when I saw the flames encircling your bed my heart shattered. Even before that. The moment you fled the library, I knew I had made a terrible mistake. I followed you – I heard you weeping – but I could not do it. You were so beautifully courageous, and I was a cowardly ass. Can you ever forgive me? I might have spared you so much agony."

Tears streamed down her cheeks as she looked up at him and smiled. "Of course I forgive you. I forgave you the moment you took me in your arms last night – in the library, I mean. And of course it was rather nice when you carried me downstairs in your wet nightshirt." She arched an eyebrow at him. "And when you brought me that blanket. I was so ill, and the memory is muddled – but I think you held me...."

"I did," he said. The very recollection of drawing her into his lap and soothing her to sleep as Netherfield burned stirred something urgent in him, and he took her in his arms again. "I was so frightened, and so ashamed of the pain I had caused you."

Elizabeth leaned into him, and she began to weep again. "I was very cross with you for being so stubborn and stupid," she laughed. "But I saw your pain, and that was just as awful." She looked up at him and laughed bitterly. "By Richard's accounting of things, if you had come to your senses any sooner, Netherfield would be a smoldering ruin at present."

Darcy gave a gentle chuckle, relishing the feel of her in his arms. The realization had come upon him so gradually, but this was just where she belonged. "If Richard does not sort Caroline out, the whole thing may go up in smoke again."

She met his eye with a teasing grin. "She has been sorting him out, but I think she really means to give in. You do not think – I believe the fire started in her room...."

"Richard was suspicious of her, but she swore it was an accident. And she was so worried for you; I believe she did not do it on purpose."

Elizabeth laughed again, her chest gently shaking against his, and she began to run her fingers through his hair. "I can well imagine it being her very first impulse upon arriving at the place."

Darcy drew back and smiled, struck with a tremendous appreciation for how easy it was to just be with her. It no longer mattered to him if Thursday ever came, so long as they could be like this together forever. He stroked her hair, and she leaned into his touch. "Is it normal to be making such jests during a proposal, my love?"

She arched an eyebrow at him. "Oh, is that what this is? Well, I suppose our courtship has hardly been normal."

"Courtship," Darcy laughed. "That is one word for it."

She grinned at him, her fingers entwining with his. "I suppose I ought to make you woo me properly."

Darcy raised her hand to his lips and kissed it, and then he dropped down onto one knee.

***

Caroline had spent the morning preparing to receive the same guests that she had welcomed the day before, but the staff was surprisingly efficient, and she was left with too much free time before Richard's arrival. Charles and Mr. Darcy had just returned from Longbourn when the two elegant carriages came into view. Caroline sprang up off the window seat the moment she saw Richard alight.

The gentlemen followed her into the foyer, but Caroline hurried outside to meet the new arrivals; Charles and Mr. Darcy trailed behind her.

Richard was leading Georgiana up the steps, while the earl helped Lady Carson and the Gardiners from the second carriage. Caroline greeted Georgiana first, and then lingered in front of Richard. "Welcome to Netherfield. It is a pleasure to see you; is it not a fine house?"

He bowed and grinned at her. "I am delighted by the sight of it."

While the other guests settled in, Richard declared that he needed to stretch his legs, and asked Caroline to show him the garden. Inevitably, they made their way to their swing. They walked in silence at first, exchanging heated looks as they drank in the sight of one another. "You were very brave last night," Caroline ventured at last.

They were out of sight of the drawing room, and Richard came to stand close to her. "So were you."

"No," she sighed, beginning to fidget. "I was stupid and petty – when I read your letter it broke my heart. I was afraid I had ruined everything – and that was before I had even burned the house down. You must think I am such an idiot."

"You are certainly quite a tempest," he laughed, touching her hair. "You are stubborn and sometimes cruel – but you are not stupid, Caroline – you must know I could never love a woman who was out of her wits."

She giggled in spite of herself, and met his eye with a bold look. "I hope I am not too cruel." She licked at her lips, really almost ready to give in, and she laid a hand on his chest. "It was very kind of you, when you brought me that blanket, and kept me quite warm last night." Now she leaned in, her body pressing against his. His arms went around her instantly, and she buried her fingers playfully in his cravat. "Perhaps I ought to be kind to you."

He smirked, but his eyes were full of tenderness. "Really?"

"I am almost there," she breathed. "Charles means to give a ball next week, and I thought perhaps you could all stay – if there is a tomorrow, if there is any future... I could become better acquainted with your family."

Richard kissed her softly on the cheek. "You wish to know my family better, eh?"

She leaned her face against his. "Yes, and I require another letter from you, sir. The last one was so beautiful – I am very sorry it burned."

His kisses trailed across her cheek and down her neck. "Are you going to tell me how the fire started?"

"No, never," she laughed, shivering from the feeling of his lips on her skin.

Now his lips brushed against hers, but he drew away just a little, though she instinctively leaned in closer. He let out a soft, throaty laugh. "Not ever?"

Her lips twitched, and she could resist him no longer. "Oh, you win, Richard," she breathed. "I want you, I have wanted you, and I cannot help myself. Is that what you want to hear?"

"Yes – is that a yes?"

She tipped up her chin, moving her mouth slowly closer to his, but Richard drew her tighter against him, burying his face in her neck. "I love you, Caroline." His fingers wound into her hair, a sensation Caroline had always found tremendously thrilling. "I am sorry for everything. Just let me love you. I have loved you for so long, and I do not want to stop."

She let out a shaky breath and pressed her face against his, nudging at him until her lips could find his again. "Shut up," she murmured. "Shut up and kiss me."

***

Richard had prepared Georgiana better this time, confiding the truth about George Wickham to her in the carriage on the way to Netherfield. She still required some confirmation and reassurance from Darcy, but the two siblings joined Richard to receive Wickham when he arrived. The conversation was warmer this time, and Georgiana was more at ease when the other guests arrived.

Now that he had made everything right with Caroline, and

she had finally forgiven and accepted him, the absence of tension was so strange it rather amused Richard. What a remarkable difference her happiness made – the drawing room felt brighter as they all gathered together, and Caroline was at the center of it, stunning and serene.

She had met his relations once before – to her, they were *Darcy's relations* at the time – and she had been all superficial civility, but today she was warm and confident and utterly dazzling. She made her guests feel welcome as she held court, and Richard only watched in wonder as she exerted her full powers of pleasing as he had never before witnessed.

Caroline found the right balance with Lady Carson, who was not quite a mother-in-law, but near enough for a particular sort of respect. With Wickham she was just gracious enough, and even with Georgiana she practiced just enough restraint to be welcoming but not overpowering. The Gardiners were quickly won over by Caroline's praise of their three eldest nieces, which Darcy and Charles contributed to with no little animation, until Georgiana was mad to meet with them.

Richard almost feared that the arrival of the Lucases and Bennets would shatter the blissful intimacy of their family party. He had been content to relish in seeing Caroline so natural in their strange new family dynamic, but the Bennets were to be family, too, and as their numbers increased, so too did Richard's pleasure in the evening.

Caroline had uncharacteristically decided on an informal dinner despite their numbers, and they were all given leave to sit wherever they liked. Richard was eager to claim a place at her side, and Elizabeth did likewise, sitting across from Richard. Darcy sat beside Elizabeth, and across from him, Georgiana sat on Richard's other side – though she made no secret of wanting chiefly to be near her new sister.

The five of them made a merry group at the end of the table; they were so lively that they nearly missed the earl's announcement. Only when his father called them out by name did Richard and his companions fall sheepishly silent.

Standing up at the center of the table, the earl stood and raised his glass. "I would like to thank my host and hostess and all my new friends here tonight for making this such a festive occasion for my family – present and *future*. I daresay the announcement I have the honor of making would be a shock enough even in London – here in Meryton I hope it is an evening long remembered...."

Richard shared a private look with Caroline, who laid her hand on his on the corner of the table. He hoped that it *would* be remembered; he was so sure this was it. All was right in the world at last. Darcy and Elizabeth smiled, too, their eyes twinkling with mirth at the earl's words.

"And now I ask you all to join me in drinking to the happiness of Richard Fitzwilliam and Caroline Bingley, Fitzwilliam Darcy and Elizabeth Bennet, and Charles Bingley and Jane Bennet. To this I would add one other name – the beautiful and incomparable Lady Amelia Carson, Mother of my son, George Wickham. She has made me the happiest of men by accepting my hand at long last."

There was a great deal of excited chatter all down the table as the earl took his seat, and Richard glanced down to the other end, where George sat with a look of wonder. They had never discussed just how he would be acknowledged, nor to what degree, but apparently the earl had made his mind up on the matter – or perhaps he had merely been swept up in the merriment and the madness of it all. Richard found it mattered not to him, for George met his eye with such a look of whole and genuine joy that all of Richard's lingering doubt was stripped away. Everything was right.

The moment passed; George raised his glass to Richard and then turned to speak with Mary, and Richard returned his attention to those nearest him. Georgiana's attention had been claimed by the effusions of Mrs. Bennet, and Richard seized the chance to speak somewhat privately with his fellow conspirators.

"I think we have managed it – what do you say?"

"I say we better not tempt fate," Caroline teased him with a roll of her eyes.

"Very well. I shall leave it for now," Richard conceded. "But tomorrow morning at breakfast I fully intend to boast that

I was right all along."

"Yes, you have been quite the martyr, to be sure," Darcy quipped, and Elizabeth nearly snorted with laughter.

"You have not suffered as I have, Darcy, for Caroline packs much more of a punch than Elizabeth."

"What?" Caroline looked at Elizabeth expectantly. "Lizzy?"

"Mr. Darcy had not been as terribly wicked," Elizabeth said with a wry smile.

Darcy looked at her with adoration. "Only you have been flawless, come to think of it. I have been stubborn, Richard has made his mischief, and Miss Bingley...."

"Oh, for Heaven's sake, do not say it, sir," Caroline chortled. "I have been abominable, but I have been in good company, and we must leave it at that."

Georgiana turned away from Mrs. Bennet now and leaned into Richard. "I believe I can guess what you are all talking of."

Elizabeth coughed, Caroline dabbed at her lips with a napkin, and Richard leaned back in his chair with a jolly guffaw. Darcy smiled indulgently at his sister. "I should imagine not."

"But of course," Georgiana cried with exuberance. "You must all be thinking how perfectly lovely it shall be to always be in such delightful company – I am sure we will be very often together, since we are all to be related by marriage now."

Richard laughed again. "Very true – you have guessed quite right, Georgie, quite right indeed."

***

Caroline spent much of the evening laughing at herself for having ever been so recalcitrant about coming to Netherfield. She had been so determined to find only misery in a place where she was now spending one of the happiest nights of her life.

Louisa took the first opportunity to mention Caroline's sudden change when chance allowed them a private moment to speak in the drawing room after dinner. "Sister, I must offer my bewildered congratulations – but how came this to happen? I thought you had never liked the colonel."

"I can see how I might have given that impression," Caroline said enigmatically. "I have not always liked him, but I love Richard so very dearly now."

He looked over at her as she spoke his name, and Caroline extended her hand, beckoning him to join them. "Ours has been a rather secretive courtship, has it not?" She smiled up at him as he came to stand beside her.

"Yes, but we have had our reasons," he said, his eyes crinkling with mirth.

"But your last letter was so beautifully written, and so utterly heart wrenching, I knew I could not refuse you any longer," Caroline said with perfect sincerity.

Louisa's eyes went wide. "You have been secretly corresponding? But how long has this been going on?"

"It is difficult to say," Richard mused, stroking his chin.

"I hope you will not mention it to Charles," Caroline said.

Louisa made a droll face. "Well, I must tell Joseph! He has long suspected there was something between you, and I think he will be delighted to be proved right." She moved away, apparently meaning to tell him *now*, but Caroline watched her go with a merry laugh.

"Another problem solved?" Richard gave her an arch look.

"I think so," Caroline said thoughtfully. "Perhaps things may be better for them now, without me in the way."

Richard drew her into an embrace. "You can be in my way whenever you like."

"I know," Caroline drawled. "And I intend to be, very often – just as soon as tomorrow comes. But tonight I must be useful wherever I can."

"Oh, my Aunt Catherine is going to love you," Richard teased her.

"From what Elizabeth has told me, that may not be entirely desirable, though I do like to be liked. But that reminds me, I meant to speak to Lizzy about Mr. Collins."

She swept away, full of purpose.

***

Elizabeth was delighted that the Lucases had been able to attend – Mr. Collins had fled with Charlotte to Lucas Lodge that afternoon in a rage rather like his tantrum the last time Elizabeth had been engaged to Mr. Darcy. Her cousin had raised all the same arguments against the match, not only on his patroness' behalf, but out of no little self-interest. But somehow, Charlotte had managed to convince him to accompany her family to Netherfield without any further objections.

Elizabeth was more bewildered by this feat than Charlotte was at Elizabeth's engagement to Mr. Darcy. This, Charlotte claimed, was just what she had seen coming since the party her family had held at Lucas Lodge. "I knew there was something in it, for he has always stared at you with such intensity. And how you were determined to proclaim your dislike! It was entirely transparent, Eliza," Charlotte chided her with mock severity.

"I suppose it was," Elizabeth laughed, relieved that she was not obliged to make the same excuses to her friend that she had supplied to her sisters and father that morning. "Mamma thinks I have been terribly clever."

"Yes, I am sure you will never vex her again," Charlotte replied.

Caroline joined them, grinning widely at Elizabeth, who suspected she knew what was coming. "Lizzy, I have been thinking about your cousin Collins."

"Oh dear," Elizabeth laughed. "I hope you do not mean to throw Richard over."

Charlotte looked astonished by the easy banter between them, but Caroline offered her a reassuring smile. "I understand you made Mr. Collins' acquaintance this afternoon, Miss Lucas."

"Yes," Charlotte said carefully.

Elizabeth arched an eyebrow at Caroline, baiting her new friend. "Having met her most humble servant, are you not now eager to meet our new Aunt Catherine?"

"Not you, too," Caroline laughed. "Richard is eager for it, which means it is sure to be a great horror," she whispered conspiratorially. "But I wonder at poor Mr. Collins, for he must face quite a dilemma, in choosing between his noble patroness and her grand connections – who are soon to be his cousin Elizabeth's grand connections. Do you suppose he will make the right choice?"

Elizabeth laughed. "I can well imagine him weighing his options even now," she observed, and the three women all looked his way; he was speaking with all his usual obsequiousness to the earl and Lady Carson.

She glanced over at Charlotte, wondering if Caroline was really right. Charlotte had never been romantic, and she would make a fine mistress of Longbourn when the time came. "You have managed him well today, Charlotte. Perhaps a little gently given advice would not go amiss."

Charlotte looked at her with wry humor in her eyes. "You wish me to advise your cousin to break with his exalted patroness?"

"If she will not say so, I shall," Caroline whispered, smirking at them. "Only think of it – he will not be a parson forever. Someday – in the distant future, I hope, for your sake Lizzy – but *someday* he will be the master of Longbourn. It does not sound like Lady Catherine has ever encouraged him to exhibit half as much good sense as any person in this room might do. If he cannot see the opportunity before him, perhaps he may be fortunate enough for the right woman to come along and guide him toward the better path. There might be infinite advantage in it."

Elizabeth was impressed, and still a little surprised by how astute her new friend could be. "Well said," she agreed, and then gave Charlotte a little nudge. "He is likely still cross with me, but I am sure you might express the right sentiments with prudence and grace."

Charlotte looked askance at her for a moment, then slowly nodded, her eyes flicking back toward Mr. Collins. "You think I really should? It would not be too bold?"

"I have come to understand that my cousin is never

shocked when the topic of conversation is himself."

Charlotte gave her friend a look of playful reprimand. "You cannot speak so meanly of a man while encouraging me to set my cap at him."

"We shall speak no more about it, then, until I hear of your success," Elizabeth replied, and watched with satisfaction as Charlotte moved away to speak with Mr. Collins.

Caroline looked at Elizabeth with a wide grin. "Shall we go and speak with your sisters?"

Elizabeth surveyed her family, who were all dispersed about the large drawing room. Lydia and Kitty were behaving well, just as they had the other times Elizabeth had been engaged to Mr. Darcy. She had to give her mother some credit, for quickly understanding what advantages the future might hold for her youngest girls once the older ones were wed so well.

"Mary is already speaking with our aunt," Elizabeth observed.

Caroline clasped her hand with a sigh of contentment. "Everything is falling into place just right, but we ought to go and help them on."

Mr. Wickham and Georgiana had joined Mary and Mrs. Gardiner by the time Elizabeth and Caroline approached, arm in arm. "We were just speaking of the delights of London," Caroline said innocuously, and Elizabeth silently applauded her friend.

"So were we," Georgiana cried.

"Mamma wishes me to purchase my trousseau there," Elizabeth said, inciting further raptures from Georgiana. "Mary, what if you were to come along? Could you manage us both, Aunt?"

"Of course I could," Mrs. Gardiner replied. "George was just encouraging the very same scheme."

"Oh, yes – he is your nephew, which makes us almost cousins," Elizabeth said, thinking aloud. "Well! That is wonderful to hear," she said, beginning to observe the looks passing between George Wickham and Mary. This was an interesting turn, but stranger things had certainly happened.

"Yes," Mr. Wickham laughed, running his hand through his hair as if suddenly self-conscious. "I have acquired a great many new relations all at once tonight."

"So have we all," Mrs. Gardiner replied, giving Elizabeth a knowing look. "I had no notion of what to expect when the colonel invited us here today, but it is a very happy surprise."

Elizabeth looked around the room in perfect contentment and leaned in toward Caroline. "If you are right about Charlotte and Mr. Collins, every person in this room will soon be connected by marriage – what a tangled web!"

Mary heard her, and let out a little gasp, but a moment later a look of relief washed over her. Mr. Wickham smiled at all the ladies, though again his gaze landed on Mary. "I have not had the pleasure of speaking much to Miss Lucas or Mr. Collins, but it is an interesting notion, Cousin Elizabeth."

Her mouth fell agape for a moment at this reminder – had she but known, when last he had called her that, how true it was! Elizabeth smiled brightly, and he took this as encouragement to continue.

"I hope it comes to pass, if only so it will be as you say. I quite like the idea that everybody present at such a significant celebration should be forever bound in such a special way."

"What a lovely thought, George," Richard said, as he and Mr. Darcy came to join the conversation. "I am sure I shall never forget the twentieth of November – we shall mark the day every year with all due reverence, is that not right, my darling?" He gave Caroline a roguish wink.

Mr. Darcy drew closer and Elizabeth instinctively slipped her hand into his. "Shall we do the same, William?"

He met her eye with a look so intense she blushed as her body tingled with longing, and then he leaned in close enough to whisper in her ear. "I shall look forward to celebrating the twenty-first."

***

Elizabeth woke with a start; there was something wet on her face, and a strange rocking sensation. She opened her eyes and sat up in her bed – Caroline was jumping on it, still in her dressing gown, bottle of champagne in hand. She looked down with unbridled glee, her wild hair glowing like a halo as sunlight poured in the windows. "Do not say I never warned you, Lizzy."

Epilogue

26 November, 1812

 The ballroom at Netherfield hummed with an extraordinary energy that was palpable and intoxicating. With four recent engagements in the neighborhood, the presence of an earl, and an abundance of handsome officers, there was ample reason for excitement. Every young lady in attendance had worn her finest, swept up in the romance of the occasion.
 The first of the weddings was to be on the morrow, for the Earl of Matlock, who had waited the longest, was determined to be first. News of it had spread through London already, along with tales of the handsome and tragic Mr. Wickham, and some of London's elites – only the Earl's nearest and dearest – moved through the ballroom, inspiring awe, but not silence, in the good people of Meryton.

It was an absolute crush, grander than anything in memory – never had Netherfield felt so alive. Wine flowed long, music and chatter filled the air, and the young crowded the dance floor as the old looked on, with pride and hope and a great deal of interest.

None looked on so happily as Mrs. Bennet; she was in as fine a form as ever tonight, and felt herself to be floating as she moved through the room, observing her daughter and making sure everyone else was doing the same. Lydia and Kitty had filled their dance cards before the first set, despite Mrs. Bennet's new stricture against the officers. Anybody unfit to dance with Miss Darcy was unfit for her new sisters. Mary had taken all the new developments in stride – she was becoming quite a favorite with Madeline, for all her talk of London, and it had put her before Lady Carson's notice. George Wickham had even called her pretty, and Mrs. Bennet began to think she really was.

But nobody shone brighter than her two eldest girls. Jane had always been her beauty, but tonight even Mrs. Bennet was in awe of her daughter's radiance. And Elizabeth, her clever girl! There was something so different about her, as if she had been lit from within.

All of her girls were dancing, and Mrs. Bennet drank in the sight of it. Years of trying to have a son, of worrying for her girls' future, the tremendous disappointment of her husband's heir – all of Mrs. Bennets' cares were washed away. Elizabeth would flourish as the mistress of a great estate, and dear Jane would be so near. They would be secure, and better still, they would be loved and treasured. She watched the way her new sons looked at their future brides, her heart brimming with joy – and a sudden notion that the weddings had better be soon.

Mrs. Bennet saw a face in the crowd that stood out, and she began to move that way. She was briefly detained by Sir William Lucas, who had rather over-imbibed. "Ah, Mrs. Bennet! What a fine thing for your daughters, absolutely splendid! And Miss Bingley's arrangements are so very elegant – I feel as if I am transported to St. James'!"

"My daughter Lizzy will be presenting Miss Darcy when

she comes out, you know," Mrs. Bennet observed – she could not resist.

"Capital! Mr. Darcy's family is perfectly charming – the earl is so very civil – and is not Lady Carson a relation of yours?"

"She is the sister of my sister-in-law, Mrs. Gardiner," Mrs. Bennet said proudly.

"Well! And I understand Lady Catherine de Bourgh was here, though she is not present tonight – I have heard of her from Mr. Collins. How well he and Charlotte dance together!" Sir William clapped his hands with excitement.

Mrs. Bennet followed his gaze, to where the simpering parson was dancing with poor Miss Lucas. "Well, very good," she tutted. *Good riddance*, she thought. "How kind of you to host him; we are so very busy at Longbourn now."

She edged a glance sideward, and saw the gypsy moving through the ballroom. Making her excuses, Mrs. Bennet hastened away from Sir William, searching the crowd. Baba Romilda smiled and moved behind a large column near the edge of the room, and Mrs. Bennet approached her with some trepidation. "They let you in?"

The old gypsy laughed. "Something like that. Perhaps for the weddings I shall actually receive an invitation."

Mrs. Bennet forced a smile; the old woman was slight but evoked a sense of power that put her teeth on edge. "Of course." She was eager to get back to the frivolity, to forget this sordid business – the impulse of a moment at the market a month ago.

Mrs. Bennet withdrew a small purse from her pocket, and handed it to Baba Romilda, who weighed it with her hand for a moment before nodding her approval. "Extra? You must be very satisfied with my results."

"I cannot say I understand your methods, but my girls are secure – they are happy."

The older woman laughed. "Nobody ever understands, but it always works." She gave Mrs. Bennet a quick wink and then moved away, and after a moment she had disappeared into the crowd of revelers.

Jayne Bamber

Printed in Great Britain
by Amazon